KT-150-217

C0000 002 476 042

SEIZURE

Recent Titles by Nick Oldham from Severn House

BACKLASH
SUBSTANTIAL THREAT
DEAD HEAT
BIG CITY JACKS
PSYCHO ALLEY
CRITICAL THREAT
CRUNCH TIME
THE NOTHING JOB
SEIZURE

SEIZURE

Nick Oldham

This first world edition published 2010
in Great Britain and in the USA by
SEVERN HOUSE PUBLISHERS LTD of
9–15 High Street, Sutton, Surrey, England, SM1 1DF.
Trade paperback edition published
in Great Britain and the USA 2010 by
SEVERN HOUSE PUBLISHERS LTD

Copyright © 2010 by Nick Oldham.

All rights reserved.
The moral right of the author has been asserted.

British Library Cataloguing in Publication Data

Oldham, Nick, 1956–
    Seizure. – (A DCI Henry Christie mystery)
    1. Christie, Henry (Fictitious character) – Fiction.
    2. Police – England – Blackpool – Fiction. 3. Drug
    dealers – Fiction. 4. Fugitives from justice – Fiction.
    5. Kidnapping – Fiction. 6. Hostage negotiations – Fiction.
    7. Suspense fiction.
    I. Title II. Series
    823.9'14-dc22

ISBN-13: 978-0-7278-6876-3   (cased)
ISBN-13: 978-1-84751-221-5   (trade paper)

To Belinda, Philip, Jessica and James

Except where actual historical events and characters are being
described for the storyline of this novel, all situations in this
publication are fictitious and any resemblance to living persons
is purely coincidental.

All Severn House titles are printed on acid-free paper

Severn House Publishers support The Forest Stewardship Council [FSC],
the leading i   our titles that
are printed o   y the FSC logo.

HOUNSLOW LIBRARIES	
C0000 002 476 042	
HJ	29-Jan-2010
AF THR	£18.99
	FEL

Typeset by P
Grangemouth
Printed and b
MPG Books

ONE

Steve Flynn was feeling just a little apprehensive. Pulling down the peak of his baseball cap to shield his eyes from the blinding glare of the hot sun reflecting off the flat, calm Atlantic, he squinted across the shimmering water, jaw rotating thoughtfully.

July and August were when the first run of the giant blue marlin passed through these waters. Flynn knew that if he were lucky enough to hook into one, it would be a big one. A 1,000lb fish had been caught not long ago and 900lb was not uncommon. The trouble was that there are no banks or shallows around these islands to hold the fish for long, like in the Caribbean, which is why Flynn was feeling the way he was. The fish were definitely out there but he knew if he didn't get a strike soon, they'd be gone. He shook his head in frustration.

'Isn't it about time you got me into a fish?'

Flynn glanced sideways at the good-looking woman lounging indolently in the fighting chair of the sportfishing boat, an ice-chilled bottle of San Miguel in her hand, resting on her lightly tanned thigh.

Gill Hartland, somewhere in her late thirties, worked in the world of celebrity PR. She had built up a thriving business back in the UK, leaving two husbands gasping in her wake like floundering fish, and this was her sixth annual pilgrimage for the big marlin that cruised through these waters each year. So far, though, this year's trek looked like being a barren one, which would be a pity for a couple of reasons.

First, this was her only real break from the hurly-burly stress of whining celebs and paparazzi. It was a chunk of time she lived for, having picked up the sportfishing bug on holiday with one of her exes. To leave empty-handed would be a gut-wrenching disappointment.

Second, though she had paid a non-refundable two and a half grand sterling up front for the week-long charter (to the owner of the boat, not to Flynn), fish or no fish, there was an additional payment on the side, and in kind, for Flynn.

However, he had been told in no uncertain terms, 'No fish,

no getting laid' – which put a lot of extra pressure on him as skipper of this little vessel, ironically named *Lady Faye*. It was an arrangement the pair had come to four years ago, the year Flynn had arrived on the island, and its no-strings-attached small print suited them both; an additional facet of the trip to look forward to, but it was totally dependent on success, meaning fish.

Flynn was determined, therefore, to get into a big fish and Gill Hartland.

She reached out and ran the cold San Mig down his bare arm, letting her eyes give his muscular body a sultry once-over. He shivered involuntarily.

'It's not as though you haven't caught anything,' Flynn pointed out. She had hooked, caught and fought numerous wahoo, barracuda and small shark, but nothing approaching the size and reputation of a blue marlin even though there had been some exciting mini-contests on the light tackle that Flynn preferred.

She pouted and gave him a narrow-eyed look, which made his muscles go weak. 'It's the big one I want,' she declared, leaving him no choice but to ensure the client got what the client paid for. And more. She sank the remainder of her *cerveza*, said, 'I need another one,' pushed herself off the fighting chair, walked across the deck and disappeared down the steps into the stateroom where the picnic chiller box containing supplies was stored.

Flynn watched her all the way, and she knew it, exaggerating her feline-like movements as a tantalizing reminder of what was on offer.

'Hey!' Jerked rudely out of his reverie, Flynn looked up to the control tower of the flying bridge and the guy presently at the helm of the *Lady Faye* as they trolled unsuccessfully in search of the big fish. 'Your tongue hanging out,' Jose laughed dirtily, letting his own tongue loll out like a dead bull's in a butcher's shop.

Flynn's middle finger made it clearly understood what he thought of the remark. Although Jose was a Spaniard, he got the message loud and clear.

'What we gonna do, boss?' he shouted over the lovely burble of the Volvo engines. 'Last day,' he added unnecessarily, and tapped his wristwatch.

Flynn shrugged his shoulders and glanced at Tommy, the third member of the crew. The teenage son of the boat's owner was bending over the bait preparation area, doing a bit of tidying up.

Time was definitely against them. They were four hours into the day, another two hours to go, so Flynn had to come up with something quick otherwise Gill Hartland would be heading home rather dissatisfied on all points.

Not one to shirk his responsibilities, Flynn came to a snap decision. One he would live to regret.

They were presently about six miles due south of Puerto Rico on Gran Canaria, trolling over some very deep water. Looking north, Flynn could see the horizon very clearly and in particular the Roque Nublo – the rock in the clouds – rising majestically up from the island. The last big fish he'd caught, two weeks earlier for a one-day charter of four drunken Scotsmen, had weighed in at an estimated 700lb from the stretch of water they were currently trolling. But there had been no joy this week. Maybe it was time for a change of scenery.

'Tommy, Jose – get the outriggers in,' he instructed the crew. He jumped on the ladder leading up to the flying bridge, gave Jose a jerk of the thumb to get out of the way – and took control.

Jose was a big brown bear of a Spaniard, born in Madrid, but raised in Tenerife, then Gran Canaria, where he'd learned his trade on the sportfishing boats out of Las Palmas. He'd been fishing virtually all his life but though he was good and knowledgeable, he did not have Flynn's innate intuition, his ability to 'smell' fish; nor did he have Flynn's recklessness – at least that's what Flynn told him anyway, much to Jose's contempt.

Despite Jose's dirty scowl and tut of annoyance when Flynn grabbed the wheel and increased the speed, Flynn shouted, 'And when you've done that' – referring to the outriggers – 'hook on the mackerel I prepared earlier. The *special* bait,' he added with a double raise of the eyebrows, designed to get Jose's goat.

'Special bait my arse,' Jose responded.

Flynn turned the boat's tail to the island with a dignified swish and powered her due south, showing how desperate, yet inventive, a man can be when his pride is threatened.

Gill Hartland was on the flying bridge next to Flynn, coming into regular contact with his bare back and arms as she swayed with the movement of the boat in the much choppier, deeper seas they were now in. Flynn was doing his utmost to ignore the deliberate touching so he could concentrate on the job in hand, but it was proving difficult.

'You need to be ready,' he warned her, 'sat in the fighting chair, strapped in for when we lay eyes.'

On this boat it had become part of the tradition to use the expression 'laying eyes' when something special was spotted. It sounded almost religious. For a heathen like Flynn it was probably as close as he came to any form of spirituality when he laid eyes on a monster fish that was going to test his skills and ingenuity to the limit. He came over all strange and humble – happened every time.

Flynn looked at Gill. She twisted her lovely mouth down sardonically and said, 'Yeah, right, as if,' like some disbelieving teenager.

As he turned his head to look forward, he mimicked her voice and said, 'Yeah, right . . .' And then he said urgently, 'Yeah, right – actually!' Excitement blasted down his spine as he caught a glimpse of that most magnificent of fish, the ocean wanderer, surging through the ocean about two hundred metres dead ahead. 'There!' he announced, pointing with gilt-edged triumph. 'And a hell of a big one.'

Gill Hartland had sharp eyes too and she'd spotted the fish only a nanosecond after Flynn. 'Get me into him,' she ordered, 'and I'll fuck your brains out and give you a thousand-euro bonus on the side.' She spun away, literally slid down the ladder onto the deck and leapt into the fighting chair. Jose and Tommy, both alerted, did not miss the opportunity to help a scantily clad woman into the harness.

Suddenly the whole boat seemed to crackle with a shot of electricity, including *Faye* herself, who came alive like a thoroughbred racehorse. Innately, Flynn knew it could not be true, but he was certain that at moments like this, she sensed she was about to be used for what she'd been built to do – hunt big fish. She literally champed at the bit.

It took Flynn almost twenty minutes of skilful but frustrating manoeuvring before the boat was in the correct position ahead of the marlin, from which it would even consider taking the bait. He trolled the mackerel expertly in spite of Jose's continual derogatory remarks to the contrary and Gill's foul-mouthed curses of annoyance, most of which were lost on the wind. Thankfully.

Initially the fish couldn't be tempted, no matter what Flynn did, and the air of excitement on board was being gradually eroded to be replaced by tension and impatience at the shy creature's reluctance.

But then it all came good. Before it went bad.

Flynn had the boat and bait ideally placed. The marlin tensed and then, amazingly, took the bait with a powerful lunge.

With a scream of primal excitement – which Flynn hoped would be replicated later that night – Gill Hartland heaved up the rod, her muscles turning to sinews of steel, embedded the forged steel hook into the fish's mouth and, grimly determined, commenced battle with what Flynn estimated to be an 800lb fish.

It was an unfair contest: Flynn pitied the fish.

Half an hour later, the struggle was still in full swing, no punches being pulled on either side.

Gill Hartland's muscles howled agonizingly as she worked the rod, keeping the pressure on, pumping the fish when appropriate, then allowing it to sound and reeling in quickly as the magnificent creature burst from the ocean depths in a series of stunning, frenzied leaps, desperate to worry the hook loose and escape this torment. Each time, Flynn's heart was in his mouth, but Gill had the measure of the beast, kept her nerve and fought it like the expert she was becoming – ably assisted by Flynn's superb boat handling, his ability to spin *Faye* on a sixpence and manoeuvre her as though she was an extension of his own being. The crew played their part too, providing Gill with a succession of energy drinks, constructive advice and buckets full of cold seawater to keep her cool.

It was ninety minutes after she had first taken the fish, after one final and unbelievably spectacular leap which could have been over a dozen feet, that Flynn knew for sure Gill had beaten it.

She coaxed the fish to the side of the boat. Flynn called for Tommy to take the wheel and he scrambled down the ladder onto the deck as Gill and Jose, who'd managed to grab the line, drew the fish alongside. Jose leaned over the side and with his safety-gloved hands, gripped the marlin's beak and held it steady, keeping the water flowing over its superb body.

As 'tag and release' was company policy these days (although Flynn understood why, he achingly missed the quayside display of a monster fish and its attendant glory), Flynn took many good quality digital photos of Gill leaning over the side of the boat, stroking her catch, a huge smile on her face. He then estimated the weight and length of the fish, tagged it and allowed Gill the pleasure of releasing it back into its habitat.

With an almost arrogant roll of its body, it dived, was gone. Flynn turned to Gill. 'Happy now?'

The boat rolled on a wave. She lost her balance. Flynn caught her and she held on to his arms gratefully, now weary and weak from the battle royal she'd just had. 'You will be,' she responded, eye to eye with him. 'How heavy d'you reckon?'

'I'm about fifteen-five,' he quipped and she punched him gently. 'I'd say seven-forty, seven-fifty . . . a good fish by any standards.' He, too, was beaming proudly, knowing just how important the photos he'd taken would be for business when posted on the website.

'Thanks,' Gill said. 'I'm famished and thirsty now.'

'Chicken mayo sarnies in the cool box, more *cerveza* in the galley fridge, if you so desire,' Flynn told her. Then he looked at Jose. 'Thanks, *amigo*.'

'*De nada*,' Jose winked.

Flynn looked up to the flying bridge, about to thank Tommy too – but the youngster rose from the chair, peering ahead. He looked down at Flynn, worried.

'Boss,' he said before Flynn could speak. 'Problem.'

Flynn's eyes were hawk sharp, but even so it took him a second or two to actually focus in, understand and identify what Tommy was urgently pointing to, some four hundred metres dead ahead of the boat. For a micro-flash he thought he was looking at a school of pilot whales, a common sight in these waters, their rounded heads bobbing about in between the rise and fall of the swell. But as his eyes and brain aligned he realized that the black blobs were not any sort of marine animal at all. The floating debris of a wrecked boat confirmed this. They were in fact the heads of people in the water – drowning people. The reason he didn't compute it immediately was because what he was seeing was so out of context with the environment: at least a dozen people were fighting for their lives in the sea, almost twenty miles due south of Gran Canaria. But then he reacted like any seaman should.

'Get the boat to them, Tommy,' he uttered. The young lad, a skilled pilot despite his age, needed no further instruction. Flynn joined him on the flying bridge, clapped him on the shoulder and said, 'Well spotted, kid,' then turned and slid back down the ladder on to the deck. He landed lightly, keeping his balance as Tommy powered up and *Lady Faye* rose majestically out of the ocean. Jose had begun to clean the deck, sluicing it down with buckets of seawater. 'Forget that,' Flynn said, 'bodies in the water, probably illegals. Could get messy.'

Jose stopped mid-throw and scowled. 'Bastards.'

'Nevertheless, bastards who need rescuing,' Flynn admonished him, increasing the length and breadth of the scowl.

'What's going on?' Gill had emerged from the salon, chicken sandwich and beer in hand, alerted by the power surge of the boat and the raised voices. Flynn quickly explained but by the time he'd finished speaking they were on the scene and words were superfluous. Tommy powered right down to a holding crawl.

'Jeez,' Flynn uttered on seeing a tableau reminiscent of something from the aftermath of a Nazi U-boat attack in a Second World War movie. The water was covered with a viscous layer of diesel oil and fuel, probably an area the size of a football pitch. And in that area was the wreckage of a small wooden boat and about twenty people bobbing up and down in the water, some clinging to wreckage, others desperately trying to stay afloat through their own efforts. Among them floated several face-down bodies, splayed out as though on invisible crucifixes. And above all that were screams for help, desperate screams.

'Freak wave,' Jose spat, assessing the situation.

'Shit boat,' Flynn said, then called to Tommy to keep *Faye* steady.

There was not one life jacket in sight and Flynn realized that a rescue had to be effected quickly, or even more would drown. He turned to Gill. 'We'll need your help – and I don't want to sound sexist, but you get the hot water boiling on the stove for tea and there's about a dozen blankets in the bulkhead storeroom. Get the tea on and the blankets out, please.'

Gill, a terrified expression on her face, nodded numbly and with one last look across the water, hurried down into the galley. Flynn and Jose leaned over the side and using a combination of life belts and a gaffe each, hooks removed, they began the task of dragging people out of the water. Some had already managed to swim to the side of the boat and were clinging to the ropes; others looked to have given up all hope, their energy vanished, nothing left inside them.

'More trouble, boss,' Tommy yelled from the flying bridge, pointing urgently.

Flynn was concentrating on reaching out with his gaffe as far as possible and getting it into the grasping hands of his first rescuee. It was a flailing black woman who was screaming desperate words in a language he did not understand.

'Come on – take it,' he yelled at her.

She lunged for it, missed and her head disappeared under the water.

'Boss,' Tommy shouted again, a worried tone in his voice.

Flynn gave him one of those irritable 'in a minute' chopping gestures with his free hand, then reached out as far as he could and made sure the gaffe was presented to the woman as she broke the surface covered in the slime of engine oil, fighting for her breath. This time she grabbed the hook and Flynn pulled her quickly and gently to the boat. Once she was within arm's length, Flynn leaned over and took hold of the scruff of her neck, hauling her thin body easily out of the sea. He'd caught and landed fish much heavier than her. He spun her around and eased her on all fours on to the deck. He pointed to the galley.

'Go,' he pushed her, 'go inside.'

She looked gratefully at him and crawled away, dragging her exhausted body. Flynn gasped at the futility of her plight, but did not dwell on it. Task was now, emotions could come later, maybe. He turned his face up to Tommy, who'd screamed 'Boss!' even more demandingly.

'What?' he said impatiently. Behind him, Jose had man-handled the first of his bedraggled bodies on to the boat, a young guy, nothing more than a kid, who flopped on to the polished deck, spreading oil everywhere – and also blood. He had a huge gouge to his inner right bicep, long, deep and very nasty.

Jose looked disgustedly at the mess, knowing it would be hell to clean up. 'Shit.'

Tommy pointed, jabbing his finger.

Flynn followed the direction of the finger.

'Hammerhead,' Tommy said. 'And mako.'

'Shit,' Flynn spat. He looked at Jose, who had also seen what Tommy was pointing at – sharks moving in. 'Get working,' he shouted.

Most of the survivors had managed to get closer to the boat now, but there were four of them whose strength had deserted them and were drifting away, unable to muster even a pathetic swim stroke against the current. Two dead bodies floated with them, riding the swells with ease.

Flynn's mind raced.

The hammerhead shark was common in these waters. Flynn

had yanked many of the strangely designed beasts out, but they were not particularly good game fish in his estimation, not really sought by anglers except on bad days. Generally speaking they were not a great threat to humans either. Even though a hammerhead is a consummate predator, attacks on people were rare occurrences under normal circumstances.

The same pretty much applied to the mako shark. Described as the most aristocratic of all sharks, they were a good game fish, but attacks on humans were pretty rare.

Unless of course the humans were in deep water, severely injured, with blood flowing from the cuts.

Both types of shark could easily be driven into a feeding frenzy by the scent of blood in the water.

For a moment, Flynn was transfixed, taking in what was happening – maybe six dorsal fins rushing towards the drowning or dead people. Flynn recognized two mako and four hammerhead. Suddenly there was a foaming flurry fifty metres off starboard as another unseen shark struck from below with terrible ferocity and took one of the floating dead bodies. The shark rose from the water and bit into the torso of the body, spun and dragged it under. The activity seemed to influence the approaching sharks and they speeded up excitedly, drawn by the bubbling, bloody frenzy.

With horror, the four drifting survivors had seen what had happened, the body of their travelling companion disappearing.

'Fuck!' Flynn breathed, feeling powerless, knowing that unless he did something, more people were going to die terrible deaths he was going to have to witness.

His mind whirred.

The boat itself was now virtually surrounded by people trying to clamber aboard. There was no way he could abandon them, because if he left them and got Tommy to spin *Lady Faye* around to deal with the weak, shark-threatened survivors, he'd put the ones at the boat in the same predicament.

Some alternative.

He looked into Jose's petrified face, then up to Tommy, equally frightened, and then to Gill Hartland who had reappeared on deck. All of them were looking to him for the big decision. In other words, 'What the hell are you going to do, skip?'

'I came here for an easy life,' Flynn moaned bleakly. He pointed at Jose and Gill and stabbed an instruction at them. 'You – both of you – keep dragging these poor souls out of the water.'

His face flicked to Tommy. 'You keep edging her slowly backwards and watch the debris,' he concluded warningly. There was no way he could allow the boat to be damaged by the floating bits of the destroyed vessel. If *Lady Faye* was holed accidentally by any of these chunks, they'd all be in deep trouble – and water.

With his orders issued, Flynn rushed past Gill into the cockpit, ducked and dived for the storage cupboard under the double bed in the master stateroom. On his belly, he yanked it open, stretched into it, running his right hand along the inner cupboard wall. He pressed the hidden catch and flipped up the front of the makeshift false wall he'd built into the cupboard, then reached inside until his fingers clasped around the cold metal barrel of the Bushmaster .223 AR-15 Predator rifle secreted there.

It was an additional piece of kit he had not bothered running past the boat's owner, put there for defensive purposes only – he would argue. There was always the prospect of encountering unsavoury people such as pirates on the seas these days and Flynn wanted to be prepared for that eventuality. He pulled the heavy gun out of the clips that held it to the bulkhead and rolled back up on to his feet. As he legged it back through the cockpit, he checked the five-round magazine, found it to be full of lethal-looking bullets and slotted it back into place. He cocked the weapon as he emerged on deck, where the others were still dragging people to safety one by one.

Once by the fighting chair, he took in the situation again.

The word 'dire' came to mind.

More sharks were moving in – at least a dozen of them. Several were engaged in ripping the body to shreds in a blood-foaming frenzy which was growing more intense. No one else had been touched yet, even the other floating body.

'Flynn, what the hell are you doing?' Gill shrieked as she dragged an oil-covered female on board. She had seen the gun in his hands and her mouth was open in shock.

Jose piped up, as he distastefully saved another life. 'Shoot all the immigrants – good idea.'

Flynn gave him a withering look, then Gill a sidelong glance. 'Diversionary tactics?' he suggested. 'Well, hopefully.' He raised the weapon to his right shoulder and peered down the twenty-inch barrel. There was no scope fitted, but Flynn was good enough not to need it at this range. Curling his right forefinger on to the trigger, he steadied himself against the roll of the boat, pulled himself physically and mentally down, controlled his breathing, controlled his heartbeat.

His target was one of the sharks just arriving and therefore furthest away. It was a fearsome hammerhead swishing through the water, its monstrous flattened head swivelling from side to side as it used each eye in turn because its optic nerves could not produce a single, combined image. This action alone made the fish seem even more sinister and dangerous than it was.

Flynn purged everything: his surroundings, the movement of the boat, the panic-stricken people in the water. His finger tightened. It was just him and the shark. He squeezed the trigger.

Even in the open, the sound of the shot was loud, but more importantly, it was deadly. Expertly using the dorsal fin to estimate where the brain would be, Flynn knew he'd hit the fish exactly where he wanted.

The water exploded and the huge shark, mortally wounded, jerked and thrashed obscenely.

Flynn lowered his weapon, satisfied, his breath shallow.

A spark of triumph seared through him as the other sharks veered away and closed in on their companion in its death throes. Flynn made a fist and jabbed the air, hoping he'd given them a little bit more time.

He propped the gun against the fighting chair and cast his eyes over the scene. Gill and Jose were dragging two more out on to the boat, the deck of which was now a horrible mess. He saw that Gill was having a particularly torrid time with the young girl she was trying to rescue. The girl seemed to be fighting her, not wanting to be saved. Flynn moved across to them and grabbed the female's wrist. With a heave of strength he hauled her over the side and deposited her unceremoniously on deck. But the girl, who looked no older than fifteen, lurched back to the rail and tried to scramble back into the water. Gill pulled her back.

'What the hell's up with her?' Flynn shouted.

The girl shook herself free from Gill's grasp, screamed and fell to her knees, gesticulating at the sea. She was hysterically upset and Flynn couldn't understand a single word. His eyes followed the desperate pointing and squinting into the sun, until he saw a tiny bundle of black rags on the surface, some fifty metres starboard of *Lady Faye*.

His heart and insides were suddenly wrecked. He stared at Gill, who had also spotted the bundle, the object of the girl's hysteria.

'A baby,' he blurted. The girl was frantically trying to claw her way overboard again. Flynn took it all in. Sharks tearing apart one dead body, others attacking their injured fellow shark, scores of fins now in the water, circling and building up courage to attack; a cluster of boat debris all around *Faye* making any quick manoeuvres completely impossible. His basic instinct took over.

He kicked off his deck shoes and began to climb onto the starboard railing.

'Steve!' Gill cried, seeing what he was about to do.

Flynn didn't hear her, but he was suddenly brought back to reality as Jose tried to assist a young black man into the boat. As the man's right leg dangled tantalizingly in the water for a few seconds too many, an immense mako shark powered out of the water like a rocket and took the bottom third of the leg into the huge cavern of a mouth containing rows of magnificent tiered teeth.

Gill screamed. The man emitted a sound that was unworldly.

But Jose clung on, his strong arms under the armpits of the man, and for a few moments it was as if he was competing in a tug o' war with the mako. Then, as the huge fish twisted away, there was an ugly tearing sound and a massive chunk of the lower leg had gone, ripped off with an elemental power. Jose fell back onto the deck with his prize of a writhing man, screaming in pain, a terrible jagged wound gushing a huge amount of blood.

Flynn watched the scene for a moment. It had seemed to happen in slow motion, like a movie. But then, without further hesitation, he jumped feet first into the water.

Despite the heat of the air, the sea was incredibly cold. As it enveloped him, oxygen was sucked from his lungs as though he'd been punched in the belly. Flynn fought through this initial shock and began a powerful crawl towards the rag bundle that was a child.

His mind didn't even start to question what he was doing. What drove him was just as inbuilt as the responses and re-actions of the sharks in the waters around him. He wasn't being brave or stupid, he was simply responding to the stimulus presented before him, even though deep down he realized that the child would be very, very fortunate to be alive. And he would be just as lucky to get out of the sea in one piece.

Instinct propelled him through the swell, adrenaline fuelled his system and he was suddenly at the rags. He pulled them towards him as he trod water and kept an eye out for approaching fins. The bundle was firm yet pliable and instinct now told him there was a child wrapped in it. As to whether it was still alive was not something he had time to dwell on at that moment. Holding the child to his chest with his left arm, he struck out with a powerful sidestroke back in the direction of *Lady Faye* – and just at that moment he caught sight of a hammerhead fin cutting towards him at a terrifying rate, maybe only thirty metres to his left.

Something deep inside twisted in agonizing panic. The shark was maybe fifteen metres away now. Coming for him.

He scissor-kicked his legs hard, trying to make himself move faster, but knew it was a futile effort. Part of him wondered what it would be like to be attacked by such a creature.

Then there was a crack, followed by another crack. The hammerhead rolled away, blood gushing out of the centre of its head.

Flynn didn't spend any time assessing what had happened. He powered back to *Lady Faye*, which Tommy was reversing carefully towards him through the debris without damaging the boat. Two pairs of eager hands reached over the side. Flynn could not begin to describe the unbelievable feeling of relief as Jose's fingers gripped his right arm, he managed to pass the bundle to Gill, and then Jose hoisted him to safety, ensuring his feet didn't dangle too long in the water.

As the Spaniard dumped him on deck, Jose looked at him in dismay and said, 'You're one crazy bastard.'

Lady Faye ploughed through the choppy waters of the Atlantic Ocean, throttles well open. Tommy stayed at the wheel, grimly piloting the boat north towards Puerto Rico, trying not to keep glancing over his shoulder at the mess on the deck behind and below him.

In total they had managed to rescue fourteen people, including the young man who had lost most of his lower leg to a shark, the mother and baby – and two dead bodies that had not been got at by the sharks.

The man with the injured leg had gone into deep shock. Flynn and Jose worked on the terrible wound as best they could, packing it with bandages and antiseptic cream from the well-equipped – but in the circumstances, painfully inadequate – first aid kit. They wrapped his leg and made one of the other refugees prop it up at an angle to help stem the blood flow by use of gravity.

The leg was a horrible mess and he had lost a lot of blood all over the deck, which kept Jose scowling and muttering because he knew he would never get it cleaned properly: human blood stained more permanently than anything gutted from a fish.

The baby had been snatched from Flynn's hands before he was even pulled on board. The young mother – and Flynn was shocked by her age, or lack of it – clutched the bundle to her inadequate bosom and Gill steered both of them into the state-room, where she wrapped them in the boat's best quilt that had been covering the double bed. Then she hovered over them, not even knowing if the baby was dead or alive. She stood there feeling helpless as the mother knelt on the bed, holding the baby tight, rocking back and forth, wailing and chanting.

Flynn stood up from the shark-bitten man then picked his way over the splayed legs of the exhausted travellers who were packed side by side on the deck. They had all been given a hot drink. Some managed to drink it, others could not and were obviously very poorly. He then had to step over the tarpaulin that had been used to cover the two dead ones. Flynn asked if any of them spoke English or Spanish, but their responses were muted and confused. Not that he felt like holding an in-depth conversation, but he wanted to know where they were from and what had happened. The Spanish coastal police were already demanding explanations over the radio and Flynn didn't have any answers.

'I don't need this,' he bleated. 'Not my scene.'

'*Como*?' Jose asked.

Flynn gestured helplessly and shook his head. '*No muy bien*,' he said. 'Not good – el crappo.'

'Fuckin' immigrants,' Jose snorted.

'Ugh – whatever . . . anyway, you mean old bastard – good shooting.'

'*Como*?' His grizzled face screwed up.

'The rifle – bang-bang.' Flynn pretended to shoot. 'Killing the shark – thanks, *amigo*.'

'*De nada*,' he shrugged, then turned back to the injured man who was convulsing. Flynn saw him, but went down into the stateroom where Gill was tending mother and child.

It was a pathetic scene. For a few moments Flynn felt his guts wrench and breathing seemed difficult.

Gill shot him a worried glance and a hopeless gesture.

'Is it alive?' Flynn whispered.

'I don't know, she won't let me see.'

Flynn's nostrils flared. He stepped in front of Gill, went down on his haunches before the woman and opened his arms.

'Please.' He jiggled his fingers to indicate he wanted her to hand over the child. She shook her head and clung on even more tightly to the bundle. Flynn persisted and edged closer, trying to look as reassuring as a drenched six-foot-two, tough-looking man could without scaring the living daylights out of her. 'Please . . . *por favor . . . s'il vous plait*,' he said as though he was multilingual. 'The baby . . .'

She continued to hold on defensively, but her expression changed as he held in there. Her grip on the infant slowly relaxed and her arms opened until Flynn knew it was OK for him to reach forward slowly and take the child. It felt like he was taking a cold, lifeless bundle and he churned inside. Maybe he should have let her keep it.

That wasn't an option now.

He placed the child, a boy, carefully on the bed and unwrapped the damp covers. It lay there lifeless and unmoving, its black skin blue with cold and lack of blood. Flynn could not prevent a hiss of despair escaping from his lips. The mother clamped her hands to her face and gagged a scream, while Gill laid a hand on Flynn's back.

He leaned over the child, his hands touching its cold, clammy skin. His first and second fingers slid up to the neck, just underneath the jaw, probing for a pulse.

'What d'you think . . .?' Gill started to ask behind him, leaning over his shoulder. He waved her to silence and returned his fingers to the search. Was there something? Or was it his imagination? Or just a forlorn wish to find something? His fingertips probed gently. He opened one of the baby's eyes and the eyeball rolled back. His own eyes watched the baby's chest. Did it rise and fall? His concentration was total, cutting out everything else that didn't matter.

He tilted back on his haunches and hoarsely whispered, 'There's a pulse . . . I'm sure of it. Hardly there, but it is there.'

'You certain?'

He nodded shortly. 'How do you feel like holding a baby to your bosom? The kid's getting no heat from Mum. Here.' Flynn's eyes flickered to the refugee. She was staring with cold terror. 'But I know you're hot stuff.' His eyes angled up to Gill. 'If the kid doesn't get some real warmth, it'll die.'

'It's a no-brainer then,' Gill said. She pushed Flynn aside, reaching for the motionless child. 'You wrap us up tight in the quilt,' she told him.

He did. 'Good lass,' he told her. 'You'll dine out on this for · months back in London,' he said.

But she didn't really hear him. She was feeling so drained and emotional. 'This is a miracle,' she said as she felt the baby move.

'That's the problem,' he winked. 'The impossible I do at once . . . but miracles . . .?' He shrugged with a wink.

TWO

D etective Superintendent Henry Christie scanned the printed crime report as he walked purposefully and grim-faced down the hospital corridor. His eyes quickly read the dry, formulaic words which, while succinctly summarizing the incident, went no way towards truly describing the sheer terror which came with it.

> *Attempted Murder/Robbery: Offenders approached super-store situated off motorway roundabout during opening hours. Three offenders posed as legitimate customers and when security guards had collected store takings from office, attacked the guards with previously secreted baseball bats and demanded the takings. One guard refused to hand over cash box and one offender produced a handgun and shot guard once in face causing serious injury. Offenders then made off in a getaway car waiting outside the store with the fourth offender at the wheel. The car was later found abandoned and burnt out on a nearby council estate. Offenders are believed to have transferred to other ve-hicles to make good their escape.*

It was the third such robbery, but the first one that had gone utterly wrong. The first two had been particularly brutal and frightening affairs and innocent people did get hurt – quite badly – because these robbers were violent, nasty people. However, no firearms had been produced and no one got shot, a fact which ratcheted number three up to another level entirely.

The MOs of the robberies were all exactly the same.

They came in from out of town into an unsuspecting back-water and targeted a security van collecting the day's takings from a superstore close to a motorway. The offenders knew exactly what they were doing, when to do it and how to get away – which meant that good planning had gone into the jobs. The only difference between the execution of this robbery and the previous two, other than the use of the gun, was that it had taken place in Blackpool, whereas the others had been committed over in east Lancashire. This meant the offenders had travelled further. As it was believed they had come in from Manchester, it was a big hike and more risky for them.

The change in venue had also caught the cops on the hop, something that was grating with Henry Christie.

'How much?' he asked.

'Forty grand.'

Henry pursed his lips. 'Definitely the same crew?' The question was almost superfluous, but he had to ask it.

'Yeah,' the detective inspector said, trying to keep up with Henry's pace as he strode down the corridor to A&E. 'Deffo Manchester crims.'

Henry flicked the crime report back at the DI, nodded stone-faced and very serious. He swung a right turn and pirouetted through a double door into the cauldron that was the A&E reception area. He stopped abruptly to get his bearings, almost causing the scampering DI to rear-end him.

'How's the security guard?' Henry asked. The shooting had happened some four hours earlier and Henry knew the doctors and nurses here at Blackpool Victoria Hospital had been working frantically on him since he had arrived with a bullet in the face. The said slug was lodged somewhere between his right eye and his brain.

'Last I heard, touch and go, fighting for his life,' said DI Rik Dean.

Henry took a steadying breath in order to regain some control over himself. 'What's being done . . . been done?' he asked, meaning what the hell had the police done so far?

'Uniform were on the scene within minutes, motorway patrols were alerted and India Ninety-Nine was put up. Statements are still being taken from some very shaky witnesses at the store, which we've shut down for the day, much to the management's annoyance. There's a big crime scene investigation going on and Manchester have been apprised of it.' The DI shrugged.

'They torched their car on Shoreside, which incidentally was stolen from Manchester, then divided up into maybe two or three other vehicles. And, of course, the residents on Shoreside aren't exactly coming forward in droves to assist. We reckon they'd be back in the city within forty-five minutes, tops.' He shrugged again.

'And all this happened when we were running a crime op in east Lancs, checking suspicious vehicles coming off the M66, to try and catch the bastards?'

The DI nodded. 'Correct.' Henry tutted in frustration. 'To be fair, though, it was a pretty high profile operation – Hi-viz jackets, marked cars and everything. Could be why they changed locations, we just displaced them.'

'Maybe we need to be more subtle in future . . . however, just make sure the crime scene is covered as though we're dealing with a murder – remember, you don't get a second shot at it, so let's miss nothing. These bastards are a dangerous nuisance and need catching.'

'Already doing that.'

Henry inhaled again. A rush of stress rose through him like a tidal wave, a sensation emanating from his heart. It had been a tough, crappy day and to get this on top of everything else was just short of giving him palpitations. He shook his tired head to rid his mind of a disturbing image, then the two detectives walked to A&E reception and waited impatiently behind a woman with a child which had a small plastic toy inserted up its nose. The harassed receptionist took details and directed her to the waiting area. Henry stepped up to the desk, flashed his warrant card and explained his mission, adding, 'There's a uniformed officer with the patient, but we can't seem to contact him . . . probably has his Police Radio switched off.'

'Still in surgery,' the receptionist said after consulting her computer screen.

'Can you direct us to the appropriate theatre?'

She sighed impatiently. 'Back through that door, end of corridor, left and left again . . . just off that corridor,' she snapped. Henry was going to ask if there was any news but decided against it. She looked under more pressure than he was. A full whingeing waiting room coupled with a scrolling LED display that declared a three-hour waiting time, and more patients already queuing up behind him, made him give her a quick nod of thanks and withdraw.

'You OK, boss?' Rik Dean asked Henry, seeing him rub his eyes in exhaustion.

Henry curled his lip, Elvis style, and said nothing, just shook his head in a 'Don't ask' gesture. The day had taken all the fight and energy out of him and all he wanted to do was go home, dive into a bottle of JD. He also knew that the whisky part of the wish wasn't even a close option. Caffeine was going to have to be his crook for the time being.

He grabbed Rik and propelled him towards a drinks machine from which Henry extracted a frothy, weak coffee that was billed as Americano, but was about as far away from that as the North Pole was from the South. He took a few sips of the burning hot liquid. Even though it was rubbish, it hit the spot quickly and fired him up a gear.

They found the PC who had been assigned to remain with the injured guard sitting outside the operating theatre, bouncing his helmet from one hand to the other like a basketball. Clearly bored. He rose sheepishly when the two senior officers appeared and slid his helmet under his arm.

Henry didn't know the lad – which was all he was, a lad – but Rik Dean did.

'PC Berry, this is Detective Superintendent Christie from the Force Major Investigation Team,' Rik made the introduction.

Henry gave the young man a curt nod – he did not particularly like anyone today. 'Any news?' He almost added the word 'son' but managed to hold it on the tip of his tongue. Being called 'son' had always irritated him when he'd been a young scamp of a bobby and he promised himself he would never subject anyone, ever, to that patronizing epithet.

'Er, no sir. He's been in hours now and there's been a lot of doctors and nurses in and out, but none've spoken to me and I felt like I didn't want to . . . y'know? Ask.'

'Yeah, OK,' Henry said. He should have added it was a copper's job to ask, but he couldn't be bothered to go there. 'When did you last have a break?'

'Dunno . . . since he went into surgery.'

'Go get yourself something and be back in twenty minutes.'

'Cheers, boss.' The PC did not need asking twice and zoomed off for some refreshment.

Henry paced the tiny waiting room outside the operating theatre, the doors to which had a red warning light above them, indicating surgery was being performed.

'What's the relatives' situation?'

'Wife contacted . . . I sent someone down to pick her up. Not landed yet. She lives in south Manchester.'

Henry stretched, cricking his neck, then sat down heavily on a plastic chair. His eyes rose up to Rik, a man he had known for plenty of years. Rik's brow creased. He detected something very clearly amiss with Henry.

Henry could still not quite believe it.

Earlier that day, at eight forty a.m. precisely, he had parked his new car, a top of the range Mondeo (having disposed of the rot-box Rover he had naively bought), on the car park near the tennis courts at Lancashire Constabulary Police Headquarters at Hutton, just to the south of Preston.

He could still not quite get his mind around getting out of the car, walking down the side of the converted student accommo-dation block in the grounds of the Police Training Centre, now the offices of the Force Major Investigation Team (FMIT), tapping in the entry code at the door – a privilege denied to him not very long ago – and trotting up the steps to the middle floor and walking down the tight corridor to *his* office.

The door had a new sign on it simply saying *Detective Superintendent Christie* – nothing more, but that was how he liked it. He unlocked the door with his own key, another privilege, entered and sat down behind his desk with an air of contentment.

His desk, his office, were provided for him as co-head of FMIT, a job he shared with two other detective superintendents.

It did not detract from his self-satisfaction, nor his cloud nine attitude, that his office had once been two separate student bedrooms that had been knocked into one several years before when the whole block had been commandeered for what was then the Senior Investigating Officer Team. It did not bother him that he vividly recalled using these bedrooms almost thirty years before on his probationer training courses; that he'd peed in the sinks (now removed, of course), been sick on the floor (now recarpeted), and had snuck a female colleague into his room and in his eagerness as a young stallion had, much to the young lady's disappointment, prematurely finished before he'd even reached home and had splattered the floor with what then felt like a bucket of man-juice. Lovely memories.

None of that bothered him because today he was a detective superintendent and this was *his* office. The stains of his past seemed only to add to its ambience.

He gave himself a little pinch just to prove he wasn't dreaming, allowed himself a couple more moments of self-indulgent reverie, then got down to the tasks of the day. These included progress checks on two domestic and easily solvable murders, a stranger rape that was dragging on far too long, and a couple of nasty armed robberies that had come his way even though they had been committed in east Lancashire. It was an area of the county he rarely covered. And that was just the tip of the iceberg.

He logged on to his computer, plugged in and replenished his coffee machine, and swept up the phone on his desk before the second ring had been completed.

Hell, he was raring to go.

'DCI . . . Sorry, Detective Superintendent Christie . . .' The words and rank hadn't yet sunk in and he still stumbled over introductions.

'Henry, it's Kate . . .' Even in those brief words, he picked up the tone and knew something was very, very wrong. He braced himself.

'What is it, love?' All the things it could possibly be swarmed through his brain.

'Henry, it's your mum . . .'

He knew she was going to die. He blinked back a tear at the thought, sat back in the uncomfortable chair and felt his stamina drain out like water down a plug hole. He rubbed his eyes, which squelched with a noise that turned Kate's stomach. They were tired and gritty and he realized he needed to get them checked. His vision had deteriorated noticeably over the past twelve months. Somehow he had to find time to get to an optician. But it was one of those things he constantly deferred, maybe because it was a tip and a wink to his own ageing process.

Which brought him right back to his mother propped up in a bed in the cardiac unit at Blackpool Victoria. The warden of the sheltered housing in which she lived had found her face down in the bathroom and had called an ambulance. With a suspected heart attack, Henry's mother had been rushed to A&E, then up to the specialist ward – still alive, obviously, but very ill.

Now attached to a machine that 'pinged' occasionally, she was sleeping open-mouthed, drugged up and, Henry was certain, very close to the end of her life.

On receiving the phone call from Kate, Henry had made some immediate calls to colleagues, asking them to cover for him.

Then he'd hurried to the hospital, met Kate there and found his
mum being treated in the cardiac unit, having been transferred
from A&E.

He had heard her voice before actually seeing her. High pitched
but croaky – and insistent: 'I think I'd know if I'd had a heart
attack, don't you?' She was clearly annoyed and upset. As Henry
pulled back the cubicle curtain, she said to the doctor treating
her, 'I don't need a drip, thank you.' He was fiddling with a
needle on the back of her left hand, trying to find a vein. She
saw her son and breathed, 'Henry,' in relief. 'Would you mind
telling this . . . this man of colour I'm here under false pretences?'

Henry stepped into the cubicle, a little embarrassed by his
mother's ingrained racism. The doctor turned and Henry introduced himself, then looked sternly at the woman who had borne
him. 'Mum, you were found collapsed on the bathroom floor.'

She blinked her glassy grey eyes. 'Was I?'

'That's why they brought you here in an ambulance.'

'An ambulance? I don't remember that.'

'Just let him give you a drip, will you?' Henry said gently.
He sat by the bed, taking her other hand. She squeezed it and
looked at him, then smiled as if she was having everybody on.
Then she presented the back of her hand to the doctor.

An hour later she was asleep. Henry was talking in hushed
tones to the doctor.

'She's actually very ill and she has had a major heart attack,
believe it or not. If she hadn't been found . . .' The doctor let
Henry finish that sentence.

'OK, what's the plan?'

'The next twenty-four hours will be critical . . . once we get
beyond that we'll have to look closely at the care she'll need.'

The conversation lasted a few more minutes and didn't fill
Henry with any great hope. He sat at the bedside and simply
stared at his mother's ashen face, more thin and wrinkled than
usual because her false teeth were smiling at him from a glass
on the cabinet. He knew she was in trouble.

Kate's gentle touch made him look around. She handed him a
cup of tea she'd cadged from a nurse and pulled a chair up beside
him, resting a hand on his leg.

Henry pulled a face that could have been jokey or desperate,
he wasn't sure which. Part of him felt hysterical, another part
completely lost. Kate moved her warm hand from his leg and

clasped it over the back of his hand, her shining, probing eyes showing deep concern for the man she had loved – on and off – for twenty-odd years. Henry raised his face and caught her expression, then out of the corner of his eye he saw his mother move and groan. When he looked properly, wondering if she had woken – she hadn't – she seemed to be nothing any more, just a ghost. Now he truly realized what the phrase 'a shadow of your former self' could mean.

It hit him like a sucker punch.

He swallowed, but could not hold it back. He began to cry.

Kate hugged him tightly until the body-jerking sobbing had subsided. Then, faintly embarrassed by his less than macho display, he disengaged himself gently from Kate's embrace, stood up and crossed to a sink. He swilled his face with cold water and rubbed himself dry with rough paper towels.

'Got a dribbly nose,' he said with a sniff and a rueful laugh. 'Sorry about the blubbering.' He pouted with his bottom lip just in time to catch a wet drip from the end of his nose.

'It's OK,' Kate said with a sad smile. 'It's what I'm here for.'

They held each other for a few seconds, then Henry felt his mobile phone vibrate in his trouser pocket and eased himself free again with a muted apology. Rik Dean's name lit up the caller ID.

'I told them not to call me,' he whined.

'It's fine,' Kate assured him. 'Answer it – it might keep your mind off things.'

He gave her a weak smile, stubbed his thumb on the disconnect call button. 'I'll call him back from the corridor. Here's not the place.' He glanced guiltily at the wall notice clearly indicating that mobile phones were not allowed.

Once in the corridor he returned Rik Dean's call. The DI informed him about the supermarket raid and the fact that a guard had been shot and was now in hospital. A short while later he went back inside and whispered to Kate.

'That's handy,' she said ironically.

'Life's full of good surprises. I'll bob down and see Rik and see what's happening.' He turned to his mother and looked at her for a few seconds, composing himself with a jerky inward sigh. He touched the back of her bony, liver-spotted hand, then left the unit, striding towards A&E. On the way he met Rik Dean, who briefed him and handed over a rough draft of the crime report. Henry read it as he walked. A few minutes later they were outside the operating theatre, inside which was a critically injured security guard with a bullet in the face.

'Ahh,' Rik Dean nodded sagely as Henry regaled him with succinct details of his torrid day hovering around the cardiac unit at Blackpool Vic. He didn't say, 'That explains it,' although it did clarify Henry's demeanour and the reason why he was already on hand at the hospital, something that had initially puzzled Rik as he'd scurried behind Henry down the corridors.

'What's the prognosis?'

'Dunno . . . not good. She's old, weak and knackered – but she is a fighter. I'm not sure I'll see her walk out of here, though,' he concluded bleakly. He sighed, 'Anyway . . .'

As he spoke, the door to the operating theatre opened and a guy who was obviously the surgeon stepped out, theatrically removing bloodstained latex gloves, then his cap. He was round faced and young. Henry and Rik stood up slowly – again, a little bit theatrically – even though Henry's right knee cracked and nearly gave way with a jolt of pain, which would have made it comic theatre if he'd gone down. He managed to retain his balance.

'Are you the police?'

Henry nodded.

'ID please.'

Henry fished out his warrant card. 'Detective Superintendent Christie. I'm in charge of this case.'

'Well in that case, officer, I'm afraid things have taken a turn for the worse. I couldn't save him and now you've got a murder on your hands.'

So Henry was right after all. It was a shitty end to a crappy day.

'That was the most moving thing I've ever done in my life,' Gill Hartland sighed reflectively.

Steve Flynn, naked, returned from the bathroom and settled himself on the edge of the king-sized bed in her hotel room. 'It was pretty good for me, too,' he cracked, bringing a punch on the arm from her.

'Not that, you idiot, although it was good,' she said rolling back onto the bed, intertwining her fingers behind her head. 'You know what I mean. Today.' She blew out her cheeks and stared at the ceiling. 'First catching that marlin, beautiful, beautiful fish . . .

then those poor, wretched people . . . unbelievable . . . and that baby.' She rubbed away a tear. 'I don't do crying.'

Flynn sighed too. 'Nine thousand boat people turned up in the Canaries last year, hundreds more died on the way. No one'll ever know how many. First time I've been involved with any. I always steer well clear of their boats.'

Gill rolled on to her side. The thin sheet slid down her arm, revealing her well-toned body as far as her waist. She reached out and grabbed Flynn's wrist. 'You're a bit of a hero, aren't you, Steve Flynn?'

'I'd've been a dead hero if Jose hadn't plugged that hammer-head.'

'Jose?' she chortled. 'Did he say he shot it?'

'He didn't say anything, actually. I assumed . . .' Flynn's expression changed. 'You did it!'

She smiled shyly. 'Nearly made the winter Olympic shooting team years ago.'

'Wow – thank you,' Flynn said sincerely. 'It was an amazing shot.'

'It was nothing.' She continued to search his face with her eyes, as though seeing him for the first time. 'But you are a hero.'

'Unsung – and I'd like to keep it that way.'

'You're too modest.' Her eyes narrowed. 'I've just realized I don't know anything about you, Mr Steve Flynn.'

'Nothing to know.' He said it with a gentle finality that Gill picked up on and decided to change the subject. 'And actually – you *were* pretty good.'

'Pretty good?' Flynn roared mock-dramatically, glad the subject had moved on. He wanted to avoid any navel gazing. What had happened had happened. He recognized he had been driven by a fundamental human force, the instinct that drove people to protect and save others, and he hadn't particularly liked it. The last thing he needed was any deep, embarrassing introspection where he might be forced to get in touch with his sensitive side. He was a man of action, did what he had to do and got on with it. So he twisted and pinned Gill to the bed. He tugged the sheet right off her, exposing her wonderful body, and stared lustfully into her eyes.

'Don't you need half an hour?' she teased. 'That's what blokes usually say, isn't it?'

'Not this one.'

'So I see,' she smirked and slid a warm hand around the back of his neck, paused eye to eye, then yanked his head down. Their mouths clashed as they kissed passionately while Flynn rearranged himself above her. Then for the second time that night they made love. The first session had been fast and urgent, driven by their reactions to the day. This time it was slow, long and perfectly timed.

An hour later an exhausted Flynn was fast asleep, snoring softly.

Gill eased herself away from him. She tied a flimsy wrap around her body and quietly made her way to the decking outside her room. The clifftop hotel situated between Puerto Rico and Mogan had a magnificent vista across the ocean, of which Gill's expensive, ground floor garden room took full advantage. She settled herself on to one of the chairs, lit up a menthol cigarette – a treat she saved purely for her holiday – and ran over the day she'd just had. Turning to look through the wispy curtains, she watched Flynn sleeping. He was well gone. She picked up her Blackberry and started to make a few calls. Even though the hour was late, the Canary Islands were in the same time band as the UK, and there were people she needed to speak to, to get the ball rolling.

THREE

B reathing heavily now, Flynn weaved his way through the narrow streets of Puerto Rico, his feet pounding the concrete footpaths, avoiding the numerous potholes and broken tiles along the way which had tripped many an unwary holidaymaker. He ran easily, descending all the time until he reached sea level at the beach, with the Puerta de Escala away to his right where *Lady Faye* was moored. For the moment, though, she was not his destination.

Cutting underneath the digital day/date/time/temperature display board by the curving sands – already reading twenty-four degrees at seven thirty a.m. – Flynn trotted down the few steps on to the beach and ran to the water's edge. He paused briefly to divest himself of his running singlet, shorts and trainers – fortunately he was wearing his swimming trunks – then ran on and plunged into the water. He began to swim powerfully across and back over the width of the bay in the tepid water. Eventually he dragged himself out after covering about a mile from side to side. He refitted his trainers, and wearing only his Speedos and carrying his other garments, he started running again. Not far this time, a few hundred metres.

Flynn's present accommodation was in a small, terraced villa backing on to the Doreste y Molina. It was a property owned by a fishing charter customer who rarely used it in the summer months. The idea of having someone in it who was sound and trustworthy had been one Flynn had sold to the owner after a particularly fruitful week of fishing in late May. He found himself ensconced for free in a pleasant two-bedroom villa, set halfway between Puerto Rico's busy commercial centre and the harbour. In October he knew he'd have to find a winter hidey-hole, but that didn't worry him. He had a few soft touches in the pipeline and this was how he'd lived for the past four years. He knew he'd be very unlucky not to be able to find somewhere cheap and cheerful, or free, to lay his hat over winter and to park his Nissan Patrol, which was presently squeezed on to the tight drive at the back of the property.

After warming down for a long ten minutes, Flynn showered thoroughly, shaved and changed into three-quarter length cargo pants, his beloved Keith Richards T-shirt, tatty baseball cap and deck shoes. Then he set off to the marina. On the way he stopped at a café run by a British couple where he grabbed a large black coffee and a full English breakfast.

Today, he knew, would be a tough day in more ways than one, and he wanted to be as fortified for it as possible.

As he stepped out from the shade of the café, the heat smacked him in the face. It was going to be another scorcher on Gran Canaria.

In contrast the streets of north Manchester were bitingly cold for a morning in late July. Henry Christie shivered, hunkered down in the front passenger seat of one of the firm's Vauxhalls and shoved his hands deep into his jeans pockets. He took a deep breath and wondered, not for the first time, about the sense in him being out here on the front line, especially with what was happening at home.

As if he could read Henry's mind, Rik Dean said, 'You don't need to be here, y'know. Besides which, it's always pretty dangerous for me being out and about with you.' Rik rubbed his thigh, recalling a similar situation in the not too distant past when he'd been shot in the leg partnering Henry on a stakeout that went skew-whiff.

Henry squinted sideways at the DI. They had known each other for a long time. Henry had been instrumental in getting Rik on to CID when he'd been a mere PC with an uncanny ability for taking thieves. Rik's subsequent promotions had been down to himself alone and now Henry was trying his level best to wangle a place for him on FMIT. 'I might as well be here,' Henry said. 'There's nothing I can be doing back home . . . I just had to get away. It was doing my head in.'

He thought back to yesterday evening.

After having received the shocking news about the security guard, Henry had decided to strike while the iron was still a bit warm. Revelling in the new-found weight that came with the rank of superintendent, he got a manhunt up and running immediately. If the robbery hadn't turned into a murder he would probably have got a fully fledged major investigation under way the day after, but the death changed things completely. He hastily convened an urgent heads-together at Blackpool nick to implement a plan of action based on what was already known about the robbers from their previous two crimes and the intelligence gathered from them.

He knew that the Intel had matched up known offenders to the MOs – i.e. persons who had committed similar crimes in the past. There were a couple of ongoing surveillance operations, each targeting a likely crook from Manchester who had a history of pulling off similar jobs. Henry quickly brought himself up to date with the current position of these operations. He found himself extremely pissed off, but not surprised to find that the last time either of these guys had been surveilled was over a week ago. Problem was that the surveillance branch had limited resources and everyone wanted them. There was a lot of good will, but a limited amount of time people would work over-time without payment, or the likelihood of getting time off in lieu.

Henry ripped the fax off the machine in the CID office. It had just arrived from the surveillance branch, showing copies of the logs relating to the two suspects. In front of him were details of their previous convictions, Intel sheets from Greater Manchester Police, and their mugshots. He skimmed through the stuff and passed it round to the detectives he'd managed to assemble, giving them all ample time to read the contents.

'These two guys are the main suspects for all three armed robberies, a suspicion based on past intelligence rather than firm evidence. Both men are very surveillance and forensically aware. They are careful, professional and extremely violent individuals. They both have a history in the use of firearms, as you can see.

'They've been followed on and off since the second robbery, but their activities have not raised any suspicions – which means nothing, of course, except that the surveillance unit were pulled off to deal with something more pressing . . .' He scratched his head and lost his train of thought.

Rik Dean noticed the senior moment and picked it up for him. 'They seem to be the best we've got at this stage. As we speak, my DS is swearing out warrants with a tame magistrate.'

'Thanks, Rik,' Henry nodded, bringing his focus back on track. 'This investigation will kick off big style tomorrow, but I'd like to get the ball rolling now. Greater Manchester are already sitting on these guys' addresses. It would seem they are both at home, waiting for us to kick their doors in. I'm pulling together two arrest squads, including firearms officers, and we're gonna hit both addresses simultaneously tomorrow morning, assisted by GMP.'

A murmur of approval rolled around the detectives like an audible Mexican wave. Most detectives liked action and that was now a feature of FMIT since Henry had moved into its highest echelon. He was a proactive leader and didn't spend much time ruminating.

The detectives spent the next hour planning strategies and tactics, a lot of time on phones.

It was after eleven p.m. when all the planning had been done and everyone other than Rik and Henry dispersed for a pint before a short night's sleep. Henry's would be shorter than everyone else's.

He had often been exhausted at work. It was the nature of what he did – long hours, often for no reward, other than the satisfaction of nailing villains. But today was very different. He had started at the normal time and it was after eleven now. That was pretty much a regular span for most adults, but the hospital interlude with his mother had seriously drained him.

'You going back to see your mum?'

Henry nodded.

'I'll come back up to the hospital with you, see how the FLO's going on,' Rik said. He was referring to the family liaison officer who'd been attached to the family of the dead security guard. He knew that the FLO and the grieving widow were still at Blackpool Vic.

Henry had returned to the cardiac unit, walking through deserted corridors until he found Kate. Loyally, she had stayed at his mother's bedside, even though their relationship had often been strained over the years.

Henry hugged her, getting a shot of much-needed energy from the embrace.

'How is she?' he whispered. He stepped up to the bed and looked at his mother. She was sleeping, her chest rising and falling almost imperceptibly. If it hadn't been for that movement, Henry would have mistaken her for a corpse. She looked no better than earlier. A lump hammer pounded in his chest and he caught a brief glimpse of himself in the mirror on the wall over the wash basin.

He too looked old and ragged. His eyes had heavy bags under them and his skin was drawn. He reminded himself of a Gulag prisoner in some Russian novel. He looked like hell.

'Stable,' Kate said. 'Comfortable.'

'Has she been awake?'

'Just for short spells. She was quite lucid. Asked where you were.'

'Damn. I should've been here.'

Kate squeezed his elbow. 'She was fine about it. Don't worry.'

He turned to her. 'I need to go out on a job early tomorrow. The security guard died, so it's a murder now. I need to supervise some raids.'

'That's OK. I'll be here.'

'You sure?'

Kate nodded. 'We'd better get some sleep then, otherwise neither of us will be fit for anything.'

Henry yawned, big and loud, showing all his fillings. He had slept soundly, aided by a microscopic Jack Daniel's, for the five hours available. Even so, he was still whacked.

He checked his watch: eight fifteen a.m. Doors were due to be battered off their hinges in fifteen minutes.

Flynn made his way across the harbour to where *Lady Faye* was moored. He could see activity on board before he got there. Jose,

Tommy and the owner, Adam Castle – the man who employed
Flynn as skipper, and to whom Flynn owed much for the man's
generosity and trust – were busy at work.

Flynn stood on the edge of the harbour and inspected *Faye*'s
decks. Jose was still dutifully scrubbing away at them, desperately trying to clear away the last vestiges of blood, going into
every nook and cranny with a power hose.

'Hey, what do you call a Spanish fireman?' Flynn called across.
The three people on board raised their faces to him. They squinted
up against the sunlight, quizzical expressions on all.

'What do you mean?' Jose asked.

'He's called Jose – but what's his mate called?'

Jose shrugged. As if he cared.

Adam Castle simply stared at Flynn with his hands on his
hips. Tommy, Adam's son, was on the flying bridge with a
lopsided teenage grin on his face.

'We need a chat,' Castle the elder said. He gestured for Flynn
to come aboard and follow him into the cockpit. Flynn's cheeks
blew out. He walked across the gangplank and stepped on to the
boat, glared at by Jose.

'Where have you fucking been?' the Spaniard demanded.

'Looking after customers' needs,' Flynn said with a click of
the tongue and a wink, just to wind up Jose.

'I've been here since six.'

Flynn shrugged. 'I'm glad to hear it, *amigo*.' He gave Tommy
a nod and went into the cockpit, his bravado a mask for what
might be about to happen.

Stern faced, Castle waited for him, ominously.

Flynn kept up the breezy pretence. 'OK, boss?'

'Siddown.'

Flynn sat uncomfortably. He looked tensely at Castle, who
had been out of town when the boatload of blood, refugees and
dead bodies had arrived back the day before. Castle owned half
a dozen similar boats throughout the Canary Islands, as well as
a small property business, a couple of well-run night clubs, a
travel agency and a business taking tourists out on tours of the
island. Of all the boats, *Lady Faye* was his favourite, mainly
because with Flynn at the helm it was consistently the most
successful in terms of catches and repeat business.

'First of all, you did a good job yesterday. I don't deny it.
As much as these immos are a pain in the rump, you did a
fantastic job in rescuing as many as you did. They're all being

held by the local authorities now, as you would expect. So, well done.'

'Thanks, boss,' Flynn said, though he could tell there was a nasty 'but' coming in from left field. He braced himself. Castle was a well laid back guy, but he also had a powerful broadside in his weaponry.

His eyes hooded. 'However, the issue of the rifle is something that concerns me. Deeply.'

Flynn swallowed. He'd made Tommy and Jose swear on their lives not to reveal anything about the weapon, but someone had obviously blabbed. Flynn realized his insistence on secrecy had been unfair on the others, but he'd half-hoped it might have lasted a tad longer, at least until he'd had the chance to ditch or hide the Bushmaster. He scratched his head, coughed nervously.

'What the hell were you thinking?' Castle roared suddenly, catching Flynn unawares and making him jump. Under normal circumstances, Castle did not raise his voice. He was a pleasant guy and very little wound him up. Except of course one of his employees hiding an unlicensed hunting rifle in one of his boats. Castle went into the stateroom and came out bearing the rifle, brandishing it angrily. 'Do you realize this could completely fuck me up if it comes out? The cops would come down on me like a ton of shit.' He was furious.

'Sorry,' Flynn said inadequately.

Castle shook his head. 'Not good enough, Steve.' His mouth clamped shut. He put the weapon down and placed the ball of his thumb over his right eye as though he had a storming headache. Then he looked at the very chastened Flynn. 'Why have you got it?'

Flynn gave a pathetic shrug. 'Pirates?' he said thinly. 'Target practice? A throwback to my army and cop days? I like guns and it was a bargain.'

Castle held up a hand in mock-surrender. 'Don't, don't,' his voice was weary. 'Look, Steve, if this comes out, even though the gun was used for a good purpose' – he emphasized the word *good* by tweaking the first and second fingers of both hands – 'there will be some really tough questions to answer. I'm hoping the illegals won't say anything. I know Jose and Tom won't – but what about Ms Hartland?' Castle looked at him knowingly.

'She'll keep quiet – promise,' Flynn said. A sliver of relief shimmied through him. He'd thought he was going to get the chop.

Castle picked up the rifle and handed it to Flynn. 'Get rid, OK?'

Flynn nodded, knowing that would be easier said than done.

The two men regarded each other, then Castle started to smile. 'Look, man, you're my best skip, so don't blow it . . . OK, today is a very big clean-up op. There's no charters booked and we won't accept any walk-ins today or tomorrow. The cops want to speak, too, so let's accommodate them. Fortunately they're as pissed off as anyone by illegal immigrants, so I don't think they'll probe too deeply.

'Tonight I want you on the door of the Purple Cane,' Castle said – the job of bouncer at Castle's club in the commercial centre was one of Flynn's other roles. 'Tomorrow, you'll be taking one of the Jeep safaris – OK.'

'Got that,' Flynn said with great relief.

'And I don't care how you do it, Steve, but ditch the weapon – preferably in deep, deep water. I run an honest business.'

With that, Castle left the boat. After composing himself, Flynn went on deck, a serious expression on his face that caused Tommy and Jose to look away guiltily.

'OK guys, I understand. One of you ratted on me.'

Jose scowled as he stood up from his task. 'We were not the ones with a rifle,' the Spaniard pointed out. He wiped his hands on a cloth. Next to him was a bucket full of blood-coloured water.

'I know,' Flynn said, backing off and realizing the wrong words had tumbled out of his mouth. 'I'm sorry.' Flynn was being very, very humble today.

'Adam's very pissed off at you.'

'He has every right to be – although the gun did save the day.'

'Hey, it don't make it right.' Jose jabbed a finger at Flynn. 'And how is the customer?' he said, changing the subject without warning.

'She's been cared for and is recovering well from the trauma,' Flynn said grandly.

'I'll bet she is.'

'And not only that.' Flynn held up a finger. 'She wanted to make a generous gesture towards us all. I told her it wasn't necessary, but she insisted.' Flynn's right hand snaked into his back pocket and reappeared with a flourish, a thin wad of euro notes between his fingers. He saw Jose's eyes widen appreciatively as he peeled off four fifty-euro notes. 'A little bonus for good fishing

and excitement – not to be revealed to the boss, OK?' Jose
nodded. His greedy mitts snatched the cash. At the present
exchange rate it was almost equivalent to two hundred pounds
sterling, money not to be sniffed at.

Flynn glanced up at Tommy, who was watching the transaction
with interest from the flying bridge. 'Some for you, too – on the
QT,' Flynn told him and waved a couple of fifty-euro notes in his
direction. Tommy's young eyes lit up and he scampered down the
steps. 'She gave us a five hundred bonus to split,' Flynn explained.
'I reckon this is fair, don't you?'

'Thanks Steve,' Tommy enthused. He was usually paid a pittance
by his dad for working on the boat, which he did for love rather
than money anyway, during downtime from school. A hundred-
euro windfall was an incredible amount for a fourteen-year-old.

'No probs. You did good yesterday. How're you feeling?'

'I'm good.'

Flynn smiled benignly at the members of his crew, aware
that a little financial recompense had smoothed the rough edges
of a possible rocky situation – and that they would never be
aware of the true share of the bonus he had taken from Gill
Hartland. He wasn't going to tell them he'd pocketed seven
hundred euros and the bonus had actually been a grand. He
justified it in his mind, convincing himself he deserved
it because he'd done all the work – particularly the extra-
curricular stuff – hadn't he?

'What're you going to do with the rifle?' Jose asked.

Flynn shrugged. 'Not thought that one through as yet. Maybe
ditch it overboard when I get a chance.'

Jose looked at him sceptically. 'We won't be out on the water
for two days – and you can't keep it on the boat, *amigo*. Adam
will not allow it.'

'I know, I'll sort it,' Flynn whined. 'So, have you finished
scrubbing the deck?' he asked, his turn to change the subject
without warning.

'It's come up well, considering, but still needs more work.'

'Better get cracking, then.'

Jose turned instinctively at the instruction, almost falling for
it momentarily, but then he glared at Flynn, his dark Spanish
eyes very menacing. 'A-ha, nearly had me then.' He wagged an
admonishing finger. 'Anyway – what was that you were saying
about Spanish firemen? Some kinda joke? I mean, a Spanish
fireman is called Jose – so what the hell?'

'The joke is, his mate is called Hose-B. Gettit? Jose, Hose-B?'

Jose stared blankly at him before returning to his blood-scrubbing duties. '*Ingles*,' he muttered. 'Sheesh.'

There was one thing Henry Christie admired about police raids in the modern era: usually, they were fast, hard and professional. A world away from the ragtag raids he used to take part in when he first joined the job. Back then they were often based on an iffy tip-off to a fat jack who stayed in the CID office, feet up, fag in gob, while the uniforms (a derisory term) 'spun the drum', as they used to say.

It was good fun, but Henry remembered at least three occasions when he'd been tasked to smash someone's soil pipe and put a net under it to catch the drugs that were likely to be flushed away by the panicked felons in the house. Only to discover it was the wrong house. On-call plumbers and joiners made a small fortune from police callouts in those days.

Nowadays more preparation time went into intelligence gathering and surveillance, and police training, before size eleven boots were applied to doors.

Which is how Henry knew for certain that the house he and Rik were covering *was* the right one, and the occupant they were interested in *was* in. And because of the speed and force of entry, he was captured in just the way Henry liked. Underpants around his ankles, reading a newspaper on the toilet.

When the first uniformed cop booted open the toilet door, the suspect merely looked at him over the top of his paper and said coolly, 'You'll have to wait your turn, pal, I'm constipated.'

His name was Richard Last – inevitably Tricky Dicky – and during the course of his relatively short life (he was twenty-seven) he'd become one of the north-west's most feared armed robbers. Even so, such villains had stomach problems from time to time. And it was fortunate he was stuck on the toilet because, as his house was searched, two firearms were discovered in the attic and one under his mattress. The latter was a fully loaded automatic pistol, probably kept there for the occasions when someone unannounced came bursting through his door.

He smelled of sleep, sweat and cigarette smoke. He needed a shower and two hours after his arrest, having been conveyed directly to Blackpool nick instead of via Rochdale, he still needed to crap.

'I'm answering none of your questions,' he stated categori-
cally to Henry and Rik in interview room number one. 'Not till
I've seen a doctor, been given a shit-pill, and then I've seen my
solicitor.' The prisoner was now wearing a white forensic suit,
commonly called a zoot suit, and sat squirming in the chair, very
uncomfortable. 'I haven't shitted for days and I feel like I'm
going to burst, only it won't come. So don't even bother asking
me anything until I have done.'

The two detectives, however, remained unmoved by the plight
of Tricky Dicky's bowels.

Henry knew that the arrests of Richard Last and his running
mate, Jack Sumner – locked up during a simultaneous raid and
ensconced in another cell out of earshot of Last, and without
either of them knowing the other had been arrested – were acts
of hope.

They were two violent robbers who fitted the bill nicely and
he guessed their arrests would probably be the first of many
fishing expeditions – cloaked by layers of solid intelligence,
obviously, just to appease the defence solicitors who would
become involved along the way. Henry knew everything had to
look above board. Actually he wasn't too concerned by the
heavy-handed nature of these tactics. Even if these guys weren't
ultimately involved in the supermarket murder, something else
– such as other offences or intelligence – was usually thrown
up by similar arrests.

Which was the case with Richard Last and Jack Sumner.

Henry knew he would struggle to put either of them at the
scene of the robbery. If they were involved, they were very cute
forensically and so far, neither the CCTV footage, witnesses nor
intelligence had come up with anything useful.

And on top of that, Henry was beginning to suspect that neither
man was involved anyway.

So the discovery of firearms at Last's house and a massive
wodge of cocaine at Sumner's hidden under floorboards, did
help matters. It gave the cops a toehold.

'I've done nowt,' Last said cockily, and not for the first time.
He was feeling better. His bowels had been evacuated and he'd
had a chat with his solicitor, a sly, deep-eyed brief from
Manchester, who sat back and watched the interview proceed
with cold detachment.

'I want to know where you were yesterday, what you did,

who you saw, who you spoke to, which car you used,' Rik Dean insisted. 'Then after I've followed all that up and spoken to the people concerned, I might believe you.'

Last took a slightly hesitant breath and his eyes flicked to his solicitor. It was an insignificant movement, but Henry saw it and hoped it would be captured on the videotape recording of the interview. He swallowed and his nostrils flared with the scent. Perhaps his earlier assumptions had been wrong. Maybe Last was involved.

'I was at home all day.'

Up to that point, Henry had tended to believe Last's denials. But no longer. There was just *something*. Henry rolled forward. 'Home all day?' he said sarcastically.

'That's right.'

Henry allowed himself a half-smile, one not captured on tape because the camera was recording the back of his head. Last saw the smile, as did his solicitor.

'I want to talk to my client,' the brief said, entering the conversation for the first time since introducing himself for the benefit of the tape. 'I think we've reached a suitable juncture . . . gentlemen?'

The guy's name was Baron. He had trailed all the way from his practice office in Rochdale to represent Last. He was a squat, powerful-looking individual with a severe haircut that made him look more like an SAS trooper than a man of the law. Most were soft and pudgy in Henry's experience, but Baron had the feel of a cougar.

'OK,' Henry said. Rik brought the interview to a halt.

'Thoughts?' Henry said. He and Rik were in the canteen on the top floor of Blackpool Police Station, sipping coffee, eating bacon sandwiches. The detectives interviewing Last's partner, Jack Sumner, were still at it, but by all accounts getting nowhere.

'Not much for us to go on if he sticks to his story.'

Henry nodded sagely, as superintendents are known to do when they have a head full of nothingness but would like people to think different. 'At first I believed him, then there was a twitch when you mentioned his whereabouts. A smidgen of doubt.'

'I saw it.'

'OK. There still officers at his house?' Henry wanted to know. Rik nodded. 'Contact someone there and get them knocking on neighbours' doors. See if anyone can cast a light on Last's comings and goings yesterday. If he's going to stick to his story, let's shove it up his arse if he is lying. Do we have someone there who could do that?'

'Yeah. I'll sort it now.'

'I'm also conscious the clock's ticking, so I might be looking at releasing these guys and doing some more work on them. And I want that surveillance operation back on them twenty-four seven from the moment they step out of custody. My authorization.'

'I'll sort that, too.'

'So unless they change their stories in the next three hours, or something turns up from the neighbours, both of which I doubt, let's bail them to come back here in a fortnight. Then we should also be somewhere down the line with the guns and the drugs, if nothing else.'

'We could keep them in custody based on what we found in their homes,' Rik said.

'Maybe we'll do that next time.' Henry smiled dangerously. 'In the meantime, let's give them enough rope and see if they hang themselves . . .'

Flynn was sweating profusely, but the hard work was paying off. *Lady Faye* was looking as good as new. He stood erect, his knees and back aching, and surveyed the deck. It was midday and he was disappointed the boat wasn't up for charter because he was raring to get out on the ocean again and hook into some marlin. The sales kiosk further down the quayside had already turned away three half-day charters – good money – and they'd gone to other boats in the marina. Flynn was tempted to take *Faye* out himself for a couple of hours, maybe dispose of the rifle at the same time.

He squinted across the quay and spotted Gill Hartland approaching, accompanied by a man Flynn didn't immediately recognize. She was talking animatedly, gesturing towards the boat in a way which gave Flynn a queasy feeling. A sensation that increased tenfold to almost vomit level when he noticed another group of people behind Gill clambering out of a hire van.

Flynn could make out the logo on the sides of some aluminium suitcases being unloaded from the vehicle by these other folks – the emblem of a very well known UK breakfast TV company. Flynn realized the luggage being placed on the quayside was in fact equipment cases. One of the people was even unfolding a large aerial of some sort.

Flynn's face dropped as the man with Gill stopped and shouted something at the people by the van, thereby confirming his fear that they were connected.

Flynn's whole being stiffened up. The man with Gill was saying things he could not hear but he seemed to be giving instructions, then he turned and pointed in Flynn's direction.

Jose emerged from the small galley with two mugs of tea. He picked up on Flynn's shocked expression and stared at what Flynn was looking at.

'What is it?'

'Not one hundred per cent, but I have a very nasty taste in my mouth at this moment in time.'

Jose handed him one of the mugs. 'Here, drink, *amigo*. Sorry it is not something stronger.'

It was one of those raging arguments held out of the hearing, but in full view of others. Two people head to head, trying vainly to keep their voices below a scream, but with their body language betraying their every emotion. One of them using open, placatory gestures, asking for reason; the other pointing, enraged, one hand slashing down in a karate-like chop into the palm of the other hand, until finally spinning away, arms up in the air; then making a strangling gesture before turning back to the other person, relenting and calming as she stepped forward and snaked a hand around his neck . . .

'Hey babe, c'mon, calm down,' Gill Hartland cooed, stepping into the seething rage of Steve Flynn, sliding a hand around his neck.

Flynn's lips had been drawn back tight against his teeth in a snarl, but her touch and soothing words gradually brought him down from the heights.

'I don't want to be on TV,' he stated. 'It's not me. I don't want to draw attention to myself.'

'Steve, you're a mega hero, shark wrestler, baby saver, people saver . . . you're an unbelievable guy.'

'You'll be telling me next my middle name should be Crocodile.' He emitted a long, steadying breath.

'Maybe it should.' She took hold of his T-shirt and gave him a gentle shake. 'You did something heroic and it should be brought to the attention of the public. And your story will also highlight the plight of these poor people. People in the UK hear things about them occasionally, but this'll bring it slap-bang into their consciousness.'

'For how long, two days? It's the breakfast time equivalent of chip paper. It'll change nothing.'

'So what? *You* still deserve the recognition.'

Flynn looked along the quayside. The TV crew and presenter stood in an impatient huddle around a camera and sound boom. Jose stood to one side of them, smirking.

'You managed to get people from a UK TV company to jump on a plane at short notice just to come and speak to me? You must have some clout.'

'Yup.'

'I think I recognize that presenter guy.'

'He's pretty well known.'

Flynn sighed for the hundredth time and regarded Gill. She raised her finely lined eyebrows. 'Think of the free advertising. The charter business will go through the roof.'

He ran a hand down his features. 'Jee-sus,' he whined. 'You did it without asking me.'

'If I had done, what would you have said?'

The corners of Flynn's mouth twisted down cynically. No need to reply to that one.

'I have advised my client to tell you the truth and once he has said it, there will be nothing more forthcoming from him. It is patently obvious, detectives, that you are on a fishing expedition' – on those words, Henry swallowed – 'and have arrested my client on a wing and a prayer.' The solicitor, Baron, sat back and invited a retort from Henry or Rik Dean.

'Let's hear what he has to say, then,' Henry said. 'Mr Last?'

'I had nothing to do with this robbery or the killing of that security guard. I was at home all day yesterday with the exception of spending half an hour in the garden. It was a nice day, but I spent most of it watching TV and DVDs. End of,' he concluded.

Henry nodded, pouted, considering the pithy statement. Then his eyes levelled with Last's. 'I don't believe you. However, you have some very serious allegations to answer anyway in connection with the firearms found at your premises. What we intend to do is this: check out your story, have the guns forensically examined and speak to you again in two weeks' time, unless something comes to light which necessitates an earlier conversation.'

'Does that mean you're giving me bail?'

'With certain conditions, yes.'

'Which really means you have fuck all on me—'

'Mr Last,' the solicitor cut in quickly, warning him with a look that said, 'Shut it.'

Henry smirked. 'That remains to be seen, Mr Last.'

It was one of Steve Flynn's most unpleasant experiences and when the rather intimately fitted microphone was extracted from his clothing, his relief was evident. He was a shy man at heart, did not like to blow his own trumpet, and retelling his deeds of derring-do (not mentioning a rifle) was arse-twitching for him. He had been cross-examined in court on many occasions but he found sitting in front of a camera being asked inane questions by a smarmy presenter was far more painful.

'You were brilliant,' Gill Hartland told him. 'Now what they want to do is go out on the boat so you can take them to where the rescue actually took place and maybe show you fishing as well.'

Flynn's face screwed up for the umpteenth time. 'Why – what are you getting out of this, Gill?'

She regarded him cynically. 'On this occasion, nothing. I'm doing it for the reasons I've already told you. I've got the connections to get this story told and the fact that you're a bit of a hunk and can string more than three sentences together – unlike most of my clients – is a bonus. You're a hero, Flynn – bask in it.'

'Y'think I could get a modelling contract?'

'Mm, age may be against you there,' she kidded, but then her eyes narrowed. 'But I could get you on a dozen daytime chat shows and you could sell your story to a women's magazine I have a contact with. I bet I could get you twenty-five grand out of all this . . .'

'Whoa – hold it right there.' Flynn raised his hands to stop her before she really got into her flow, her eyes sparkling with possibilities. 'Let's just leave it at this, shall we? I've already had my fill of the media, ta.'

'Wouldn't the money come in useful?'

'Any money would come in useful, but not this way. Not my scene.'

'OK babe, fair enough,' she relented.

'Besides which, I don't want some greedy agent taking twenty per cent of my hard-earned dough.'

FOUR

F elix Deakin had become a creature of habit. He knew better than most that routine could be fatal in his line of work, because once the enemy, whoever they might be, whichever side of the fence they might be on – law or lawless – got to know where you were and what you might be doing at any point in the day, they could use that knowledge and move in for the kill. It was a fact of life, and regularity and predictability were things Deakin had been at pains to avoid ever since he'd learned as a youngster on the streets that the packages his father asked him to deliver were not full of caster sugar.

But for the moment he was past caring and couldn't give a toss who knew where he was and what he was doing at any time of day.

The first habit he'd got into was waking up at six forty-five a.m. precisely every morning. Then he would lie in his king-sized bed, his hands clasped behind his head, listening to the twitter of garden birds in the trees outside and the gentle breathing of the woman next to him. The heat of the Mediterranean day was already rising.

An idyllic peace.

Next he would turn to the woman who, familiar with his habits and needs by now, would flutter open her eyes, blink the sleep away and gaze adoringly at him.

'Hi, hon,' she would always whisper in that throaty, early morning way.

'Darlin',' he responded with a half-smile.

She would snuggle in close, her voluptuous naked body hot and soft against him from the night's sleep. He could feel every contour of her and would start to respond as her fingertips danced lightly across his hairy chest, down over his stomach, making his muscles quiver as she took hold of him. This forced a grunt from his throat as she worked him deftly. Then at the right moment her tousled head would disappear under the single sheet.

Afterwards he would clamber sleepily out of bed into the

en-suite shower for a long hot soapy wash, followed by a close wet shave and the application of a soothing balm to moisturize his face and keep his skin young looking.

As he returned naked and refreshed to the bedroom, his woman would be propped up on a bank of pillows, a sultry smile on her face . . .

. . . And Felix Deakin's dream would then abruptly turn sour as the cell lights flickered on behind their protective cage, the screws would start to bang and shout, and another day would begin in Lancashire Prison at seven a.m. All Deakin's pleasant thoughts would evaporate in to the ether and another round of prison life.

He cursed. With an expression of distaste on his rough, unshaven countenance, he swung his legs out of the top bunk and dropped barefoot on to the carpeted cell floor, ignoring the guy on the bottom bunk and the third prisoner squeezed into the cell on a camp bed. He went to the stainless steel toilet affixed in the corner of the cell and pissed away his erection, furious that this was the reality of his life: the fixed routine of a prison where he had no choice about where he was and what he was doing; where it was all chosen for you, whether you liked it or not, even if you wielded a huge amount of power inside the joint, as Deakin did. It had been his routine for almost the last four years, and would be for at least another six unless he did something drastic about it.

'Hit me with it.'

Deakin's solicitor looked across the table at his client.

'Bad news, innit?'

The solicitor nodded. Deakin deflated inside. His appeal against his conviction had been turned down, one of his hopes for early release or a retrial at least. Now he faced six more years inside, taking him up to ten of the sixteen-year sentence the bastard Crown Court judge had handed down to him. The halfway mark in a sentence was often when prisoners were released, but that judge had recommended that Deakin serve a minimum term of ten for the crimes he'd committed.

'On what grounds?'

'No new evidence, the trial was fair, and you were found guilty of all offences, including witness intimidation,' the solicitor said. His name was Barry Baron, the same solicitor who had represented Richard Last at Blackpool Police Station. He was a much sought-after defence solicitor in the Manchester area, especially by high-level criminals, and made a very good living – particularly from Deakin. Deakin knew he had worked hard behind the scenes at the trial, doing his best to discredit the cops, witnesses and evidence – everything, in fact, including the intimidation – through a third party, of course. Yet still the Crown had won.

Deakin got to his feet, breathed and paced the solicitors' interview room at the prison.

'Six more years. I'll be forty-four when I get out of this shit hole, and that's only if I stop myself from killing a screw or a queer. Forty-bloody-four. My life will be as good as over.'

'Forty-four isn't old.'

'It is if you get sent down at thirty-four,' Deakin snapped. He paced a few more steps then retook his seat, pondering for a while. 'What other news have you got for me?'

Baron squirmed slightly. 'Dick Last and Jack Sumner got arrested.'

Deakin inhaled the news, said nothing.

'The last robbery went tits-up,' Baron said. 'Dick Last had too much crap up his nose, it clouded his judgement and a security guard got whacked.'

'Idiots! I said no shooters,' Deakin spat vehemently. He wiped the corners of his mouth.

'Fortunately the cops are just locking up all the usual suspects and because we're careful, there's no forensic links and the gun's been disposed of. The only way they'll get anything is if either blabs or gets careless. I reckon the cops'll be keeping them both under surveillance for a while now, so we need to keep a low profile.'

'But other jobs are planned.'

'I know – we'll just have to keep them on the back burner.' Baron paused, hesitant. 'There is something else . . .'

Deakin's eyelids half-covered his pupils. 'That would be?'

'They're both getting greedy. They want danger money, more of a slab than the thirty-five per cent.'

Once more Deakin allowed the news to filter in. 'On the whole, this consultation hasn't been very positive, has it?'

Baron could see the tension in the prisoner's being, the calm before the violent storm. Deakin's jaw jutted and he ground his teeth. 'You tell them they can fuck off, OK? That money is mine. I do the planning, they subcontract whoever to help 'em out and

pay them from the takings. That's the way. My money,' Deakin
snapped and banged his palm down on the table – just the once.
Then he whispered, 'My retirement fund. Because the bastard
cops have virtually seized all my friggin' assets. Money I won't
see for another six years at this rate. How much did we take
from the job?'

'Forty thousand, give or take.'

'That's fourteen grand for them, less four for their hired numpt-
ies, which makes five grand each for Last and Sumner.'

'And you get twenty-six without getting your hands dirty.'

Deakin's triangular features sharpened. His eyes burned into
Baron, who held up his hands defensively. 'Their words, not
mine.'

'OK, forty per cent for the next one.'

'They want sixty.'

The short, derisive laugh from Deakin said it all. 'No way.'

'And at the moment the money from the last one is still in
their possession. They won't hand anything over until they make
a deal with you.'

Deakin's lips pursed. 'They're taking the piss.'

'There is an element of that, but they hold the money.'

'In that case I'll have to do something about it.'

'Such as?'

'How much does Dick Last love his itty-bitty brother?'

A grin spread across Baron's face. 'A lot, I'd say.'

Deakin sniffed up. 'But having said all that, my circumstances
haven't changed. I'm still in the slammer. I need to be out of
here, Barry. Legally or illegally, even if it means on the run –
and I'll need all the money I can get if I break out . . . as if I
could.'

Baron's face clouded over. Deakin picked up on it instantly.
'What?'

'Maybe there is something . . .' he said thoughtfully, eyes
narrowing.

The young man was in the gym, working out hard: weights,
cross-trainer, rowing machine, the full works. Up to date equipment and even large-screen TVs were dotted around the walls
to ease the burden of exercise.

Jamie Last was twenty-three, just a tad too old to find himself
in with young offenders. Now he was part of the man's world
of grown-up prisons. Not that he cared. He was a tough kid,

brought up on the estates of Salford and Moss Side, a gang member, gun carrier and knifer – which is how he'd finished up inside. A gang fight that went too far, guns and knives brought out and hand-to-hand combat on a bleak car park just outside Manchester city centre. He'd found himself tussling with a nasty black kid who whipped a pistol from his waistband, but in the heat of battle dropped it in the grit. Jamie managed to kick it away and plunge a four-inch shiv into the lad's neck. Only the lucky intervention of mob-handed cops and an ambulance had saved Jamie from being up on a murder charge.

But he was happy enough to do time, excited by his promotion into the world of the adult, not in the least afraid.

He was on the mat now: press-ups, sit-ups, burpees. He sweated and pushed himself hard, determined that the day he walked back on to the streets he would be tougher, fitter and harder than ever. He was concentrating, in his own world, not aware that the few other users of the gym had been silently beckoned to leave. Only as he stood up following fifty press-ups did he realize he was alone in the room.

He shrugged, unconcerned, turned to the treadmill facing a wall and a TV screen affixed out of the reach of mischievous hands. He began a slow trot, intending to complete 5k, after which he'd call it a day.

The TV screen went blank.

Again, Jamie wasn't bothered. It was only boring daytime stuff they were allowed to watch. He hunched his head down, controlled his breathing and imagined himself pounding the pavements.

The blow from the dumbbells floored him. Struck with agonizing force somewhere between the base of the skull and the shoulder blades, Jamie went down hard, smacking his face on the electronic control panel of the treadmill, sagging to his knees which were suddenly the consistency of jelly. The momentum of the rubber roadway dragged him back and deposited him behind the treadmill on the gym floor.

Then somebody stomped on his head. It felt as though his skull went out of shape for a moment and he was underwater, until his senses returned. He groaned and twisted on to his back when a 125kg spinlock bar – the steel bar on to which dumbbells are slotted – was slammed across his unprotected throat. Then Felix Deakin's out-of-focus face came swimming into Jamie's vision, his mouth a twisted smile.

'Mornin', Jamie.'

Jamie struggled to raise the bar, but despite his strength and fitness he could not hope to dislodge Deakin and the men at either end of the bar assisting him. He tried to wrench himself free, but the trio pushed down harder until all their victim's fight dissipated and he gagged for breath.

Only then was the bar raised a little, allowing air to gush into his lungs, and he was allowed to roll away, clutching his throat.

But if the young man had even begun to think it was over, he was cruelly mistaken. With no explanation for their action, Deakin's two heavies began to beat him with fourteen-inch spin-lock dumbbell handles, raining blows about his head, neck, arms and lower legs. It was a relentless assault carried out with ruthless efficiency.

Deakin stood back and watched coldly until he said, 'Enough.' He jerked his thumbs at the two men and they dragged an almost lifeless Jamie across the gym and propped him up against the wall. His head lolled and blood poured out of his busted nose and broken mouth.

Using a digital camera, one of the men took numerous shots of the injured victim. Then they left him and walked out of the gym. Deakin nodded a quick thanks to the prison guard, who entered the gym and took care of the mess.

'Brief's back to see you.' The screw did not enter Deakin's cell, stood a respectful two feet outside on the landing. The authorities had learned it could be a dangerous place.

Deakin was on his bunk, grinning as he tabbed through the camera holding the digital photos from the recent beating he'd supervised. Jamie Last, brother of Dick Last, was a very nasty mess – at least on the surface. Deakin's two men, the ones he shared a cell with, had done a good job but not gone too far. They were pros and knew how to deliver any degree of assault. Deakin knew Jamie would soon recover. This was just a warning of what could happen should his brother Dick – and Jack Sumner, his partner in crime – get awkward over financial matters.

Deakin sighed at the interruption and propped himself up. 'He's back again?'

'Yeah, you know where to go,' the officer said.

'At least he can deliver the photos,' he said and swung himself down from the bunk. He was puzzled as to why Baron should be back so soon. Still, he thought, solicitor's privilege.

He exited the cell and made his way along the metallic landing, trotting down a staircase into an association area where a number of inmates were watching a big-screen TV. Deakin gave the TV a cursory glance. He had his own TV and DVD in his cell. He saw they were watching some crass mid-morning bollocks but as he turned away he heard a name he recognized spoken by one of the presenters. His head jerked back to the screen and as if drawn by a magnet, he threaded his way between the seated prisoners and stared open-mouthed at the screen. He was in the way of several people, but not even the man he pushed out of a chair in order to sit in his seat complained. He was riveted by what he was seeing. When the piece came to an end, he turned and demanded, 'Who's got the remote?' Another prisoner held up the black box. 'Rewind it back to the start of that interview.'

There was no question as to why. The man just did it, using the digital rewind facility that came with the satellite package.

Deakin watched it again, all the way through. Then he rose in a sort of trance and made his way through the gaol to the screws' office on the ground floor landing. After a cursory search during which the digital camera wasn't even challenged, he was shown through to the interview room where Barry Baron waited impatiently.

'Couldn't they find you or something?' Baron said sarcastically, making a show of checking his watch, then regretting it when he saw the expression on his client's face.

'Yeah, I went out for a fucking stroll,' he snarled. 'What are you doing back so soon?'

'I said I knew there was something,' Baron explained. 'Which, if it's combined with something else, could give you that *something* you want,' he said mysteriously.

'And as we're talking in riddles, there's something else just come to my attention which could go into the pot. But what say we cut the crap and say what we mean, OK? We both know this room isn't bugged, not like next door, and we can speak freely.'

'Trust no one, is what I say,' Baron said. 'But, yeah, we should be OK in here.'

Deakin said, 'Just get on with it and stop fartin' around . . .'

Baron smiled grimly. 'Johnny Cain's due to appear shortly at Preston Crown Court—'

'I know – so?'

'You know lots of things about Johnny Cain, don't you?'

'Enough to send the bastard to prison for a thousand years . . .'
Then the realization hit Deakin. 'Fuck me, that's a good idea.'

It had been another extra long day for Henry Christie. On the
previous evening he'd been late at work, then very late at the
hospital where his mother had become 'stable'; then he'd
managed about four hours' sleep before crawling back to the
hospital for an hour at the bedside, before driving to his office
at headquarters for a day of getting everything straight.

Not that there was much chance of that.

The one thing he'd discovered about being a superintendent
was that the work that *needed* to be done was always superseded
by less important tasks, such as attending meetings, seminars
and general tick-the-box crap.

At five thirty p.m. that day, other than attending a tactical
tasking meeting – which was important – and going to all the
other dross, he'd done nothing that he wanted. All those things
now had to be achieved outside his supposed eight hours, but
then again, the eight-hour working day had always been a fallacy.

At last he was on the phone to Rik Dean, who was bringing
him up to speed with the superstore murder/robbery investigation. There was little to report. The police were going through
the motions, surveillance was up and running, CCTV tapes were
being scrutinized, witnesses interviewed, and a stolen car had
been found burned out by some garages in Rochdale that could
have been used as a second getaway car by the robbers. Its location fitted in with the addresses of Richard Last and Jack Sumner,
but didn't prove anything.

Henry hung up with a heavy heart. He hoped that everything
that could be done was being done. His gut feeling was that
these two guys were involved and it just needed persistence and
a bit of good luck to uncover the vital chink that would open
the floodgates and nail the fuckers.

He had to make some more calls. There was an ongoing
stranger rape in Lancaster, a domestic murder in Fleetwood
(solved but with complications) and several other investigations
that needed pushing along.

He picked up his desk phone, keeping his finger on the disconnect button while he tried to recall the extension number he
needed, when the phone rang unexpectedly, making him jump.

'It's me – Rik. Some bad news just in, Henry.'

'Go on,' he sighed.

'Last and Sumner have shaken their tails. The surveillance team has lost them.'

'Oh, brilliant . . .' Henry couldn't be bothered to get angry. 'Keep me up to speed, please.' He hung up, his finger still on the button, and the phone rang again. 'That was quick!'

'Well you know me, Henry,' came a low, female voice at the other end, one he recognized instantly. It always sent a shiver of anticipation down his backbone.

'Sorry, I thought it would be someone else, not Naomi Dale, prosecutor extraordinary, unless I'm much mistaken.'

'As ever, right on the button.'

'What can I do for you?' He checked his watch. It was going on six thirty, time to be getting back to the hospital.

'Johnny Cain,' she stated.

'What about him?'

'He's about to go on trial for murder. I know you're not involved.'

'No, but I'm up to speed with it.' Henry knew that Cain had been committed for Crown Court trial some time ago. He hadn't been involved with the job and the investigation had been headed by the previous head of FMIT, Dave Anger, who was now pending serious charges of his own – not linked to Cain. Henry thought everything was done and dusted, even though Cain was pleading not guilty to the charge.

'I need to have a word with you about it. Something's come up,' Naomi Dale said.

'Oh fuck me, the brief is back. Woo-woo,' Dick Last said, shaking his hands to imitate fear. 'Look at me – scared.'

Barry Baron inhaled deeply and sat down in the alcove next to Last. He glanced around the bar, which was quite empty. The pub they were in was situated high on the moors between Rochdale and Rossendale. On a bad day it could be bleak and barren. That evening, though, it was warm and sunny, a pleasant enough place to hang out.

Richard Last and Jack Sumner often visited the place. Their main haunts were dives in Rochdale town centre, but sometimes they gravitated to this pub, known as Owd Betts, to have a quiet pint in a location the law probably wasn't watching. And because Last had realized that he and Sumner were under surveillance, the duo had spent a good deal of time that day ensuring they shook off their followers. He was certain the police were not watching them when they met Baron.

It was a mistake that would cost them dearly.

Last cut to the chase.

'Been to see him, then?'

'I have.'

'What's he say?'

'He's not impressed,' Baron replied, unfazed and not intimidated by either man. In the world of the crim, he was pretty untouchable.

'He's not impressed?' Sumner shot forward, jabbing his finger. 'He's not the one doing the work, is he?' He thudded back against the padded seat and grabbed his pint petulantly.

'No one was supposed to get shot,' Baron said evenly.

'Well someone did,' Last iterated. 'Tough shit, shouldn't have been a hero.'

'However,' Baron continued calmly, 'I did relay to him your suggestion about upping your percentage and explained your position to him.' Both men eyed him greedily, waiting. Baron gave a short shake of the head. 'No deal.'

There was a beat of silence before the reaction.

Last leaned forward again. 'In that case you can tell him where to stick it – *and* that we're keeping all of the last one. All of it. Every last cent.'

Baron pursed his lips, then slid his hand into his jacket pocket, extracting an envelope. 'Let me remind you that even though he is inside, he wields more power than you could ever imagine. This is just a small example.' He held out the envelope. Last snatched it, tore it open. The recently downloaded and printed set of digital photographs splayed out on the table between the men's pints.

Last picked one up slowly. Baron watched the blood drain out of his face. His eyes took in the image and flickered to Baron and back.

'I'd advise you not to get mad with me,' Baron warned. 'But the message is that sixty per cent is unacceptable. He'll go to forty and no more. And the next job must be done without shooters. *And* the money from the last one must be handed over, otherwise he will start to spread his net . . . more family.'

Last's face became a mask of rage. His eyes widened. His lips pulled back into a snarl. 'He did this to Jamie – the bastard.'

Baron interlaced his fingers in front of him and leaned back. He knew these two wouldn't touch him but he still had to be cautious. The reaction to the news he had just presented to them could easily end in a violent outburst. 'Jamie will be all right. It looks worse than it is and you should consider that.'

Last seethed visibly, his chest rising and falling, fist clenching. He was an unthinking, dangerous man usually fired by drugs – hence the shooting – and his rage always required some kind of outlet. His eyes became opaque and the skin on his face tightened to a surface like the side of a box of safety matches.

Sumner put a calming hand on Last's forearm and spoke to Baron. 'You can tell him he just made the wrong move on us and now he'll pay for it in more ways than one. Financially and personally.'

'He could easily have let a lot worse happen to Jamie. He could be in a body bag right now and if you threaten him, he will be.' Baron rocked upright. 'Now, I expect to collect the money you owe tomorrow and back to business as usual. I don't have the time or inclination to talk or counsel either of you. That's the way it is.'

Last's arms were now folded as tight as a wire rope around his chest as he held on to his volcanic rage. He hissed, 'Tell him no deal.'

Baron nodded. Guys like this were very expendable and he'd been told by Deakin to do whatever was necessary to get the money back, or deal with them with finality. He stood up, keeping his eyes on Last, then turned and walked out of the pub.

It was still warm outside, the sun slowly dropping behind the coarse hills. Baron exhaled a long breath, then trotted to the car park, pausing by the door of his Mercedes. He glanced back at the pub, raised his chin and in a subtle, prearranged way, ran his right forefinger across his throat. Anyone watching would have thought he'd scratched his neck, not given the gesture that meant 'Kill them.'

She was petite, maybe five four, but had a seductive voice that made Henry want to breathe heavily, and doll-like looks which had not diminished with the twenty tough years she'd spent as a CPS prosecutor in Lancashire. Although she still regularly attended court, where her looks and stature belied a tigress-like tenacity and a devious brain which had caught out many an unsuspecting defence solicitor, she spent much of her time working alongside the police on complex major investigations. She pulled together intricate files which, more often than not, delivered guilty verdicts. Henry had known her for many years, and had always been impressed by her professionalism and annoyed by her complete lack of interest in him. She was also a workaholic, unmarried; he thought she had a fairly lonely life, from what he knew about her. She needed a bit of excitement in her life, Henry thought.

She was based at the Crown Prosecution Service office in Blackpool, which meant it was easy for Henry to make his way across to meet her before going to visit his mother in hospital.

They did not meet in the office, however, but at a pub just off Marton Circle, the motorway roundabout which was the last junction of the M55 outside the resort.

'Hope you don't mind meeting here,' Naomi Dale said, climbing out of her Mazda coupé. She was still in her practical business suit of grey pinstripe, which sounded dull but clung tightly to her curves and which Henry thought was extremely sexy: a woman in uniform, almost.

'Not at all. It's on my way home.'

She regarded him oddly. 'Of course, you live over here, don't you?' They shook hands and walked side by side to the pub. Henry let her step in ahead of him, gallant as ever. The main bar was sparsely populated and they were served quickly, a gin and lime for her, mineral water for him. They moved to an alcove and sat opposite each other at a brass-topped table. Henry had trouble keeping his eyes off her. Despite now being a super-intendent, he acted like a nineteen-year-old trapped in the body of someone with almost half a century behind him.

'How are you, Henry?'

'I'm good.'

'How's the Dave Anger fiasco panning out?'

He wasn't surprised she knew about the corrupt Dave Anger, previous head of FMIT and Henry's nemesis. But he was a little taken aback by the question.

'Still bubbling away. Don't think it'll disappear for quite some time, but the stench of a corrupt cop always lingers.'

'I expect it does.' She sipped her drink and her eyes focused on his left hand. 'You're married!'

'Remarried, as in ex-wife, now wife again.'

'Mm, I think I heard that. Congratulations,' she said flatly. Henry gave her an equally flat smile. 'Anyway, to business. Johnny Cain, one of Dave Anger's cases.'

'His legacy lingers in more ways than one, but the reality of it is, all he did was oversee the investigation. Others did the graft.'

'It was a good case, but even good cases can use a bit of assistance sometimes.'

Henry nodded. Despite Dave Anger's deep-rooted corruption, he had a good clear-up rate. It was hard for Henry to admit, but it was a silver lining in Anger's very grey cloud. The Johnny Cain file was a case in point. Cain was a top-line drugs dealer and suspected for a number of years of killing a business partner who had been skimming deals. It had been a very nasty execution, an object lesson in persuading other people who were thinking of doing the same thing to Cain to think otherwise.

It had taken a three and a half year investigation for a small team directed by Anger to finally make links to Cain and ultimately secure an arrest. Henry acknowledged the gruelling work involved, but he had heard a rumour that there were still some tenuous threads in the case which could possibly be snapped by a smart defence barrister. These were mainly procedural things linked to surveillance and phone tapping, on which a lot of the evidence relied.

'There is no doubt that Cain knew John Swann,' she said, naming the victim, 'but we have to convince the jury of that. Once that connection is firmly established, Cain is well and truly screwed . . . but a lot of it depends on interpreting phone calls and conversations couched in, shall we say, innocent terms or euphemisms.'

'A bit like the Mafia. All those phone taps used by the FBI to bring down some big Cosa Nostra families,' Henry said.

'Yeah. Plus there's no forensic links, which is a bit of a bummer. Three and a half years from finding the body to making an arrest. However, I am confident the Crown has a good case, but it could always be better.'

Henry sipped his drink, then shook his head slightly. 'So how can I help?'

'Ever heard of Felix Deakin?'

Henry's guts hit the ground with a thump at the mention of the name. He tried to hide his reaction. 'Yeah, I've had experience of him.'

'What do you know of him, then?'

'Big time crim, used to be one of our top targets . . . now in prison for importation, distribution, serious assaults, threats to kill. Got sixteen years, if I remember rightly. Once suspected of killing a seventeen-year-old lad who was one of his mules.'

Naomi nodded. 'I've had an approach from his legal representative, literally only hours ago, so it's not something I've been sitting on. Johnny Cain is due to go to trial in the next few weeks and Deakin is offering to give evidence against him.'

'What evidence?' Henry asked dubiously. Naomi shrugged. 'Not to put too fine a point on it, I wouldn't trust him as far as I could chuck him.'

'Me neither.'

'What's he offering?'

'I have actually no idea, but I've arranged to go and see him in prison tomorrow. But I'll need a cop alongside me.' She raised her eyebrows. 'One of appropriate rank and influence and at a level to make serious decisions.'

'Good Lord,' Henry said, 'that must be me.'

FIVE

The two men eyed each other venomously. Henry Christie breathed shallowly, gritting his teeth and holding himself from leaping across the screwed-down table and tearing the shit limb from limb.

In turn, Deakin watched Henry with a smug degree of readiness, probably fully expecting that to happen.

Henry and Naomi Dale had arrived at Lancashire Prison about twenty minutes before. After the customary searches and ID checks, they had been shown into the interview room where they had to wait for Deakin and his solicitor to be brought to them.

As the inner door opened and prisoner and brief stepped in, Henry felt a jolt. Not only due to his past encounter with Deakin, but because the solicitor was none other than Barry Baron, the guy who had represented Richard Last, the suspected robber and killer. Henry looked from one to the other, his mind suddenly whirring with the implications of the connection. It made him uncomfortable. Maybe he was being far too suspicious, but the first thing he asked himself was how did this fit together? He screwed it through his mind, then told himself not to be silly. Barry Baron represented a lot of criminals, just like any number of solicitors did, and this was probably just a coincidence. What the hell else could it be?

After some stiff formalities, Baron, his eyes shifting between

Naomi, Henry and the sheaf of papers he'd brought in with him, said, 'First things first . . . My client, Mr Deakin, wishes you to know exactly why he has decided to come forth with his knowledge and what he expects to gain from his . . . opening up.'

Naomi and Henry waited patiently, letting Baron fill the gaps.

'The bottom line is this . . . he feels he has a public duty to perform by giving evidence against Cain as he is very much a reformed character since being in prison.' Henry stifled a guffaw at this. 'But also, and being completely honest, he does see this as a possible way to get his sentence reduced. It is a combination of altruism and selfishness, but he would like to say that even if he does not get a reduction in sentence, the fact that he has done a public service will be good enough for him.'

Henry looked quickly around to see if he could find a sick bag. The 'I'll bet' remark just about managed to stay on his lips.

'He does expect wheels to work within wheels in the justice system to get a further review of his sentence so that he can be considered for parole in a year's time. That's all he seeks – the public good and an opportunity to get out of prison a little bit sooner.'

'Is that all?' Naomi said.

'Not quite,' Baron said. 'Johnny Cain is a very dangerous man. He controls a sophisticated criminal organization. He is a killer and has people who kill for him. So, also in return for his testimony, my client wishes to be protected. That means a transfer from here to a prison where his safety can be guaranteed and then, on his early release, entry into a witness protection programme and all that entails.'

Henry held back another snort. His eyes stayed trained on Deakin, wondering what the hell was going on. People like Deakin did not do things for the public good, nor did they grass on their fellow crims – unless they'd had something very wrong done to them. And as far as Henry knew, Deakin and Cain rubbed along OK in the free world. Maybe not as the best of mates, but . . .

'Before I can make any promises, I have to know what's on offer,' Naomi stated.

'I understand that, but I can assure you that what my client has to say will be gold dust to you. It will make your case against Johnny Cain rock solid and will send a bad man to prison for a long time. And we know your case has certain . . . gaps . . . in it.

My client is more than willing to stand up in the dock and be counted. He will face Cain and give evidence.'

Naomi glanced at Henry. 'Short break?'

'Don't like it.'

'Nor me.'

'Just how strong is the case? What's the chance of a conviction?'

They were in the corridor outside the interview room, whispering hoarsely to each other under the bored but watchful gaze of a prison officer, out of his hearing.

'Sixty-five, seventy per cent.' Naomi rocked her hand.

'Thirty per cent chance of him walking. What'll be the stumbling block?'

'Confirming, without any shadow of a doubt, the connection between Cain and the victim, Swann.'

'Therefore if Deakin plugs that gap, you'll be laughing?'

'It wouldn't go amiss in the grand scheme of things.'

'I don't trust him,' Henry said. 'And there's something else I just can't put my finger on.' Henry shook his head.

'We can at least listen to him.'

Henry nodded.

'What's your connection with Deakin?' Naomi asked. 'You can cut the tension between you two with a chainsaw.'

'Water under the bridge.'

She regarded him suspiciously. 'Don't let it cloud your judgement, whatever it is.' She touched Henry's arm.

His lips tightened. 'He threatened my family once,' Henry admitted. 'It's the way he operates.' He shrugged. 'Threats and more threats.'

'Do you feel you can go on with this?'

'As I said, water under the bridge.'

Henry nodded to the prison officer and they were allowed back into the interview room where Henry saw Deakin pass a yellow Post-it note to Baron. He didn't give it much thought: client–solicitor privilege.

Everyone had backed off and Steve Flynn was feeling a lot better. The publicity machine so quickly assembled by Gill Hartland had retreated and Flynn hoped he would now be allowed to get back on with his life.

It was a great sensation, simply to stroll along the quayside in the steaming hot sunshine wearing the Keith Richards T-shirt and ragged shorts after a swift cola in a nearby hostelry, knowing that all the crap was over with. Awaiting him a hundred metres away was the spick-and-span vision that was *Lady Faye*. Maybe she wasn't his boat, but she was as near as dammit.

She looked wonderful, back to – nay, surpassing – her previous glory, having been worked on and cleaned remorselessly by himself and the crew.

'Nice, nice,' he whispered on his lips.

He looked diagonally back across the quay towards the built-up area he'd just left. Sitting on a stool outside a bar was the aforementioned Gill Hartland who, having discovered her latest celebrity, had decided to stay on an extra few days just to calm down the poor chap. Her presence was much appreciated by Flynn, though she'd done little to calm him down in the ardour stakes – but their frenetic lovemaking did have the effect of keeping him sane in his brief flurry of fame.

He sighed contentedly and gave Gill a quick wave before stepping on to the boat to take charge for a half-day charter of a group of Irish guys who didn't want to leave port too early. They hadn't turned up yet, but they'd paid upfront so Flynn wasn't worried by the no-show. He guessed the charter would be a short one anyway, as it was obvious the group had booked on a whim in a week of otherwise being drunk and chasing skirt. They'd be seasick and pining for dry land before they got an hour out, Flynn guessed. But at least he'd be at sea, instead of being all at sea as he had been for the past few days.

His mobile phone hung in a waterproof pouch at his waist. It vibrated and he answered it. As he drew it to his ear, he glanced across the harbour at Gill who had her phone to her ear.

A smile cracked on his tanned face as he flipped open the phone, not even glancing at the caller display. My God, he thought, his male ego taking over, she really can't do without me, can't bear to let me go.

'Hiya babe,' he crooned into the phone.

'Dad, is that you?'

An eerie sensation coursed through his veins as these few words registered with him. Even so, he did then automatically check the display, and saw that although the number was not shown, it told him it was an international call. He pressed the phone to his ear.

'Dad?'

Flynn's knees suddenly went weak. He steadied himself on the fighting chair, then swivelled round to sit on it, otherwise he would have toppled over.

'Craig?' he asked breathlessly.

'Dad, Dad?' It was an urgent whisper.

'Yeah, Craig, it's me – your dad.' He licked his lips and wiped the sudden sweat off his brow.

Jose, who had been working in the cockpit, emerged rubbing his oily hands with a rag. He'd seen Flynn take the call and witnessed the unusual reaction to it. He watched him with a faintly concerned frown – but not too concerned.

Flynn was stunned. His son Craig was on the phone, completely out of the blue. The son he hadn't officially been allowed to speak to for almost four years. All contact had been via furtive, occasional phone calls like this one. Craig, now fourteen years old. Flynn clamped his eyes tight shut and tried to imagine what he might look like. Fourteen, a young man growing up fast. He opened his eyes and a tear balanced in the corner of them, blurring his vision.

'Dad, you OK?'

God, the voice, so grown up.

Flynn, as though struck by a demolition ball, struggled to control himself. 'Yeah, Craig, course I am. It's just such a . . . pleasure to hear your voice. How are you? Is there something wrong?'

'No Dad, I just wanted to speak to you.'

'Does your mum . . .?' Flynn started to ask, but didn't even have to complete the question.

'No,' Craig whispered conspiratorially, two thousand miles to the north. 'She doesn't know I'm calling you. She'd have a hissy if she did . . . I saw you on telly, being interviewed about those immigrants, y'know? Dad, it was really magic to see you.' Craig's voice crackled with either static or emotion, Flynn couldn't quite tell. 'I still miss you, Dad. I love you.'

'Yeah.' Flynn's voice definitely crackled. 'Love you, too.'

'Er . . .' Craig hesitated, not knowing what to say next, a fourteen-year-old boy not used to making small talk to adults, Flynn guessed.

'Hey – did you get my Chrissy present?'

'What? No . . . Mum said you didn't send any.' The bitch. Flynn nearly chewed the end off his tongue. He kept his voice level.

'Gotta go – she's coming,' Craig said hurriedly. 'Love you, Dad.' Then the phone went dead.

Flynn was gutted. He stared at his phone, then eased out a long breath.

'You OK, *gringo*?' Jose asked.

'That was my son,' Flynn said proudly. He smiled and gave a short laugh, suddenly so pleased they'd spoken. 'Maybe some good has come from the TV appearances after all,' he gushed and punched the air with a whoop.

'You know I can't discuss any points of the case with you,' Naomi Dale said sternly to Barry Baron. 'To reveal the prosecution evidence would be unethical.'

'But we all know your case will go to rats if you can't prove a direct link to Cain and Swann – otherwise it's all circumstantial.'

'I'm not at liberty to say.' She gave Baron an even harder glare.

'OK, have it your way. But what if I was to say that my client's testimony will prove that Cain knew Swann, knew him personally and knew him well?'

'It would have to be direct evidence, evidence of what Mr Deakin saw or heard Cain do, not circumstantial. Otherwise we're wasting time.'

Deakin cut in. 'I've been in Cain's presence on numerous occasions when Swann was also there. Just three of us on several occasions. I can give evidence that he knew Swann, that Swann worked for him, went boozing with him, went away for a weekend with him once. And that Cain even once told me he suspected Swann of skimming from him and if he ever found out for certain, he'd kill him . . . which he obviously did.'

The revelation stunned Naomi. She tensed up and for once her prosecutor's composure deserted her. She came upright and shot Henry a look of excitement.

Henry, on the other hand, remained cool and unsettled. Maybe it was because he wasn't involved in the case personally and was somewhat detached from it. In fact he felt nothing, other than a deep-rooted mistrust for Deakin and his motivation. And a sense that the whole thing seemed a bit contrived.

Although Steve Flynn had never suffered from it, he knew that one of the worst ailments anybody can have is seasickness.

The condition is compounded when the sufferer is surrounded by others who are not affected and refuse to offer any form of succour, condolence or hope – and just take the piss instead.

Flynn glanced down from the flying bridge and sympathized with the sole member of the charter who was hanging over the side of the boat, retching dreadfully on a now empty stomach while his three mates steadfastly refused to listen to his pleas to return to shore. Instead they took it in turns to tell him that to be cured he should sit under a tree. All found this highly amusing except the sick one, who crawled on all fours into the stateroom and flopped on the bed, closing his eyes.

Not a good move, Flynn knew. The blackness behind the eyelids just made things a whole lot worse. Better to keep moving and concentrate on the horizon.

However, not his problem – except the sick man had earlier tried to do some fishing, but his state of nausea meant he did not concentrate or care and he managed to 'bird's nest' one of the reels, much to Jose's anger, who had to put it right. At that moment, the Spaniard was still unpicking the mess with a scowl on his face that made him look as though he was munching gravel.

Instinctively Flynn knew it was three p.m. Another half-hour, then back to Puerto Rico. Then a night on the town with Gill was his plan. Eat, drink, dance, fuck. The circle of life.

He smiled contentedly. The last couple of days of trials and tribulations were over. He knew he'd have to give evidence regarding the deaths of the immigrants, but that was way ahead and would be a low-key affair. The Spanish authorities were not overly concerned with the fate of people trying to enter their country illegally and didn't put much effort into investigating how their deaths came about. Much to Flynn's relief.

'Hey, hey, hey!' screamed one of the trio of fishermen as a line zinged out.

Flynn got his mind back into gear and reacted.

He had fish to catch. From the way the line was shifting he could tell it was a barracuda, vicious, nasty – a handful.

Henry Christie had never bothered to delve too deeply into the theory of the psychology of criminality, even though offenders and their motives did fascinate him. He was more concerned with being the hunter bringing down his prey, and would be the first to acknowledge that he probably allowed the deep-rooted

element of his psyche that was still 'man the hunter' to mani-
fest itself in his job. He worked on instinct when it came to
dealing with people and always believed he could read others
well – with the exclusion of women, that is. But he knew crims,
knew what made them tick; he knew when he was being lied to
and tricked – usually. That had been one of the reasons he'd
been a good thief taker in his younger days and an excellent, if
flawed, SIO in his later years.

Which is how he knew he was being twirled by Felix Deakin.

Problem was, there was no way of proving it.

It wasn't anything Deakin had said. He'd uttered all the right
words. Nor was it in his body language. He'd used open, reassuring gestures, maintained eye contact without overdoing it,
not clamped up, been pleasant . . . so what was it about him?

Henry pondered. Maybe, he thought, it's because I simply
cannot be swayed to trust a single freaking word that comes out
of his mouth.

And, on reflection, that was probably the root of Henry being
a good jack. He started every investigation on the basis that
everything he heard was a lie. It was a bit like gathering corn,
sorting the wheat from the chaff. Everyone's a liar until proved
different. Even the witnesses.

There was a flicker of a smile on Deakin's cruel lips.

Naomi and Baron had retreated to the corridor to discuss some
legal points, leaving Henry and Deakin alone in the interview
room, across the table from each other.

'I get the impression you don't like me.'

'Not only do I not like you, Felix, what's much more important is that I completely and utterly mistrust you and your motivation. That's the key,' Henry said, using his forefinger to emphasize
the point. 'Plus anyone who threatens my family is not top of
my Christmas card list.'

'That was just words.' Deakin flicked a dismissive gesture.
'Nothing meant.'

Henry gave a disbelieving snort.

'It's true, Henry. Wives, girlfriends, kids – all out of bounds
as far as I'm concerned. The players, however . . .' He shrugged
innocently. 'Anyway, it's old hat. But the truth here is that I am
being selfish. I want the chance to get out of this shit hole before
I'm an old guy and if I can do it by bringing down another crim,
then, hey! And perform a public service too. Y'know, ying and
yang?'

It was transparent that Henry's face displayed his disbelief. 'To coin a phrase, you're a lyin' sack of shit and I don't believe anything, so I'll be keeping a close eye on you if the CPS are stupid enough to go along with this charade. Pardon me for being an old cynic . . .' Henry would have ranted on, but the door reopened and the two briefs entered. From their faces, Henry saw that they had reached an agreement and his opinion from now on was purely academic.

Earlier that day two men sat quietly in the international departure lounge at Terminal 2 of Manchester Airport. They had suffered the indignity of the intrusive customs searches and now they waited patiently within sight of one of the departure monitors, sipping coffees bought from Starbucks, scanning newly purchased magazines and exchanging occasional words.

They were wiry, tough-looking individuals, having the look of ex-soldiers perhaps. They exuded an air of menace that made other passengers give them a wide berth.

When the monitor declared that all passengers for the flight should go to Gate 32, they picked up their hand luggage and sauntered in the right direction. Hand luggage was all they had. They travelled light, without encumbrance. They seated themselves at the gate and continued their patient wait until the flight was called.

A few minutes later they were settled in their seats, strapped in.

At eleven thirty-five a.m., the jet rumbled on to the runway. The engines powered up, the brakes were released and seconds later the plane was rising steeply towards the clouds, the start of their four and a half hour flight. Destination Las Palmas, Gran Canaria.

Flynn guided *Lady Faye* into harbour at four p.m. Although the heat had gone out of the day, there was no breeze in port and it was stifling – just how he liked it. With the ease of an expert, Flynn manoeuvred the boat into her allotted mooring and Jose leapt on to the quayside to tie her up.

The seasickness sufferer scrambled ashore and within seconds of being on dry land he had recovered. His three mates, satisfied by the afternoon's fishing, clapped Flynn on the shoulder and shook hands. It had been a good few hours from a customer point of view, with barracuda, roughtail stingray, angel shark, bonito, wahoo all caught, as well as two red snapper that Flynn claimed for himself. The guy who'd made the reservation slipped Flynn a hundred euros before climbing ashore and the four of them bounced away, knackered, suntanned and in one case, relieved to be ashore.

Flynn watched them go, giving them a captain's salute as they turned and gave him a cheer.

He split the euros – forty to Jose, twenty to Tommy and forty to himself. Then he selected a chilled beer from the icebox and washed away the tang of salt with a long swig of Cruzcampo. It tasted amazing. Its icy tentacles slithered through his chest. He turned to Jose. 'Good afternoon?'

The Spaniard nodded approvingly and rubbed the euro notes between thumb and forefinger. '*La cuenta*,' he said.

'*Si* – and what's your plans for tonight?'

'Home – wife – paella – fucky-fucky.'

'Sounds good.'

'You?' As he asked the question, his eyes glanced past Flynn's shoulder and he went, 'Ahh.' Flynn looked around. Gill Hartland was strolling along the quayside. 'She leave tomorrow – *si*?'

'*Si*.' Flynn found it a heartbreaking word to say.

'In that case, *amigo*, Tommy and me will clean up and lock up . . . you go and enjoy your last hours together.'

'You certain?'

'For a forty-euro tip, I'm certain. You know, most Brits haven't yet realized that one euro is worth almost a pound, have they?'

'And long may that continue.'

Flynn picked up the red snappers and dropped them into a carrier bag. He thanked the two guys and almost ran off the boat to meet Gill. She looked stunning. Not because of how she was dressed – a red basketball top, blue cut-offs, flip-flops and sunglasses, nothing special. She simply looked amazing to Flynn, whose heart whammed a little too wildly for comfort. He wondered if the no-strings agreement was beginning to look a bit creased around the edges.

'Hey – look what I got.' He showed her the fish in the bag. 'Fancy a bit of alfresco tonight? These babies are beautiful on the barbie.'

She flashed her eyelashes at him. 'Sounds ace.' She upped on to her toes and pecked him on the cheek, twisted around and slid her arm into his. They strolled comfortably along, chatting amicably, passing all the boats and then the first bars and restaurants.

They were so engrossed in each other that neither noticed the two men sitting at a table in Pablo's. Men who watched the two lovers silently as they went by.

SIX

F lynn cleaned the barbecue, filled it with charcoal briquettes bought from the local Aldi, and lit them. He filleted and scraped the red snappers, gutted them and sliced off their heads before stuffing them with herbs and garlic, brushing them in extra virgin olive oil and wrapping them in foil. He fixed the grill pan high over the heat and set the fish to cook gently while preparing a tossed salad and some dirty rice.

The sun had set by the time the food was prepared and he and Gill sat out in the tiny front garden, drinking chilled white wine and eating.

'This fish is delicious,' Gill enthused. She was right. It was thick and meaty and full of flavour. 'As is everything else. I've never had dirty rice before.' She raised her glass to Flynn, who smiled modestly, took a sip then placed his glass on the patio. They were eating off plates on their knees and everything seemed perfect. 'This is much better than hotel food.'

'Thanks.'

When they'd eaten, Flynn swilled the dishes then returned to the patio to finish off the wine.

'I've had a great time,' Gill told him, 'despite the tragedy.'

'Me too – despite the TV people.'

'Sorry . . . but I've had loads of magazines wanting interviews with you, men's ones as well as women's. I don't suppose . . .? There'd be good money in it.'

Flynn held up his hand. 'I want to retreat back into my shell, please.'

'OK, OK,' she relented. She relaxed back into the slightly unstable folding chair and inhaled the sweet aroma of the bougainvillea and the dampness of the recently watered lawns beyond the garden wall. Her chest rose and fell jerkily. She shook her head. 'Don't wanna go home. Can't believe I'm saying that, but it's true.'

Flynn's own chest started to tighten. 'You've got all those clients clamouring for your attention.'

'Screw 'em,' she sighed, blew out her cheeks. 'I'm usually raring to get back 'cos I love my job, but . . . this island, as developed as it might be, has really got to me.' She turned to face Flynn. 'And so have you.'

He almost choked on his wine.

Henry Christie was back in his office at police headquarters, having decided to review a copy of the case files on Deakin and Johnny Cain. It took him less than ten minutes of skimming, and knowing what he was looking for, to see the glaring hole in the police evidence against Cain.

'Shit,' he said. There was no way he wanted Deakin involved in Cain's trial, but looking at the case, the knowledge he claimed to have simply couldn't be ignored. Out of the blue, Felix Deakin had become a vital witness.

His desk phone rang, the tone indicating it was an internal call. 'Detective Superintendent Christie . . .'

'Boss? Rik Dean . . .' There was a hint of urgency in the DI's voice. 'We've got a problem of sorts.'

They had a hurried conversation and Rik, who was presently in Blackpool, arranged a meet at Henry's house in forty-five minutes. Henry gathered his files together and tidied his desk, leaving his office locked and scurrying to his car. As he hurried, he was on the mobile to Kate.

'Any change?'

'No, love, she's still as she was.'

'Look, sweetie, I have to turn out to something . . . going to be a late call I think . . . I know.'

'It's OK. I'll visit her shortly. There's nothing you can really do.'

'Other than be there like a son should be?'

'Well at least Lisa's arrived.'

Lisa was Henry's younger sister and only sibling, three times married, three times divorced, feckless and rootless. Henry was surprised by the news. He'd dropped her a quick text to say Mum was poorly, but hadn't expected her to turn up until the fat lady sang. Or at least until Mother died. Then she'd be around for the crumbs. 'Jeepers,' he said and slid into the new car.

'I've told her she can have Leanne's room for the time being.'

Henry's face showed displeasure at the thought. His kid sister was always best kept at arm's length. 'Whatever,' he muttered resignedly.

'She has come up from London.'

'I know . . . it's just that . . . look, I'll see you soon. I'm meeting Rik at our house, then going on in one car. I just phoned to keep you in the picture.'

'Thanks. Appreciate it, love.'

To keep in regular contact was one of the things Henry had promised Kate since they'd seriously got back together and ultimately remarried. One of many things that had irked Kate about him was his inability to pick up the phone. Now he tried his best to do this, even though it didn't come naturally for him. There was something inbuilt that made him feel he was being supervised, even though he realized other couples kept in touch as a matter of course. 'It's part of being a committed couple,' Kate had insisted.

He pulled away from headquarters, his mind on his sister whom he hadn't seen for about three years. He wasn't really relishing the encounter.

They walked around the outer harbour wall with the easy pace of a holidaying couple, pausing to gaze out across the Atlantic. After a few minutes with Gill settled in front of him, his arms wrapped around her, they strolled down the steps and then back past *Lady Faye* until they reached the beach bars and restaurants. Flynn steered her to his favourite bar, owned by a Spaniard who often bought fish from him. They found two big comfortable cane chairs with soft cushions right on the sand and ordered cold beer. There seemed to be no need for anything fancier. The bars were busy, but the hubbub was just background to Flynn and Gill. Flynn had to do a quick internal double take when he, fleetingly, thought he might be falling A over T for this woman. The feeling terrified him.

'Y'know, I've been coming here for six years now,' Gill started hesitantly. 'I've seen you for four of those years and we've met and fucked and caught fish, then said *adios*, but' – here she screwed up her face – 'I don't know a damn thing about you, other than your prowess at sea and in the sack.'

'When you have a no-strings arrangement, that's the way it goes, I reckon.'

'Mm,' she said doubtfully and sipped her beer. 'About that arrangement.' She turned and faced him squarely. 'I'm not sure I want it to continue.'

Flynn's insides slumped dramatically.

'Certainly not in its present format.'

'Oh?'

Her eyes played over his face. Flynn eventually got it.

'Oh,' he said again, but more like an 'Ooh', 'OK, who's supposed to say it first?'

'You,' Gill said firmly.

'Well, I, er . . .' he began. If he'd had a shirt collar to pull on, he would have been tearing it by now. 'I kind of think I've fallen for you.' He gave a simple smile and shrugged.

'That it?'

He looked at her in bewilderment. 'Um, I love you?' he whispered.

'Better.'

'Maybe I should get a couple more beers.'

Rik Dean and Henry drew up outside Henry's at the same time. Henry would have pulled into his drive alongside Kate's Ford Focus, but a battered Mercedes coupé was in his parking spot. It was an old model, one Henry usually thought of as a tart's car. In this case the tart happened to be his sister, Lisa. He was unsure of her present surname. It depended on her mood as to which one she chose to use.

He climbed out of the Mondeo and went to Rik, still in his car. 'I need to bob in and say hello to my sister.'

Rik perked up. 'Your sister? Younger? Older? Married? Single?' Rik was a serial womanizer and his radar was always erect.

'Younger, but older than you, single, fit – and out of bounds,' Henry responded. He wagged his forefinger at Rik. 'And I mean it. She's a very vulnerable person at the best of times – in other words she's barking mad – and doesn't need a guy like you.'

'Vulnerable is good,' Rik said.

'Down, boy. I'll be back in a few minutes.' He headed up to the house.

As ever, Lisa looked stunning, and he had a hard time believing she was really his sister. At forty she was slim, attractive and as flighty as a bumblebee. She threw her arms around him dramatically and began weeping into his shoulder. He gazed over her head at Kate with an expression of terror in his eyes.

'Henry, oh Henry, I can't believe she's so ill,' she said when she pulled away. Her meticulously applied make-up had run with her tears, smudging her eyes. 'Will she live?' she snuffled.

'She is eighty-eight, but let's hope so.' He eased her away to get a good look at her. Despite himself, her tearful appearance did have an effect on him, and with a surge of emotion he dragged her back to him and fought to quell his own tears. 'Thanks for coming. She'll be overjoyed to see you.' A fact which stuck in his throat. As was so often the case, the wayward member of the family was the one most adored. Those who stayed and did their steadfast duty were usually merely tolerated. Henry knew for a fact that Lisa hadn't seen Mum for six years, and a little part of him hoped she wouldn't even recognize her daughter. It was a mean-spirited hope that he immediately shelved.

'You're not coming to the hospital?' Lisa said accusingly.

'I have to go to the other side of the county.'

They were in the hallway, just inside the front door, which was open. Contrary to Henry's orders, Rik had followed him up the drive and now stood on the front step, a few feet behind Henry.

Lisa spotted him and her eyes zoomed in. 'Is that a detective too?'

Henry twisted around and frowned at Rik. 'Yeah – not for much longer, though.'

Lisa edged past and strode, hand outstretched, to meet the DI. 'I'm Lisa, Henry's sister.'

Henry caught Rik's eyes appraising her quickly and liking what he saw. He turned back to Kate, enraged.

'Two rutting . . . somethings,' he muttered. 'What's her present situation?'

Kate was unable to conceal a smirk. She had two brothers and they all got on well, a sane, well-adjusted family. 'Not sure yet – manless, in debt probably, a mess left behind, I'd hazard.'

'If she's here for any length of time, I'll lay odds he'll be up to the maker's name before the week's out. Fortunately, they'll just toss one another aside.' He rubbed his face and was aware this was not a good way to talk about his sibling. Outside, Rik and Lisa were inspecting the Mercedes, Rik hanging on her every word. Henry gave Kate a quick kiss and a hug. 'Whatever happens, I'll pop in and see her later – Mum, that is.'

'Do you have to go?'

'If I didn't, I wouldn't.'

'OK.'

He strode out, cocked his finger at Rik, then jerked his thumb at him to get back into the car. Lisa watched them drive away

with a sad pout and a come-hither stance that had Rik transfixed, even though he was driving.

'Eyes on the road,' Henry snapped. 'Erection lowered.'

Flynn knew there was a saying that men talk to women so they
can have sex with them, and women let men have sex with them
so they can talk to them. That evening didn't quite follow the
pattern, because both of them suddenly opened up to each other
in a torrent, before and after the sex.

Flynn began hesitantly, finding that probably for the first time
in his life there was someone he could confide in. Even so, he
prefaced each major revelation with a warning and one of those
statements that went, 'I'll understand if you want to get up and
leave after I've told you this and I won't blame you if you do.'

There was something about Gill he hadn't seen before, and
he wanted to tell her everything in the vain hope that there could
possibly be something solid between them. And that wasn't
something he considered lightly. He hadn't opened up his heart
to a woman for many years.

'There's some bad stuff,' he said.

Gill regarded him over the rim of her wine glass. They had
gravitated to a bar within one of the hotel complexes overlooking
the harbour, found two chairs in an elevated position with a good
view of everything going on around the resort. She saw a tough-
looking man, bronzed by years of sea fishing, with hard muscles
and secretive eyes. Up until the moment he had dived in to rescue
that baby and put his life in jeopardy, she had seen him as nothing
more than a great lay and an extra treat on her yearly blow-out.
His incredible bravery and then his genuine modesty had capti-
vated her whole being. Somehow, this ruthless career woman
had had her heart melted by what could only be described as a
rough diamond.

How the hell a relationship like this could work was another
matter.

'Somehow, I guessed,' she said. 'You're not on the run or
anything, are you?'

'Nah, nothing like that. I came out here to lick my wounds.
It was a place I'd come to for years and I was comfortable here.
I wanted to keep my head down, get my life on an even keel
and get a job on a boat. I managed all three.'

'And to keep women at arm's length, metaphorically
speaking?'

'Very much so.'

'And have you – maybe – come out of that phase?'

'To put it in *Cosmopolitan* terms, do you mean am I ready for a relationship?' He didn't need to tweak his fingers to emphasize the last word. 'I'd never actually thought about it until now, I suppose. Maybe the immigrants thing was the catalyst. Us two involved. A life and death thing.'

'Incidents like that can draw people together.'

'Quite often people who have no possible future together.'

'People who are sucked in by the moment and don't realize they're going to make fools of themselves in a completely unworkable relationship.'

'But then again,' he said, his eyes softening as he looked at her. He had known what a stunning woman she was, that she was high powered and ambitious – his complete antithesis . . . but when he'd seen her dealing with that child, the expressions on her face, he'd been breathless. 'I know it's a corny line, but it's better to lose in love . . .' He felt stupid saying it, but Gill helped him finish it off. Both raised their glasses and said, 'Than to never love at all.'

Then, both highly embarrassed, they burst into fits of giggles.

Rik hit the M6 within twelve minutes of leaving Blackpool, veered south, then cut on to the M61, then the M65, east across the county.

It was a pleasant enough evening. A bright orange sun was setting behind them and the sky ahead was cobalt blue, sliced across by stiletto-like clouds. Henry had always loved skies. When he'd been a kid he had been able to let his eyes mist over, defocus and imagine he was heading into another world, usually populated by knights and dragons. But that evening, as lovely as the sky was, he knew the world he was heading towards was grim and violent.

He emitted a low whistle then blew out his cheeks before his jaw clanged open. It was one of those moments of stomach-churning disbelief, causing him to wonder what the hell made him stupid enough to be a detective investigating murder.

'Times like this,' he said out of the corner of his mouth, 'I wish I'd kept my shiny wide arse fitted firmly into a comfy chair in a comfy office at headquarters.' Even as he said it, he knew it wasn't true, because investigating murder was what he believed he'd been set on this earth to do. It was just that, occasionally, the enormity of the task, or the sheer brutality of a crime scene, slammed into him like a sledgehammer.

It had been the smell that first alerted the suspicions of a neighbour. A smell of rotting, decomposing flesh creeping out from a slightly open window. A smell that wafted on the breeze, just catching the neighbour's senses, making him raise his head while out in his back yard, sniff up and wonder. Did he smell it, or not? Until eventually the smell was always there. Putrid, clawing, nauseating.

That's when he'd been drawn to the house, flipped open the letter box when his persistent knocking had failed to get a response, looked inside and was overpowered by the whoosh of stink. And without ever having smelled something so awful before in his life, the neighbour knew instinctively he smelled death. It was one of those odours already implanted in the brain.

When Henry and Rik pulled up at the end of the pleasant terraced cul-de-sac in the area known as Strongstry on the Lancashire/Manchester border, the smell hit them too as they climbed out of the car.

'Hell, I'd know that whiff anywhere,' Rik said.

Henry looked along the terrace. He knew the place, having attended occasional jobs there when he was a PC on the crime car in Rossendale in his early years on the force. It was a well-tended, picturesque row, formerly houses for workers in now non-existent mills, now inhabited by the younger end of the Manchester commuter fraternity. A BMW sports and an Audi coupé were among the tightly parked cars on the narrow street, once cobbled, now tarred. Flower baskets hung from many of the house fronts.

Residents milled about with cautious interest at the police activity. If Henry had taken a photo in black and white, other than the clothing and the cars, it could almost have been a pre-war scene.

But death had visited this street at one of the houses halfway down the left-hand side and each person was holding a handkerchief or cloth to their nose.

Two marked police vans prevented any vehicular access into the street. There were two plain police cars, a van inscribed 'Scientific Support' and a muster of bobbies, more than necessary, drawn to the scene by the prospect of a gore-fest. Cops are cops: they need to see things like this.

Henry spotted a Jaguar XK9 parked a short distance away and recognized it as belonging to the Home Office pathologist.

The two newest arrivals on the scene went to the Scientific Support vehicle, where they were kitted out in the requisite crime scene gear – baggy paper suits, slip-over shoes, a mask – and booked on to the scene by a uniformed PC who recorded all comings and goings.

As they got nearer the front door, the stench strengthened, sweet and sickly at the same time.

Rik fitted his mask. Henry tutted, stretched his own over his head and let it swing around his neck.

They ducked under the crime scene tape stretched outside the house and approached the front door where they were met by the local DI, a sound, grizzled jack near to the end of his service, someone who'd seen many things over twenty-nine years. He looked shaken.

'Bad 'un,' he said. 'Tortured.'

Henry and Rik eyed each other. If Bill Hendry said it was bad, then . . . Henry decided to fit his face mask. And a few moments later he was having that moment of doubt about the wisdom of being a murder investigator.

Body one, white male, late twenties, naked, was in the lounge strapped to a dining chair by plastic ties. The chair seat had been cut out so his backside and genitals hung below the level of the chair, as though he was sitting on a toilet. The ties tightly fastened the wrists, forearms and ankles to the arms and legs of the chair, digging deeply into his skin, effectively securing him to the chair as though he had been superglued to it.

The reek appalled Henry, his hand instinctively covering his nose and mouth even though he wore the mask. Even so, he was fascinated by what he saw, even the deep black pool of viscous body fluid that had formed underneath the chair, drip by drip, from the guy's anus as his insides had rotted away. Henry could see the puddle was alive with a squirming mass of insect life.

He stepped into the room, cautiously using the preordained pathway around the edge which everyone entering or leaving was obliged to follow.

The dead man's head was tilted backwards acutely, his mouth agape, the angle suggesting a broken neck. It was more than a suggestion, Henry thought.

The man had been savagely beaten, that was obvious. He'd also been burned and the triangular imprints on his chest, stomach and legs from a steam iron confirmed this.

Drip. A blob of something plopped from underneath the man on to the carpet.

There was also a noose of some sort of cord around the dead man's neck.

Henry leaned in close, still trying to keep his distance from the body, but needing to see. The cord was actually the stuff found in builder's yards, where it was used to keep bricks together: a thin, metallic strip. Henry knew it well. Early in his service he had carried a length of the stuff inside his peaked cap. It came in handy for breaking into cars; it could be slipped down inside between the window and door and used to click up the locking mechanism, though it wasn't so useful on modern cars. It was handy, flexible and very strong stuff.

Henry's eyes worked down the body.

The face had been beaten into a mush, probably by a bat of some sort. The hands had been crushed, the fingers splayed and broken at all angles. Knife slashes were whipped across the chest. The knees looked as though they had been sledgehammered and Henry could tell from the unusual shape of the shins that they had been broken.

''Kin' 'ell,' Rik's muffled voice came behind him.

'Someone spent a lot of time in here,' Henry said, 'having fun.'

Body two was in the front bedroom above the lounge. Another white male, again naked, he had been tied to the double bed, his arms stretched and fastened to the headboard, his legs splayed and attached to the rail at the foot of the bed.

Henry approached the figure slowly, using his eyes to take in as much of the scene as possible because he knew he would never be able to replicate this moment again. As he got closer, he almost leapt out of his skin as a white-clad figure appeared from a crouching position on the opposite side of the bed, backlit from the diffused lighting filtering through the drapes.

'Hell's teeth,' Henry gasped, recognizing the man – his big ears, which stuck out of his head at right angles, giving the game away. It was the Home Office pathologist, Professor Baines, a man Henry knew well. He had covered many of the murders Henry had been involved with over the years. The two had often shared a few pints after a grisly post-mortem to discuss its finer points.

'Heard you creeping upstairs. Thought I'd give you a thrill.'

'Cheers, Prof . . . I can feel fibrillation a-go-go.' Henry patted his chest. He was standing about three feet away from the body. Behind his mask his face screwed up with distaste at the sight. There was a cut throat, dismemberment and deep gouges across the chest of the corpse in the shape of a cross.

Baines stood by the corpse. He was a very proactive path-ologist and liked to visit murder scenes, rather than just be presented with a body on a dissecting table in a mortuary. He never did anything at the scene but look, being very aware of the need to protect and preserve evidence, and Henry always trusted him not to interfere at the scene of a killing. Not like some others who waded in like their TV counterparts as though they were running investigations. Baines knew his role in the overall scheme of things.

'Bit of a compendium, this, before you ask,' Baines said.

'A compendium?' Henry's muffled voice asked.

'This one, for example, has been mutilated – dismembered and slashed across the chest.' Baines pointed out what Henry had already seen. 'A bit like a combination of Jack the Ripper and the Da Vinci Code.'

'I know about the ripper but not the Da Vinci thing . . . Having said that, do you think we're dealing with a religious nut or something?'

'Doubt it.'

'Why not?'

'Well,' he said, stretching the word, 'unless these two guys are high priests on the run with a secret that will ruin the Vatican, they've simply been tortured and murdered by two people having fun doing what they were doing . . . acting out some scenes in books and films they liked . . . But don't quote me, I'm not a psychologist.' He moved carefully around the bed and stood next to Henry.

'What about the one downstairs?'

'Ever seen *Casino Royale*, the new James Bond movie?'

'Nope – read the book though.'

'When Bond gets tortured by the baddie?'

'Oh yeah.' Henry visualized the dead man downstairs, strapped to a chair with the seat cut out. Bond had been tortured in the same way, having had his dangling genitals smashed with a carpet beater. Bond had screamed in agony. 'Two people, you reckon?'

'As a minimum,' Baines said.

'And why not religious fanatics?'

'Because even though these two men were mutilated, they were tortured in the good old-fashioned way to get information out of them – by breaking bones and fingers. Tried, tested, usually with great results. There are no leads to God here – at least in my humble opinion.'

Henry went silent, ruminating.

'So, old adage – find out how they lived, find out why they died,' Baines said.

'I already know how they lived,' Henry said, looking at the body of Richard Last, suspected bank robber. He adjusted his face mask because the smell was beginning to overpower him.

SEVEN

It was the first joint decision of their relationship. Catching a taxi from the harbour in Puerto Rico up to Gill's hotel, where they could spend the remaining hours of the night together and get some sleep – possibly – in a big, comfy king-sized bed, as opposed to the 'seen better days' three-quarter width one in Flynn's villa. They could have a leisurely breakfast and a morning by the pool before Gill left for the airport. She had to get home. Work was stacking up, clients were whingeing and there was a lot of straightening out to do.

It was five a.m. before they fell asleep, following a long, slow bout of inventive lovemaking that had Flynn scraping the headboard with his fingernails as Gill's dug into his buttocks leaving an arc of scratches.

Five a.m., though, even at the best of times, is a low-ebb hour for anyone. Coupled with the evening of boozing and sexual debauchery they had just enjoyed, they were zombies at four minutes past that hour and were unable to react in any meaningful way to what happened when a nightmare became reality.

At four fifty-seven a.m. Flynn was taking a long piss in the bathroom, admiring himself dreamily in the multi-mirrored room. That was when he saw Gill's fingernail digs in his arse and smiled stupidly at the memory – and the pain – while tensing his gluteus maximus. That had been a good moment, when both of them realized they were howlers in bed. He finished, yawned, then trudged wearily back to bed. Gill was already asleep, curled up tight.

Flynn flopped gently on to the bed so as not to disturb her, eased up the single sheet. In a flash he was asleep, just a moment after he'd spotted the time on the bedside digital clock: 4:59.

Then he was out of it.

It couldn't have been timed better.

Not that a forced entry was required. The hotel room was on the ground floor, part of an annexe situated by the cliff edge, and each room along that section had a large terrace and a small wall. The two men simply bided their time and enjoyed the sounds and occasional glimpses of energetic lovemaking between Flynn and Gill through the net curtains wafting at the open French windows. They even winced when Gill dug her nails into Flynn's rump.

They were patient guys, which is why they were so successful in their chosen trade.

They gave Flynn four minutes to fall asleep, knowing the poor soul would be exhausted. Not that it mattered if he was asleep or not, but it was preferable.

They rose from the shadows, stepping silently from their hiding place, approached the French windows and edged in – then it all happened very quickly.

They grabbed Flynn as he slept, yanking him violently from the bed, twisting him on to his face and smashing him to the floor.

In moments he was trussed up with cable ties. His hands were fastened behind him, his ankles then bound together with duct tape – and only at that moment did he really wake up. To find himself being dragged bodily across the room by his ankles, his head being repeatedly punched before he was dropped face down on the tiled bathroom floor. There he was kicked savagely about the head, unable to protect himself from any of the blows.

He tensed hard, arching his head away from the feet and generally thrashing like a fish.

'You bastards!' With a ferocious scream, Gill launched herself through the bathroom door and laid into one of the attackers. He turned, parried her blows and hit her once in the face, a well-placed decisive blow that crushed her nose and sent her spinning

back into the bedroom on her arse. The man who'd hit her stepped
out with her while the one standing over Flynn smashed his boot
down on his temple, sending him into instant blackness.

Dawn did not want to come. The previous day had been like a
proper summer's day but overnight clouds had scudded in from
the Pennines and settled low across the county. Henry had spent
a long night in the east, ensuring the double murder scene had
been properly dealt with. Even though he now ran murder investigations without the prospect of someone pulling the rug from
under him, those cold times he'd spent on every callout rota
possible, just to stay in the investigative loop, had drilled some
particularly good habits into his noggin. Mainly: get the ball
rolling as quickly as possible; seize and secure evidence; start
trolling for witnesses. And always remember that the first hours
of a murder inquiry were critical.

Hence he worked until four a.m. with an increasingly grumpy
Rik Dean. But at least Henry knew that if they only got three
hours' sleep each, they would hit the ground running later in the
day.

The pair drove back to Blackpool, the sky behind them light-
ening dismally in the east, but the day refusing to get going.
Rik's head sagged a few times at the wheel, but Henry punched
him hard and kept firing questions at him, putting hypotheses
to him, opening the window to give him blasts of icy wake-up
air.

'I'm goosed,' the DI admitted. 'It's hard working with you.
You keep rotten hours.'

'I'm tired too . . . So, our armed robbers have bitten the dust,
eh? Richard Last and Jack Sumner . . . So what's it all about?'

It was a conversation they'd had several times over the last
few hours.

'Money – always is with lowlifes like them.'

'Well if they fell out between themselves, they did a helluva
job on each other.'

'Third party,' Rik said. 'Mr Big, or a sleeping partner. I'll bet
it's fuckin' money.'

'This is serious stuff, though . . . Why the torture? Why the
mutilation? Why not just shoot them?'

''Cos someone wanted to know something.'

They had reached the motorway junction at Marton Circle,
the Blackpool exit.

'You want dropping off at home?'

'Nah – I want a McDonalds. Go to the twenty-four hour drive-through on Preston New Road.'

'A McDonalds?' Rik said in disbelief.

'Famished.' Henry rubbed his stomach.

'You're the boss.'

'My favourite phrase.'

Flynn's chin lolled and rolled on his chest. Blood cascaded down his nose. Pain arced through him like a pickaxe in an ice face, under and around his brain. He forced his eyes open as consciousness ebbed back and he realized he was propped up on the toilet, naked. There was something awful in his mouth. He spat it out, trying to aim between his thighs into the toilet bowl. Instead he splattered it down his lower stomach and pubic hair.

His neck muscles screamed as he raised his head and tried to focus on the man standing in front of him. He could feel the side of his face ballooning out like some sort of movie special effect. It almost creaked as it swelled.

'You're two tough guys,' Flynn said through a mouthful of phlegm and blood. Something hard crunched in his mouth. He spat out a broken tooth. 'Knocking women out . . . pathetic bastards.'

The man snorted a laugh. He was lean, but wide shouldered with a dead-fish expression, which even then told Flynn he was face to face with someone cold and dangerous.

'You haven't seen the half of it,' he said, smirking with a twitch.

The second of the two men stepped into the bathroom rubbing his hands with delight. He was the one who'd pounded Gill and heaved her back into the bedroom, smacking her hard and repeatedly, knocking her into a state of insensibility. 'That felt good.' He smiled genuinely at Flynn.

Flynn said nothing, but inside the rage burned like a furnace. Without warning he launched himself head first at the guy, trying to get a grip for his bare feet on the blood-slippery bathroom floor, but he slid and went down on to one knee. This made it easy for the first guy to use Flynn's own momentum, place his hands on the back of his head and drive his face into his knee.

Something broke in Flynn's face. He went down on to the floor, then the men dragged him back up and rebalanced him on the toilet.

The one who had assaulted Gill stepped out of the bathroom briefly, returning a moment later.

'Look what I got!' He held the item aloft for his companion to see. 'A travel iron.'

'Nice one.'

'Not as effective as its steam cousin, but they do get real hot.'

Flynn retched and slid off the toilet woozily.

'I'll plug it in. Only take a mo.' The second man left.

'Now then, Flynn, my boy,' the first one said.

'If you've hurt her, I'll kill you,' Flynn croaked.

'Don't be silly,' he grinned. 'An unwise thing for a man to claim in your position.'

'What the fuck do you want?'

'We just need something sorting.' He squatted on his haunches, getting down to Flynn's eye level. 'Need a bit of a repayment . . . I think you know what I'm saying – don't you?'

At the drive-through, Henry bought a sausage muffin, hash brown and a coffee. Rik passed on everything.

'Drive me up to the hospital. Drop me off there and after I've blagged my way in to see my mum, I'll walk home.'

'Hell, that's a long way.' Rik estimated it was at least two miles from hospital to home. 'You'll be leaving for work before you know it. You'll be meeting yourself coming up your own arse if you're not careful.'

'I reckon I can get a couple of hours kip in.' Henry unwrapped the muffin and bit into it. It tasted completely wonderful. The perfect dawn breakfast after a long night at a murder scene.

'I reckon you're kiddin' yourself.'

'I don't feel sleepy now. Ooh . . . idea.' Henry fished out his mobile phone, tabbed through the contacts list, selected a number and dialled. 'Jerry, it's Henry . . . yes I know it's friggin' early . . . I'm watching the shit rise in Blackpool as we speak. Look, get yourself into work ASAP and read the circulation about a double murder in Rossendale . . .' Henry went on to explain what he wanted the groggy DC Jerry Tope to do, but whether he took it in was another matter. 'Anyway, hope I didn't wake you,' Henry concluded and snapped his phone shut. 'He likes to feel wanted,' he said to Rik with a quick grin.

'Unh,' Rik grunted, exhaustion creeping over him like a shroud. He drove Henry to the front of the hospital and Henry swung his legs out of the car. 'It's a long walk home,' he said again.

'I'll be OK. Sleep's for wusses.' He was about to push himself out when Rik said, 'That's your kid sister, isn't it?'

Henry followed Rik's line of vision. Emerging through the revolving door was in fact his sister Lisa. She looked tired, but still breathtakingly gorgeous, even Henry had to admit. She turned towards the car park, not having spotted Henry.

For a brief moment, Henry considered letting her get on her way. The thought of an encounter with her at this time of day was almost too much to bear. Rik immediately pounced on his hesitation. 'You gonna shout her?'

Henry grunted, then called her name. She spun around, surprised, but at least her face showed pleasure.

'Henry!'

'You been here all night?' he asked as she trotted across to meet him. They embraced stiffly.

'Mostly.'

'Not absolutely necessary.'

'Just trying to do my bit. I know you're busy.' She bent a little and looked into the car, smiling at Rik. 'Hey there, you,' she said like a teenager. Henry gave him a warning scowl that the DI, for some reason, didn't seem, or want, to notice.

'Hi Lisa, you OK?'

'Yeah – tired, but good.'

Henry edged a couple of inches sideways to put himself between them, not sure which one he was trying to protect, or if he was trying to protect himself. 'How is Mum?'

'Er, OK,' Lisa said, bringing her attention back to Henry. 'Stable, but she had a bad night, which is why I stayed. She's sleeping now.' Her eyes constantly tried to find Rik.

Henry heard the driver's door open. Rik got out, stood up and leaned nonchalantly on the car roof. Henry felt a surge of anger, but could not understand why. Clearly these two were going to end up bonking each other's brains out and there would be nothing Henry could do about it.

'Can I give you a lift back?' Rik asked.

'No, it's OK – got my own car.'

'Course you have, how foolish of me.'

Henry speared another look at Rik and saw the DI's expression had morphed to pick-up mode, with the lopsided grin – which Henry was certain he'd pinched from him – designed to melt any woman's heart. At that moment, Henry gave up the ghost. He could tell the deal had been done. It was one of those unwritten moments and Henry was now powerless.

'I'm going to go and see Mum,' he said to Lisa. To Rik, he

said, 'See you later – take your own transport across and I'll
meet you at Rawtenstall nick at midday.'

Rik flipped him a cheeky-chappy salute and Henry started to
walk across to the hospital, head shaking angrily, kicking at
imaginary stones.

Then he heard Rik shout, 'Jesus Christ, he's got a gun.'

Henry turned, and saw Rik pointing at the hospital. Henry spun
back as a man slid out of the revolving door some twenty mctres
ahead of Henry, a pistol held down his flank, which he raised
and steadied on his left hand and aimed in Henry's direction.

Things started to happen in a swirl of slow motion, as they
often do in times of great stress and action. Henry shouted something that came out of his mouth in a primeval roar. His whole
body twisted back around as his innate protective instincts kicked
in. With huge force he pushed Lisa away. She screamed something unintelligible and staggered to one side. Henry went with
her, covering her with the bulk of his body.

The gunman fired twice, a double tap.

As Henry drove himself into Lisa he was aware of the rear
side window of Rik's car disintegrating, of Rik's hands flying
up as though he was doing a backstroke and howling in agony.
And then Henry was on top of Lisa, grabbing her and forcing
both of them to roll down the grass banking which angled down
to the main road in front of the hospital. They completed about
four three-sixty-degree rolls before coming to a crunching stop
on the footpath. Henry's elbows connected with the concrete
with a bone-jarring smack.

He pushed himself up.

'Stay here,' he ordered her.

He crouched for a moment, his eyes searching, and then uttered
a curse when he saw the writhing figure of Rik Dean down by
the driver's door. One – or both – of the bullets had struck him.

Henry scrambled back to him, his shoes slipping on the dewy
grass, keeping his head low.

'I've been hit, Henry.' Rik clutched the left side of his rib-
cage, just below his heart. Blood covered his fingers.

'Hang in,' Henry gasped. He rose to his haunches and took a
glance through the car windows, fully expecting the gunman to
be there, coming in for the kill. He rose another few inches,
holding on to the front wing of the car to steady him. The man
had gone.

*   *   *

The travel iron had heated up nicely.

Steve Flynn, unable to move other than fractionally, clamped his teeth together and swallowed repeatedly as terror gripped him. He was unable to speak, as duct tape had now been wrapped over his mouth. He braced himself for the agony he knew was coming. He was now sitting on the dressing-table stool which the attackers had brought into the bathroom.

The guy with the iron tilted it slightly and spat on it. The saliva sizzled with bubbles and a hiss.

'Oh, nice and hot.'

Flynn was no coward, but the thought of being touched by the iron made him groan, writhe and shake.

'God, you're pitiful,' the other man said. He went to stand behind Flynn, then grabbed his head, circling it with his arms, and held Flynn steady. 'There, there, mate, this won't be too bad. It's just a bit of a message to you about how bad things could get if you don't cooperate.'

The guy with the iron approached. He had a crooked smile on his face. His eyes burned with pleasurable anticipation. The iron and the saliva still sizzling on it transfixed Flynn.

He writhed powerfully, but to no avail. He was trapped and was about to be tortured.

'How about a nipple?' the man with the iron asked his colleague.

'Oh, God yes, a nipple would be great.'

'I'm chock full of ideas.'

He stood in front of Flynn, then jammed the iron down on Flynn's right nipple.

There was a sizzle and the smell of burning flesh as the man pressed the iron hard into Flynn's skin, then tore it away with a flourish and a ripping of melting skin.

Agony coursed through Flynn's arched body and the man holding him from behind had difficulty keeping him down as he contorted and fought. The scream behind the tape was muted, but awful.

The last thing Flynn heard before passing out was another scream – was it his own? he wondered – and then a deafening ringing noise. He put it all down to his body's reaction to the hell it had just endured.

EIGHT

'This,' Henry Christie said irritably, 'is a sideshow I can do
without.' He pushed himself up from the table and paced
the room. 'I've got a double murder to run and on top of
that, some bastard took a pot shot at me and my DI and wounded
him, something which may or may not be connected to the
murders. And here I am, waiting for the production of an untrust-
worthy criminal who is, I'm sure, scamming us.'

He returned to his seat and sat down heavily, looking around
the high-windowed interview room at Lancashire Prison,
simmering nicely.

Deakin was in conference with his solicitor, Barry Baron, a
conflab that had been going on too long now.

Henry inspected his watch. He swore under his breath, then
glanced sideways at Naomi who sat primly next to him. 'Sorry
– a lot on my plate all of a sudden.'

'I understand . . . but you also understand why I need someone
like you to take this on, don't you?'

'Yeah.' Henry picked up on the phrase 'someone like you'
and wondered why he hadn't tried to get another superintendent
to do this, or maybe delegated it to a chief inspector. But he
knew that his colleagues' workload was just as horrendous as
his own, and he also had an inability to delegate. Not necessarily a good managerial trait, but Henry often operated on the
maxim that if you wanted a job doing, it was best to do it yourself . . . Plus the Deakin scenario intrigued him. Just what was
the slimy bastard up to?

Henry shuffled out his mobile phone, ignoring the signs clearly
stating that their use was prohibited. The signal came and went
anyway, but he dialled.

'Jerry? Henry Christie . . .' Henry heard the man at the other
end of the line utter a muted groan. 'How are you getting on
with the job I gave you earlier?' Henry listened, uttered a few
'Uh-huhs' then said, 'Got something else for you too.' He outlined
some further thoughts before the signal went. Although he stood
up and moved around the room, holding his phone high and at
different angles, it refused to be found again. 'Shit.' He knew
his language was crude and said 'Sorry' to Naomi again before
sitting next to her. 'Where is he?' he demanded, annoyed. He
realized that he was not in the best frame of mind to be doing

this right now, but Johnny Cain's looming trial meant it was something that needed to be done PDQ.

He sat back, closed his eyes, breathed in, then exhaled a long breath to steady himself, get some equilibrium; then he sat forward and leaned on his elbows, his head in his hands, and his tired mind whirled back to the shooting outside the hospital . . .

He clearly saw the man with the gun emerging from the revolving door. He'd been wearing a balaclava over his face and a black zip-up top, jeans and trainers, and had fingerless gloves on. Only when Henry was sure he'd done a runner did he rise up from behind the car to his full height, his breath tight in his chest.

'Oh God, oh God.' Behind him Lisa had scampered up the banking to Rik and was kneeling by his side, his head on her lap, a terrified expression on her face.

'Henry, he's been shot.'

'I know.'

'Hell, Henry – every time I come on a job with you,' Rik moaned and winced.

'At least you've still got your sense of humour.' Henry bent down next to him, his eyes still searching, not convinced the gunman had actually gone. 'Where's a nurse when you need one?'

'I'd prefer a doctor, please.'

People began to appear on the scene. At least Rik didn't have far to go to A&E . . .

Henry rubbed his eyes and reached for the insipid coffee in a plastic mug one of the prison guards had supplied him. It was awful stuff, the colour of grey slate with a taste of dust to it. 'Times like this you realize the good side to cocaine,' he said and smiled at Naomi, who reached out and touched his shoulder.

'You must be exhausted.'

'Just this side of delirious. If I start making stupid errors, dig me in the ribs, will you?'

'No problem.'

Henry sat back, tilted his head, exhaling through puffed-out cheeks . . .

A paramedic team that just happened to be pulling in for a break had taken Rik to casualty minutes later. Once Henry had ensured he was being treated, he returned to the scene, got on his mobile and started acting like a general, ordering in the troops. Within half an hour there was a Crime Scene Investigation team covering the scene, four firearms officers scouring the hospital and grounds for the offender, a detective reviewing CCTV footage and various uniformed officers of all ranks tasked with jobs. He was going through the motions, didn't truly expect to turn up anything, but it had to be done. When a local DI turned up, bedraggled after being rudely heaved from his pit, Henry handed him the whole shebang and went back to A&E.

'They're pretty sure the bullet just skimmed my rib cage,' Rik told him dreamily, now stuffed with painkillers. 'I was lucky . . . two inches east and I'd be dead, shot through the heart. You really are a bad guy to hang out with.' Twice before, Rik had come a cropper while out on jobs with Henry. Once a psycho had stabbed him, another time he'd been shot in the leg by a desperate drug dealer.

'The run of bad luck stops now, OK?'

'I think it has.' Rik smiled and raised his bleary eyes past Henry to Lisa, who was standing at the foot of the bed. 'Lisa was brilliant,' he said. Henry couldn't avoid the sardonic twist of his lips, or the roll of his eyes. He looked at Lisa. 'I'll go and see Mum.'

She was asleep and Henry sat down wearily next to her, watching her withered face and the pitifully small rise and fall of her chest. He thought about her. She was eighty-eight and, to coin a cliché, had had a good innings. He wondered how much longer she would be batting for. There had been other health scares recently, but none quite as grave as this one. He had a very bad feeling about it and guessed that the odds of her leaving hospital were slim. And even if she did leave, what were the implications? Where would she live, who would care for her?

He closed his eyes and promptly fell asleep.

'Mr Christie – sorry to wake you.'

Henry stirred, sucked up his dribble, and looked at the middle-aged nurse gently shaking him awake. He shook his head like a cartoon character. 'Sorry, must've dozed off.' He glanced at his mother, still asleep and far more exhausted than he was.

'It's OK,' the nurse said.

'How long . . .?' He checked his watch and answered his own proposed question. He'd been out for about twenty minutes and now felt dreadful. He needed his bed. He took a last look at the patient, blew her a mental kiss, then wandered back to A&E to find Rik and his sister.

She was at his bedside and they were in deep intimate conversation that stopped abruptly when Henry swished into the cubicle. Both had seriously guilty faces, but Henry decided to make nothing of it. What would be, would be.

'How are you doing?'

'Going to be discharged,' Rik said. He looked ill and in pain. 'Confirmed the bullet just creased me. I've been injected, disinfected and a dressing's gone on. Just waiting for the doctor to say adios.'

'Good. I'm going back to the scene to see if anything's been recovered. And then, sis, if possible' – he looked Lisa in the eye – 'I'd like a lift home.'

Lisa exchanged a worried glance with Rik. 'I was going to . . .'

Henry picked it up instantly and weighed it up. Rik lived alone and he would need some sort of assistance over the next day. 'OK, Rik, you give me your car keys. Lisa, you sort him out – how about that?'

'Sounds great, boss, whatever.'

'Always look after the welfare of my staff,' he said and snatched the car keys from the top of the bedside cabinet.

The scene had yielded little of evidential value, other than the possibility of a shoe print that could have belonged to the offender. The CCTV footage hadn't been properly analysed yet.

He was about to leave the scene when his phone rang. He spent the next hour explaining the incident to the chief constable, the deputy chief, an assistant chief and a detective chief super, making him realize that although he was now a superintendent, he was a long way down the food chain. He managed to get to bed at nine a.m., set the alarm for eleven, was back in Rossendale to kick off the double murder inquiry at noon, then met Naomi Dale at Lancashire Prison in order to conduct an interview and take a statement from Felix Deakin at four.

Gill Hartland closed her eyes slowly. A breath shuddered out of her savagely beaten body, then she twisted gingerly out of the taxi and placed her feet painfully on the kerb. Flynn reached for her arm to assist her upright. She brushed him off with a flap of the hand.

'I'll do it myself.'

Flynn took a reluctant step back. He watched her rise slowly and gain her balance. 'Just get my bags on to a trolley, will you?'

He went to the back of the cab and took her bags from the driver, before heaving them on to a luggage trolley. He paid the fare and followed Gill into the departure lounge at Las Palmas airport. She walked stiffly in front of him, shuffling her way towards the monitors announcing flight departures.

Flynn joined her.

She could hardly see. Her head had swollen on the right-hand side about a third larger than normal. Her right eye was black and swollen, virtually closed. The other side of her mouth had cuts inside where it had banged against her teeth – two of which were loose – and had been stitched and twisted out of shape. The back of her head was a mass of egg-sized lumps and where her hair hadn't been shaven away, it was matted with blood.

She drew looks of horror from other passengers in the terminal.

'Check-in desk opens in twenty minutes,' Flynn told her.

'OK . . . I need to sit.' She wobbled unsteadily towards a row of plastic seats and eased herself cautiously into one. 'I look awful.' She tilted her head down to hide her features and pulled on a floppy hat.

Flynn sat next to her. 'You shouldn't be flying.'

'I need to get home. My sister will meet me.' She squinted at Flynn. 'So what was that really all about?'

'I don't know.' He could not return the look. Not because of her injuries, but because he did not have the answer for her. 'Just violent robbery, I think.'

'Liar,' she whispered. 'That was more than a robbery. They were torturing you.'

'They wanted to know where the money was in the hotel room. And your jewels.' He gasped. He too was beaten, but the pain inside him pumped from the triangular burn across his left nipple where the travel iron had been branded on him.

'No . . . but you do know what it was about, don't you? Those men weren't interested in my tat jewellery.'

His eyes dipped. 'I don't know what they wanted.'

'Is it connected to the immigrants?'

Flynn shook his head. 'Can't see that.'

'What then?'

'I don't know for certain.'

'But you have an idea?'

He shrugged. 'I said I don't know.'

'Ugh!' Gill said disgustedly and angled herself away from him. She held her head, which hurt dreadfully. This was the first real conversation they'd had since the incident and her insistence on discharging herself from the hospital against his and the doctor's wishes.

The intruders' intentions had been rudely interrupted by the fire alarm – the source of the ear-splitting ringing Flynn had heard in his head before passing out. It had been set off by Gill. Having been very badly beaten and left semi-conscious on the floor of the hotel room, she had managed to drag herself to the door. She had pulled herself up on the handle, crashed out into the corridor and, screaming for help, smashed the fire alarm. The sound had been deafening and within moments doors were opening, guests and staff were appearing, followed not much later by the fire service, the police and an ambulance.

'You told the police nothing?' Gill asked.

'Nothing to tell them, other than to describe the blokes.'

'Know something, Steve? I don't actually care. I thought I did, but I don't. I don't want to be part of this.'

Flynn's heart pounded like a lump of molten lead in his chest. He could barely breathe through the emotion he was experiencing. Something he believed he would never find again.

'Gill,' he said plaintively, 'I truly don't know what they wanted. I have an idea – maybe – but that's all. They didn't get the chance to say what they wanted. Until I make some inquiries, I won't know for certain.'

'But you won't share your thoughts with me? Thought not.'

On the taxi ride back to Puerto Rico Flynn could not believe just how awful he felt. He had known Gill for four summers and had only fallen in love with her literally just hours before. Now it had been ripped away from him. He couldn't grasp why he felt so bad.

The lone taxi ride was a descent into hell for him.

It wasn't the physical pain of the beating that had left his body creased with agony, it was the inner hurt of losing Gill after having had her for such a short time. The worst of it was that Flynn had never felt so strongly about a woman before, not even his ex-wife. There was an incredible emptiness in him, a feeling he hardly recognized but which began to shred him. Was this what love felt like, he asked himself. Is this what it was like to have a love snatched away for a reason he had no control of? Or was he just being a soft bastard? Yet, in the back of that cab, he could hardly get his breath as he railed against the stupidity of the way the split was affecting him. After all, he had only admitted falling in love a matter of hours before. But within that time a whole new kind of existence had opened up for him, with a range of previously unthinkable possibilities that came with being with someone: loyalty, friendship, great sex, anticipation and the multitude of other things that came with a proper 'relationship'. Things he'd never thought he needed, but which had suddenly become precious to him.

Then, in one fell stroke, they had all been cruelly sliced away from him by the arrival of two dangerous men from a time and place he could only guess at. A violent visit that had injured Gill, terrified her and made her see that being with Flynn would be a danger to her life.

The taxi dumped him on the Doreste y Molina outside the El Greco apartments opposite the marina. Flynn stood there unsteadily for a few moments, blinking, feeling the heat after the air-con of the cab. Then he crossed the road and entered the complex of beach bars and restaurants. He took a seat at the first bar he came to and ordered a Cruzcampo and Jack Daniel's chaser.

The descent into hell was always best accompanied by a drink.

Henry took his time over Felix Deakin's statement. Two hours and more of careful questions and cross-checking the answers. He was desperate to trip up the crim, but Deakin was well prepared and stuck to his simple story without embellishment. He often smiled superciliously at Henry as though he understood the cat and mouse game Henry wanted to play, but was having none of it.

In the end, Henry finished up with a competent enough statement that directly implicated Johnny Cain in murder – exactly what was wanted to tie up the loose ends of the case and get a conviction. Neat, tidy, spot-on, just right. It sucked.

'Anything more you'd like to add?' Henry asked finally. He knew he had done well despite his exhaustion. He'd got himself mentally prepared to face Deakin, done the business and knew he'd gone as far as he could. Now it just needed winding up. He wanted a decent meal, a shower and a JD on the rocks – then to hit the sack. Then he winced internally because he knew he had to drop into the office on his way home and get some progress updates.

'That's everything, officer,' Deakin smiled.

'And you're sure you want to go through with this?'

'What are you getting at?'

'Johnny Cain is a very vindictive man.'

Deakin laughed silently and shook his head. 'Not half as vindictive as me.' His laugh became an expression of evil.

Henry swallowed, picked up the statement forms after they'd been signed and slid them into a folder which he handed to Naomi. The prison guards came in for Deakin and led him away.

As Henry tidied his things up, he said to Barry Baron, 'I presume you heard about Richard Last and Jack Sumner.' He watched for a reaction.

'Mm, yeah – but I suppose guys like those are always on the edge. At least I won't have to represent them now.' Baron's eyebrows arched. 'Always felt uncomfortable, truth be told. Anyway, bye.' He left the room, Henry's eyes burning into his back. An example of how little solicitors cared for their clients.

Naomi grasped his forearm. 'Thanks for doing this. It'll make the case, you know.'

'Either that or cock it up completely – or am I just being cynical?' He gave her one of his sardonic sidelong looks, the twist of the mouth, the raising of the eyebrows. The Henry Christie look, number two in the catalogue he'd built up over the years. Number one was the boyish shrug of the shoulders, tilt of the head and half-smile, the deadly weapon in his women-chasing arsenal – the one he was sure Rik Dean had used on his sister. Had he been less tired and had it been eighteen months earlier in a time before his remarriage, he might have tried that one on Naomi. But he couldn't be bothered any more. Instead he yawned like an old lion and tried to hold back a fart.

The door opened and a warder leaned in. 'You guys finished?'

'Yeah, guess so,' Henry said, pushing himself up. Naomi went out ahead and the officer followed them towards the reception area.

'Success?' the guard asked behind Henry.

Looking over his shoulder, Henry grunted something that sounded positive, although it wasn't any of the guard's business.

'Not that I know what it's about,' the guard rambled on.

Henry grunted something again.

They reached an inner security door. The guard reached over Naomi's and Henry's shoulders, slid a card down a slot, typed a four-digit code into a keypad. The door buzzed open and Naomi stepped through into a secure sterile area before the next door. As Henry was about to follow, the guard slipped a big hand around his biceps, preventing him from moving behind her. Into his ear he said, 'Got a minute, boss?'

Henry gave Naomi a shrug as the door clicked shut behind her, effectively separating her from the two men.

'What is it?' Henry took in the guard, a big, kindly looking man in his forties, smelling of sweat, mustiness and cheap deodorant. Maybe a whiff of booze, too.

'I wanted to speak to you alone.'

'You got me.'

'Does the name Jamie Last mean anything to you?'

'I know Richard Last,' he corrected him. 'Why?'

'Jamie is Richard's younger brother. He's in here for a knife job.'

Henry slitted his eyes. 'Tell you what, tell me what you want to tell me, eh?'

'Er . . . it's just that you're dealing with Felix Deakin, yeah? I don't know why you are, though there's enough whispers going around. I just thought you'd like to know that two of Deakin's goons in here – and Deakin, I think – kicked the livin' crap out of Jamie, a real badass kicking. We can't prove it, even though we know who did it, and Jamie won't say because he's shit scared, so it isn't going anywhere. Just a snippet for you. Do with it what you will.'

It was a long time since Flynn had purposely got himself into a fight. But that evening, as his bleak, self-pitying mood deteriorated, he found himself hunched angrily over his third beach bar of the night, staring glumly into the depths of a Bushmills, convinced he was the innocent victim in all this. He was feeling very sorry for himself, a state of mind he was unused to – and the drink didn't help matters, either.

A group of boisterous young men, British tourists, barged into the bar and lined up alongside Flynn, jostling him and other punters raucously, laughing and leering drunkenly. One shoved up against Flynn, who was resting his chin on the palm of his hand, his elbow wedged at ninety degrees to the bar. The man deliberately jerked his arm against Flynn's, making Flynn's head drop as though he had nodded off unexpectedly. Flynn reacted instantly, rising from his stool and angrily facing the new arrival.

'Hey pal, watch it.' Not the most original warning, but in that moment Flynn was willing to let the incident go.

'Why? What you gonna do about it, old geezer?' the man sneered.

Flynn's mouth suddenly went dry as the insult hit home. He frowned and focused on the man. He was early twenties, shaven headed, tattooed, a little overweight and bigger than Flynn, dressed in cut-off jeans and a short-sleeved shirt. His tattoos extended up the back of his neck and around his throat. His watery eyes betrayed the amount of drink he'd consumed that day and his demeanour said he was good and ready for a brawl.

So was Flynn. 'You've one chance to apologize,' Flynn told him in nothing more than a whisper.

The drunk laughed, then flicked Flynn's ear. And it hurt. 'Fuck you, old guy.'

He started to turn away from Flynn with a look of contempt.

And Flynn's mask of red mist slotted down.

He swung round and drove his fist into the guy's stomach, but because of their relative positions, the blow landed at an angle and not as hard as Flynn would have liked. The man staggered back, but didn't double over. Flynn saw the mistake he'd made when the guy turned like a bear, roared and bore down on him, trying to grab his head in a lock.

Flynn ducked to one side and laid a punch into the side of his face – but again it didn't connect as he would have liked. The man's head went out of shape for an instant, but he recovered immediately, turned and launched himself at Flynn.

Bar stools crashed over. A roar went up from the other punters, some women screamed and the two men laid into each other, punching, tearing, biting.

Flynn pounded the guy, aware of the man's sweaty face, stinking breath and body smell.

They rolled over. Tables disintegrated, glasses smashed, people leapt out of their seats. Then they crashed out of the bar on to the beach where they came apart, faced each other and circled like wolves.

Flynn was glad to see his opponent was breathing heavily.

'Now who's an old man?' he taunted.

'C'mon, cunt.'

The man charged. Flynn sidestepped, turned low and swung a double-handed punch into his guts, getting the result he wanted this time. The man staggered down to his knees, all breath out of him, coughing up his guts into the sand as he dropped on to all fours.

Flynn knew he should have left it there and walked away. But the concoction of adrenaline, alcohol and mood was deadly.

He wanted to finish it – wanted it badly – in the sense that he now wanted to really hurt the guy who had stepped into his space and who was now going to carry the brunt of his situation.

He lined himself up next to his spluttering adversary.

It was going to be one hell of a rib-kick – but it never landed as two of the guy's mates leapt on Flynn. One put an arm around his neck in a stranglehold and bent Flynn double, pounding his face with a fist as he dragged him to the sand. The other booted and kicked him as he went forward. Flynn realized he was into something that might not have a happy ending.

He writhed and twisted and used his elbows, but the new attacker had a solid hold of him and continued to punch his face with his free hand.

Then Flynn heard something like a roar and, despite his untenable position, he smiled.

Suddenly the second man no longer had an arm around his neck and the third man wasn't kicking any more.

Flynn hit the beach, scrambled back up to his feet and turned to see the two men laid out cold on their backs, while the rotund figure of Jose hopped painfully around in a circle as though he was doing a rain dance, cradling the knuckles of his right fist.

A semicircle of onlookers watched from a respectful distance, drinks in hand, enjoying the entertainment.

'Jesus, man,' Jose said, 'I think I dislodged my knuckles.'

Flynn said, 'Thanks, *amigo*.'

The man who had borne the brunt of Jose's huge fists stirred in the sand, while the third one pulled himself upright on to his knees. Flynn's original attacker sat up on the sand and was sick.

'Never call me old,' Flynn warned him.

'Sorry . . .'

'Look, look!' Jose grabbed Flynn's arm and yanked him bodily to look across the harbour at the flames rising into the night sky from one of the boats moored in the vicinity of *Lady Faye*.

'C'mon.' Flynn started to run. Jose rumbled behind him. Even from that distance, Flynn knew this was going to be disastrous.

'Who the hell was I kidding?' Henry admonished himself in his office, speaking the words aloud, though there was no one else to hear them.

It was gone nine and he had only intended to drop into the office and get a quick situation report on all the things he was dealing with. That had been hours before. Then one thing led to another, one call to the next, and the time whizzed by unnoticed until he received an irritable call on his mobile from Kate, Mrs Henry Christie twice over. That had stunned him and made him realize he should call it a day.

His mobile rang again.

'Henry, it's me, Naomi.'

'Oh hi, how's it going?'

'Good. Look, I've been going through Deakin's statement and seeing where it fits in the overall picture . . . I just wondered . . . I know it's late and all . . . and I'm assuming you're still at work . . . and my place is more or less on your way home. Any chance of you popping in for a few minutes? See what you think?'

Henry lived on the outskirts of Blackpool. Naomi lived some-where in Kirkham, a small town between Preston and Blackpool, definitely more or less on his way home.

On his way out of the office, he checked his ruffled appear-ance in the long mirror on the back of the door.

If he had been completely honest with himself, he would have seen a tired, grizzled, middle-aged man who tried to keep fit but was always two steps behind the journey his body was taking. His clothing was rumpled after having spent too long in it. His five o'clock shadow was four hours older than it should have been and his face looked like a prison blanket.

All that, however, didn't stop him giving himself a double raise of the eyebrows, then flattening them down with a damp thumb – they were getting a little overgrown – and giving himself a double-click from the corner of his mouth.

'Hot man,' he hissed, and touched his thigh with a sizzling fingertip. 'Burning man.'

By the time they reached *Lady Faye* she was well alight, the fire inside her having spread and grown like a raging monster.

It was too late to save her.

Flynn and Jose, along with a number of others, raced around the quayside, but the heat of the flames cowed them as they neared the boat and there was no way they could get within fifty feet. They were forced to simply stand and watch, shielding their brows with their forearms, seeing the flames rise high into the sky, feeling incredible heat rolling across the quay.

Flynn was mesmerized and appalled. He watched open-mouthed, the heat drying out his mouth. Then he realized what could happen and turned desperately to Jose.

'The gas bottles,' he shouted.

Jose's face froze in shock.

Behind them a crowd, mainly tourists, gathered, gawping at the unexpected spectacle. In the distance was the sound of sirens.

Flynn turned. 'Back, everyone get back,' he screamed, gesturing with his hands as though herding cattle. 'There's gas bottles on board, they could blow. Get back,' he shouted into the lit-up faces that reminded him of Bonfire Night.

The fire was relentless.

'Go – people – get away,' Jose said, attempting to get people to move. 'Very dangerous.'

'Come on, folks – move!' Flynn shouted again.

Behind him there was a huge crackling noise from the boat. He turned, and gutted, he saw the flying bridge, engulfed by flame, begin to waver, then suddenly collapse like blocks in a game of Jenga. Then he saw that the fire had leapt over to the boat moored alongside *Faye*, another sportfisher.

'Shit, where the hell's the Bombas?'

He saw blue lights coming down the Doreste y Molina. Maybe a quarter of a mile away.

But they were too late for *Faye*. There was one loud *pop* – the first of the three gas bottles. Then, in quick succession, the others went – *pop-pop* – and *Faye* erupted.

The explosion was immense and intense. A huge boom followed by a whoosh of burning air that flattened all the onlookers like a bowling ball smashing down ten pins. About thirty people, Flynn and Jose included, were mown down with unbelievable force. Some hit the ground hard, others were swept off their feet and deposited like animals in a twister. And among all that blast was the debris of the boat and chunks of the adjoining boats.

Flynn felt everything leave him, as though he'd been inserted into a crushing straitjacket pulled tight by racing cars going in opposite directions. Every ounce of breath was forced from his lungs and his whole body was lifted as though by magic. For a moment he hung in mid-air, then the propulsion of the explosion pounded into him and he was flung across the quayside and slammed into something, he didn't know what. And then even more was squeezed out of him as he smacked hard on to the concrete floor and lay there blinking up at the mushroom cloud from the explosion.

For a few moments he was disorientated, had no idea where

or who he was, what had happened, what he was or whether he was even alive. He closed his eyes.

For certain, he knew he was dead.

'*Amigo, amigo.*' Jose roughly shook the prostrate, splayed-out figure of Steve Flynn. With a great rush, air shot down into Flynn's empty lungs. He gasped and gulped as consciousness returned. He opened his eyes and saw Jose over him. The Spaniard's head looked as though it had been sliced off. Flynn then realized that Jose's scalp had been ripped from his head and was now flapping by a thread over his left ear, exposing the top of his skull.

Jose slumped down next to Flynn and groaned as he touched the top of his head. 'What the hell has happened to me?'

Flynn's senses flooded back, even though he felt like a train had hit him. He gradually propped himself up, trying to make sense of his surroundings.

It all came back as he saw a scene of devastation.

Bodies were scattered along the quayside. Some did not move. Others did. The fire service, cops and ambulance had arrived. Dozens of people were racing to the scene.

He looked at Jose. 'Jesus, you're a mess.'

'Oh, mama,' Jose uttered, then his eyeballs rolled back in their sockets like a doll and he slumped across Flynn's legs. Flynn looked at the huge flap of hairy skin hanging loose as though a knife had scalped him. Flynn had no idea how it might have happened. Many objects had scythed through the air with the explosion and Flynn realized that both he and Jose were lucky to still be breathing. Whatever had hit Jose, had it been an inch lower, would have sliced his head off like a spoon removing the top of a boiled egg at breakfast. Any lower than that and he could have been decapitated. Flynn could easily have been lifting a severed head.

Flynn leaned forward and touched Jose's neck. There was a good strong pulse and his breathing was steady. It would take more than a fine haircut to kill him off. He eased the big man's shoulders off his legs, pulled himself out from under the dead weight and gently lay him on the quayside, arranging him in the recovery position. Then he stood up slowly, teetering unsurely until the balance came back.

He wiped his nose and mouth with the back of his hand, seeing a swatch of blood there, but not knowing if it was an injury from the explosion or the fight beforehand. He was pretty sure he had escaped anything serious himself, though.

He took in the scene. Devastation. Bloodshed. Possible death. Some people lay in positions on the quayside that looked as though they could only be dead. Others stood screaming. Some stood mute and traumatized, their minds completely baffled by incomprehension. Smoke drifted lazily between the figures as the emergency services started to take control. Cops were on the scene. Paramedics. Blue lights, red lights, sirens.

Flynn staggered a little then moved to the edge of the quay, looking at the place where *Lady Faye* had been moored.

Other than some floating debris and fuel on the surface, still aflame, she had gone. The boats either side of her had been extensively damaged too, and they burned.

A wave of nausea coursed through Flynn. He stepped backwards before gripping his head between his hands and sinking to his knees, realizing that something else had now been taken from him.

'Bastards,' he said.

'I've completely reworked the summary to include Deakin's statement . . . what d'you think?' Naomi Dale handed Henry four sides of close-typed A4 paper. He was impressed by the amount of work she had done over the past few hours since they had left prison. She had obviously been pounding away at the laptop.

Henry's mouth twitched down at the corners as he nodded appreciatively and his experienced eyes scanned the hastily rejigged summary that would be the basis of the Crown's case against Johnny Cain. It would, with the verbal embellishment of the prosecuting barrister, basically be the opening speech of the trial. Henry, who had only recently boned up on the case, found it a well-written document, telling a vivid tale of underworld murder, double-cross and intrigue, written in subtly emotive language designed to get under the skin of each jury member. He had written many such summaries himself and appreciated Naomi's turn of phrase. He assimilated the words quickly, smirking at one or two points.

'Looks good,' he commented, his eyes rising from the text above the top edge of the sheets.

Naomi watched him expectantly, apparently relieved at Henry's reaction. They were in the front room of her spacious terraced house in Kirkham. The furniture was soft leather, a shade of grey. She sat on a large armchair, Henry was tucked into one corner of the settee. She had changed out of her work clothes into a white blouse, three-quarter length cargo pants and flip-flops. Her hair had been liberated into a well-cut bob that framed her features. All traces of make-up had been scrubbed away and her complexion was fresh and fine.

In her right hand was a glass of red wine, the bottle on the coffee table. Henry had declined a drink.

'Yeah, excellent,' he confirmed, laying the sheets on his lap. 'The cops can prove Cain knew Swann, but Deakin's testimony really nails the connection. It reads well.'

'Thanks.'

She held his gaze for a couple of seconds longer than necessary. There was a familiar stirring somewhere in the pit of Henry's stomach. It wasn't many moons ago when Henry might possibly have been forward enough to say, 'You and I both know I haven't been invited around here to check your summary, don't we?' And sooner rather than later he would have been taking Naomi on a roller-coaster ride to heaven and back. But that was the old Henry with a devil on each shoulder, one trying to outdo the other. Now he was a reformed character, recently remarried and dedicated to the cause. But then he had a thought: maybe he *had* been invited round here just to read the summary.

'The trial begins soon,' she said, confirming to Henry that he had been brought around here for purely legitimate reasons and the look she'd given him had been clearly misinterpreted.

A very large part of him – his sad, male, sexual ego – was suddenly quite deflated. 'Bugger,' he internalized.

'The prosecution team will have to move quickly to get all the papers across to the defence, who could, of course, kick off big style. But we have given them notice of a possible new witness and at least they're prepared for it. I don't think we want any adjournments at this stage.'

'Suppose not.' Henry's body language shifted.

Seeing this, Naomi rose, came across and sat next to him. Very close – and took the papers from him. Henry inhaled. She had showered and smelled of scented soap and cleanliness. He swallowed.

'How quickly can you get stuff together?' she asked.

'What do you mean?'

'Won't Deakin have to be escorted to court and back?'

'I suppose he could hardly go by taxi.' They chuckled together at that quip. 'I think that owing to the nature of what's happening, there'll have to be an armed escort of sorts . . . not sure about the extent of it, of course. Maybe a low-key affair.' He screwed his face up as he mulled it over. 'I need to speak to the Operations Superintendent. It'll be his job, not mine. But, if what Deakin says is true, and he does give evidence, you can make the assumption his life will be in danger. No two ways . . .'

'Will you keep me in the loop?'

'Sure.' Henry rose to leave. 'And will you e-mail me a copy of this?' He pointed to the summary.

'Not a problem.'

'Brill – OK, then.' He walked out into the hallway and shivered faintly at the narrowness of it. Bad things had happened to him in hallways. Things bad enough for him to have nightmares about. He went to the door and Naomi followed. He stopped, turned and faced her. She had both her hands tucked into her back pockets. Once again, their eyes locked. Henry had a palpitation as her lips parted a fraction and she ran her tongue over them.

'I really want to kiss you,' she said. Her eyes played over his face. She moved towards him.

Henry's nostrils flared. Fleetingly he hoped his rampantly growing nasal hairs hadn't sprouted too far down his nose since this morning. 'It'd be a silly thing to do. I mean, your boyfriend, man friend, whatever . . . I'm assuming . . .' His words petered out pathetically.

'There is no one.' One of her hands shot out and snaked around the back of his neck. She didn't need to pull him down to her. Henry suddenly had his own need. A desire to kiss her, feel what her lips tasted of, things he just had to know. He leaned forward, cocked his head slightly and their lips came into contact. He knew instantly his curiosity would not be disappointed, particularly when her tongue slithered into his mouth.

Steve Flynn sat on the quayside, legs dangling over the edge. It was past midnight and it was all over bar the shouting. The police had cordoned off the scene, but had allowed Flynn to stay within the tapes once they realized they would have to arrest him to remove him. A lone cop stood guard, directing people away or around the scene.

And Flynn sat there.

The drink had left him. The explosion and its aftermath had sucked it out of him. He stared down at the water, debris still bobbing in the mini oil slick.

Footsteps approached from behind. 'Señor Flynn?'

Flynn looked around reluctantly. He recognized the man – a detective, one of the few down this edge of the island. He was the one who had dealt with the alleged robbery at the hotel, or at least the incident Flynn insisted was a robbery.

He squatted next to Flynn. 'A terrible coincidence,' he said, 'the robbery, then this.'

'Mm, isn't it just,' Flynn said, knowing the detective had not believed a word Flynn had told him. 'This your case, too?'

'No.'

'Then why are you here?'

The detective – a young, good-looking man, but with old eyes – sighed and laid a gentle hand on the centre of Flynn's back.

And in that instant, Flynn knew exactly why he was here.

They looked sharply at each other and the expression on the detective's face served only to confirm Flynn's knowledge.

'I'm sorry,' he said genuinely. 'It seems that Miss Hartland suffered a brain haemorrhage on the flight back to the UK and there was nothing that could be done. She was dead before they touched down.'

NINE

'It's a tricky one.' The Operations Superintendent adjusted his glasses and looked at Henry. 'He definitely needs protection, but as you suggest, a low-key approach might be the order of the day. Maybe a top-and-tail job. Deakin and his guards in the middle car, security escort vehicles either side with armed personnel, outriders back and front.'

'I like the sound of it,' Henry said. He was a little distracted, his mind not completely on the proceedings. He was still tired and guilt gnawed away at his insides. He got a grip of himself and glanced at the other person in the HQ meeting room. PC Bill Robbins was a firearms officer and trainer and very experienced in putting together operational orders in respect of security escorts where firearms were involved.

'It's all we can do anyway,' the superintendent said, 'bearing in mind that we're fetching Johnny Cain to the same court at the same time – and he gets the full hit.'

'Yeah – a real stretch of resources,' Henry sympathized. Several firearms officers were involved in transferring Cain back and forth between court and prison. 'So, Bill – can you put the op order together?'

'Yep. I'll do the risk assessment, site and route recces and have it ready for approval, say by lunchtime day after tomorrow – that OK?'

The higher-ranking officers both nodded.

Henry said his goodbyes to the other superintendent, then left. He was in the main headquarters building at Hutton. He walked along the ground floor to the office housing the Intelligence Unit and entered after rolling his thumb on a pad and keying in a code. He walked to a desk about halfway along the office that belonged to Jerry Tope, Henry's 'tame' intelligence analyst. At least that was how Henry liked to think of him, but in truth Tope was a free spirit and something of a subversive.

He plonked himself on the chair at the end of Jerry's desk and waited for the DC to finish what he was doing on the computer. Henry wasn't in a hurry. He was lethargic and annoyed with himself, and found himself scratching the back of his neck and emitting strange groans, yawning continually.

Eventually Jerry tapped the Enter key with a flourish and gave his full attention to Henry. 'Mornin', boss.'

'Jerry,' he answered grumpily.

'To which foreign clime will you be taking me this time?' the DC asked. Tope still displayed his chagrin about once missing out on a jolly to Cyprus and getting the booby prize of a trip to Liverpool instead.

'I could go a breakfast bap if you're interested?' Henry checked his watch. It was short of ten o'clock and breakfast was still being served.

'Chuck in a coffee and I'm all yours,' Jerry said, locking the computer. He picked up a thin sheaf of papers and the two men made their way to the dining room where they served themselves and got a coffee each from the machine, then found a table.

'What've you got for me?'

Jerry bit a large chunk out of his bap and wiped his chin before speaking. Henry watched him, did not hurry him. Other superintendents, he guessed, would have been snooty about a mere DC making them wait, but Henry couldn't have cared less. Jerry Tope was pure gold as an intelligence analyst. Not just because he could put two and two together, but also because he was a computer whizz and had the knack of interrogating databases he should not really have access to. In fact, his cyber-snooping had recently got him into bother with the FBI, but they had been so impressed by him they quite fancied him on their books. Henry had told them where to get off, but he knew that a decent package might lure him away from the constabulary.

'Connections,' Jerry said. He placed the bitten bap on his plate and picked up his papers. 'First, Deakin. I won't dwell on his past, which you know reasonably well, but he does know Johnny Cain, though it's hard to say how well, or how friendly they were . . . or at least it was initially.' He skim-read a few lines. 'I did most of my digging in Lancashire's and GMP's databases, but then I cast the net wider. I'd accidentally picked up on an associate of Cain's from Liverpool, a guy called Tomlinson, who Merseyside were watching for some local drug stuff a while back. Cain met up for several chats with this guy and an unknown man was along for the ride . . .'

'Deakin?'

Jerry nodded. 'Bearing in mind all this is about five years ago. But I only know it was Deakin because I got on the blower to a DC I know in Merseyside who did a manual search for me and came up with some surveillance shots on file, from which I ID'd him.'

There was suddenly a splurge of questions Henry wanted to ask. Trouble was that intelligence gathering was such a nebulous thing. He wasn't surprised that no one seemed to have identified the man with Cain and Tomlinson as Deakin.

It was as if Jerry sensed the questions.

'Merseyside were on to Tomlinson for their own reasons. The meeting he had with Cain and Deakin was just a side issue that wasn't even given a second thought. Just entries in logs. They weren't interested.'

Henry nodded. 'So we know Cain and Deakin knocked about together and could well be friends, though there's nothing in the files that suggests very much at all.'

'Correct.'

'Any other connections?'

'Deakin also knew the dead guy, Swann, the one Cain is on trial for killing. Lots of sightings together – again, just entries in logs.'

'So it's possible Deakin knew Cain well enough to be told by Cain he was furious at Swann for short changing him and threatening murder?' Jerry nodded. 'Is there anything that puts all three together?'

'No.'

Henry blew out his cheeks. He felt his mobile phone vibrate in his pocket. He saw it was Naomi Dale calling. His hell froze. He put the phone on the table and watched it dance until it stopped. He closed his eyes for a despairing moment.

'You OK, boss?'

'Yeah – so the bottom line is that we know these three guys, Deakin, Cain and Swann, were together in various combinations, but we have nothing that places all three together.'

'No.'

'So Deakin's tale could be true – that he knew Cain well enough to be told by him he was going to murder Swann for skimming.' Henry's face tightened. 'The only thing is it's pretty common knowledge how Swann was murdered and Deakin puts in his statement how Cain planned to commit the murder. He could just be telling us what we already know and adding his twopenn'orth to gild the lily, like he was the man on the inside, which is what he wants us to believe. I'm not cock-a-hoop about Deakin.'

'A man who's just had his appeal turned down,' Jerry stated.

'And one who's just had all his known assets seized and could be in prison for another ten years.' Henry bit his own bap. It tasted fantastic, one of life's simple but wonderful pleasures.

'But giving evidence against Cain won't get him out earlier,' Jerry reasoned.

'No, but it'll look good on his CV.'

'Ever thought he intends to do a runner from court?' Jerry suggested. 'Get sprung from custody?'

'It's something that would take a lot of planning and resources, which on the face of it Deakin hasn't got. Unless the assets seizure team have missed some.'

'Is there any way you could put the kibosh on it?'

'Doubt it, but I'll try.' Henry finished the bap – sadly – and looked at Tope. 'What more do you have?'

'On a different theme, something very, very interesting indeed: torture.'

'You know I have to ask you this, don't you?'

Steve Flynn nodded at his boss, Adam Castle. They were at

a table in the Sun Bar, an establishment run by a British couple who Flynn was on good terms with. They had an espresso each, sharp and bitter, making Flynn's mouth turn down at the corners. The look matched his mood.

But, angry and emotional as he was, he knew he had to give Adam his best attention because this was one of those moments when his future might be in the balance.

'Having said that, Steve, you look horrendous. I'm really sorry about Gill. You were getting it together, weren't you?'

'Up to a point.'

'Anyway, sorry mate.' Adam reached across the table and gave Flynn's arm a comforting, manly tap.

'But there's still something you need to ask me, isn't there?'

A couple of beats of uneasy silence passed between the two men. Flynn had known Adam long before he'd come to live on the island. Flynn had holidayed on Gran Canaria many times since getting the sportfishing bug and he'd got to know Adam through that. They'd often joked that when Flynn retired he might come and work a boat for Adam, or if anything went tits-up, as it did – big style. So Flynn had scampered to the island and found Adam to be as good as his word. Flynn had turned out to be the best skipper he'd ever employed, surpassing even the indigenous guys who had been brought up on these waters.

Adam ran a relaxed but firm business, but didn't like it when things went off-beam.

'I don't really know how to . . .' Adam wriggled uncomfortably in his skin.

'Let me make it easy for you,' Flynn said gently. 'You want to know if what happened over the last couple of days is anything to do with me, don't you? The robbery in Gill's room, her murder and the sinking of *Faye*? That about the long and short of it?'

Adam nodded, a little embarrassed.

Flynn picked at his eyelid. He moved fractionally and tensed with the pain and exhaustion. He shrugged, 'Truth is, I don't know. The guys who broke into her room did tie me up and start to hurt me, but didn't get chance to ask any questions because Gill raised the alarm, bless her soul. As for the boat . . .'

'First indications are it was a deliberate act, but that's not really based on much yet,' Adam said. 'We need to salvage as much as possible for a forensic team to have a proper gander.'

'Was she insured?'

'She was, but that's not the issue, Steve.'

'I know – I'm the issue. It could have some connections to the illegals I rescued,' Flynn said plaintively, knowing it was untrue.

'Maybe . . . I just wondered. You came here under a cloud, though. Anything to do with that?'

Flynn had once told Adam the whole sorry truth of his exit from the cops in the UK and he was right to speculate.

'I don't know for sure,' he said honestly. 'It could be, but why I don't know. I certainly don't know the guys who broke into the room, but I do know one thing for sure – I'm going to find them . . .' He ended the sentence there, but his gaze hung across the table in a way which made Adam shiver, even in the heat.

Henry Christie said, 'Torture?'

'The flat-iron business.'

'Gotcha,' Henry said, vividly recalling the branding on the bodies of the two suspected armed robbers who had met grisly deaths in a backwater town of Lancashire. 'You know something?'

'From GMP files, which I shouldn't be accessing.'

'Jerry, you've accessed the deepest FBI files,' Henry said, 'so GMP should hardly be a worry to you.'

'I'm doing this with your consent then?'

'We're going off task here.'

'Whatever, just trying to cover my back is all,' Jerry shrugged. 'About four years ago, there was a series of very nasty assaults in Manchester, mainly on gangland bosses, so there were never any formal complaints. They were recorded, but never acted upon by the cops. Intel was that two guys, acting on behalf of another boss, were combing the streets for information about some missing drugs.'

Henry's eyes hooded over. 'Rufus Sweetman,' he said dryly.

Jerry raised his eyebrows. 'You remember?'

'Sweetman ended up dead, as did a major player from Spain called Mendoza.' Henry had been involved in the affair, which had been a complex murder investigation linked to a small nucleus of corrupt detectives in Manchester. It had all started with the murder of a low-level drug dealer whose body had been dumped just inside Lancashire and Henry had ended up investigating it. He sat upright and trawled his brain for some of the detail that came out after Sweetman's death. 'Sweetman suspected other gang bosses of ripping him off,' Henry said enthusiastically, 'and to find out who he sent a pair of nasties around to ask questions in a less than subtle way. I remember now, but it was only a side issue to the main inquiry.'

'Yep – but I'd say that "nasties" is a bit of a namby-pamby term to describe these guys. In their quest for information, they snipped off a guy's foreskin with hairdressing scissors, but without anaesthetic, did straightforward beatings, even tried to set fire to an Asian guy after stacking tyres around him, like they used to do in South African townships. But, part of their MO was to steam-iron people. Connections?' he said hopefully. 'These guys specialize in scaring the shit out of handy people. Maybe they went too far this time. Very dangerous dudes.'

'Names?'

'Tony Cromer and Edward "Teddy Bear" Jackman.'

'Where are they now?'

'No idea.'

It was a tough day but Flynn knew he had to keep at it to stop himself crumbling. If he stopped it would hit him harder than anything he had ever experienced in his life before, and he knew he didn't want to face the fact he had brought death and destruction to the people he had come to love and respect.

He spent the day carrying out a salvage operation on *Lady Faye*, assisting a couple of professional divers from a local company to bring ashore as much as they could lift of the remains of the boat. Much of it had been destroyed. The blast had torn the poor girl to shreds, but some things were still in one piece. A couple of rods survived, some of the navigation system, surprisingly, but mainly just odds and sods. They brought her up piece by broken piece and Flynn worked furiously at it, the physical nature of the task keeping him from thinking of anything. Eventually all that lay beneath the surface of the marina were several of the larger chunks of the hull and superstructure and the bridge, items that would require specialist lifting equipment.

Exhausted, Flynn dragged himself on to the quayside at around four o'clock. He pulled off the facemask, humped off the oxygen bottle he'd borrowed and raised his face to the afternoon sun. A shadow crossed him.

'Thanks for all that,' Adam said. He and Tommy, his son, had been working alongside Flynn and the other divers and everyone was drained.

'Least I could do,' Flynn said, squinting.

'Join me for a drink at the Sun? You'll be needing one.'

'Nah, thanks anyway. I'm going over to see Jose – he's back home now, and I'm hoping to do a bit of nosing around.'

'Don't get into any trouble, Steve,' Adam said gravely.

'I won't.'

Flynn towelled himself down on the quayside and allowed the still hot sun to dry him off completely. His hair was rough and matted from a day under the water and he needed a proper shower. After cleaning off the diving equipment and looking forlornly at the wreckage of *Faye*, he started to make his way around the marina, but Adam beckoned him back.

'I almost forgot . . . I don't know if you fancy it, but I need a driver for a jeep safari tomorrow. You up for it?'

'Er . . .' Flynn did not want to refuse, but neither did he want to accept.

'A couple of girls you took out last year actually asked for you personally at the booking office. I didn't recognize them, but they looked pretty nice. Might cheer you up . . . not that I made them any promises.'

'Usual time and place?'

'Good man.'

Flynn headed across the quayside. Taking out jeep safaris was his secondary role with Adam's company. He had a special permit that allowed him to go off road in the rugged mountains of the interior and a good day was usually had by all – but he didn't feel any enthusiasm for tomorrow's jaunt. He would do it because he owed at least that much to Adam. He'd do it, put on a smiley face and give the tourists a great time. That's what he got paid for.

Even though he had turned down Adam's offer of a drink, Flynn still needed one. He sidled into the beach bar he'd been fighting in and ordered a large Cruzcampo, downing about a third of it in one. The taste and its ice-cold fingers were wonderful, displacing the salt superbly. It was his intention to shower, change, pay a quick call on Jose, then go on the hunt for two very dangerous men. Then he was struck by the impossibility of his task. He was going for two men he'd not even got a proper look at, whose names he didn't know. And he had no idea where they might be, or even if they were still on the island, which they probably weren't.

He had a very shaky moment when he considered getting himself comfortable on a bar stool, slapping a wodge of euros on the bar and drinking himself into a stupor.

A brainwave stopped him.

It was a pretty long shot, but worth trying. He fished out his mobile phone, checked the time – now four fifty-five p.m. – and dialled the UK code followed by a number that was imprinted in his brain.

Time to call in a favour, even if it was over two thousand miles away.

Henry spent the remainder of the day in his office, trying to get back on top of things while steadfastly avoiding speaking to Naomi Dale, sidestepping her calls although he knew he would have to converse with her at some point. He decided to wait for Bill Robbins's assessment of the security escort that Deakin would require from prison to court before speaking to her.

Consequently, most of his time was spent on the blower talking to detectives involved in the supermarket shooting. Henry didn't want any false assumptions made that the two dead men, Last and Sumner, were the main offenders in the robbery. He was pretty sure they were, but pretty sure did not mean certain and he didn't want to end up with egg on his face by not keeping an open mind. He also wanted to get someone locating Tony Cromer and Teddy Bear Jackman because they were good suspects for the double murder. And he looked at making links between the two jobs, because his gut feeling told him there was a connection.

He jotted a few things down.

> *Supermarket murder/robbery – Last and Sumner – who's got the money?*
> *Barry Baron representing Last and Felix Deakin (connect?)*
> *Felix Deakin, failed appeal/wants to get out?*
> *Beats up Jamie Last in prison (speak to him ASAP)*
> *Jackman/Cromer – bad ass bully boys – steam iron – Rufus Sweetman*
> *Shot at, at hospital – whose feathers have we ruffled?*

Even so, Henry thought, despite Deakin having beaten up Richard Last's brother, the only other link in the chain was Barry Baron, and he represented a lot of low lifes. Maybe his presence was just a coincidence?

Henry guffawed at the thought. 'My arse,' he said to himself. 'But what exactly is happening?'

His desk phone rang. From its ring tone he could tell it was an external call. He reached for it automatically, then his fingers stopped a centimetre above the handset, allowing it to ring, then stop, an agonizing twenty seconds.

Next his mobile phone started to vibrate and dance around the desk top, moving around like a mini-hovercraft. He picked it up and saw the number calling was withheld.

Then he thought there was no way a superintendent should be uncontactable. Not answering the phone was tantamount to desertion of duty. He steeled himself and answered it, his Adam's apple sticking in his throat as he uttered a short request to any god that might be listening for it not to be Naomi Dale on the other end.

'Detective Superintendent Christie,' he answered nervously.

'Boss? It's Jerry Tope. I thought you were still at work.'

'I am.'

'But I just phoned your office.'

'I was having a pee, if that's OK?'

'Oh, right.'

Henry checked his watch. He needed to get across to Blackpool to see his mother, who had had a comfortable day, apparently, and also to check in on Rik Dean, who was also doing well. He probably needed to see Naomi Dale, too. 'What do you want, Jerry?'

'Need to come and see you.'

'Urgently?'

'I'd say so.'

Henry closed his eyes and screwed up his face, then got a grip. 'You know where I am,' he said without a trace of irritation.

There was a knock on the office door. That was hellish quick, Henry thought. 'Enter,' he said imperiously, only to receive a slight jolt when the door opened and Bill Robbins filled the frame with his stout, but agile and fit body.

'Got a few minutes, boss?' He waggled a paper file at Henry, who waved him in with a broad sweep of the hand.

Bill and Henry knew each other well. They'd been PCs together briefly in the eighties and had come into regular contact since. Henry had tried to get Bill a transfer on to FMIT, but the chief constable wouldn't allow it and Henry had to agree reluctantly that there was no room for a firearms PC in the department. Henry had suggested that Bill could become his batman, but even Bill baulked at that one.

'I've done a recce on the security escort from Lancashire Prison to Preston Crown and back again,' Bill announced. He shook the file. 'No great problems route-wise. It's only a short journey, just about eight miles, and I reckon it can be done with a sandwich job: Armed Response Vehicles front and rear, a couple of outriders.' He shrugged.

'Don't you mean a shit sandwich?'

'Knowing what I do about Deakin, yes. But what exactly is the threat?'

'He's giving evidence about a gang leader from Manchester who killed a guy in Lancashire – or at least the body was dumped in the county. His life could be in danger. At the moment it's all under wraps and the prosecution are going to keep it as tight as they can, but they will have to disclose soon as the trial's going to start soon.'

'At what stage will his evidence be needed?'

'Early on, I'd say. We'll know more when the barrister's had a proper look at what Deakin has to say. But if he's to be believed, he provides the glue for everything else that follows.'

Bill nodded. The two men looked at each other and smiled.

Henry said, 'Having said that, you need to watch out for any possibility on the road because there's just as much chance that Deakin'll try and do a runner. You need to be aware of that.'

'I'll write it into the operational order.'

There was a soft knock at the door. It opened and Jerry Tope slid in, a little put out to see Bill sitting there.

'OK, thanks, Bill,' Henry said.

Bill rose, nodded at Jerry and left the office. Jerry replaced him on the seat.

Neither man spoke. Henry raised his eyebrows encouragingly.

'Erm,' Jerry winced, 'I don't know how to put this, but I think I've done something silly and a bit unprofessional.'

'And you need to tell Uncle Henry?'

'But there is a good side to it.'

'I'm listening.'

'I think I might know where Tony Cromer and Teddy Bear Jackman are, or were very recently.'

'That's the good side, I assume. What's the downside?'

'I just got a phone call from an old acquaintance of mine. He wanted a bit of information from me. Ha! Talk about connections,' Jerry chuckled forcibly. 'This guy wanted to know if I knew two heavies who went about torturing people using irons.'

'And why did this guy want to know that?'

'Because they'd just tried to iron his chest.'

Henry shot forward.

'Well, two guys fitting their descriptions.'

'In other words, Tony Cromer and Teddy Bear Jackman.'

'Well, yeah, I suppose so.'

'I take it you told this guy to come in immediately and make a statement – him being an old acquaintance and all that?'

'I . . . uh . . . well, not exactly.'

Henry jerked a hand at him. 'What?'

'Well, y'see . . .' He rubbed his forehead with his thumb and finger. 'It wasn't that simple.'

'Let me get this straight. You're telling me you failed to ask someone who'd been assaulted by two guys suspected of committing a double murder to come in and make a statement, and look at some mugshots? What wasn't simple about that?' To be fair, Henry was enjoying this in a strange, knife-twisting way. He knew Tope was a straight down the line guy, excellent at his job, even if in this case Henry was picking up some odd signals. 'Let's begin at the beginning, shall we?'

A short time earlier Jerry had been at his desk when a call had come through from the HQ switchboard. 'Can I help you?' he inquired. As instructed, he did not give his name or reveal he was in the Intelligence Unit just in case it was a crank or a crim calling.

'Jerry Tope, old mate.'

Tope instantly recognized the voice. He quivered like a shot of electricity had jerked through him.

'Steve,' he said, his voice hushed, his eyes flicking back and forth around the office. 'Flynn,' he whispered almost inaudibly.

'Yep, none other.'

'How you doing?'

'I'm OK. You?'

'Good, yeah. Still sifting through intelligence documents,' Jerry said.

'It's what you do best.'

'Yeah, it is.' Tope's voice was shaky. His body had heated up with fear. 'What can I do for you?'

'As you can guess, this isn't an old mates' catch-up call.'

Tope's throat constricted. 'I gathered.'

'I'll keep it short, pal . . . it's payback time. You owe me a favour, buddy boy.'

Tope hung his head and swallowed dryly. 'I never thought . . .'

'That I'd come a-knockin' on your door?'

'Something like that.'

'Knock, knock,' Flynn said as dangerously as those two words could be made to sound.

Jerry looked to be on the verge of tears. Henry kept his expression unforgiving.

'Ex-cop Steve Flynn, you say?'

Tope nodded, his nostrils flaring.

'That's a name to conjure with.'

'Oh yeah,' Tope gasped. He held his head in his hands. 'It's not so much he came to ask for a favour to be repaid. I mean, I never expected to hear from him again . . . it was just the nature of the favour and the fact I blabbed out some pretty sensitive stuff and then – whap! – too late.' He held up both hands, palms out, as though he was about to be hit by a bus. 'I blabbed. Old blabbermouth me.'

'What did you tell him?' Henry's voice was as unforgiving as his facial features.

'That the guys who assaulted him could be Cromer and Jackman . . . and that they were suspected of a double murder . . .'

'Anything else?'

'Well, he asked about Felix Deakin for some reason. And I told him about his upcoming court appearance, even though I know it's pretty bloody sensitive.'

Henry's brow furrowed. 'What were the circumstances of the assault on Flynn?'

'He didn't say . . . and I didn't ask,' Jerry said meekly.

'So these two goons assault Flynn and he asks about Felix Deakin, who we know he is historically connected to, don't we? And these two goons could have killed two guys, one of whom has a brother in prison who was beaten senseless by Deakin?' Henry inserted the tips of his thumbs into his eye sockets either side of his nose and pressed up into his throbbing cranium. 'Cromer and Jackman don't do anything off their own bat, do they? They always work for other people, don't they?'

Jerry raised his head, cautiously optimistic. He nodded. 'So the Intel suggests.'

Henry went on, 'Could they be working for Deakin?'

'Every chance.'

'They kill two men – after torture – on Deakin's orders. Next they assault Steve Flynn. What exactly did he tell you? What did they want from him?'

Jerry grimaced. 'As I said, he didn't say.'

'A one-way conversation then?'

Jerry nodded childishly.

'And you got nothing from him?' Henry's mind spun. 'What the hell's going on then?' He regarded Jerry severely. 'You've divulged sensitive information to a non-police person, which if stretched could be a sackable offence.'

A groan escaped from Jerry's lips.

'You've just had a verbal bollocking,' Henry said. 'Superintendent's prerogative. Matter dealt with.'

'You sure?'

'Yeah. Did Flynn say where he was? I haven't heard of him in ages.'

'No.'

'Oh, for goodness sake, Jerry, I thought you were a detective?'

'I do know where he is, though. I saw him on telly the other day – breakfast TV.'

Henry sighed. 'Explain.'

Which Jerry did, telling Henry about Flynn's appearance on national TV. 'He's a bit of a hero,' he concluded, as though this made his blooper OK.

'To some, maybe,' Henry said bitterly. 'To others he was a cop with a cloud of corruption hanging over him . . . including the allegation made by Felix Deakin.' He thought back to Rik Dean's assessment of why Richard Last and Jack Sumner might have died: money. And with the appearance of Steve Flynn on the scene, Henry also thought the same. Chase the money. 'And why did you owe Flynn something he could cash in?' he asked Jerry.

'Um . . . he saved my marriage.'

TEN

Flynn found his way into a bottle just after eight that evening. Following the call to Jerry Tope, he'd made his way to his villa and changed into his running gear. As bad as he was feeling, he needed to get out on to the streets. Though he had grafted all day, the euphoria brought about by a three-mile run and a dip in the sea was something his brain and body needed, especially after the news he had just extracted from Tope. It was still burning hot, the August sunshine relentless even late on, but Flynn had to do it. He ran back up the Doreste y Molina, then cut right on to the pathway clinging halfway down the cliff face that took him across to the shell beach at Amadores. There he turned and ran back along the same route. The exercise purged his system and after the run, followed by a swim across the bay, then a long, hot-cold-hot revitalizing shower, he was almost human again.

After a flying visit to see Jose, who was recovering well from the scalp injury, his mood unfortunately darkened once more when he found himself in a bar in Puerto Rico's commercial centre. He began to repeatedly mull over his conversation with Tope and the nugget of information he'd drawn from him. Nugget may well have been a euphemism unless, of course, the name Deakin was a gold tip on a killer bullet.

As he sat there, his suspicions started to come together to make some sort of sense. Although still not certain why the two men had come for him, he did know he was now involved in a deadly game that he could either run from or face.

He ordered a selection of tapas to accompany a bottle of Rioja and a litre bottle of Cruzcampo, then moved to a seat in a quiet area of the bar. He dipped a Canarian potato into a saucer of mojo sauce, bit on it and washed it down with a mouthful of the beer. He sat back, one eye on the large TV screen at the opposite end of the bar. His mind silently cursed the invention: if it hadn't been for the box, he wouldn't be in this mess. He munched his way through the food and his memory shifted back several years to a different time, place and way of life, which was still all too vivid and real to him.

Five minutes to midnight.

Detective Sergeant Steve Flynn was in the locker room at Blackpool Police Station, shrugging himself into a stab vest, ensuring his rigid handcuffs and extendable baton were hooked on to his belt, that his personal radio was secure and worked and was on the correct channel for that night's operation.

Flynn looked at his partner, Jack Hoyle, and nodded. 'OK, pal?'

'Well good, mate.' He rubbed his hands together enthusiastically. Flynn and Hoyle had worked together on and off for the best part of twenty years. First as cops on the beat, then plain clothes on targeting teams; next on Support Unit and eventually, via CID, on to the Drugs Branch, their present posting. 'Tonight's the night,' Hoyle said.

They gave each other hearty backslaps, both eager to get on with the task ahead.

They walked into the briefing room where they were faced with about a dozen cops, uniform and plain clothes, and a dog man. A local DI sat at the edge of the room, watching the proceedings with detachment. This was a drug squad raid and he wasn't particularly interested.

'OK guys, time to listen up,' Flynn announced loudly, getting everyone's attention. The idle chatter died down. 'Thanks for turning up. All being well you should be treated to some fun tonight, so be prepared to break heads where necessary.' This elicited a small murmur of approval.

Sitting in the bar in Puerto Rico, Flynn visualized himself that night.

He'd always been a fitness freak, and that, coupled with a ruthless and sometimes violent streak, made for a cop with a reputation. He was six-three and just under fourteen stone, all of it muscle. He knew he looked bloody good in his gear that night – the stab vest, the dark blue T-shirt underneath, the tracksuit bottoms and steel toe-capped boots. He held his head high and was proud of the fact that most of the crims he dealt with were shit scared of him, that he often got results without recourse to the bureaucracy of the cops. He could have been seen as a dinosaur, but he knew how to survive the minefield of the law and come up smelling of roses.

He was keen and conscientious in the pursuit of criminals, but if he couldn't pull them legally, he did so illegally.

In truth, Flynn thought as he reflected, he'd believed he was riding on the crest of a wave. He hadn't realized he was actually on a knife edge, ready to have his balls cut off – as the next few hours would show.

But at that particular moment, standing in front of those officers, directing an operation of his own making, he'd thought he was untouchable.

'Right, I'll keep this short and sweet before I hand over to DS Hoyle here, who'll go through tonight's tactics for you.' He flicked the button on a remote control and the data projector affixed to the ceiling came to life. An image shot on to the whiteboard at the front of the room. 'This man is Felix Deakin and I have been after him for eighteen months. Without a shadow of a doubt he is one of the biggest and most dangerous drug barons in the north of England. He works out of Manchester, but his empire – and it is an empire – spreads right across Lancashire, Cheshire and Cumbria, and West Yorkshire. We've been running a job on him for a long time without success. He's slippery and very canny. Surveillance and forensic conscious. Also, he rarely gets his hands dirty, except where money is concerned. He likes getting the stuff in his grubby mitts and *that* is his weakness.' Flynn paused. 'He is suspected of ordering murders on rival dealers, shootings, beatings, etc. Unfortunately we don't have evidence to convict him of such things. However' – and Flynn recalled smiling wickedly at this point – 'tonight will see him begin a long period of incarceration. We have enough evidence to get him to court on drug trafficking, importing, supply and distribution and tonight will just be the icing on the cake. We're going to catch him counting his cocaine-tainted cash.

'He has a series of transient counting houses across the north-west and every so often he likes to do a collection himself. And tonight's the night. Over the past month a lot of money has been collected from drug sales and there will be a count at a terraced house in Blackpool. Deakin's collectors have been arriving and departing all day and a couple of women employed by Deakin have been counting the cash, protected by three goons armed with knives and coshes. The last money is due to arrive in half an hour. Deakin is then due to arrive in an hour, where all the money will be re-counted in front of him. He'll be there about an hour and at the end of that time he'll pocket about fifty Gs.'

A susurrus of appreciation rippled around the room.

'It's the nail in his coffin,' Flynn said. 'And now Jack Hoyle will go over the tactics . . . Jack.' Flynn turned to his partner and friend. 'Over to you.'

Flynn drove his fork into a slice of pan-fried chorizo and popped it into his mouth as he thought of Jack standing there beside him in the briefing. They had joined the cops together as nineteen-year-old rookies and made a drunken pact to be crime-busters together, smashing down crims wherever they operated. And if they couldn't get them lawfully, they'd deal out their own particular form of justice.

Over the years they'd dealt out a lot of it.

'OK, guys . . .' Jack had taken the projector remote from Flynn and the screen now showed a row of terraced houses in South Shore, Blackpool. 'We know that this is the address of Deakin's counting house here in the resort . . .' He thumbed the button and the photo changed to one showing the front elevation of a specific house.

Thing was, Flynn thought he knew Jack well. After all, they'd been close buddies for a long time. They'd watched each other's backs, got drunk together a lot, lied for each other in court. They knew each other inside out. At least that's what Flynn thought . . . still thought . . . He walked back from the bar with another beer and sat down at his table. A couple of middle-aged women had blundered into the place and were sitting on stools at the bar, constantly eyeing him. A week ago he would have been up there chatting them up, cocksure of making a threesome. Now he scowled at them. A week ago he hadn't been in love. A week ago he hadn't had a future of possibilities snatched from under his nose. The beer went to his lips and he drank half of it, not even tasting it.

Twenty minutes after the briefing the team was ready to strike, but not until they got the word from Flynn, who had sneaked into an empty house opposite the target address where an observation point had been established. Two detectives manned the cameras and binoculars.

'He's not landed yet,' one informed Flynn.

Flynn settled down for a wait. The world of drug dealing and counting ill-gotten gains does not necessarily run to a timetable and the strike team had been warned to expect delays. But Flynn was certain Deakin would be coming. Because even though he probably hadn't realized it, Deakin had slotted into a routine, albeit one that may have come about accidentally. Flynn and Hoyle had seen it, a pattern of visits, one confirmed by an informant of Hoyle's working on the periphery of Deakin's business.

Flynn didn't get time to make himself comfortable.

He was about to reach for a flask of coffee and pour himself a much-needed slurp when the detective with the binos said sharply, 'He's landed.'

Flynn lurched to the window and peeked through the black net curtains to see a big Audi move slowly along the road and drive past the house. It disappeared, then returned two minutes later. Flynn pegged this as the recce car, the front-runner vehicle for Deakin, checking out the neighbourhood, getting a gut feeling for how the land lay. The car did a couple more passes, then left the scene. It would be returning to a meeting point where the occupants would report their findings and feelings to Deakin.

Flynn hoped the cops had been good enough. That the strike team was parked far enough away and hidden well enough not to arouse suspicion. The next minutes would be critical. Flynn's arm jerked nervously as he poured the coffee from the flask.

There was just time to take a few mouthfuls. He tried to control his breathing.

This was the culmination of a long investigation, during which he had done everything right, totally by the book. Flynn was proud of the way he'd pulled it together, the biggest hit of his career. He just hoped he hadn't overstepped the mark with this little operation, which had not been rubber-stamped by his bosses.

Flynn snorted a laugh and glanced around the bar, his thoughts back in the present. Suddenly Gill Hartland walked into the bar. He snapped upwards, ready to call out her name, but the woman turned and it clearly wasn't Gill. Gill was dead – murdered – and his mind was starting to play tricks.

'Tosser,' he admonished himself, settling back with a scowl of self-loathing, still recalling that night in Blackpool.

The headlights came down the street. Two sets, one on the lead Audi, the scout car, the second set belonging to Deakin's 4x4 Lexus.

'He's back,' one of the observers said.

'Let him get into the property,' Flynn said. He wanted him literally red-handed, fingers on the money.

The cars drew up. A passenger from the Audi leapt out and ran to open the rear nearside door of the Lexus. Deakin hopped out, pulled his jacket tight, tucked his head down and crossed the pavement to the front door which, rather like 10 Downing Street, opened just at the moment of his arrival. He ducked in with the passenger from the Audi. The drivers of both vehicles stayed with the cars.

Deakin was expected to be inside for up to sixty minutes. Flynn gave him five, then said, 'Go,' into his PR. The strike team rolled into action.

Eight officers, plus Flynn, Jack Hoyle and the dog man, raced to the front of the house.

Four others emerged from shadow and smashed the windscreens of the two cars with pin-hammers. Their job was to neutralize the drivers as quickly as possible to prevent them from warning the occupants of the house. They did the job well. Surprised and over-powered, the drivers were dragged out and pinned to the ground.

Those with Flynn and Hoyle charged at the front door, expecting to have to smash it down, but they discovered that even drug dealers get careless. The door was unlocked.

Flynn burst in, followed by the strike team, and chaos broke out.

A man appeared in the hallway. A uniformed officer went for him and rugby-tackled him down. Flynn leapt over the tussling bodies and turned into the front room, which he knew was the counting room. He was dimly aware of Jack Hoyle running upstairs . . . And as he relived those moments while getting drunker and drunker in a bar in Puerto Rico, he scowled even more. Why had Jack done that? That wasn't part of the plan, was it? He tried to remember.

But it was gone.

And Flynn was in that front room of a terraced house and face to face with Felix Deakin for the first time ever. Deakin was standing at a trestle table at which two women sat counting untidy wads of notes. First estimate, forty grand. On the floor beside them were buckets full of so far uncounted notes and coins.

Deakin's face registered shock.

Flynn could hardly keep the triumph out of his voice as he slammed Deakin against the wall.

'Fuckin' nicked,' he yelled in Deakin's ear as he pinned him there. It was a phrase that, in a subsequent written statement, would morph into, 'I told him he was under arrest for supplying and distributing controlled drugs. I then cautioned him and he replied . . .'

Deakin said, 'Cunt.' That word did appear in the statement.

Flynn cuffed him in a flowing, expert motion and the two female officers who had accompanied the arrest teams dealt with the women tellers.

But then Flynn's heart sank as he heard a plaintive, 'Put the gun down,' from one of the officers in the hallway.

A man had appeared unexpectedly from the back room, drugged up and brandishing a revolver.

Which was then fired.

Flynn winced at the memory. He took a drink of the locally produced whisky he'd acquired.

'Man down! Man down!' were the words he could hear ringing in his ears.

Being averse to confrontation, Henry decided to bypass Kirkham on his way home and head straight for Blackpool instead. It was late when he arrived at the hospital, and the corridors were strangely deserted and spooky as he made his way to the cardiac unit. He was allowed into the room in which his mother lay and wearily took a seat next to the bed.

She was sleeping, her mouth open, false teeth removed, and dribble eked out of the corner of her mouth.

A nurse gave him a quick overview of the current situation: still very poorly, but comfortable (whatever that meant). Henry sighed deeply and listened to her mild snoring. She looked old, ill, and Henry was depressed by the thought he might soon be an orphan.

It was a curiously strange sensation to think there was a good chance he might have neither parent soon. He'd been close to both of them, his father more so than his mother, and when his dad had died a few years earlier Henry had been devastated for a long time. But he only ever remembered crying once.

He wondered why. Wasn't grief supposed to be some massive outpouring, tears, screaming, all that shit? Henry often castigated himself for not showing more emotion but he knew it was bottled up inside him. One day he expected an explosion, but it never seemed to come.

He looked at his mother and took her right hand, the one without the intravenous drip. It had originally had a needle in it, but sometime the hand had been swapped. Henry saw that the hand was flecked with liver spots and heavy bruises.

She stirred, but did not waken.

He sighed again and let go of the hand, feeling dithery.

Suddenly he wanted some form of solace. He needed something, someone. And for a terrible reason he could not explain, he didn't want it to be Kate.

'Shit,' he breathed quietly.

He did not want to talk, didn't want anything other than bodily contact and an escape from the reality of this moment. He pulled out his mobile phone, which was on silent. The display told him he had two missed calls, both from Naomi Dale. He blinked and his lips tightened as his thumb hovered over the keypad.

As he looked at the phone, the screen changed to announce an incoming call.

It was a crap Eastern European gun, with crap home-made ammo, brandished by a man more frightened than the cop staring down the business end of the barrel. But that didn't stop it blowing off most of the cop's left shoulder, chunks of it splattering around the hall. The cop staggered backwards, screaming with pain; in a panic, the goon tried to fire again but the hammer hit a dud, and Jack Hoyle and another cop floored him and beat the living daylights out of him.

In terms of arrest and seizure, the raid should have been judged a success. Forty-eight thousand in cash was confiscated and two kilos of high-grade cocaine recovered, a small fortune in itself. Deakin was arrested (and found to be armed) and his drugs empire was taken apart at the foundations.

Two things completely overshadowed these points.

First, the shooting of the cop, which resulted in an injury that meant the guy could no longer work. This was followed by a huge civil claim against the police for negligence (upheld) and a hefty sick pension payout.

Second was the missing money. The alleged missing money. Not the forty-eight grand. That was all accounted for.

But the million pounds. The alleged million pounds.

Not one penny of that was accounted for.

Henry's mind was a blank as they made love. He had withdrawn into a world where nothing mattered other than to be engulfed in a physical encounter, hardly any words being spoken, just an exchange of looks of passion as the two of them moved around the bed from position to position. Henry lost himself in her and she in him, and although he could not manage it for them to come together, she came first in a series of gasping thrusts and he came a minute later with a judder that shook the both of them to the core.

Then he stayed where he was, slowly taking every last drop of sensation until he withdrew and rolled next to her, sweat rolling through his scalp and down his neck. He blinked until he fell asleep.

ELEVEN

Flynn woke with a sense of foreboding. He blinked at the ceiling and watched a tiny lizard emerge from a crack in the wall and stop in a glint of sunlight coming through the blinds. For a moment he thought someone was in the bed next to him. Wrong. Imagination playing up again. He pushed himself up, aware he had been sweating heavily all night and that his sheets now reeked like a dog basket. He was past caring.

He heaved himself out of bed and fell towards the bathroom. After peeing for an inordinately long time, he checked the mirror and didn't like what he saw. He could not be bothered to do anything with it, though. Unshaven and smelly was what the tourists would have to bear that day.

His battered Nissan Patrol with fitted bench seats was parked under the awning at the back of the villa. It was dirty, caked with mud from the last jeep safari he'd done for Adam's company up in the mountains.

He'd bought the vehicle a couple of years earlier from a fisherman in Las Palmas knowing it would add another string to his bow in terms of getting work. He now did occasional safaris for other companies as well as Adam's and enjoyed the experience. This was mainly because he had never yet taken out a safari without getting laid. He was the tanned, muscled, good-looking bastard of a tourist guide with the gift of the gab and a breathtaking tour that always got the ladies' hearts a-beating.

Not today, though.

He eased himself stiffly into the driver's seat, slotted the key into the ignition and fired up the sluggish-sounding 2.4 litre diesel engine. He reversed carefully out of the tight parking space, then drove up to the centre of Puerto Rico close to the bus station, the usual meeting point for safaris.

To be honest, Flynn enjoyed taking out safaris. Not as much as skippering a boat, but it took a creditable second spot. Most tourists visiting the island rarely saw its stunning interior and Flynn felt honoured to be able to drive up into the mountains to show people exactly how fantastic it was. The mix of lush valleys, sleepy villages, rough peaks and fabulous views all interconnected by dusty trails, often clinging to the edges of dramatic vertical drops, always drew awed gasps of appreciation from the clients.

As he drove, his spirits began to lift.

Maybe today would turn out to be a good day. Having to concentrate on something entirely different from the fates of Gill, *Lady Faye* and himself was a good distraction after a couple of days in a bottle, trying to work out exactly in which direction to travel, metaphorically speaking.

The options were limited, but they still gave him a headache.

Maybe a day of not dwelling on things would clear his mind.

As he pulled up at the meeting point, things definitely took a turn for the positive. Lounging idly by the roadside were his two passengers. Female, early twenties, dressed in hardly anything, legs on display, tummies showing . . . Flynn's mind flashed to a grainy image of three in a bed. Suddenly he regretted the lack of a wash and a shave, though as he caught a glimpse of himself in the rear view mirror, he thought he looked like a rakish tomcat, especially when he flashed his most charming smile and leapt athletically out of the Nissan.

'Ladieees!' he beamed and approached them, rubbing his hands together and adopting his best lounge lizard look. 'I take it you are waiting for the arrival of the Castle Tours Jeep Safari?'

They shared a secret glance with each other, giggled, and tiptoed towards him. Flynn knew that a triple-whammer was not out of the question. Already he had the day mapped out in his mind. An exciting safari, lots of shrieks from the rear, lunch at a romantic hillside restaurant, then back down through the hills to an unused, but still flowing, mountain water irrigation channel where they could strip down and bathe. After that back down through the hills to a bar in Maspalomas for a few drinks, a drop-off back here and make arrangements for a meet-up later in a beach bar. Shelling peas, he thought.

'My boss says you asked for me specifically,' Flynn said over his shoulder as he gunned the Nissan out of Puerto Rico towards Puerto Mogan. The wind blew warmly and the two girls in the back of the vehicle clung to anything they could as Flynn flung it around the tight bends. Already their hair was everywhere, blowing in the wind; although they fought desperately with it, the battle was already lost. Hairstyles were the first casualty of any jeep safari. Flynn's voice was lost in a combination of the wind and a double scream from the girls as he took a corner too quickly, both lost their grip and slid down the bench seat. It felt like a dangerous manoeuvre, but Flynn knew exactly what he was doing. No one got hurt on his safaris. He concentrated on his driving, feeling undeniably happier.

As the road rose, he glanced back at Puerto Rico. It was a place he'd come to love, almost to call home. He knew that feeling was part of the decision-making process he was working through as regards his way forward. Should he simply get his head down, forget what had happened and get on with his life, forget any thoughts of revenge?

He wasn't sure he would be allowed to do that, though. He had been sought out and it didn't take a genius to see that someone, somewhere, had unfinished business with him.

Flynn rejected such thoughts for today. He was determined it was going to be a fun ride all the way.

If only he'd had a shower and shave.

*   *   *

He knew the route intimately and did not plan on any detours for these ladies. It would take about four hours, including the pre-paid lunch stop and a couple of other breaks. One of the girls leaned into the cab of the Nissan through the open rear window and shouted in his ear.

'I need a piss,' she announced, a phrase which jarred somewhat with Flynn. Not terribly ladylike. 'There's some bogs at the car park in Mogan.'

'Yeah,' he nodded, knowing she meant the car park behind Amadores beach.

She sat back, touching his shoulder suggestively. He cast a quick glance over his shoulder and she gave him a cockeyed grin, an eyebrow raise and a blown kiss. Not the subtlest of women, he thought, but he wasn't on the hunt for sophistication today. Something more akin to prehistoric pleasure was his agenda – and theirs, from the looks of it. He concentrated on the road ahead, already feeling a movement in the groin and a smirk on his face.

He drove on to the car park and drew up by the toilet block.

'We both need to piss, thanks,' one of the girls said.

'No problem,' Flynn said and flashed them a debonair smile.

They clambered out in unladylike fashion, making him wonder just how much they'd had to drink already. By the time they'd downed their free wine at lunch and been for a dip in the irrigation channel – the time when they'd be really dusty, tired and feel the need to strip – he was pretty sure they would be eating out of the palm of his hand.

He still couldn't place them from last year, though. Not that it worried him. Most safaris consisted of eight people at a time and he couldn't remember everybody. Taking two was unusual.

He watched them walk out of sight and enter the *señoras*, then sat back tapping his fingers on the steering wheel, head tilted on the headrest, eyes closed for a few moments. He sighed at the warmth of the day and tried to concentrate solely on double-headboard conquest. He wanted nothing to spoil the da

'Have a good day, have a good day,' he intoned to himself mantra that did not last long.

He knew the day was completely fucking ruined when his d was yanked open and a handgun was jammed into the side o neck and screwed tight. At the same time the back of the N dipped from the weight of someone clambering on board. A mc later another gun barrel was shoved into the back of his ne

'We meet again.'

Flynn's head remained immovable with fear, but his eyes managed to look left, into the face of the man who had assaulted him in Gill Hartland's hotel bathroom. In his hand was a large calibre pistol. 'I think it's only fair that you know my name is Tony Cromer.'

'And your mate is Teddy Bear Jackman,' Flynn said.

'You've done a bit of homework.' Cromer was impressed.

Flynn made to take his hands from the wheel. Cromer repositioned the muzzle of the pistol and ground it into his cheek. 'Do not fucking move.'

Flynn allowed himself the slightest of nods. 'Gotcha.'

'Now then,' Cromer said. 'I'm going to walk round this vehicle and get in the other side. My friend, Mr Jackman, who you know, will remain right behind you and if you do anything silly, he'll blow your throat out. Won't you, Mr Jackman?'

'With pleasure.'

Cromer eased the gun out of Flynn's cheek, then walked slowly around the front of the Nissan. Flynn stayed deadly still, Jackman's weapon at the top of his spinal column. His breathing had shallowed to almost zero. Adrenaline flooded through his system. His heart pounded, whammed up against his rib cage, and he sweated again.

Cromer climbed in, a pleasant smile on his face, and sat alongside Flynn, his gun resting on his lap, pointing at Flynn's pelvis.

'Now, as they say in all good movies – drive!'

'Where to?'

'We're on safari, aren't we? Let's go safari-ing . . . safari, sogoody,' Cromer chuckled. 'Waited years to use that one. We'll go on the usual journey.'

As Flynn accelerated away, the two girls emerged from the toilets and waved excitedly.

'How much did they cost?' Flynn asked.

'A hundred euros well spent.' Cromer laughed quietly. 'Holiday chicks . . . Enough chit-chat for the moment . . . take us on the ride of our lives, Stevie, babe, then all will be revealed. But I warn you, if you do anything silly, I'll start by putting a bullet in your hip and then things'll get real nasty.'

Flynn nodded.

He drove north out of Puerto Mogan towards the inland village of Mogan, beyond which the road filtered into a track and rose into the mountains. The two men didn't speak until that point and Flynn wasn't too inclined to attempt conversation. He had

in his vehicle the two guys who had, deliberately or otherwise, killed Gill, tortured him and probably destroyed *Lady Faye*. He was adding up all the possibilities, weighing up the pros and cons, wondering if he could kill them both, or at least one of them. That was what he put his mind to and try as he might, he could not keep a smirk of superiority off his face.

They passed through several small, boiling hot villages such as El Palmito and Los Navarres. The safari usually passed a few lakes while negotiating the trails towards San Bartolome, picking through dusty tracks and throwing up a cloud behind.

'Find a nice quiet spot, then let's stop for a chinwag,' Cromer said, raising his voice above the level of the diesel engine and the scrunch of gravel under the tyres. Flynn glanced often in the rear view mirror and watched Jackman clinging to the rails on the side of the Nissan, being bounced around uncomfortably, but still holding the gun steadily aimed at his back.

'Whatever, Tony,' Flynn said.

Cromer looked sharply at him and his face cracked into a smile. 'You think you're a tough nut, don't you?'

'Hardly.'

'Anyone who joined the Marines at sixteen, then the cops at twenty-three must be pretty hard.'

'You've done your homework too.'

'I was briefed. I never liked homework.'

'By Felix Deakin?'

'Too much talk. Find somewhere picturesque – and quiet.'

'Everywhere's quiet out here,' Flynn said. He steeled himself to continue driving, thinking that the best way out of this might be to drive them all, himself included, off a ravine. There were plenty of those in the mountains.

He cut across the hills and mountain tracks until he reached a lake known as Los Cercados.

'Somewhere pleasant around here will do,' Cromer said.

He drove on for another couple of minutes, then cut on to a flat circle of pine trees by the lakeside, knowing it was a place where they were unlikely to be disturbed. The other safari groups out for the day would still be hours behind and there was a window of about two hours before anyone else would show up.

'This do?' he asked, drawing the Nissan to a halt under the trees at the lakeside. A cloud of dust engulfed them, making Jackman choke.

'This'll do fine,' Cromer said. 'Keys.' He flipped the fingers of his left hand and Flynn dropped the ignition key into his palm, which he noticed was soft looking and a little podgy.

Jackman swung down from the vehicle and Cromer said, 'Out.'

Flynn obeyed the instruction slowly, his eyes taking in every possibility, every angle – including the back of the Nissan.

Cromer cackled. 'You've no friggin' chance,' he sneered. 'Not even if you were James Bond. Just do as we say and try to make this as painless as possible all round.'

'Yeah, right,' Flynn said sarcastically, dropping to the ground.

Jackman was behind him and Flynn was given the first indication that 'painless' was going to be a relative concept. Jackman swung hard with the butt of his pistol and smashed it into the area above Flynn's kidneys. It was a beautifully delivered blow, borne of great practice, Flynn guessed. His back arched and his head snapped back as agony seared through him. Jackman followed this by side-footing the back of Flynn's right knee, causing it to crumple. Flynn went straight down as the knee gave way and Jackman pounded the gun into the back of his neck, sending him on to all fours. He reached out for the front wing of the Nissan, a conditioned reflex to pull himself back up. By that time Cromer was in front of him and smashed the butt of his gun on to the back of his open hand, very, very hard. Something cracked in Flynn's hand, maybe a knuckle, and he pivoted headlong into the dust.

He expected to be kicked. Instead Cromer bounced down on to his haunches and looked at him as though he was inspecting a flower.

Flynn twisted his head out of the gritty ground and pushed himself up an inch. Terrible pain coursed through the back of his chest and his hand burned.

'Now then, cocker, me old lad. Neither me nor my mate fucks around. Not with anyone – get my drift? We do our jobs and then get gone, so as long as you cooperate with us, this encounter can be short and sweet. Understand?'

Flynn gasped and nodded.

'Right – get to your feet and don't do anything to make me cross.'

Flynn slowly eased himself up but as he reached his full height, Jackman again assaulted him, crashing his pistol into the side of his face, catching him on the mouth and nose. Another good shot. Flynn reeled backwards against the side of the Nissan, then bowed double, clutching his face. His top lip had split having banged on his teeth, one of which was now loose. Jackman smacked the gun into the back of Flynn's head again, and again he hit the ground. He cursed through the pain.

Jackman heaved him back upright and hit him in the stomach. Flynn had managed to tense himself, but it still hurt. His six-pack wasn't what it was. His breath whooshed out of him with the groan of a tennis player and he didn't know which part of his anatomy to cradle.

But he didn't have time for self-nursing as Jackman brought him back up by the scruff of his neck, tearing the beloved Keith Richards T-shirt.

'You know you killed her, don't you?' Flynn spat a mouthful of blood which tasted bitter and strong.

'Killed who?' Cromer asked. He had been watching the beating with dispassion.

'The woman at the hotel. She died of a brain haemorrhage because of your assault.' Flynn's eyes caught Jackman's. The big man shrugged his shoulders, the statement obviously meaning nothing to him.

'Collateral damage,' Cromer said. 'Like the fancy boat.'

A spark of rage ignited in Flynn's chest, surpassing any of the pain he was feeling.

'OK, bud ... this is what this is about – money.'

'What money?' Flynn wiped spit and blood off his face with the back of his hand, then shook it like a rag, splattering the dry ground with red spots that instantly turned brown.

'I need to be honest with you, Steve,' Cromer said, stepping up to him. 'I – we've – been given a job to do ... don't neces-sarily like it' – he grinned at this point – 'but I'll do it to the best of my ability. I simply want to know the whereabouts of what remains of the million pounds in cash you stole from Mr Deakin. You've had it for four years, so we know some of it will be spent – fair do's – but you don't exactly lead a rock-star life out here, so we'd be content with nine hundred grand back.'

'I don't know what money you're talking about.'

'The money you stole when you raided Mr Deakin's counting house.' Cromer spoke as though he was addressing a special needs kid. 'He wants it back.'

'There never was any money.'

'Not how he sees it, apparently.' Cromer paused. 'Look, you might as well tell us now – where it is, how we can get it, all that kind of shit, then take us to it. I don't suppose for one moment you banked it.'

'There's no money,' Flynn insisted. 'He claimed there was to muddy the case against him. It's all bollocks – you've got to believe me.' Flynn looked at the two men, then he winced with pain. 'I swear it.'

Cromer gave Jackman a conspiratorial glance. 'Looks like we're in for a rough ride. Waterboarding's a piece of cake compared with what you're about to experience, Steve.'

'You guys know all about torture, don't you?'

'It's our specialist subject – all self-taught, of course.'

'Amateurs, then,' Flynn said. But he knew they were good at what they did, that only after a sustained period in their company would they realize he was telling the truth. He had no idea where the alleged missing money was. The money that was supposed to have disappeared in the fuck-up of a raid he had been responsible for organizing.

Flynn measured the distances and angles but the two men worked in sync. As one got closer to him, the other pulled back out of range. If he attacked one, the other would be in a position to defend.

Cromer grinned as though he knew what was ticking over in Flynn's mind. 'Naughty – tut-tut. Look, Steve,' he went on reasonably, 'tell us, show us – and maybe you live. Screw about, you get hurt, then maybe die. It's a no-brainer.'

'Move away from the car,' Jackman said.

Flynn had to make his move now, while still near the Nissan. Once he got too far away from it, he would be beaten. 'Look – I'll tell you, OK? But first I need a drink. That's fair, isn't it?' He gobbed out another mouthful of blood. 'Need to clear my mouth.'

Cromer angled his face with suspicion. 'What do you think, T-Bear?'

The bigger of the two men shrugged noncommittally. 'Makes no odds.'

'Where's the drink?'

'Underneath the back bench seat.' Flynn jerked a thumb. 'In a cool-box.'

Cromer nodded, still wary.

'What? You think I'm going to come after you with a monkey wrench?'

Jackman guffawed.

'Get it, be quick about it,' Cromer gestured impatiently. 'I'm too fucking soft.'

'I need the key for the padlock.'

Cromer fished out the key ring on which the ignition key, plus one other, hung. He tossed them at Flynn.

Flynn gave a short nod of thanks, walked to the Nissan. His captors stood a few paces back, watching him carefully, their guns at the ready. He swung up into the back and bent over to unlock and unlatch one of the bench seats, which he opened on its hinges. There was indeed a cool-box under the seat. Flynn pulled the lid off and looked inside. Swimming in tepid, melted ice-water were four cans of Coke. He took one and flipped up the ring pull, downing half the can in one. The liquid was warm but refreshing. The cans had been there since his last safari about a month ago.

'Either of you guys want one? Thirsty work, this.' He placed his can on the cab roof.

Jackman, who'd done most of the work, looked hot and bothered, a good bet he could do with some liquid down him – but it was Cromer that Flynn wanted to say yes.

'You?' Flynn nodded directly at him.

'Yeah, go on,' he said reluctantly. Flynn reached into the cooler and got out a second can of Coke. He lobbed it underarm at Cromer who had to take his eyes off Flynn and stretch to catch it, but it fell just short of him.

'Sorry, mate.'

'Arsehole,' Cromer said.

Flynn bent and dropped his hand as if he was going for a can for Jackman. He saw Cromer stoop to pick up his can, taking his eye off Flynn again. Jackman had put his pistol down by his side and his left hand was held out lazily for the can Flynn was reaching for.

Flynn had to move fast.

His fingers closed around the stock of the Bushmaster rifle. He'd found he could not bring himself to dispose of the weapon, but didn't know what to do with it. So while he'd been thinking about the best way of getting rid of it, he'd secreted it badly under a bench seat in the Nissan, shut away and secured by a crappy padlock from a suitcase.

But it was no easy weapon to use in a fast-flowing situation like this, where speed was of the essence. This was a rifle that required time to aim, get your breathing right, not like a Heckler & Koch MP5 machine pistol, which would have been the ideal weapon to spray the two bastards with bullets.

Beggars could not be choosers, though.

With his right hand, Flynn reached into the cooler for the Coke, tossing it hard in Jackman's direction as he rose.

At the same time he picked up the Bushmaster with the other
hand, pulled it into his hip and aimed at Cromer, who was just
coming upright with his Coke in his hand. He saw Flynn and
the rifle and he opened his mouth to shout a warning.

Another factor playing against Flynn was that only two rounds
remained in the Bushmaster from the shark shoot-out. He needed
to be incredibly fast, accurate and deadly. Even then his mind
told him he had made an irreversible decision. Pulling the gun
had opened a door. Before that, there'd been a slim chance of
him coming out of this alive, even though a parallel thought told
him it was unlikely. Now it could only go one of two ways: he'd
end up dead, or they would.

He knew there was one in the breech and one in the magazine. He flipped the safety off with his thumb and his forefinger
curled onto the trigger. Cromer's face was a mask of horror,
coupled with anger, as he threw down the Coke and brought up
his gun.

But Flynn had spent seven years in the Marines practising
almost daily with weapons like the Bushmaster. Even though
that was over twenty years ago, it had been drilled into him.
What he was doing was second nature, even if it was buried
deep within.

He pulled the trigger immediately. He saw the round enter
Cromer's upper left chest, then exit via his shoulder blade. Flynn
did not look to consider what he'd done. It was enough to put
the man down – that was the important bit. Now he wound
around and aimed at Jackman, who had caught his can of Coke
at his chest. Flynn gave him no chance, fired, and the second
and final round drilled into Jackman, going through the back of
his hand, through the can of Coke and into the centre of his
chest, exiting by way of the spine. He was propelled backwards,
then fell. Instinctively Flynn knew he was a dead man.

He breathed out, dropped the Bushmaster and vaulted over
the side of the Nissan to inspect Cromer, suspecting he could
still be alive. He was, but would not be for much longer. Flynn
stood over him. Cromer's mouth popped open, bubbles of bright
red blood forming on his lips, then bursting with a fine red spray
as he coughed. His eyes were opaque, unfocused. He swallowed,
coughed once more and a gush of blood rushed out of the chest
wound.

'No one,' he whispered hoarsely, 'no one has ever . . .' He did
not manage to complete the sentence.

TWELVE

The next few weeks were a fraught time for Henry, personally and professionally.

The double murder inquiry into the deaths of the two armed robbers got nowhere fast. The two prime suspects, Cromer and Jackman, seemed to have leapt off the face of the earth (something Henry was not too far off the mark in thinking, although he didn't know it), even with the snippet from Jerry Tope's old mate, Steve Flynn, who in turn did not seem to want to be contacted. Henry concentrated the murder squad on back-tracking the original robbery, the one during which the security guard had been shot in the face, murdered, he suspected, by either Last or Sumner and their gang. Henry was convinced there were definite links between the two cases, not least of which was the bridging presence of Barry Baron, defence solicitor. Henry had actually tried to get authorization to stick a bug in Baron's home and car, but his request had been turned down by the chief constable, who accused him of clutching at straws.

Both investigations had lost momentum and Henry was starting to feel the pressure from above. He desperately needed something to break, but it seemed that the jobs had gone on too long for that to happen. But he kept his teams at it, pushing, knocking on doors, asking questions, getting into people's faces.

The mysterious shooting of Rik Dean was also something he was getting nowhere with, despite a big investigation and lots of media coverage.

There were times when he sat in his office, feeling tightness in his chest and blood pounding through his veins as the stress of it all got to him. He even bought himself a home blood pressure monitor just to keep a check on things. It didn't reassure him when one reading was 172/105, though mostly they hovered around the 125/85 mark, which he thought reasonable for a guy of his age.

At least one of his problems dropped off the radar: his mother. She had made a slow recovery from the heart attack and became well enough to be discharged from hospital. Now she was back in her flat at the sheltered accommodation she called home. Henry had tried to persuade her to move into a home with better caring facilities, but the old lady refused point blank. It had taken him long enough to get her out of the big rambling house she'd shared with his father into the sheltered accommodation in the first place. Now she was settled and Henry could tell from the steel-like glint in her misty eyes that the lady wasn't for moving again. Any further upheaval would probably be detrimental to her shaky health, so it was an issue he didn't force. She had age, status and resolution on her side, and he was just her son. So he let it be. At least she seemed sprightlier than she had been in a while. He did not want to jeopardize that.

Unfortunately another problem that refused to go away, which in fact seemed to get bigger, was that of his sister, Lisa.

Once their mother had been sent home, Henry expected – nay, rejoiced – at the thought that his fickle sister would do the same and he could wave bye-bye with a great big sigh of relief. It didn't happen.

Instead she seemed to claim his daughter Leanne's bedroom as her own, spent a lot of time nursing Mum, letting Henry know how much she was doing for their beloved and only parent. It made Henry sick to the stomach. And as a sideline Lisa was also nursing the recovering stallion that was Rik Dean, DI of this parish. He was convalescing nicely from being shot by the mystery gunman.

One Friday, Henry had come home after a heavy day to find that Lisa had invited a very mobile and obviously rampant Rik to the house, and that they were up in Leanne's bedroom screwing the living daylights out of each other.

Kate was sitting ashen-faced in the living room, hands clasped between her knees, wondering what to do.

Henry erupted in rage, but Kate held him back from chasing Rik from the house with a pitchfork and kicking his wound. He bided his time over a glass of cheap whisky. When Rik left, after popping his head around the living-room door and giving a cheery wave, Henry confronted the two of them as they embraced and kissed in the entrance hall.

'Rik, get out of this house,' he said evenly with a very clear undertone.

'Henry – how dare you?' Lisa admonished him.

He leaned into her. 'It's not a question of daring. This is my house and I lay down the rules of behaviour. And I'm not having you two fucking in my daughter's bedroom, or anywhere else come to that.'

'Henry,' Rik warned.

Henry's face turned to his friend's. 'You have something to say?'

They maintained eye contact for a few moments, then Rik backed down. To Lisa he said, 'I'll see you tomorrow.' His look at Henry should have, by rights, sliced Henry's head off. A surge of something told Henry that things between him and Rik would never be the same again. One of those moments between friends when a woman comes along and screws everything up.

Rik opened the front door and walked down to his car, Henry hot on his heels.

'Don't get involved with her,' Henry said.

Rik turned fiercely. 'Who the hell are you to tell me that? We're consenting adults . . .'

'Well go and consent in a Travelodge or your place – not mine.'

'And we're in love.'

Henry paused, blinked and retorted, 'All right, Rik – I'll tell you this once and once only: she falls in love with every guy that half-smiles at her. She fucks every guy she can. She's fickle and will let you down. She has a history of bad relationships. She's on antidepressants. She's got a teenage son she hasn't seen for years and fuck knows what's going on in her head at this moment in time, why she's really come up north and what she's left in her wake. She's certainly not up here for Mother. She's got bad debts coming out of her ears. I wouldn't be surprised if the guy with the gun was coming after her.'

'You finished?'

Breathless, Henry nodded.

'Most of what you said there could apply to you, mate,' Rik sneered. 'So – two peas out of the same pod. Think about it.' Rik hobbled, dropped into his car and drove off, leaving Henry dumb-struck and hurt. Particularly as he reflected on the fact that in so many ways his description of Lisa could well have applied to him to a lesser degree – although without the financial problems.

He turned to see Lisa at the front door. She gave him one of her killing looks, then flounced into the house.

Kate appeared at the door. She and Henry shrugged helplessly at each other, shaking their heads sadly.

Felix Deakin was not required to attend Preston Crown Court until the first day of the third week of Johnny Cain's murder trial. Not unusually for such a complex and serious case, the trial had commenced with numerous legal submissions and arguments,

criss-crossing from prosecution to defence and back rather like a
slow tennis game. There were also arguments about the make-up
of the jury, which took several days to resolve, Cain's defence
team being as legally obstructive as they could be. After many
days of wrangling, the trial proper commenced on the Tuesday of
the second week when the first terrified witness took the stand to
testify. Deakin was to be produced on the Monday after that.

That day was an early start for Henry, the Monday after the
Friday bust-up with Rik Dean. He was up at five and at police
headquarters by a quarter to six, exhausted after a weekend of
family fallouts and work callouts.

He parked in the deserted car park behind the FMIT block
and walked over to the training block that housed the Motor
Driving School, the department that provided the expert drivers
for Deakin's security escort. Officers from the firearms training
unit would accompany them, including Bill Robbins, and motorcyclists from the road policing unit.

They were being briefed in one of the first floor classrooms in
that block. As Henry pushed the door open just before six, the
aroma of toast and coffee in his nostrils made him achingly hungry.

The officers sat around chatting, yawning and consuming food.
Bill Robbins was at the front of the classroom setting up a laptop
connected to a ceiling-mounted data projector.

'Morning, Bill.'

'Boss. Brew and toast over there if you need it.'

Henry collected a couple of slices of thick buttered toast and
a mug of steaming coffee from the grizzled MDS inspector, who
seemed to have taken on the role of chef at the four-slice toaster
and kettle. He and Henry exchanged pleasantries, then Henry
took a seat in the horseshoe-shaped arrangement of chairs as
other bodies arrived, got their rations, sat and waited.

This was obviously Bill's show and he briefed them well,
being cool, relaxed and quite funny. Henry thought it ironic that
a PC should be doing this. In his earlier days in the job, everything had been done by rank. PCs were the lowest of the low
and given little credibility. In the last ten to fifteen years things
had changed for the better, Henry thought. Officers' skills and
abilities were used to their full potential now, regardless of rank.

'OK, any questions?' Bill concluded. There were none. 'In that
case' – Bill checked the time – 'let's chill for a few minutes before
we hit the road. Firearms officers recheck their weapons please
and MDS and motorcyclists carry out last-minute vehicle checks

. . .' He glanced at Henry. 'Anything you'd like to add, sir?' Henry shook his head. 'OK, the prison's expecting us bob-on seven.'

The officers rose and sauntered to their tasks. Henry hovered in the classroom as Bill stowed away his gear.

'You happy with this, Bill?'

'As can be.'

'I know the other escort team has Cain sorted,' Henry commented, referring to the security escort team bringing the defendant Cain in from Manchester Prison and depositing him at Preston Crown Court, then reversing the journey at the end of the day. They'd been doing this since day one of the trial, a high-profile, bells and whistles escort that would discourage any sort of rescue attempt.

'Yeah – it should be clockwork. Our plan is to get Deakin to court before Cain arrives, then house him in the police room, under guard and secured, to keep him separate from Cain. That'll be the job of the officers in court, of course.'

Henry's mouth twisted at the thought of this. 'I think that looks like a weak point. The police room isn't designed to be secure.'

'He'll have armed cops for company and four support unit PCs and prison guards.'

'OK, I see your point. But do not ever trust the bastard, Bill. He's a slimy rodent and if he got chance to go, he would.'

As those words were being spoken, the slimy rodent in question was just returning to his cell having had an early shower and shave prior to his court appearance. Deakin strolled casually along the landing and turned into his cell, where his clothes for the day had been laid out for him on his bunk. His two cell-mates watched him from their beds, saying nothing as he climbed into a well-tailored suit and patted himself down.

At ten minutes to seven, two prison guards appeared at the door.

'Boys, nice to see you,' Deakin beamed.

One of the guards beckoned him with a crooked finger. 'Out here, pal.'

They slammed the door behind him. One said, 'Spread 'em, pal.'

Deakin turned to the wall and propped himself against it while one of the guards purported to search him. He made it look good, but in reality there was no body search at all.

'OK, stand up straight,' the guard said, smirking.

'You two'll get nice bonuses,' Deakin said just loud enough for them to hear. One pushed him along, keeping up the pretence.

'That way, Mr Deakin.'

The prisoner smiled smugly and walked on as instructed. He failed to see the man hiding in the arch of a cell door a few feet away, a man who watched the little charade with burning, vengeful eyes, but with a feeling inside him that there was nothing he could do to stop Deakin in his tracks.

Wincing painfully, Jamie Last waited until Deakin and his escort had gone out of sight and then emerged from behind the cover of the door to walk in the direction of the kitchens, where he had secured a job as a trusty.

Henry watched the security escort roll off in formation: two motorcyclists to lead, an ARV with two armed officers on board plus an MDS driver, a second vehicle that would carry Deakin staffed by a driver and an unarmed PC; then the following vehicle containing another duo of armed cops and a driver. All the cars were liveried. They crept up the main drive at headquarters, past Henry. He nodded at Bill in the lead car, who returned a Yank-style salute. They turned right at the top of the drive and left on to the A59. It would take less than ten minutes to get to the prison.

Henry did not really envy them, although there was a healthy adrenaline rush associated with such jobs. Now all he craved was peace and quiet, but somehow that eluded him. He shook his head and returned to his office.

Something he'd said in anger over the weekend had stuck in his mind and he wanted to check it out. Then he wanted to get down to Preston Crown Court to be ready and waiting for Deakin's arrival. In the office he picked up a phone and dialled Jerry Tope's home number, a nasty little smile on his face.

'Mornin', Jerry.'

'Unph! Henry, are you making a habit of phoning me early? It's like having a stalker. Not funny . . .'

'And nor is failing to get details of the whereabouts of two murder suspects and blabbing police intelligence to a third party,' Henry retorted.

'You're not going to let that drop, are you?'

'Not until you've paid your dues.'

'What you want?'

'Need you to do some digging for me.'

'You mean unauthorized snooping in other people's or organizations' computer systems?'

'How dare you . . . well, actually, you could be on to some-thing there.'

Henry dodged his way recklessly through the early morning logjam of traffic from headquarters into the centre of Preston. He found a space in a municipal car park not far from the court and went down into the holding cells where the Operations Chief Inspector could be found. This was the person responsible for coordinating the security surrounding the Johnny Cain murder trial – the armed escort to and from Manchester Prison and the discreet presence of armed cops inside and outside the court building. As well as a sniper on the multi-storey car park opposite.

The guy looked jerky and nervous, continually checking his watch and cocking his ear to the two PRs on his desk. One was tuned into the channel used by Cain's escort, the other dedicated to Deakin's escort.

He had a hunted expression. The kind of face worn by a man who expected the very worst to happen – which was much to Henry's delight because the man was no other than CI Andy Laker, a brown-nosing git who had a massive downer on Henry. The feeling was mutual. Laker saw himself as a go-getter, a man with a future in the job, Association of Chief Police Officers potential. He saw Henry as an obnoxious dinosaur who for some unaccountable reason had his nose permanently up the chief constable's rectum.

Laker had once been the chief's staff officer but the chief had soon realized he didn't like the arse-licker one little bit and booted him out of post unceremoniously. Since then he had flitted between various operational roles before actually taking Henry's old job in the Special Projects Team, which no one else would touch with a bargepole. Henry had learned recently that Laker had made such a pig's ear of it that the team had mutinied and been disbanded, Laker being dumped on the Operations branch.

'Andy, my boy,' Henry beamed.

Laker's scowling face turned to Henry. 'It's you.'

'The one and only. How's it all going?'

Laker's eyes surveyed his predicament. 'You work it out.'

'Exciting stuff,' Henry said, recalling a fairly recent occasion when Laker had collared Henry in a corridor at HQ when they were both chief inspectors, and given him a right royal dressing down for undermining his authority. Laker had expected to fly past Henry in the promotion stakes and Henry guessed that the fact he now sported the rank of superintendent rankled with

Laker no end. He hoped it gave him heartburn. But Henry wasn't one to gloat.

There was an awkward pause, then Henry said, 'Right, how are we doing?'

'The pick-up at Lancashire Prison was effortless and they should be here within the next few minutes. Cain is en route from Manchester as we speak, no problems.'

'Is everything in place for keeping the two parties apart?'

'Yes.'

One of Laker's PRs blared out. 'Lima Charlie to Chief Inspector, now Ring Way, two minutes from destination.' It was the voice of Bill Robbins.

Laker grabbed the PR. 'Roger that.' He leaned out of his office and spoke to one of the private security guards in the reception area. 'Doors, please.'

The guard sauntered to the roll-up door situated at the rear of the court and pressed a button. The metallic door clattered upwards just in time for the car containing Deakin to drive in and stop. The remainder of the escort vehicles pulled up and stayed in the compound.

The back door of the car opened and a manacled Deakin was helped out of the seat by a prison guard. He caught Henry's gaze.

'Mr Christie,' Deakin declared. 'Here I am, here to do my public duty.' He held up his bound wrists. 'I hope these won't be staying on and that I'll be looked after.'

Henry turned his back and made his way through a series of security doors to the main court area on the ground floor. He emerged into the public mezzanine and immediately bumped into Naomi Dale, carrying a multitude of files. He thought of doing an about turn, but she spotted him and there was no escape.

'Hello, Henry,' she said demurely if a little coolly. Since their encounter, Henry had kept her at phone's length. He'd been extra proud of himself that he hadn't succumbed to her on the night he called around on his way home, even though it had been a close-run thing. He was also just as proud that on the night he thought he needed someone like Naomi, the night when he thought about being on the verge of becoming an orphan and needed a refuge in meaningless sex, he'd gone home and had exactly the opposite with Kate. Henry knew this meeting was inevitable and that their extra-curricular relationship would have to be dealt with. Everything had been done by chilly conversations since. 'Long time, no see.' She regarded him cynically. 'It's still available,' she said. 'And I still feel scorned by the way you left that night and the way you've not spoken to, or avoided me since.'

'It's not happening. I'm married and happy with it,' he said unconvincingly.

Her look was similar to the one he'd given Andy Laker earlier. His feet seemed to turn to liquid in his shoes, but suddenly her face softened. 'I'm not after a relationship, nor am I after busting up yours. I'm free, single and like having a bit of fun – and I'd like to have some fun with you, Henry. So there it is, out in the open. Now, let's move on to the real reason we're here, shall we?'

Relief flooded into Henry's shoes as though he'd wet himself. He tried not to show it, just in case she was messing with him. 'That'd be good, thanks.'

'Doesn't mean to say I won't be after you, though.' She gave him a wicked half-smile and her eyes twinkled mischievously.

Henry's feet went to lead this time. He wondered, with a hint of cruelty, how many bunnies Naomi might have stewed in her time.

'Let's get a coffee and chat about Mr Deakin, shall we?' she asked. Henry followed her meek as a lamb to a coffee machine which dispensed two plastic mugs of grim-tasting liquid. They retreated to a consulting room where they could be alone. Naomi plonked herself on one side of a table, Henry sat opposite, about as far away as he could without seeming rude. 'I take it he's arrived safely?' She slammed her court files on the table top with a hefty slap.

'He has.'

'That's a good start. No problems encountered, then?'

'None.'

'Will you be using the same route each day?'

'I don't know. Not up to me, but I guess they'll vary it as much as possible. He's only likely to be here two or three days at most, isn't he?'

'Yes.'

'Why the question, then?'

'Just curious.' She brushed some hair back from her face, then changed the subject. 'I really thought you'd be back that night, you know?' she purred. He wondered what a tiger's purr sounded like. His mouth remained tightly clamped. 'Don't worry,' she laughed, 'just teasing.'

'Mm,' he said, unconvinced. 'Have you managed to slide Deakin into the scheme of things to have the best effect on the trial?'

'The barrister thinks so.'

'How's it all going?'

'More up than down. Deakin's evidence will be critical, though – if he sticks to his statement, that is.'

'I still can't work out what he's up to. There doesn't seem to be any mileage in it for him. If anything he'll just piss Cain off and get a bullet for his troubles. Even witness protection isn't one hundred per cent.'

'Let's not be bothered by his motives, shall we? Let's just be thankful for what he's doing.'

Henry shrugged. It wasn't his problem, but he still didn't like it.

'How's the wife?' Naomi asked suddenly.

Henry stood up from the table and walked out of the consulting room.

Once Johnny Cain had arrived at court, Henry left. There was a DCI in charge of the case and the presenting of the evidence was nothing to do with Henry. Having satisfied himself that Laker had all the security in place, he got back to his day job – trying to catch murderers.

His first stop was thirty miles due east in Rossendale, where he attended the briefing of the team investigating the double murder of Richard Last and Jack Sumner. Henry watched the proceedings with a cool detachment, realizing it was completely stonewalled even though it was now combined with the supermarket robbery-cum-shooting. This joint investigation was now focused on Manchester, the main hunting ground of the dead men. But the estates they frequented put up a wall of silence and no one seemed to want to stick their heads above the parapet.

Henry's thoughts turned to Steve Flynn, somewhere out in the Canary Islands. Attempts to recontact him had failed, but Henry remained intrigued as to why Flynn had suddenly been visited by Cromer and Jackman, two men renowned for their less than subtle ways of getting information out of people. Henry thought it through. Cromer and Jackman were basically information and debt collectors . . . Perhaps Last and Sumner owed a debt . . . perhaps Flynn owed a debt . . .

'Money,' Henry said, coming to the same conclusion once again. That was the answer. It had to be. Owed money. Last and Sumner owed money and got visited. And maybe Steve Flynn also owed money . . . lots of it. He left the briefing and found an empty office, where he dialled Jerry Tope's internal number. 'Get checking the flights to and from Gran Canaria from all north-west airports around the time Steve Flynn contacted you,'

Henry told him without pleasantries. 'If Cromer and Jackman went out, maybe they've come back, so speak to airline companies, immigration, CCTV at the airports, see what you can turn up. Also, get back in touch with Steve Flynn.'

'I've been trying.'

'Try harder.'

'OK . . . but I've come across a couple of things you may want a face-to-face about. One is about Flynn, the other about that delicate matter you asked me to look into.'

'Is it bad?'

'Could be.'

Henry floored it back across the county to HQ. It took about forty minutes, then he almost dragged Jerry to the canteen where he plied him with victuals and made him divulge what he'd discovered.

THIRTEEN

As it turned out, Henry didn't have time to deal with either of the issues Jerry Tope had unearthed for him. As he walked back across the sports pitches from HQ to FMIT, his mobile phone rang. He fished it out and answered with a gruff 'Hello.'

'That Henry Christie?'

'Yeah, who's that?'

'You dealin' with Felix Deakin?'

'Who is this?' Henry insisted.

'You need to go and visit Richard Last's missus – now, in person. She won't talk to anyone else.' Behind the voice, Henry heard a metallic clang and echoing voices. 'But she'll talk to you, 'cos I told her to.'

'Who is this, please?'

'Just do it. I can't talk to you. I've already had a whackin' just 'cos I got a brother – who's now dead. Go see her. You need to.' There was another metallic clang and a shout behind the voice. Then the line went dead.

When he'd answered the phone he hadn't bothered looking at the caller ID. On checking, surprise, surprise, he saw the number was withheld. He hurried the last fifty metres to FMIT

and went to his office on the middle floor, sighing in agitation
at everything. He phoned the murder incident room he'd left
ninety minutes earlier at Rawtenstall nick and got through to the
office manager, a DS Henry knew well.

'Bernie, Henry Christie – I need the name and address of
Richard Last's wife.'

'OK, hang fire.' Henry heard tapping at a computer keyboard.
'Sharon Dawn Last, née Roche.' He read out the address. It was
in Rochdale, but wasn't the one Henry had raided in his initial
arrest of Last. 'Why do you need to know, if you don't mind
me asking? She has been spoken to, and a statement taken.'

'Can you put the statement up on the screen?'

'Yep, already done that.'

'Anything of interest?'

'Mmm, not much really. They were actually separated, but
still saw a lot of each other . . . in fact she had a kid by him a
few years back. Not much to tell, though.'

'Is anyone free up there?'

'Everybody's out, I'm afraid.'

'Bernie, make out an action sheet for me, to revisit her today.
I've just had a call from an unidentified male, must have got my
number from the media circulation, asking me to go and see her.
I'm pretty sure it was Richard Last's brother, Jamie, who's in
prison at the moment. Is there a phone number for her?'

Henry took down a landline and a mobile, frustrated. He didn't
really want to traipse back across the county, but he shifted
himself into action.

Always one to move several paces behind technological advances,
Henry had only recently had a SatNav fitted to his new car.
Although he knew Rochdale reasonably well, he used the device
to take him on the last stages of his route through the streets of
what had become a pretty mean town on the outskirts of Greater
Manchester. He drove there via the M61, M60 and M62. Not a
long journey, but a depressing one with little to recommend it.
It did nothing to revive his mood, which was as bleak and edgy
as the moorland he crossed.

He followed the directions, spoken in a tone he soon found
annoying, and found himself driving across the town and towards
Whitworth, which was actually in Lancashire. Sharon's address
though was just in Rochdale – a tiny terraced house off the main
road out of town.

He parked at the end of the street and called Sharon Dawn Last's mobile number.

'Shazzer here,' came the accented voice.

'Sharon, I'm Detective Superintendent Christie from Lancashire Police . . . I believe you want to talk to me. Are you in at home?'

'In at home?' Her voice rose immediately. 'In at fuckin' home? You must be jokin', pal. Have you seen the friggin' state of the place?'

'No,' Henry said, getting a mental image of the sort of woman he was dealing with. He could even hear her chewing gum as she spoke. 'So where are you? Can I come and see you?'

'How do I know you are who you say you are?'

'Look, I've just had a call from Dick's brother,' Henry said impatiently. 'From prison, saying you wanted to see me.'

'I'm in hiding – at my sister's house in Whit'orth,' she said, pronouncing the name in the local manner.

'In hiding from who?'

'Felix Deakin and his crew.'

'And you've run to your sister's house?' Henry tried to conceal the sarcasm in his voice.

'Couldn't think where else.'

'Have you spoken to the police about this?'

'Beg pardon, but you're a shower of shit. No offence, like.'

'None taken. Give me the address.'

Henry implanted it in his memory, then inputted it into the SatNav. He then drove slowly down the terraced street he'd parked on, stopping outside Sharon's address. The front door and all the windows had been boarded up and the scorch and soot marks on the stonework surrounding them told the story. The place had been gutted by fire.

Henry was immediately on to the murder incident room at Rawtenstall asking if anyone knew about this. The answer was no, so he requested them to get details of what had happened, if possible, from the police at Rochdale.

On the way up through Whitworth, Henry had to avoid several ponies in the road, a hazard everyone living in that area knew well. The main road sliced through a large area of common land on which animal owners through the centuries had exercised their ancient grazing rights; sheep, cattle and horses were allowed to roam freely on land that, lawfully, could not be fenced. He drove on to a small private estate and parked outside the address

Sharon had given him, a semi-detached dormer bungalow that had seen better days. There was a fridge on the front lawn, a wire contraption of some sort that Henry could not identify and an old Ford Fiesta on three wheels and a stack of bricks. A wheel brace and various other tools littered the drive.

There was a front door, but it was the side door that opened before he had chance to knock. A young woman peered out.

'Sharon?'

'You Mr Christie? ID please.' She jiggled her fingers.

Henry approached her and extracted his warrant card. She gave it a brief glance, then said 'Come in.'

The door led into the kitchen, every surface of which was stacked with clutter. Clothing, broken electrical goods, a carburettor, a hamster cage with no sign of life in it; broken crockery, cutlery. The sink was a precarious mountain of dirty washing up. Newspapers were stacked high on the floor and Henry had to step over a long, green tarpaulin, which could have been wrapped around a tent or a dead body. He hoped it was the former. It was difficult to tell because a blanket of cigarette smoke polluted the atmosphere. He followed Sharon through to the living room.

She was dressed in a tracksuit and the loosely fitting bottoms had slid down to expose an expanse of skin at the base of her spine. Henry saw a thong and a strange, oriental sort of pattern tattooed across the space, which on closer focus was revealed to be the words *Love Fucking*.

The living room was desperately untidy, with the added nicety of a kiddie's potty on the floor, containing liquid and solid deposits from a child who didn't appear to be present in the house.

Henry had been in much worse.

Sharon sat in an armchair and pointed to the settee for Henry. He shifted away a pile of washing and found room while Sharon produced a ciggie and lit up. Henry caught sight of the tattoos around her neck as she tilted her chin upward and exhaled smoke through pursed lips.

'I'm sorry about Dick,' Henry said.

Sharon squinted at him. 'You and me both, but you mess with the big boys, you get fucked, doncha?' Her voice was matter of fact and she wafted the subject away with her hand.

'Still, doesn't make it right,' Henry said, raising his eyebrows. 'What happened to your house in Rochdale?'

'I got a visit from the taxman,' she said. 'Don't know the guy, but he was after dosh that Dick owed.'

'To whom?'

'He didn't actually specify – but I knew it was Deakin.'

'How did you know that?' Henry asked, astounded by his piercing questioning skills. All those training courses had come in useful after all, all those grab-a-granny nights in town with the rest of the detectives in his classes.

'I have ears, I see things, too.'

'What exactly did you see and hear?'

'Dick and Jack were last employed' – and while her cigarette hung at the corner of her mouth, she tweaked her fingers to indicate ironic speech marks around the word 'employed'. Henry saw her nails were chewed to the quick and the first two fingers of her right hand were stained nicotine-brown, something Henry didn't see too much of these days. He almost had to pinch himself at being in the presence of an almost perfectly stereotyped council house tenant, even if neither this house, nor her own, was council owned. She continued – 'by Felix Deakin. Some of his guys did the legwork for the jobs and stupid Dick and Jack did 'em, bringing their own muscle in to help out. They got a cut, Deakin got most of it, thick twats, but it's what they did. The last one went to rat-shit, though.'

'The one with the security guard?'

'Aye, poor sod.' She took a deep drag of the cigarette and blew out a grey cloud.

'So how did it work?' Henry asked, amazed anyone could be dim enough to carry out robberies on someone else's behalf. By the same token he knew that was how much of the organized criminal world ticked over. Those with power and influence used those without. Maybe that was just the way the whole world operated, he thought cynically – and was reminded of the famous nugget of wisdom from the movie *Forrest Gump*: 'Stupid is as stupid does.'

'Like I said, Dick and his crew took a cut and the rest went to Deakin.'

Henry's eyes narrowed. He had an awful lot of questions to ask all of a sudden and needed to get a long statement from her, but this wasn't the place to be doing that. He had to get the lovely Shazzer down to the nearest cop shop pronto, but without frightening her off. He shuffled ideas around in his mind.

One of the questions he knew he needed to ask was, why did she suddenly feel the need to blab? But because the interview had gone the way it had, it was something he would leave till later. He didn't want to look a gift horse in the mouth by spoiling things. They would come to it in good time, he guessed. For the time being he would go with the flow and let her speak.

'I assume they fell out,' Henry prompted.

'Proper little Poirot, you,' she chided him with a smile, pronouncing the name of the famous Belgian detective as 'Pwarrott', revealing an array of stained teeth that matched the colour of her fingers. 'Yeah, it were all over that last job. I don't know the ins and outs, but yeah, as ever, the dimbos fell out about money.'

'And yet Deakin's in the slammer. Someone must be acting for him.'

Sharon snuffled a snort. 'Every crim's favourite brief . . .'

And the connection finally slotted into place like the dovetail joint Henry had made for his woodwork O-level. 'Barry Baron?' he asked cautiously.

'The one and only.'

It was Henry's moment of epiphany, the coming together of all his subconscious ideas. His ring piece twitched almost uncontrollably. Had he been Poirot he would have twiddled his moustache. In Henry's case, his arsehole simply tightened like a drawstring being pulled on a pump bag.

'Cunt's on a retainer,' Sharon revealed. 'Does a shit-load of work for Deakin and goes around scaring the living shite out of people, creepy, nasty bastard. And if he doesn't get what he wants, he gets the heavies in.'

'He wasn't the one who visited you, though?'

'Nah, some numpty gofer with a brain like a brick, came asking me where Dick'd stashed the money from the robbery. I told him to eff off, I didn't know owt, didn't know anything about where the money was . . .' At this point she looked Henry squarely in the eye as if daring him to challenge her on this. Then she adjusted her large saggy boobs in her brassiere.

Henry was fascinated, could hardly contain his interest. 'So Deakin, through Baron, kept his business interests ticking over when he was in prison?'

'Sort of, I suppose. I don't know *everything*.'

'But what I know about Deakin doesn't necessarily fit in with armed robbery,' Henry said, puzzled. He even scratched his head like a confused silent-movie comedian. 'He's a big-time drug dealer, not a blagger.'

'I just know he was short of dosh, needed some, and set up the robberies that Dick and Jack pulled for him.' Her face dropped sadly. 'Fools.'

'And then they fell out about money? About what, percentages?'

'Hey, I don't know exactly . . . me and Dick weren't living together any more, so I didn't know everything he was up to. We were still mates, though, and we used to meet up for, y'know – rumpy-pumpy. He is the father of my kid, too . . . at least he thought he was.' She shrugged. 'No point telling him any different if he kept paying up, was there?'

'Suppose not,' Henry agreed. 'What I don't get is why Deakin organized three armed robberies from his prison cell, one of which went wrong when a security guard got shot . . . You don't happen to know who pulled the trigger, do you?'

Sharon reddened and shook her head. 'I just know that Dick came back from it in a bad way, that's all. Take from that what you want. He didn't give details, but he was as jumpy as fuck.'

'And he has a history of using firearms.'

'You do the sums, you're the detective, right?'

'Right,' Henry said, storing this away, 'but why did Deakin go to all that trouble to diversify? Did he need the money to prop up his drug business, which presumably was wobbling while he was locked up?' Sharon said nothing. Henry regarded her. 'Why did Dick's brother tell you to talk to me?'

In return she regarded him. 'Because he'd be a dead man if he got a visit from the cops while he was in prison. He's already suffered because he was Dick's brother. He wanted me to tell you he's pretty sure Deakin had Jack 'n' Dick killed.'

'Why did he get hammered?'

'To encourage Dick to straighten out the money thing.'

'OK,' Henry said. He waited. 'What do you know?'

'Look – I'm no snitch and nor is Jamie, not even on Deakin. Not usually, anyway, because anyone who grasses on him suffers, yeah? Get my drift?'

'Loud and clear.'

'But I know here . . .' – she held the palm of her right hand over her heart – 'that he killed Dick and Jack over the money from the robberies. Money which I don't know where it is, yeah?' she said in a convoluted manner. Henry nodded, didn't believe a word, said nothing. 'But I pretty much resent being firebombed out of my house on top of all that, so he deserves someone to grass on him.'

Henry guggled encouragingly, hoping a point was about to be reached.

Then she said, 'Point is, I know why Deakin went into the robbery business so late in the day.'

Henry's arse twitched again. 'That would be?'

'He needs cash – and robbery's a pretty good way of getting shitloads of it if you have the bottle. Pullin' a blag takes a real sorta bottle – I mean a real job, not a poxy off-licence or something. Just the sorta numb-headed bottle that Dick and Jack had. It's all they'd done all their wasted lives. Fuckin' robbed people, or robbed people for other people. They loved the buzz.'

Henry was intrigued. Not by the antecedents of the two dead robbers, who were probably now causing havoc for the devil, but why Deakin needed money and fast. He had a good idea, but he was keen to get this overweight dumpling estranged wife of a dead bank robber to confirm what he thought he knew.

'Go on then, Sharon – why has he turned to robbery?' Henry urged her. It was obvious she had picked up his eagerness and she was now playing him like a flounder. She rubbed her thumb and forefinger together – the international sign that meant 'cash'.

'How much?' she said.

'How much for what?'

'Good information.'

Henry sat back. A spring stuck in his back. 'Let me ask you something, Sharon. Do you believe Deakin ordered the hit on your husband because they'd fallen out about money?'

'Estranged husband,' she corrected him. 'Yes, I do – and I also know that Dick and Jack met with Mr Creep himself, Barry Baron, a couple of days before their bodies were found – to discuss matters, is what Dick told me. I never saw him again after that meeting.'

'Why didn't you tell this to the detectives who've already spoken to you? You hardly said anything in your statement.'

Her lips twisted slightly. ''Cos at that stage of the game I was keepin' me head down. Then I got the nasty visit: "Where's the money?" "Don't know." Then my house got firebombed – and luckily I was out back havin' a fag and I realized I was in danger because they obviously didn't believe me. Listen,' she leaned towards Henry, 'If I knew where the dosh was, I'd be off to the Costa, not sat waiting for a Molotov cocktail to come flyin' through the window.'

'Fifty quid?' Henry suggested.

She snarled. 'Two-fifty. Remember I'm a single penniless widow, on benefits and no income from a dead husband who never worked in his life, except for being a robber.'

'I haven't got that sort of money on me.'

'It's worth it,' she promised.

'Come with me to a cashpoint. Down to Bacup town centre.

I'll withdraw it and pay you.' Although she was playing an agonizing game with him, his cop instinct told him this was transitory. She needed to be kept sweet. It would be worth it.

'OK.' She rose with difficulty, hitching up her tracksuit bottoms over her wide waist.

'I need to know, though, Sharon,' Henry said. She scowled at him and puffed cigarette smoke out of her nostrils like a dragon. She pounded out the fag end in the overflowing ashtray. 'Deakin's raking in money – yeah? Getting it in fast. Why? Bad debts or what? Come on, tell me. I won't welch on the money.'

She stared at him. He saw that her eyes were actually devastatingly beautiful. Emerald green, oriental looking.

'Like I told the git that came to lean on me, I don't know where the money is, but I know exactly what the bastard's up to – 'cos it's an open secret in the clink, according to Jamie.'

Henry's mind jarred. 'You told your unwanted visitor you didn't know where the money from the robbery was stashed, but you knew why Deakin wanted it?'

'I just said I did – as I was chucking him out of the house.'

'In the heat of that moment, did you mention you were going to tell the police what you knew?'

'Might've threatened it, but I didn't mean it at the time.'

'And then you got firebombed – at what time of day did you get firebombed?'

'About midnight.'

'When you should have been tucked up in bed?'

'Suppose so.'

'But you were out having a fag and you weren't hurt?'

'Like I said. Why?'

'Do you think they wanted to kill you or just scare you?'

'Kill me,' she guessed thinly, starting to see where Henry was going with this.

'And you're still alive.'

They stared at each other as the implications settled on her brain.

'I don't think he's finished with you, Sharon. I might be wrong, but I think it might be as well if you get your things together and come with me. You need some protection. Where's your kiddie?'

'Out with sis – should be back in an hour. Do you really think . . .?'

'Tell me why Deakin's after the money, Sharon.'

'Run money,' she said.

And those two words completed Henry's jigsaw.

'Shit,' he said. 'You need to be in a place of safety.' He stood up.

'Oh, get to fuck!'

'OK: scenario. You tell the heavy you don't know where the money is. Then as you kick his arse out of the door, you tell him you know what Deakin's up to and that you're going to tell the cops. This gets reported back to Deakin,' Henry waved his hands expressively to accompany his hypothesis, 'and next thing you know – boom – firebombed! At a time of day when you should've been asleep, perhaps the only time ever a fag has saved somebody's life. Seriously, Sharon, do you think that's the end of it?' He looked closely at her. 'Get your stuff together, call your sister if she has a mobile, arrange a meet and we'll pick up your kid. If I found you with one phone call, it won't take long for them to find you.'

'You're a fuckin' drama queen, Mr Christie.'

They faced each other over the turd-filled potty on the carpet.

'But you know what I'm saying is true. Next question is – when is Deakin going to run?'

Henry glanced towards the large front window. He registered that it was a single-glazed unit with a wooden frame which was rotting and that the petrol bomb arcing towards it, thrown from the right hand of the hooded figure standing on the front lawn, would easily smash the thin glass. Particularly as it was a milk bottle taped to half a house brick. And as it spun spectacularly through the air like an oversized Catherine wheel, the blue petrol flames whipping around, the figure hurled another one immediately. Two petrol bombs were about to smash through the window.

Henry saw they were well aimed – a calculation confirmed as the first one hit the centre of the window and crashed through into the lounge.

Sharon emitted an ear-piercing howl of terror as the first bottle smashed and the petrol exploded with a *whump*.

Henry twisted back to her, grabbed her tracksuit top and heaved her to the door as the second bottle exploded and the room was instantly filled with flames.

He bundled Sharon out of the door, pushing her roughly through the space while feeling a smack-smack-smack on his back as he was splattered with globules of burning fuel. Then one hit him on the back of his neck with the force of an airgun pellet.

He screamed as he fell through the door behind her.

She lost her footing, stumbled, twisted and overbalanced in front of him. Henry's weak right knee gave way as he contorted and the pair of them fell in an untidy heap in the narrow hallway. Henry landed slap-bang on top of Sharon, whose legs parted accommodatingly. And again, as Henry's mind was prone to do in the most inappropriate circumstances, he pictured himself making love to her, but the terrible burning on his neck ensured he didn't dwell on this image.

He was on fire.

Flaming petrol had sprayed on to his back and started to burn his jacket.

He reared off Sharon – was that a look of disappointment in her eyes? – thumped on to his knees beside her.

'You're fucking burning,' she yelled.

Henry knew he had two things to do.

First, despite the flames sizzling on his back, he launched himself at the living-room door and slammed it shut to contain the flames. Next he dragged his jacket off, now melting with fire, hurled it to the floor and stamped on it, dancing like a madman to extinguish the flames. At the same time he smacked the back of his neck with the flat of his hand to douse the fire on his skin. Hell, that hurt.

Sharon got to her feet, stunned, hitching up her trackie bottoms again, but not before Henry glimpsed most of her backside and the thong wedged up the crack.

As he continued to jump up and down on his jacket, he realized the need to call the fire service, but only when he felt his mobile phone, in one of his jacket pockets, crunch underfoot.

'Get out of here,' he said. He picked up his ragged jacket, spun Sharon round and propelled her towards the kitchen. And let me catch that bastard out there, he thought.

He shoved past Sharon, who seemed to be whirling around in circles, and headed for the side door, bursting out on to the driveway that ran up the side of the house. He ran to the front – but stopped in his tracks at the corner of the house. He expected to find the guy who'd thrown the firebombs to have legged it, either in a car or on foot, but he was completely wrong.

The one who'd thrown the bombs stood at the bottom of the drive – hooded, slightly built, wearing a black top and jeans. But an accomplice, a bigger chap, flanked him, similarly dressed. And both brandished sawn-off shotguns, held at hip level.

Henry cursed. He'd been right. The job on Sharon hadn't been finished and they were back. Probably just two hired thugs, nothing more than kids wanting to make names for themselves.

Nevertheless, just as dangerous as a professional assassin. Maybe more so, because they would be reckless and wouldn't give a monkey's about collateral damage. And on top of that, they wouldn't know Henry was a cop . . . not that that seemed to matter much in the present day.

The smaller guy jerked back a trigger and fired.

Henry dropped to the right, rolled, was up and racing back to the kitchen door as the two guys advanced menacingly. He shot back into the kitchen and slammed the door behind him, sliding the chain lock on and turning to Sharon.

'Two with shotguns,' he gasped.

Just to confirm this, two figures appeared at the other side of the door, their outlines misted by the frosted glass, but not so difficult to make out that Henry couldn't see one of them raise his weapon.

Henry ducked and staggered across the kitchen as the window dissolved behind him, spraying the room with a shower of glass and buckshot. He forced Sharon back through and closed the kitchen door, catching a glance of the sawn-off stock of a shotgun being used to smash out the remnants of the broken window and a gloved hand come through to slide the chain lock free.

They were only seconds behind.

As the inner kitchen door clicked shut, it exploded as another shotgun blast peppered the wood.

Henry twisted into the hallway with Sharon and one burning room ahead of him – and the front door down at the end of the hall. The door to the dining room was to the left.

'In there now,' he ordered Sharon and gesticulated at the dining room.

She moved faster than she'd probably ever done in her life as another shotgun blast took out most of what remained of the kitchen door. The blast whipped past Henry's face.

He turned and raced down the hallway, hoping to hell the front door was unlocked. The last thing he wanted was to be found trying to yank it open as the two guys stepped into the hall.

Mercifully it was open.

Henry went out and slammed it hard behind him, hoping they would think their prey had legged it out with him, hoping too it would give him some advantage.

Outside he had another inappropriate thought: run to safety.

But he didn't. As a tongue of flame licked out through the

front window up the dormer, Henry stood for a moment, then bent down and scooped up the wheel brace he'd noticed on arriving at the house, next to the three-wheeled Ford Fiesta. With his back to the wall of the house, getting a good grip on the piece of iron, he sidled quickly up to the kitchen door and turned in. The gunmen were four steps ahead of him, their backs to him; one stood behind the other, the lead guy being in the hallway. Henry guessed they were debating their next move. He didn't know – but what he did know was that he was in a dangerous situation which could turn fatal if he hesitated even momentarily about his next move.

Two strides and he was across the kitchen floor, stepping over the tarpaulin, the brace rising in his right hand.

He brought it down as hard as he could on to the back of the man's skull nearest to him. It landed with a dull clunk. The guy went down silently and instantly with legs that had turned to water.

The man in front hadn't even realized his mate had been poleaxed. This was fortunate for Henry as he stepped over the crumpled body, swinging the wrench less effectively in the confined space.

Some instinct must have told the guy all was not well.

He twisted tightly, his head jerking around, saw the wrench coming down towards his head, his eyes opening wide behind the balaclava mask he wore. He ducked away and tried to bring the sawn-off around to blast Henry.

Henry was an instant quicker and hit him hard across the side of his head.

The shotgun jumped up and discharged with a deafening blast, somewhere above Henry's right shoulder.

The man sagged sideways against the wall, dragging a picture with him. He managed to regain his balance, swung the shotgun around again, one-handed, to fire it again at Henry who was open, vulnerable, believing for an instant he was about to be killed. Using the wrench as a baton, he knocked the gun sideways and at the same time punched the man in the face with his left fist. The shotgun discharged into the ceiling, blasting away a light fitting. Henry followed up the punch with another blow of the brace, crashing it down on to the man's shoulder with a satisfying connection.

He screamed, a sound muffled by his mask, and cowered away.

But Henry's rage was up. He hit his assailant once more across the side of the head with the brace, somewhere in the region of his jaw joint, and no further sound came from him as he fell to the carpet.

He stood over the two gunmen, breathing heavily.

FOURTEEN

By the time the fire service arrived with two appliances, the house was blazing. Flames from the living room spread upwards to the bedroom above, setting the wooden-clad dormer alight.

Henry, coming shakily down from his adrenaline sluice, watched from a distance while standing guard over two unmasked, moaning prisoners. The two gunmen he'd dragged roughly from the burning house were now deposited on a neighbour's lawn and handcuffed together using the pair of rigid cuffs he carried in his car.

The local cops were being directed by an inspector, sealing the avenue, evacuating nearby houses where necessary and treating the whole area as a crime scene.

Two ambulances had also arrived. A paramedic had inspected the petrol burn on the back of Henry's neck, squirted some cool cream on and covered it with a gauze and plaster.

'These guys look as though they've had a good whacking,' the paramedic said to Henry, pointing to the two offenders.

Henry nodded. 'I hit them as hard as I could,' he admitted – and would say no different if he ended up in court over the matter. He had no illusions about this: he might well have disarmed and disabled two people prepared to kill, but there was every chance he would find himself answering charges and facing a judge in this topsy-turvy world of criminals' rights. But he didn't give a stuff. If they'd both been dead at his feet, he would've been glowing with pride.

'Better get them to hospital,' the paramedic said.

'Yeah.' Henry beckoned the inspector across. 'I want three officers to go with each of these boys and I want you to arrange an armed guard for them while they're there. They're dangerous bastards.' He glanced down at them. They were nothing more than kids, as he'd initially suspected. 'They shouldn't be trusted. I've arrested and cautioned them, so when they've finished their treatment I want them back at Burnley nick ASAP.' He stuttered a long breath, feeling himself returning from the heights.

'OK boss,' the inspector said.

Henry squatted down on to his haunches. There was a severe pain in his right knee and he winced as his joints cracked. The two gun-boys glared at him, disrespectful and scowling despite their injuries. 'You guys got anything you want to say to me? Like who sent you, who you're working for? No? Don't think there's a rescue package in place, guys. You're out on a limb here. I just hope it was worth it.'

'Fuck you, twat,' one said.

'Likewise,' the other backed up his pal.

But Henry could see the flicker of uncertainty in their eyes, so he added, 'You'll be going down for a long, long time for this. Life probably. Get used to the thought of friendly shower times, because young kids like you are just meat.'

He watched the two ambulances drive away – he'd insisted they be kept apart as much as possible – then looked at the scene.

The circus had turned out and the place was crawling with detectives, uniform and CSI, fire service and the press. He found Sharon at a neighbour's house down the street.

'You OK?' he asked.

She looked at him through slitted eyes and blew out a fog of smoke. 'First time I've ever had a cop on top of me.'

Henry raised his eyebrows. She was OK. 'Witness protection – at least for the short term while we sort this out.'

She nodded glumly.

'And going back to the point we were at before being rudely interrupted by a Molotov cocktail, I asked you about Deakin. When is he going to run?'

'Today.'

'I can't help thinking I wish you'd told me that up front.' Henry looked at his watch, then scurried out of the house towards the inspector and almost dragged the man's PR from around his neck. The devices came equipped with the facility to directly call another officer anywhere in the county by simply typing in his or her collar number, as well as a mobile phone/text facility.

Henry typed in Bill Robbins's collar number.

Court finished at three that day.

Johnny Cain was bustled down to the holding cells and from there into the waiting prison bus. Once his security escort had organized itself, the roll-up doors clattered open and the convoy moved off. It headed north up the A6, varying the route, to join the M6 at Broughton, and then headed south towards Manchester. It was a smoothly run operation, no hitches, no signs of anyone showing interest in the progress other than annoyed motorists either held up or swept aside.

When it was certain that Cain had gone, Felix Deakin, who had not been called to give evidence, was brought down from the police room. His escort vehicles were reversed into the secure garage beneath the court. Handcuffed, he was put into the middle car and flanked on the back seat by prison guards.

A check that everyone was ready – and on a signal from Bill Robbins in the lead car to the outrider motorcyclists, the escort emerged into daylight, swung into the Preston traffic and headed down Ring Way out of the city.

The journey, a reverse of the morning's, was planned to take less than fifteen minutes. Deakin would then be ushered back into his cell for another night of incarceration.

It was an uneventful journey. The escort left the city limits on to the A582, crossing the River Ribble, and staying on that road before cutting on to Flensburg Way, across the roundabout at Schleswig Way, then turning right at the lights on to Dunkirk Lane and into School Lane/Ulnes Walton Lane. Lancashire Prison was about two miles along, nestling alongside the more established prisons of Wymott and Garth.

The journey along Ulnes Walton Lane was non-negotiable. Whichever way the escort chose to leave or return to the prison, Ulnes Walton Lane, a quiet country road with high hedges, hardly any traffic and no pedestrians, had to be driven along one way or the other because no other road led directly to the prison.

The lookout secreted on the corner of School Lane simply phoned ahead to give the ETA of the convoy.

As the convoy approached a right-hand bend near Norms Farm on the left, the tractor driver had a good clear view of the leading police motorcyclist. With perfect timing he emerged from the concealed entrance, swerving into the path of the cop on the bike. Affixed to the front of the tractor like two massive horns were a deadly pair of sharp-ended baling spears. The motorcyclist saw the point of one of them coming, but could do nothing to avoid it as it pierced his chest and impaled him like a whole chicken on a kebab.

The cars behind screeched to a halt, already going into anti-attack mode, but the rear motorcyclist lost control. The bike wobbled then slewed from under its rider. He slid off, ripping gaping holes in his leathers and slicing his skin off as the bike skidded and wedged itself under the rear end of the last police car, which had already started evasive measures by reversing. The two vehicles were mangled together as one.

On cue, two stolen Toyota Land Cruisers burst out from behind the high hedges at the roadside. They had been fitted with huge bull bars across the radiators and came out like two massive charging buffaloes, hammering into the sides of the front and rear police cars, smashing them sideways into the drainage channel on the opposite side of the road, effectively trapping the occupants.

The middle vehicle, the one carrying Deakin, was untouched.

The masked drivers of the Land Cruisers leapt out as four other hooded men emerged from specially cut gaps in the hedge, armed with a variety of weapons between them. Two held sawn-off shotguns with which they blasted the front and rear tyres of Deakin's car. Two held Skorpion machine pistols aimed menacingly at the vehicle. Then a fifth man appeared and pointed a .357 Magnum revolver at the driver.

As this was happening, two Transit vans appeared on the scene from their hiding place on a farm track, reversing up to the convoy.

The door of Deakin's car was wrenched open and, still manacled, the prisoner was heaved out from between his guards and bundled into the back of one of the Transits. The vehicle set off as all the remaining men leapt into the back of the second Transit, which also left the scene.

Bill Robbins sat shocked and shaken in the front passenger seat of the lead police car. He was unable to move as he was trapped against the driver, with the huge nose of the Land Cruiser right up against him, having crushed his door. He was unhurt – amazingly – and was unable to take his eyes off the police motorcyclist skewered on to the baling spear on the front of the tractor. His body still twitched and jerked obscenely in its death throes.

The whole enterprise had taken perhaps thirty seconds.

The mobile phone facility on Bill's PR started to ring.

By the time Deakin's getaway van had reached the first corner, his handcuffs had been snipped off his wrists by bolt cutters.

The van sped across the flat, tight, winding roads from Leyland across Longton Moss before coming to a stop on Wholesome Lane, near the village of New Longton. There he was transferred into a waiting Range Rover with smoked-out windows. The Transit van did a tight U-turn and accelerated away in the opposite direction. The other Transit was nowhere to be seen.

The driver of the Range Rover drove unhurriedly on to the A59, never once speaking or acknowledging Deakin, who sat winded but exhilarated in the passenger seat. They drove past police headquarters and into Preston, then on to Riversway Docklands, the city's old port. It had been redeveloped into a retail park, marina and apartment blocks, some new, some converted warehouses. The driver stopped near Victoria Mansions, a warehouse now converted into apartments, and handed Deakin an envelope with an address on it and a key inside.

The driver pulled away almost before Deakin had set foot on the ground.

The key opened a first floor apartment with a balcony and a view across the marina – which had once been the port itself – to a supermarket, a McDonalds and a DIY store. Deakin entered, sure that no one had seen him get out of the Range Rover or walk into the apartment block. Once inside he bolted the door and heaved a sigh of relief, a smug expression crossing his face.

First part completed. Now all he had to do was get his cash together and get out of the country.

'So what are you telling me?' Deakin demanded. His face tilted aggressively.

His solicitor blinked nervously. 'That these guys cost a quarter of a mill – up front.'

Deakin's jaw dropped. 'Up front, you say?'

'Look, you wanted out without mistakes. I had to get the best people – and these guys are the knees.'

'OK, I understand that. They were good, fast, effective.'

'Worth the money.'

'So where does that leave me?'

'You've got the residue from the two robberies, say sixty grand.'

'And?'

Baron hesitated. 'That's it.'

'Sixty grand?' Deakin said in disbelief.

They were in the rented apartment, now behind locked doors, closed curtains. Baron had brought round an Indian takeaway and more beer and spirits. The remnants of the feast were spread around the coffee table in the lounge.

'Yeah, not bad.'

'Sixty grand is shit. A quarter of a mill, you say?'

'Yeah.'

'So that leaves, what, sixty grand plus . . .?'

'Plus nothing.'

'The money from the last job, the money you were supposed to retrieve? Forty grand?'

'Never found.'

Deakin stood, paced the room. 'Let me get this straight. You're saying that Dick Last and Jack Sumner didn't tell Cromer and Jackman where the money was?'

'That's what I'm saying.'

'Even though they were tortured and mutilated?'

'That's what they said.'

'And so you sent these two jokers to find out where my other money went, the money that the cops stole from me – *one million fucking quid!* – and now Jackman and Cromer have disappeared? Doesn't that tell you something, you stupid, dim twat?'

'What – they found your money and did a runner with it?' Baron asked incredulously.

Deakin leaned into his face. 'Yeah – one million and forty Gs of my money!'

Baron shook his head. 'No, I don't believe it. They're solid and had a good rep.'

'Every fucker has his price. And . . . and . . . what about Dick Last's missus? You've been leaning on her. What's the result on that? Did she tell you where the money is?'

'No, but she did threaten to grass on you.'

'Did you deal with that?'

'She got a warning.' Baron was unwilling to go into detail, not wanting to complicate matters any further, or get Deakin any madder.

'I need more money,' Deakin said. 'I need to get out of this shit hole of a country with more than sixty grand. I'm talking about a lifetime here, a life on a beach somewhere, greasing the locals and keeping my head down. That costs more than sixty grand. I want that million back. That's what I want. Why do you reckon you haven't heard back from the deadly duo then, if they're so friggin' honest?'

Baron shrugged. 'I don't know. But I do know they located Flynn . . . From that point, who knows?'

'And Flynn's still alive?'

'Far as I know.'

Deakin sat down heavily and picked up a foil tin containing the remains of a prawn bhuna. He scraped some of the sauce up on his finger and sucked it off. He was thinking hard.

'Flynn's a hard bastard, isn't he?'

'Supposedly.'

'Maybe too hard and devious even for Cromer and Jackman? Maybe he scared them off – or worse?'

'I really don't know.'

Deakin slid his finger through the sauce again, sucked it off with a pop. 'That money must still be knocking around some-where – and I'll bet he's got it.'

'Him or his partner, Hoyle.'

'He's dead, isn't he?'

Baron shrugged. 'The body was never found.'

'So Flynn's got it.' He ran his finger through the sauce again and pointed it at Baron. 'I know a lot about Flynn. Made it my business to know my enemy – and I know just how to get it back.' Once more, he sucked off the sauce.

FIFTEEN

It had been a good day at sea. Six hours of superb fishing with a determined party of two businessmen, experienced big gamers, resulting in the tag and release of two blue marlin, each somewhere in the region of 250lb. Both contests had been hard fought and the businessmen were buzzing with excitement all the way back to port.

Flynn, too, was excited and relaxed, at the helm of the new, second-hand boat that had replaced *Lady Faye*. This one had been renamed simply *Faye2* and although she was a very different boat in terms of handling and manoeuvring, Flynn had got the measure of her by the end of a month.

He glanced down at the charter from the flying bridge. Jose was serving them a chilled bottle of Cruzcampo each, and one for himself. All three looked up at Flynn and held up their drinks in acknowledgement. Jose removed his cap and wiped his sweaty brow, giving Flynn one of those deep-leg shudders as he saw Jose's damaged head. His scalp had almost completely been removed by the explosion and had been refitted and stitched back on by a plastic surgeon who must have been under the influence. His scalp was misaligned, skew-whiff. If it hadn't been so tragic it would have been hysterical.

In truth the repair hadn't completely healed yet, not by a long way. Flynn had told Jose not to come back to work, but he needed the money and insisted.

Flynn gave them the thumbs-up and turned forward, increasing the power of the engines. *Faye2* dug her stern into the water and rose with a burble.

For Flynn, the last few weeks had been a decent period of rehab. Adam Castle had dithered for a few days as to whether to keep Flynn on; at the same time Flynn had seriously thought about the move south to Cape Verde. But Castle's problem was that Flynn was the best skipper he had. He did not want to lose him.

When the insurance money paid out (amazingly quickly and without too much haggling), Castle could have pocketed the cash and used it to prop up the other facets of his business. But he was a dedicated big game fisher himself and it was the most enjoyable side of his business. What was more, Flynn was in demand from new and repeat customers. The sooner he got him back on board, the sooner he'd be making money again.

When he told Flynn he didn't want to part company, there were tears in the eyes of both men.

Flynn had spent a few days salvaging equipment from *Lady Faye* when Adam appeared at the quayside with a sheaf of almost a hundred papers – ads for sportfishing boats for sale that he'd downloaded from the Internet. He and Flynn spent a couple of hours shortlisting until they whittled it down to about half a dozen worthy replacements, berthed from Madeira to Ibiza and back down as far as Banjul in the Gambia.

'I want you to look at these, test them, make a decision on one of them, then buy it for me. I'll arrange a banker's draft.'

Flynn stared at him. 'Me? Why? How?'

'Well, you ring the owners, make an appointment, book a flight,' Adam said, gesturing emphatically.

'No, no, I don't mean how . . . I mean, why? Why me?'

'Because despite all the crap, you're my number one skip – hotly contested, I might add, so don't get arrogant – and I trust your judgement about boats. Travel as cheaply as you can, I'll pick up all the tabs and get back on the water as soon as.'

Emotion welled up inside Flynn. He said simply, 'Thanks, man.'

They clinked glasses. Next day Flynn had picked up a spare
seat on a charter flight en route from Manchester to Banjul, which
had stopped for refuelling and to drop off passengers at Las Palmas.

Even though it was a tough, full week – stretching to eight days
– Flynn enjoyed himself immensely. Eventually he chose a boat
moored in Ibiza Town. It was underused and undervalued, but
Flynn saw through the crap and the faintly worn air and agreed
a price with the owner, who was only too eager to offload it. Three
days after a survey and financial completion, Flynn returned to
Ibiza with the recently patched up Jose. After a night on the town,
they packed the boat with supplies and fuel and sailed it back to
Gran Canaria, with a stop in Tangiers on the way.

Flynn exhaled, powered down and manoeuvred the boat into
its mooring in Puerto Rico.

One of the businessmen pushed five hundred euros into his
palm and they all arranged to meet for dinner that evening to
celebrate the day's fishing. Flynn split the tip fifty-fifty with
Jose, then the two of them got down to the task of cleaning the
deck and tackle ready for next day's pre-booked charter. Flynn
was anticipating the evening. Nothing special, just a shower, a
change of clothing and a meal down by the beach. A few beers,
a hook-up with a woman he knew from Holland who sold water-
park tickets from a kiosk on the quayside. Then sex at her apartment, and home for a good sleep.

As he worked and chatted, his mind drifted to Gill Hartland
and something inside him died a little again. He stood upright, a
fishing reel in one hand, and gazed skywards. Maybe they would
have come to nothing as a couple, but – *fuck!* – Flynn would have
given anything to find out. She was a terrible loss and he wasn't
sure how long he'd take to get over her.

At least she had been avenged, but that hadn't felt good.

The two bodies of Cromer and Jackman were dumped in a
deep, tight, inaccessible gully near the Roque Nublo and by now,
with the help of scavengers, they should be nothing more than
bleached bones. He had no remorse about what he'd done. It
had clearly been them or him.

Yet he still didn't completely understand what they were after.

Felix Deakin's money, that's what.

Money Flynn had never seen, which he believed had never
existed up to now because it had never been conclusively proved
it had existed. But yet why would Deakin send out his best
heavies to get it back?

He shook his head, not wanting to think about it, hoping it had now all gone away. That was a previous life, one he'd left behind, which had no bearing on his present circumstances – even if it had crept up on him and almost killed him.

'You OK, *amigo*?' Jose asked.

'Just thinking.'

'Yeah, I know. She was a good woman.' It wasn't hard to read Flynn's mind.

He swallowed and returned to the task, cleaning off the reel, rubbing hard on the steel surface so it shone.

The two of them took over an hour before everything was to their satisfaction. It was six by the time they'd finished and every piece of equipment, every corner of the boat sparkled.

'A good day, *amigo*,' Flynn said as they crossed the gangplank on to the quayside, Flynn behind the Spaniard.

'*Muy bien*,' Jose agreed, stepping on to dry land.

Suddenly Flynn halted as though he'd walked into an invisible force field. 'A good day, turned bad,' he muttered on seeing the person rushing along the quay in his direction. 'What the hell are you doing here?' he demanded.

The woman was breathless, dishevelled and looked exhausted. None of these negative traits, however, detracted from the fact she was a stunning woman, with short-cropped auburn hair, piercing green eyes and a curvaceous body that could make a grown man cry.

'It's Craig, it's Craig,' she babbled.

Oh my God, Flynn thought. His son was dead!

'He's got Craig,' she said. 'He's taken my son!'

Then Steve Flynn's ex-wife threw herself at him and clung on tight, sobbing uncontrollably, her face pushed into his chest, her legs going weak underneath her and her whole body convulsing with huge wracking sobs.

Flynn did not understand. 'What d'you mean?' he asked, trying to disentangle himself from her arms. He held her away from him at arm's length. 'What d'you mean, he's got him?' Then the words she'd said permeated into his dumb brain and a terrible sensation filled his chest with horror. 'Who's got Craig?'

Faye Flynn looked up at him, eyes streaming with tears, and said the two dreaded words: 'Felix Deakin.'

*   *   *

'OK, right, calm down . . . c'mon,' Flynn cooed. He had all but carried Faye to the nearest bar, shouting for two whiskies to be brought to them as he sat her down on a seat near the beach. On the short forced march, though, he noticed she'd already had a skinful. Probably on the flight, he guessed.

She lit up, angling the cigarette upwards between her lips, blowing the first lungful of smoke up in the same direction, tightening her bottom lip as she directed the smoke. Despite the way she had treated him in the past, this little move – lighting up, exhaling – had always somehow got to him. He found it full of sexual innuendo, even though it was usually just Faye gasping for a fag. He watched her movements, saw the rise and fall of her full breasts, and the back of his throat constricted. Bitch, he thought. Bitch still has me. He coughed, wafting the smoke away. 'What's happened?'

She took an extra long drag, filling up her chest, blew it out and got a grip on herself. She rubbed her forehead. 'Need a Nurofen – or three. Head feels like it's about to crash.'

Flynn ground his teeth in frustration and went to the bar, returning with a blister pack of aspirin. Faye popped two and swallowed them down with her whisky, then pulled Flynn's untouched glass towards her. He bristled inside.

'I got a phone call yesterday, early on. A guy said he'd got Craig. Picked him up on the way to school.'

Flynn was unable to comprehend what was being said. 'What do you mean? He picked him up? How could he have . . .?'

Faye squinted at him through her headache. 'You don't know, do you?'

'Know what?' Flynn's hands flew up in bafflement.

'Deakin escaped from custody. Apparently he'd been to court to give evidence at some trial or other and he escaped when they were taking him back to prison. A cop got killed. You really don't know?'

Flynn said no. Over the last weeks he hadn't read any newspapers or watched TV, just thrown himself into a world of work, sex and sleep, excluding everything else. It was easy to do this two thousand miles south of his homeland. He wouldn't know if the UK sank into the sea. 'How long ago was this?'

'Two, two and a half weeks. Dunno. It was all over the news for days.'

'I didn't know,' Flynn admitted again. 'Hell – so why Craig? What's going on?'

'Deakin wants that money back from you – the million you and Jack took. You give that to him, Craig goes free.'

Flynn sat upright. 'He's talking bollocks. I never had that money, even if it existed.'

'Maybe Jack did,' Faye said simply – words that hit Flynn like a spade slamming into his chest. His mouth went dry, nausea waved through him.

'Well, you'd know, wouldn't you?' But even as he spoke, he knew it was a rhetorical question. Of course she fucking well knew. The two were lovers, having a torrid affair behind his back, mocking him and sneering at his naivety and trust. Fucking each other as soon as he left the house. His nostrils flared at the memory of the betrayal which still lived with him.

'I don't know if he did or not,' she said.

'Why don't you just go and get it from *him*?'

'Something else you don't know?' she asked as if he was thick.

'What?'

'Jack's dead.'

Flynn stood up and took a deep breath. He walked out on to the beach where he stood, hands on hips, for a couple of minutes, his brain a mush. He became aware of Faye positioned just behind him.

'I don't know anything because I didn't want to know anything.'

'The hard man with a soft heart.'

Flynn looked at her. 'That's me.'

She staggered slightly. Flynn instinctively grabbed her and she shuffled into him, her body pressing against him. For a moment he went weak, especially when she looked up at him and moved her face to be kissed. He nearly fell for it, but he moved her gently away and said, 'You need to tell me everything. What's important here is Craig.'

She nodded, edged further away, aware of the rebuke.

'How much have you had to drink?'

'Since yesterday? Who's fucking counting?' She slumped into a chair, misjudged the distance and slithered off it on to the plank floor, where she passed out.

'Shit.' A lot of booze had gone into her, Flynn guessed. He heaved her up once and then lifted her up right across his shoulder, causing many a raised eyebrow, picked up her shoulder bag which seemed to be all the luggage she had, and carried her out of the bar. He'd briefly considered slapping her to bring her round but knew it would be a useless exercise. She was either one of two states when drunk. This one – pissed and passed out – or pissed and argumentative. Neither state made getting useful information out of her easy. On top of that, Flynn suspected she probably hadn't slept for a day. She needed to get some, then get sobered up and in a long hot shower before he'd be able to get a logical story out of her.

As he carried her through crowds of holidaymakers to his villa, he began to seethe angrily. Why the hell couldn't she have turned up compos mentis instead of blind drunk? If what she had blabbed was true, Craig was in serious trouble. Flynn guessed that she had been told to get her arse out to Gran Canaria and get him personally. This made him suppose there could be some time to play with, but not much. And Faye being drunk ate into that precious time.

He carried her through the public gardens and, reaching the villa, through to the bedroom. Having dumped her raggedly on to the bed, he regarded her for a few seconds, wondering if he should undress her or not. Not, he decided. She turned on to her side and started to snore.

Flynn drew the blinds and went to the kitchen, where he poured himself a glass of mineral water and ice. There would be no time for alcohol now. He sat out on the patio and pulled out his mobile phone. As well as avoiding the media, Flynn had not used the phone over the last few weeks – other than, ironically, when he had made a secret phone call to Craig. It had been a very general conversation. Flynn wouldn't even have thought to mention Felix Deakin.

It was seven thirty p.m., as it would be in the UK, and although it was late he decided to try his luck. It took a few moments for the satellites to connect, and then for the extension to be reached.

'DC Tope. Can I help you?'

Flynn exhaled a sigh. 'Jerry, Steve Flynn.'

'Ah, shit, what the frig do you want?'

'I want to know what's going on in the cop world.'

'Steve, I only just avoided deep shit from talking to you last time by a gnat's todger . . . I'm not going to get caught out again.'

'In that case, find a secure phone and call me back on this number.' Flynn gave him the landline number of the villa, a phone he rarely used. 'Otherwise I'm on the blower to Mrs Tope to explain to her how you begged me to lie for you all those years ago. It might have been a while back, but adultery is adultery. There's no limitations to proceedings, y'know.'

The word Tope uttered was lost as he hung up.

Flynn went inside to get the cordless phone, then back out to sit in the hot evening and ruminate.

Faye and his partner, Jack Hoyle, had been the two people he most trusted in the world. Old story, he supposed. Nothing new in that. But it had hurt like a dagger through the heart and, now resurrected with Faye drunk-asleep in his bed, he found the pain was still there.

He hadn't heard about Jack's death. It had come as a shock to him, again bringing very mixed feelings to the surface. Close partners for years, living in each other's pockets, saving each other's lives – and yet Flynn never suspected what was going on behind his back. Something that only came to light after the debacle of the raid, and the whirlpool of accusation and counter-accusation that followed. When his and Jack's lives were being scrutinized and their personal lives went to rat-shit. That was when the affair came out and Faye decided she and Craig were better off without Flynn, but with Jack. And she left, taking the son he loved, preventing all but the barest contact with him. It drove Flynn to despair. That, plus the way he was treated at work, the powers that be deciding he should never come into contact with the public again. Humiliation, basically, eventually resulting in his resignation and upping sticks to Gran Canaria and the fishing boats . . . no son, wife or partner.

And the ironically named *Lady Faye*, the only female of that name he could control.

'Flynn,' he said, picking up the phone he knew would ring.

'Me,' came Jerry Tope's hesitant voice. 'And don't think your threat has anything whatsoever to do with me calling you back. I don't submit to blackmail. I just see you as a potential source of Intel with regards to the whereabouts of two men suspected of murder.'

'Whatever.'

'What do you want?'

'Tell me about Felix Deakin.'

'Not much to tell. He hired a professional team to spring him from custody and he's still on the run almost a month later.'

'Where is he?'

'If I knew that . . .'

'Where do you think he is?'

'Out of the country, we assume. Why?'

'I want to know.'

'OK, so I've told you. Now you tell me about Jackman and Cromer?'

'Who?'

'Oh, up yours, Steve.'

'What happened to Jack Hoyle?'

'Jack Hoyle? What's he got do with . . . Ahh.'

'Ahh, what?'

'Deakin's after that money, isn't he?'

'What money?'

'As I said, up yours, pal.'

'Tell me about Jack.'

'Not much to tell. One day he disappeared, missing presumed drowned in a fishing accident off Conwy, North Wales. Overturned boat, big seas, no body ever found.'

'And you fell for that?'

'Not up to me to fall for. North Wales police investigated. As far as I know he's somewhere in the Menai Straits. Crab food.'

'He was an experienced angler and boatman.'

'Happens to the best of us.'

Flynn growled doubtfully.

'So why are you phoning, Steve?'

'Who's leading the investigation to catch Deakin?'

'Henry Christie.'

Flynn's heart sank to a new low. 'Right . . . OK.' He hung up without any further formality. His head tilted back and his eyes closed. 'Fuck-shit-damn-bollocks,' he uttered. 'Not that bastard.'

His next idea was to phone Craig's mobile, which he did from his own. As it connected, it clicked automatically to the answering service. He hung up, rocked forward and got to his feet. He went in to look at Faye who was fast asleep, murmuring something unintelligible. She looked to be out for the count and although the temptation to shake her awake was intense, he resisted.

Instead he walked through the bedroom to the en-suite shower and cleaned the day off himself. He dressed in the bedroom, his clattering about doing nothing to dent Faye's sleep. He cancelled his date with the Dutch kiosk lady, which she took with only a mild shade of disappointment. Next he prepared a chicken casserole with two breasts he bought from the nearby Netto store. It cooked slowly in the small oven.

Then he waited.

Faye came to at midnight. She ambled through the villa with a sheet wrapped untidily around her.

'I need a fag and a shower and a drink,' she moaned. 'Not necessarily in that order.'

Flynn was still out on the patio in shorts and T-shirt, sipping water, wishing it was whisky, and staring into the distance. He frowned at her, then took her back through the bedroom and turned on the shower for her. 'I think everything you need'll be here. Your bag's in the bedroom.'

He left her to it. She reappeared twenty minutes later with damp hair, wearing one of Flynn's T-shirts, which dropped to about halfway down her thighs. She sat next to him and lit up. He never liked her smoking but loved the action of it. She crossed her slim legs and he couldn't fail to notice the lack of underwear.

'Jeez, that's better,' she said after a long drag. 'Now a drink,' she declared but caught his disapproving eye. 'Just one, or two,' she said meekly.

'Red wine or beer?'

'A beer, then a wine.'

Flynn's eyeballs rolled, but he got up and waited on her, bringing a plateful of chicken casserole with the drinks, including a plate for himself. The chicken was tender, falling to pieces. Faye took a mouthful and groaned in a heavenly way.

'I'm so hungry,' she said approvingly.

'Enjoy,' Flynn said, 'and speak at the same time.'

'It was just a phone call out of the blue. Corny sounding, but scary, too. Y'know – if you want to see your son alive again, go to such and such a place.'

'Where to?'

'On the front at Blackpool, near North Pier.'

'What happened?'

'I was stood there and a guy brushed past me, shoved a padded envelope in my hand and was gone – phtt! I opened it and it was Craig's mobile, switched on. It started ringing and I answered it and it was Craig. God, he sounded so cool, but said he'd been kidnapped and if I wanted to see him alive again I had to do certain things.' She screwed up her face. 'After my initial panic, I thought it was a big hoax. I told him to stop messing about, but then he cracked and I could tell it was for real.' She took a steadying breath. 'Poor little lad.'

'Keep talking,' Flynn said hastily.

'I was told to look at a video clip on his phone, then the call finished. I did. It was Craig sitting there. He was tied to a chair with a hood over his head, then someone took the hood off and held a gun to his head . . . never came in shot, though.' Listening, Flynn went ice cold with fury. Every muscle in his body tensed, his teeth grating. Faye was finding it difficult to carry on, the memory affecting her. She placed her fork down and gathered herself together. Flynn resisted putting a hand on her arm. 'And that was it. I was standing in a crowd of holidaymakers and had just been told my son had been kidnapped.'

'Then what?'

'Dunno. I was in a panic trance of some sort. I just went up and down the prom, bumping into people, just didn't know what I was doing. Then the phone rang again. A man said, "Steve Flynn has got a million pounds of my money and I want it back, or else your son is a dead son." Exact words, stuck in my brain.'

'Did he say it was Felix Deakin?'

She shook her head. 'It could've been somebody else.'

'Then what?' Flynn said again.

'The line went dead. The number had been withheld, so I couldn't call back. I just sat in a tram shelter. It started to rain and the tourists seemed to disappear and I was by myself and I didn't know what to do. I must've sat there an hour, holding the phone, looking at it, couldn't believe any of it. Then it rang again.'

Flynn waited for her to compose herself. 'And?'

'Same voice said if I told the cops, Craig would be killed. All I had to do was contact you and get you to pay up. Simple.'

'What did you say?'

'That if I phoned you, you'd think it was a stupid ex-wife trick and wouldn't take me seriously. So they said I had to convince you. I said I'd only be able to do that face to face. They said, do it. So here I am, Steve. Do you believe me?'

'Would you tell me a lie about Craig?'

'No, never.'

'Then I believe you. Did you bring Craig's phone?'

'It's in my bag. But what about Craig? Do you' – her bottom lip began to quiver – 'think he's really in danger?'

Flynn considered the question. 'All I know is that Felix Deakin is a violent, brutal man who wouldn't think twice about killing someone, or having someone killed, including a kid. So, in answer to the question – yes, he's in mortal danger.'

'And can you save him?'

'Yes, of course I can. He's my son, isn't he?'

Faye sobbed uncontrollably. Flynn's face set hard and he held himself together – just, not remotely certain he could achieve what he had just claimed.

*   *   *

Faye dragged herself wearily back to Flynn's bed half an hour after she'd eaten and drunk three glasses of wine and a beer. She was still pretty much in a daze as she removed Flynn's borrowed shirt and stood there naked in front of him. He hadn't seen her body in about five years, but everything looked in first-class order.

'I'd like you to come to bed with me,' she said simply.

Despite himself – and the situation – Flynn stirred, but he shook his head and retreated to the patio where he butt-ended two plastic chairs, grabbed a couple of cushions from the settee and settled himself down, deciding that a single shot of Jack Daniel's would come in useful.

He had the glass on his chest, his feet up across the chairs as he lay looking at the stars. He knew he would be unlikely to get any sleep. His head began to hurt, a painful throbbing behind his eyes.

It was his intention to get a flight back to the UK next day, hopefully the one Faye had a ticket for, but if that wasn't possible he'd pay the admin charge to have her ticket reallocated to him and she would have to return later. He wanted to get to the UK and deal with this himself. Not sure how. He'd have to wait for the next contact and take it from there.

He switched on Craig's mobile. Flynn's missed call beeped.

Then it rang.

Flynn jumped and answered it.

'Flynn,' he said suspiciously.

'Dad, it's me, Craig . . .'

'Dad, I'm OK . . . honest, they haven't hurt me yet,' came Craig's childlike voice.

'They'd better not, you goddam tell 'em, they'd better not.'

'I am OK . . . Dad, just do what they say, please . . .'

'Yeah, yeah,' Flynn gasped desperately on hearing his son's voice. 'Don't worry, bud, you stay cool.'

There was a movement behind Flynn. He glanced over his shoulder to see a bleary-eyed Faye standing there, the sheet wrapped around her, having been woken by the ring tone and Flynn's voice. She started to say something. Flynn held up a silencing finger. 'Listen, buddy,' he started to say to Craig, but was then interrupted by a male voice he didn't recognize. Could have been Deakin, but he wasn't sure.

'No, it's you who needs to listen, Flynn. This is a simple scenario. I've got your kid and all I want is my money back.

The equation's easy. Your kid for my million. It's that straight-forward. I want the money you and your bent partner ripped off from me, couldn't be simpler. You have four days before I send you the first bit of him. And that'll be an eyeball.'

'This is bang out of order, Deakin,' Flynn said, now certain it was him. 'Bringing family into it. He's innocent in all this. Let him go now and let's negotiate.'

'Fuck you, Flynn. This isn't honour among thieves, this is payback time. I just want what's mine and you can have what's yours. I'm not messing about here. I'll kill the little fucker, enjoy it and not think twice, and you know I will. And no cops . . . If I sniff 'em, he's dead.'

'You're dead if you even touch my son. You know that, don't you?'

Deakin laughed harshly. 'Shut it and listen. I'll contact you again in four days on this number. That'll give you enough time to get the money together.'

'I don't have your money, don't even think it ever existed.'

'Oh it fucking existed all right. So get it, or Craig gets his eyeball gouged out with a fork and sent to you first class.'

The line clicked dead. Flynn stared numbly at the phone in his hand, then looked at Faye. 'Four days, then it starts,' he said hope-lessly – and then it became all too much and his world imploded.

Faye swooped down on her knees to him, the sheet falling from her shoulders, and held him tightly as massive, shuddering sobs wracked his body. He held on tight until she took his face between her hands, wiped away the tears with her thumbs, then kissed them away before placing her lips on his.

When she drew away, she said, 'We need this, you and me, we need this . . .'

Much of what then transpired was a slow-motion blur to Flynn. Rising to his feet, holding Fay's naked body to him, feeling himself harden, and then suddenly they were in bed. Holding her wrists above her head, her nipples in his mouth, entering her willing body and making desperate love as though he was in a parallel world while the real Steve Flynn watched disapprovingly from the sidelines. They shared joint orgasms and he stayed deep inside her; then, as he subsided, collapsing his weight on to her, completely drained, physically and emotionally. She ran her fingers up and down his spine, then clung to him and they cried together.

Eventually Flynn rolled off her. She fell asleep, while he sat on the edge of the bed before putting on a pair of shorts and padding back on to the patio, settling himself in the two butt-ended chairs. He picked up Craig's mobile and selected the video menu.

He woke early, stiff and chilled. He dressed quickly without disturbing Faye. He scribbled a brief note to say he'd be back later and went to see Adam Castle. Flynn knew that thanks to his ownership of a travel agency among his various other enterprises, Castle had a good 'in' to plane tickets. He found Castle in his small office in the commercial centre and sat down in front of him.

'Boss, I owe you a lot and I'm not sure I'll ever be able to repay all your kindness and generosity . . .'

'The bullshit precursor to a favour,' Castle said amicably. 'Or a kick in the nuts.'

'Something's come up,' Flynn said hesitantly. He looked at Castle, knowing he had to tell him straight.

Half an hour later Flynn left the office having got a seat on the same flight as Faye, leaving Las Palmas at nine that evening and landing in Manchester four and a half hours later. Castle also booked a car for Flynn, to be picked up at Manchester Airport for a period of two weeks, refusing to take any payment for either purchase in spite of Flynn's pleas.

'Sounds like you'll need all the dosh you can get,' Castle had said.

'I'll pay you back,' Flynn promised.

'I know you will. Just do what you have to, OK, then get back here in one piece and work like a Trojan for the next ten years. Then we'll be even.'

'I will.'

They shook hands.

As Flynn emerged on to the shopping concourse, he had a full day of tension to get through before arriving at the airport a couple of hours before the flight. He needed to stay cool, but that was a big ask. A sensation of uselessness overwhelmed him. He needed to be doing something. He was a man of action and hated kicking his heels, and he knew the best medicine was moored and waiting for him down at the harbour.

A four-hour charter was booked, ten till two, and being out on the water was the best thing he could possibly do to keep his mind from the fact that when he stepped on to that plane later in the day, his life would never be the same again.

SIXTEEN

The high-level review of the Deakin case had not gone well. A squirming Henry Christie – a butterfly on a wheel? – had been obliged to report on the progress or otherwise of the investigation into Deakin's escape and the violent death of a good cop who'd left behind, as they always seemed to do, a grieving widow, pregnant with their second child.

And Henry really had been squirming. Faced with what amounted to a panel of his contemporaries and peers, and chaired by Robert Fanshaw-Bayley, or FB, Lancashire Constabulary's chief constable. The head of Human Resources was also there, along with two chief superintendents, one being from out of the force to provide an objective view of the slaughter.

'Can I just return to a point you made earlier?' one of these chief supers had said. He was a divisional chief superintendent with a long, undistinguished detective career behind him. Henry knew him well. Although the participants were sitting around an elliptically shaped conference table in a room at the training centre as though they were all equals, Henry was very much under the cosh.

He'd raised his chin defensively as the chief super spoke, with a queasy feeling in the pit of his stomach for this return to the point. No doubt it would be the point of a dagger.

'You mentioned you had reservations about the wisdom of even allowing Deakin to attend court to give evidence. As it transpired, these were well founded reservations, if indeed you really had any at all.' Henry's face became tight at the allegation. 'So, Henry, if you did have these reservations why were you not more vociferous in raising your doubts? Why no banging of the fists on the table?'

Henry tried not to rise to the slur. 'Deakin's evidence was crucial to the case. It made a vital connection between murderer and victim, something the case lacked. It was a compelling reason to get him on the stand. Greater powers than me decided to take him to court. I voiced my opinion and if it had been my choice, he'd still be in jail.' There was no way Henry was going to take the rap for that decision, even if it made him look like he was passing the buck – which he was.

The chief super nodded. 'Thanks for that, Henry.'

Henry reached for a glass of iced water. His throat was parched. He took a gulp, then said, 'And of course it seems that the evidence was absolutely crucial to the trial. As we know, the trial collapsed yesterday and Johnny Cain is now a free man.'

'OK, then,' the chief constable said, leaning his considerable girth forward, his large round belly creasing above and below the table. 'So where are we up to with it, Henry?'

Henry shuffled his notes and gathered his thoughts. 'We think there's every likelihood that Deakin is out of the country. He amassed quite a bit of money from a series of armed robberies he, er, masterminded from jail. Although the high court ordered the seizure of his assets, amounting to somewhere in the region of five million pounds, there's every reason to think there's a similar amount hidden away elsewhere. Our financial investigators are working on that.' He glanced around the table, seeing several heads with brains in them bigger than his shaking with disgust. 'We're also making inquiries to trace the team who sprang him from custody. We think they're the same professional gang who sprang a prisoner en route from Lancaster Crown Court about a dozen years ago. They've assisted in escapes in London, Paris and Madrid.' The Lancaster escape was one Henry had been involved with, too, but it had been even more violent. 'Anyway, there is a very big investigation under way and a lot of positive leads are being followed up. I'm sure we'll have the break we need soon.'

'Henry,' the chief super who'd previously spoken leaned forward, 'to be fair to you, you should know we are seriously considering replacing you as head of this investigation. It's a mammoth task, one requiring someone with vast strategic and tactical knowhow.' Henry's insides twisted again. 'However,' he relented – and Henry's balls felt like they'd been released from a vice. 'For the time being you will remain in charge, but do note that we are extremely concerned by the lack of progress with this and other inquiries you are currently heading. We feel that new blood may well be necessary to give fresh impetus. So basically, you've another three days to convince us and show some results.'

'I'm doing absolutely everything that needs doing,' Henry responded pathetically.

'Henry,' the chief super said with a smirk, 'you might well be hitting all the right notes, but not necessarily in the right order. We need some out of the box thinking, something creative now.'

'In other words, get your finger out,' FB cut in curtly.

'OK, anything else to discuss?' He glanced sharply around the room, his look challenging anyone to come up with something. 'OK, review closed. Henry, you're still I/C, but it's a dicey thing.'

Henry collected his things as though a little cloud was raining over his head alone. Everyone filed out except FB, leaving the two of them sitting opposite each other, staring silently for a few moments.

'I headed off a vote of no confidence before this meeting,' FB told him. Henry nodded glumly. He and FB went back a very long way, knew each other well, though the relationship was very much biased in FB's favour. 'Talk is that you've been promoted beyond your capabilities,' FB added for Henry's information.

'So I'm no different to the rest of the other high-ranking officers in this force,' Henry said childishly.

'Cutting.' FB's lips pursed. 'A statement that doesn't make you sound good.'

'Sorry boss. Just feeling it, that's all.'

'As is every other cop in the force. It's fucking tough, pal – and when you stick your mush up over the parapet, you have to suffer all the slings and arrows with equanimity. Because every bastard is out to get you, especially your peers. Welcome to the jungle. I mean, I know you've taken a lot of shit historically, but it's just that you've now got much, much further to fall.'

Henry nodded.

'Fact is I promoted you because you never give up, never have done, never will, which is why I fought your corner.' FB pushed himself and his chair backwards, raised his bulk up. 'Having said that, I quite liked the Morecambe and Wise reference, the "all the right notes" thing.' He chuckled and walked to the door. 'Let's have a bit more of the old Henry Christie on this one, shall we?' He gave Henry an exaggerated wink, then went out. Henry gathered his stuff and scuttled out after him, catching up as they walked across the training centre car park.

'I want to bug Barry Baron,' Henry said.

'The brief?' They reached FB's new car, parked on the disabled-only hatch markings. It was a huge, four-wheel drive monstrosity that could have single-handedly put a hole in the ozone layer. 'Not a well thought out plan.'

'I'm a hundred per cent he's involved.'

'To get that authority would mean me talking to the Home Secretary, an ex-lawyer by the way. He could take some convincing.'

'I don't have time. Three days, remember?'

'OK, do an application and submit it through normal channels. If it makes sense, I'll talk to the Home Secretary, but it will take time. In the meantime, get the ball rolling, wink, wink. But don't embarrass me in the bargain.' He climbed into his spacious car and opened the window. 'Truth is, Henry, even though those numb-nuts don't know it, you are the best detective for this job – so if you aren't going to play by the rules, at least make it look as though you have done. Get my drift?'

Open-mouthed, Henry watched him drive away, trying to get his head around the last five minutes. FB giving him a motivational speech and then the wink-wink go-ahead to get a result by whatever means possible, both of which the chief would deny if pressed.

He decided he needed some sustenance in order to do some serious cogitation. He sauntered to the training centre dining room and got himself a frothy coffee from the machine, carrying it to the far corner of the room. There he could sit facing out of the floor-to-ceiling windows with his back to the activity inside, and watch the genteel life pass by across the quadrangle, a bit like university – with uniforms instead of gowns. He placed his mobile on the table.

The coffee was surprisingly good, giving him a jolt of caffeine that seemed to energize him.

It had been a relentless investigation. Deakin escaping, the cop dying, Richard Last's wife being targeted (as well as Henry himself in the crossfire), plus the gruesome deaths of Last and Sumner. Not forgetting the security guard who'd been killed, probably by Last or Sumner. Henry had tried to bring all these threads together and it had been like spinning plates. The whole thing had taken its toll. The squad had worked hard, putting in long hours while knowing that only a fraction of the overtime worked would be paid. But they'd done so because a cop had been killed. Unfortunately it was effort that could not possibly be sustained. People were now drained, not at their best, losing momentum, particularly since no results had been forthcoming.

Henry was bitter about the message coming from the review team. Maybe he should have been more vociferous about not allowing Deakin to go to court, but beyond that everything else he'd done was watertight.

Problem now was that time was passing. A cop had died horrifically and there was obviously a panicky feeling about that someone's head needed to roll. And it would be Henry's, if he wasn't careful, no matter how much the chief might say he supported him. That was a carpet that would be pulled PDQ if FB felt under threat.

And on top of that was Henry's personal pride. He knew he was doing a good job, but the situation spoke for itself.

In respect of the supermarket robbery/murder – no arrest. It wouldn't be so bad if he could prove that either of the murdered robbers, Last or Sumner, had pulled the trigger, but he couldn't.

In respect of their double murder – no arrest yet.

In respect of Deakin's breakout and the death of a cop – no arrest.

A sorry tale of woe.

His gut told him that Deakin had left the country, although he had no evidence to back this up. The way to get to the escapee could be much closer to home in the shape of Barry Baron, the man who must know everything. The solicitor who acted for Deakin like a *consigliere* to a Godfather. If only he could sweat the bastard.

Obviously he'd interviewed him about his meeting with Last and Sumner, after which the pair were never seen alive again, and about Deakin's escape. But the conversation had been frustrating and fruitless. Henry hadn't wanted to make too many unfounded allegations either, so in spite of wanting to toss the smug bastard into a cell and beat the living crap out of him, he had not burned any bridges by revealing any of his unsubstantiated suspicions about Baron. He was playing the long game, sure his day would come.

On top of that he was still dealing with his prodigal sister and a very poorly mother, neither of whom he had time to sort out.

His phone vibrated and did a little dance on the table. The number calling was withheld, but he answered it.

'Henry, it's me.' He instantly recognized Naomi Dale's voice. 'How did the review go?'

Henry hesitated. Having basically set the whole ball rolling, Naomi, through the machinations of the CPS, had insisted on being kept abreast of all developments in the investigation, a decision rubber-stamped by FB despite Henry's protestations. She had persuasively argued that the CPS had a vested interest in its progress and as such she should be assigned virtually full time to keep a consultative brief on the criminal law side. When Deakin was finally arrested, the CPS wanted everything to be watertight. Sullenly, Henry was economical in what he gave her, keeping her at oar's length, much to her chagrin.

'Well enough,' he said flatly, failing to add the tempting, 'But it's none of your business, lady.'

'What does that mean?' she asked in a chill-factored tone.

'It carries on the way it has been.'

'And you're still in charge?'

'Why wouldn't I be?' he retorted irritably.

'I'd just heard that . . . oh, no reason,' she corrected herself.

'Heard what?'

'OK – through the grapevine I'd heard you were going to get stiffed and chucked off the investigation, if you must know.' She sounded indignant, then her tone changed. 'Look, I'm sorry all this happened. I, we, the CPS, thought it was the right thing to do to get a conviction when all along, Deakin just wanted to escape.'

'Duh,' Henry said.

Her voice softened again. 'And not everything was horrible, was it?'

He sighed and relented. 'No, suppose not.'

There was a slight pause while Henry visualized himself in Naomi's arms in the few seconds before panic struck and he did a runner. He could recall her body, her smell.

Then she said, 'So how is the investigation going?'

'Well, in terms of it being a well-structured, well-led, well-run investigation, it's going spiffingly. In terms of catching any of the miscreants, that's where it all seems to be going down the pan.'

'Surely you must have some leads?'

'We think Deakin's abroad. Unfortunately because his organization pretty much crumbled while he was in prison, there's no one really to put any pressure on. The gang who freed him are based in southern Europe and they've split up, which they always do after pulling a job. They won't resurface until the next one . . . My gut feeling is that the door we need to be banging on is closer to home . . .' He faltered, then clammed up.

'What do you mean?'

'Oh, nothing,' he said vaguely, sensing he'd said too much. It wasn't that he didn't trust her, but it would have been idiotic to reveal his suspicions about Baron. Cynic that he was, he truly believed all solicitors pissed in the same pot. Telling Naomi only to find it whispered in Baron's ear via a very efficient grapevine would be too much of a chance to take. 'Anyway,' he said, drawing the chat to a close, 'I'll keep you posted . . . Sorry, someone's just come in the office and I need to speak to them urgently,' he lied. 'Byee.'

He ended the call and stared at the phone. Then he took another sip of his coffee and continued to gaze out of the window at the quad.

How to kick-start the investigation? he thought. How the hell do I get the drive back into it? Motivate nearly seventy detectives and thirty other members of staff?

As these considerations tumbled formlessly through his brain, he became aware of the presence of someone at his shoulder. Turning forty-five degrees he saw it was DC Jerry Tope.

Jerry held his hands together at his chest, wringing them. Henry almost expected him to say, 'I'm yer 'umble servant,' or something equally Dickensian. The fact that Jerry had recently allowed his sideboards to grow long and thick didn't help. He looked like a character straight out of *Oliver Twist*.

'What is it, Jerry?'

'Err . . .'

'Goz it out.'

'Got someone to see you.'

Henry craned his neck a little further to glance behind Jerry. There was no one there.

'Remember I mentioned Steve Flynn?'

Henry's hackles began to rise. 'How could I forget?'

'Well, he's back over here from Gran Canaria and I sort of said it'd be OK for him to see you.'

'Really?'

'Uh-huh.'

'Where is he?'

Jerry jerked his head. 'In the foyer.'

'Why does he want to see me?'

Jerry had moved around in front of Henry so as not to put a permanent crick in his boss's neck.

'Because I think I can help you, Henry.'

Henry spun in his seat again. Steve Flynn now stood there, healthy, big, broad, tall, bronzed, good looking, though with an edge of weariness to his demeanour. Around his eyes he looked tired. Behind him, Henry noticed two probationer policewomen entering the dining room who couldn't keep their eyes off Flynn. They giggled unprofessionally as they shared a sharp intake of breath and walked to the coffee machine. Henry shot them a disapproving look, but it went right over their heads. They had no idea who he was, the power he wielded.

Flynn thrust out a hand, but Henry recoiled a fraction and said, 'This is all I bloody need.'

Despite his serious misgivings, he ungraciously invited Flynn back to his office. On the short walk back to the FMIT block, there was no small talk, but Henry thought about Flynn and how their lives had crossed in the past.

Their clash had come after Flynn's badly conceived raid on Deakin's counting house and the subsequent shit-on-fan fallout.

Fortunately for Henry he had not been involved in anything connected with the raid, and he thanked heaven for that mercy. But following it, he had been requested by the Professional Standards Department – or the rubber heel squad, as they were otherwise known, the cops who police the cops – to look into the allegation made by Felix Deakin. Namely, that mysteriously, almost a million pounds of drug money had disappeared into the pockets of Flynn and partner Jack Hoyle, even though a more realistic fifty grand or so had been seized from the raid.

To do this, Henry had to spend some time looking at the careers of the two detectives, and he didn't like what he found. Two jack-the-lads operating on the edge, often alleged to use strong-arm, intimidatory tactics to get results. Maybe Henry didn't like what he found because he saw a blurred reflection of himself – without the tough-guy approach – in Flynn particularly. Investigating Flynn was a little like investigating himself.

As it happened, both Flynn and Hoyle were resolute in their stories and recollections about the raid and could not be budged. They'd made a fifty grand seizure in cocaine-tainted wads of cash, plus a substantial amount of cocaine itself, so why wouldn't they have basked in the glory of seizing a million if it had been there to grab?

Henry recalled believing Flynn more than Hoyle, but couldn't remember why. Both were obviously sleazy cops, coming across as devious and sly, but Flynn seemed a more pleasant character. Henry thought that having a guy like Flynn behind him in a touch and go situation would be a good thing. In the end, though, he didn't take to either man.

During the internal investigation Henry had been required to interview Deakin about the allegation. Deakin had lost his temper with Henry when it was suggested he was making up the story about the missing money just to put up a smokescreen. Deakin's OTT reaction had been to threaten Henry and his family, and it was then that Henry saw Deakin for what he was – a cornered tiger, lashing out at everything and anyone just to get free.

And yet . . . a little worm continued to eat away at the back of Henry's mind, even though he couldn't prove if the money existed or not.

Finally Henry recommended there was no case to answer. But because there were many unfounded allegations against the duo historically, including intimidation of suspects, unproven assaults and heavy-handed tactics, he suggested that both men be taken off the front line and given menial jobs which kept them from coming into contact with the public. This recommendation was upheld and Flynn and Hoyle found themselves ignominiously removed from the sharp end, stuck in dusty offices in cop shops at opposite ends of the county. The powers that be made it hard and uncomfortable for both men and Henry wasn't surprised when he heard Flynn had subsequently resigned.

That little job had only been a minor side road in Henry's career and he'd soon forgotten about it . . . until Deakin re-appeared in his sights.

In his office he sat loftily behind his desk, indicating with a regal wave for Flynn and Jerry to park their backsides opposite. Jerry, still looking humble and a little terrified, remained standing.

'Should I stay, boss?'

'You brought him here,' Henry said bluntly. 'So sit down.'

Jerry shot into a chair.

'OK, Mr Flynn – you've got a maximum of ten minutes to make your pitch.' Henry made an exaggerated show of checking his watch, adding, 'I'm extremely busy, y'know.'

'I'm just going to come to the point,' Flynn said. 'I won't dwell on any past history between ourselves or anything like that.'

'One minute's nearly gone.'

'I'd like to come in and help in the investigation to recapture Felix Deakin,' Flynn said simply. 'I know the guy, how he operates. I know a lot of his cronies and I also know something you don't.'

'And that would be?'

'He's still in this country – right under your nose.'

SEVENTEEN

Henry went home via his mother's bungalow in the sheltered accommodation complex. He let himself in loudly, rattling his keys, banging the door and announcing his arrival with trepidation. Every time he visited her now, he expected to find her dead on the bathroom floor. There was no pleasure in entering the house until he confirmed she was alive and kicking.

'I can hear you, no need to shout,' came her screechy voice from the lounge. 'I'm not completely deaf.'

'Other than when it suits,' Henry said under his breath. He exhaled with relief. At least she'd made it through another day – although, as Henry found her in the living room still dressed in grubby night attire, he guessed she'd been sitting in the same position all day. The meals on wheels service had obviously been and delivered lunch, evidenced by the tinfoil cartons on the tray at her feet, but there was nothing that said she'd had anything else all day. Henry's blood began to boil when he went into the kitchen and touched the cold kettle.

'How are you then, Mum?' he asked on his return.

'Old, knackered and not completely deaf,' she said, touching her ear.

'What've you had to eat today, other than meals on wheels?'

'I don't know.' She looked at him through milky eyes. 'I could murder a brew, though.'

He collected her tray and made her a mug of tea. He threw out some mouldy bread, defrosted a few slices from a loaf in the freezer and made her a ham sandwich. He made a cuppa for himself, too, sitting with her as she ate ravenously. She hadn't lost her appetite, but the chewing noises she made turned his stomach.

After she'd finished, Henry switched the TV on for her, then wandered through the bungalow. Her bed was unmade and starting to whiff slightly. Discarded clothing surrounded it, which Henry collected into a bundle to take home. The toilet was unflushed and stinking, so he flushed it, found some bleach and cleaned the pan.

His ire continued to rise. The evidence was that she'd been alone all day.

Dispirited, Henry did a bit of tidying up, made the bed with

fresh sheets and added the ones he'd removed to the bundle of
washing. He spent another half-hour with her, reprogrammed the
TV and found a satellite comedy channel, helped her to the loo,
found a change of night attire for her, then left her with a brew
and some chocolate biscuits.

Outside, he sat in his car for a few minutes before calling Rik
Dean on the mobile.

'Hi, boss,' Rik answered cautiously.

'Rik, how you doing mate?' Henry asked perkily, so as not
to put him on guard. 'Just a quick welfare check. Wondering
how you were doing. I've been up to my neck in it as you know,
so apologies for not calling sooner.'

'Hey, no problem.' Rik sounded relieved. 'The quack says I can
get back to work next week – light duties. I'm raring to get back.'

Not as raring as you could be, Henry thought. Rik's liaison
with Lisa had put his eagerness to return to work on the back
burner. 'How's things with Lisa?' Henry asked, hoping it sounded
innocent, especially when he added, 'Just by the by, I'm OK with
you two. I think it was just a big brother thing initially. But, fact
is, you're two grown-up people, so it's none of my business –
although bonking in my house is still strictly a no-no.'

Rik uttered a laugh of relief. 'I'm really glad to hear that, H.
It's going well and we had a great day today. She drove us up
to the Lakes – Ambleside and all that. We're meeting up for a
meal at eight. I think she'll be spending the night at my pad.'

'Yeah, whatever.' Henry now tried to sound uninterested.
'Anyway, glad you're feeling better.' He ended the call on a friendly
note and snapped his phone shut. His face was screwed up with
anger. He started the car and screeched away from the kerb.

Flynn let out a stream of muttered curses following his meeting
with Henry Christie. Having thanked Jerry for fixing it up, he left
police HQ and drove back to Blackpool, flummoxed as to how he
was going to deal with his precarious position and save his son.

Depending on how Deakin was marking the hours, there was
a maximum of three days left, time that was sifting through his
fingers like fine sand. And he'd heard nothing on Craig's phone,
which was constantly at his side.

He wasn't even sure what he'd hoped to achieve by his half-
baked plan of speaking to Henry. Yes, he was. He wanted Henry
to take him on board as some sort of 'consultant' in the hunt for
Deakin. The idea was that Flynn would be able to glean enough

information from the investigation as to Deakin's possible where-abouts to enable him to wade in before the cops could move and liberate Craig, while killing Deakin if necessary.

That's how dumb and uncoordinated his thinking was. There was nothing joined up about it and now he was floundering.

Henry had been no help, but Flynn accepted that was his own fault as much as anything. Despite his grand claims, there had been nothing to offer, even though it was true Flynn knew as much as anyone about Deakin. After all, he'd spent months building up a huge intelligence and information dossier on him, much of it unused (and Flynn had a thought there that went nowhere), leading up to the ill-judged raid. If the raid had gone well, Flynn and Hoyle would have been covered in laurels as opposed to shite.

But the reality was Flynn knew nothing helpful to Henry. His claim about Deakin being in the country may well have been correct, but where was the proof to back it up? Other than revealing that Craig had been kidnapped and Deakin was demanding money with menaces, Flynn simply had zilch. And he didn't want to say anything to Henry about Craig because if Deakin got wind the cops were involved, Craig would be dead for sure. Flynn was positive that Deakin would either kill him outright or abandon him to die.

It didn't help Flynn's case when Henry asked him about why he'd phoned Jerry to ask about Jackman and Cromer, either. Flynn's evasive answer and body language told Henry Flynn wanted everything on his terms, and that wasn't the game Henry was going to play.

Hence the flea in his ear.

As much as Flynn did want to handle things his way, make the running, take the initiative, the means to do this eluded him. And time was running out.

He drove back to Faye's house on a small, neat estate in Blackpool South. It was actually the house they'd shared as a married couple until it all went sour. She had originally left, then had Flynn thrown out and came back to live with Jack. It was strange for Flynn to pull up outside the property that was once his.

He'd crashed out in Craig's room on arriving from Gran Canaria, avoiding the offer of a shared bed with Faye. Although they'd shared a passionate incident in Puerto Rico, it had been of the moment, not to be repeated. She got the message with a sad, understanding face.

For the first time ever – Faye wasn't strong in the kitchen department – there was food waiting for him on his return.

A beef casserole and jacket potato that Flynn wolfed down with a mug of tea, observed by Faye while she picked at her food and spun a tall glass of Chardonnay by its stem as she sat opposite. She held back the questions until he finished eating.

'How did it go?'

'Dead end.' He swigged the last of the tea, which tasted wonderful. It was something he couldn't seem to recreate on the island. He declined the temptation of a beer because he wanted to keep his system clean now until this whole thing was over. 'Henry Christie obviously despises me and even though I pleaded with him, there was nothing I could offer him. I need to start turning stones over by myself if I want things to happen.' He sat back, squinted at Faye. He still found her hellish attractive and knew if she tried to cast a spell, he'd probably dance to it like the mop in *Fantasia*. 'Tell me about Jack,' he said.

'What do you want to know?'

Flynn considered the question for a moment. 'Why did he leave you?' He had to keep a note of triumph from his voice. He knew Jack had left his wife and moved in here when Flynn moved out. Flynn had then resigned from the force and gone to Gran Canaria. What he didn't know was how soon Faye and Jack had split after that. Because she had denied him access to Craig, Flynn had decided quickly, and probably misguidedly in hindsight, to sever all ties as he was hurt so badly by the betrayal. At that time it had seemed the right thing to do if he was to operate as a human being; it was only Craig's occasional secret phone calls that kept him and his beloved son in contact.

'I don't know,' Faye answered the question. 'He talked about the pressure of the situation, how his own wife was making life hell for him, which she was – bitch! His kids had turned against him, his other workmates didn't want anything to do with him, working under a cloud of suspicion.'

Flynn's mouth twisted sardonically here, resisting the urge to say, 'And? What did he expect?' Jack had had the audacity to stay in the cops and try to tough it out despite the incredible internal pressure.

Faye went on, 'He just upped and left one day, no explanations, nowt. Never saw him again, then I heard about the boating accident in Wales.'

Flynn nodded. 'I don't think you know how much you hurt me, both of you,' he said.

'Sorry. Maybe we could . . . when all this is over . . .?'

Even as she spoke, Flynn's head was shaking. 'Let's just concentrate on getting Craig back in one piece.'

She took a long drink of the chilled wine and refilled the glass.

'Did Jack ever speak of the money?'

'Only that the allegation was untrue. He always denied it, saying Deakin was just being a stirring bastard, claiming the cops were bent. Were you?'

'Never dishonest. Overzealous to get results, maybe.'

'I knew that of you,' she confirmed to herself, 'but not of Jack. Not that I ever saw any evidence of the money.'

Flynn's mind was working overtime, many simultaneous thoughts tumbling alongside each other, past, present, future. It was one from the past that grabbed him at that juncture as he recalled what had jarred his mind when he'd earlier been thinking about the information he'd gathered about Deakin. 'When was the last time you went into the loft here?' he asked.

'I've never been in the loft,' she said, puzzled. 'Going into lofts isn't a woman thing.'

Flynn got to his feet quickly and went upstairs. The entrance to the loft was above the landing. He could easily reach the bolt to release the hatch, which swung down to reveal the black space in the rafters.

'Where's the ladder hook?' Flynn was tall, but even he couldn't reach high enough to grab the extending ladders, the ones he'd fitted a lifetime ago. Faye was on the stairs, looking perplexed. 'Y'know, the long piece of wood with a hook in the end you drag the ladders down with?'

Faye thought hard, her features scrunching up. Then it came to her. She went into the spare third bedroom. Flynn heard her muttering and moving a few things around, then she emerged bearing a length of cane with a hook screwed into the tip, another great piece of DIY created by Flynn. He was amazed at how skilled he'd been. Fitting the ladder had been the hardest thing he'd ever done, DIY not being one of his strongest points.

He dragged the steps down, climbed up and peered into the loft. He flicked on the light switch affixed to one of the joists and was surprised when a weak light came on. It was a mess up here. Boxes, old suitcases, Craig's Scalextric. Flynn experienced a momentary emotional lapse, remembering he'd bought it for Craig on his eighth birthday.

'What're you after? The missing money?' Faye called.

'I wish. No, an old file from work.' He hauled himself up and

perched on the edge of the hatch, legs dangling. He reached in
and moved a few things around. 'Here we go,' he said, finding
a foolscap document wallet, fastened by a rubber band. He turned
the light off and came down the steps, sliding them back into
place and closing the hatch.

The file was a good inch thick. Flynn opened it on the dining
table, a trickle of trepidation tingling through him. This was the
unofficial file he'd kept on Deakin while building up his case against
him. Flynn had a habit of doing this, keeping a file that ran parallel
to the official one. While it contained and mirrored much of that
file, there was stuff in it for his eyes only. He did this because he
was acutely aware of the disclosure rules in criminal cases, where
the prosecution were obliged to disclose virtually everything to the
defence, even scraps of paper with notes scribbled on by detectives.
Things that might not be evidentially valuable, but could be crucial
to tripping up an investigation. Flynn knew what he did was wrong,
but sometimes things got written down baddies shouldn't see.

He leafed slowly through the file. Much of what it contained
was pretty harmless and he didn't actually know what he was
searching for – if anything. There was a lot of background information on Deakin and his organization, its structure and finances.
Flynn knew much of this had been sanitized into court-friendly
documents. It included lists of associates, family, contacts, and
in a separate envelope some names of possible informants in
Deakin's set-up. One of the names had a pink highlighter line
over it. This puzzled Flynn. He could not recall why he'd done
this. There was a question mark next to the name – *Dennis
Grant?* – but the mists of time had dimmed his memory as to
why. There was an address alongside the name.

He sat back thoughtfully.

'Something?' Faye asked. She had been watching him.

'Name Dennis Grant mean anything to you?'

She was tipping the last of the Chardonnay into her glass,
shaking the bottle to get all the drops out. Flynn recalled that
drink had always been a bit of an issue with her. 'Nahh . . . huh!
Dennis the Menace,' she hiccuped and belched quietly.

'No, this is serious. Dennis Grant,' he said firmly, then, 'Look,
getting arseholed won't help our cause here.'

She stared at him through watery eyes, lips pursed. Then she
dissolved into tears. 'I know,' she wept. 'I just don't know what
to do, how to handle it. Suppose Craig gets murdered . . .' Her
shoulders shuddered and she covered her face with her hands.

Flynn touched her arm. 'He won't, I'll make sure of that.' And then a thought struck him: Dennis the Menace. He and Hoyle had spent a lot of time gleaning information from inform-ants. Some they shared, some they dealt with properly – by the book – and some they kept to themselves, not even allowing the other partner to know their informants' identity. Much of what he and Hoyle did was completely against regulations concerning the handling of sources, but they had always flown by the seat of their pants and never cocked up. They respected each other's rights to have their own personal informants, even if they did constantly try to discover their identities, usually unsuccessfully. A little game both played.

Flynn remembered that when they were closing in on Deakin they had used a lot of info gleaned from one of Jack's sources who, he claimed, was close to the target. It was information provided by this guy that eventually led to the raid on the counting house.

Flynn racked his brain. Something had clicked in a deep recess. A memory of a fleeting conversation with Jack. Hardly anything, but one where Jack had realized he'd said too much about an informant he had referred to as 'a right menace'. He'd become worried, coughed and changed the subject – quickly. Subsequently Flynn had gone through the unofficial file, highlighted Grant's name and speculated whether or not this was Jack's informant. Now he remembered dismissing the idea after checking Grant's criminal record and Intel file. He was too low level to be providing anything useful.

Or maybe Flynn had been wrong. Perhaps Grant *was* the source: *Dennis the Menace.*

Flynn found Grant's record at the back of the file. It was basic stuff: name, address, date of birth, etc. The connection to Deakin was that Grant was a low-level gofer, a fetch-me, carry-me man, delivering and collecting drugs, money, guns and occasionally people. The man who would get caught and take the rap. A mule. Low down the chain, his position of importance probably exag-gerated by Jack. But maybe Grant was in the know or had heard something vital – like the janitor no one ever thought about.

His address was in Blackpool, a flat in North Shore. But it was five years ago, every chance he'd moved on. There was a mobile number for him, too. Once again, every chance it had been replaced a dozen times.

For Flynn, though, it was a start.

*   *   *

Henry tapped on the bedroom door. Behind it he could hear a hair drier on full blast and music blaring out. He knocked louder and both sounds stopped.

'Come in, I'm decent,' Lisa called.

Henry opened the door, annoyed he had to knock for permission to enter a room in his own house. Inside, it was a mess. Clothing and underwear was strewn over the bed, on the floor. A strong smell of perfume hung in the air and in the middle of this, clad in frilly lingerie, which included the briefest of panties, little more than a lace G-string, was Lisa, Henry's sister who had commandeered Leanne's bedroom.

'Hi, Henry,' she beamed.

'Lisa,' he said sonorously. He had to admit she was stunning looking, but boy-oh-boy was she hard work. He tried to mask his anger when he said, 'Can you cover up? It's a bit distracting.'

'Ooh, sorry.' She eased herself into a flimsy gown of the finest material.

'Have you had a good day?'

'Fine, fine.' She checked her watch.

'I haven't had time to get around to Mum's today with all this shit at work. I just wondered how she was doing. I'll get around tomorrow on the way in to work. I know you've spent some time with her today.'

He'd prepared his lie and the body language to accompany it. Lisa hadn't had time to do the same, so when her eyes fell and her shoulders shifted uncomfortably, he could tell she was about to lie back. 'She's really good.' She swallowed. 'Doing OK, really pulling through.'

Henry nodded. 'I lied – I have been round.'

'What do you mean?'

'I've been round to Mum's and no one has been to see her today, except the meals people.'

'Well that's not true.'

Henry held up a hand to stop her. 'I also spoke to Rik. I believe you had a nice day up in the Lakes. A bit of convalescence for him.' He stepped forward with a faint air of menace and pointed at her. 'Don't lie to me, Lisa. I deal with people who lie to me every day.'

She lowered herself on to the edge of the bed. 'Sorry,' she said timidly.

'Lisa, I don't know if the penny's dropped here, but Mum's dying. Bit by bit, hour by hour, she's going downhill. Coming out of hospital doesn't mean she's better. All right, we haven't reached the need for twenty-four hour care yet, but it's not far away. She needs help getting dressed, getting washed, getting food and drink. I'm working on getting social services to help with these things, but it'll be a while before I can pull that off. I thought you came up here because I sent you the text telling you she was ill, to help out. Or was it just a coincidence?'

'What do you mean?'

'That you were on the run from a difficult domestic situation at the same time as Mum had a heart attack?'

'Difficult domestic situation?' She looked fiercely at her older brother.

'Lisa, I'm a cop. I never take anything at face value – and your reappearance on the scene got me wondering.'

'You checked up on me, you bastard.'

Henry didn't even bother to respond to that because it was true. He'd asked Jerry Tope to do some digging for him in the Metropolitan Police's incident files to see what he could unearth. He found that the police in Chigwell had attended a series of increasingly violent domestic disturbances involving Lisa, an irate wife, a wayward husband and a father-in-law who might very well be connected to the mob.

'I got threatened,' she capitulated. 'I mean, seriously threatened. The cops advised me to go, so I ran . . . So, yeah, it was a coincidence. Happy now?'

'Not specially.' He shook his head despondently, wishing that in spite of everything he didn't love her so much. He found it hard to be really judgemental because he saw a lot of himself in her. He sat next to her on the bed so they were thigh-to-thigh. He took hold of her hand and marshalled his thoughts. 'You want to tell me about it?'

'No. It just got ugly and messy. I got involved with them through the jewellery business and they turned out to be dangerous people, so I cut my losses and got the hell out.'

'Leaving a broken marriage behind?'

'Um – yeah.'

'What are you going to do now? Have you thought that through?'

'Not really.'

'Right, well, what about staying here and getting your head together?' He could hardly believe his own words, yet couldn't seem to stop himself blabbing. Lisa's face suddenly brightened as though the sun had risen across it.

'You mean it?'

'I haven't run it past Kate, yet, but I'm sure she'll be OK.
There is one thing – no shagging in this house. At least not while
we're in and listening. And you put the time in with Mum. That's
a given, too. She needs all the care we can give her at the moment.
I have a feeling she won't be here much longer.'

Flynn had lost count of the number of doors he'd kicked down
in places like this, big terraced houses turned into flats and
occupied by the underbelly of society. A subculture of the popu-
lation he and Jack Hoyle had often invaded uninvited. And there
was nothing to beat bursting in unannounced and catching your
fish. Often they were tiddlers, occasionally marlin.

Flynn trotted up the steps and inspected the bank of doorbells
on the wall next to the front door. Some had names taped alongside, some had flat numbers, but he couldn't see the name or
number of the one he was interested in. The front door was
locked, so he rang every doorbell and waited for a response,
checking up and down the North Shore street that ran at ninety
degrees to the promenade. He could hear the waves slapping
against the sea wall. It was a high tide tonight.

One of the occupants buzzed him in and he stepped into the
ground floor hall, checking the flat numbers. He was after Flat
4, which was obviously up on the first floor, so he climbed the
uncarpeted stairs, the heel of his trainer crunching a discarded
syringe, like stepping on a cockroach. He emerged on the first-
floor landing and the first door he looked at had a number four
hanging upside down on it.

Flynn fished out his mobile phone and dialled the number he
had earlier keyed in for Dennis Grant. He watched the display:
'Dialling', then 'Connecting'.

Stepping closer to the door and listening hard, he wished and
prayed, knowing he was operating on a wing and a prayer.
Holding the mobile to his ear he heard it ringing out, or at least
giving an audio-digital impression it was ringing. There was a
slight delay, then from inside the room he heard a mobile phone
ring tone. 'Result,' he said.

'Yuh, who's that?' a male voice answered. Flynn heard the
echo of the voice inside the flat.

'Is that the Menace?'

'Who's that?'

'Jack Hoyle, remember me?'

There was a beat of silence. 'You're dead.'

'Very much alive, actually.'

Grant hung up instantly.

Flynn grinned, placed his phone in his pocket, then slyly tried the door handle to Flat 4. Locked. He gave the door a gentle push and saw it was a little loose within the frame. He stepped back, gathered his strength, picked his spot by the lock and powerfully flat-footed the door. Flynn was a strong, powerful man. Four years of deep-sea fishing, hauling in 800lb marlin and sharks, living a life of physical exertion, had honed every muscle in his body. Smashing down the flimsy door of a shitty flat was nothing to him.

The door almost crashed off its hinges with the first kick. Flynn barged in, getting his bearings instantly as he entered what was nothing more than a one-room bedsit, with a toilet and shower room off it.

Dennis Grant was hunched on a low single camp bed positioned under the window. His mobile phone was still in his hands as he looked at it in disbelief. He looked up stupidly when Flynn came through the door before any reaction kicked in. Next to Grant was a bedside cabinet with three blood-filled syringes on it, an overflowing ashtray crammed with dog-ends and used condoms and two empty beer bottles.

A scrawny fifty-year-old junkie dressed in a pair of ragged boxers, he shot to his feet to protest. But before he'd even reached his full height, Flynn had kicked the door shut and had him by the throat.

It was like grabbing a skeleton. A lifetime of substance abuse had robbed this man of all his muscle and strength. All he could do to fight back was wriggle and kick out pathetically.

For Flynn it was no contest. He held Grant with one hand around his chicken-like neck and lifted him across the room, where he pinned him against the wall. Even by then, as muzzed as Grant's mind might have been, he knew he was beaten. All he had left was the power of speech, though even that was controlled by the pressure Flynn used on his windpipe. He gagged to say something, trying to prise Flynn's finger ends out of his flesh.

Flynn's face closed on Grant's. 'This can be short and relatively pain free, Dennis. Or I can draw it out and give you pain like you've never felt before.'

'What do you want?'

'Know who I am?'

'Yeah, Jack Hoyle's partner.'

'Good memory. Now, then.' For good measure Flynn slammed Grant's skeletal body against the wall, hearing the hollowness of his skull bounce against it. 'I'm going to let you down, but don't even think that this act of kindness means I'm weak. If you try anything, or yell out, I'll just break your neck – got that?' Grant nodded. 'I'm not a cop any more, so I don't play by the rules, OK?'

He nodded again. Flynn eased him down and let go. But Grant's legs, having gone weak, couldn't hold him up. He slithered down the wall on to his haunches, knees clicking obscenely. He massaged his neck with his fingertips and gulped air.

'Fuck – no need for that.'

Flynn towered over him threateningly, then hauled him back up by his T-shirt. He groaned in terror. Flynn held him up easily.

'Quick questions, quick answers.'

'Man, I need a fix,' Grant whined. 'I can't handle this sorta shit.'

'Tough.'

'Look, whaddya want, man?' Grant gestured in a way that said he understood nothing.

'You were Jack Hoyle's informant on Felix Deakin, weren't you?'

A pained expression crossed Grant's deeply lined, drug-addled face. 'Is that what this is about?'

Flynn's right hand squeezed Grant's neck slowly and he sucked for air. A wide-eyed expression of dread came to his face as his bloodshot eyes almost popped out of their sockets. His breath rasped and panic gripped him as Flynn increased the pressure. Flynn could feel every contour of Grant's windpipe, felt as though he could slide his fingers all the way around it and tear it out of the throat if necessary.

'Answer the questions, don't ask, OK?'

Grant nodded. Flynn released the grip. Air rushed back down to the lungs. He coughed and spluttered.

'I was Jack's informant,' he declared.

'Was it you who told him about Deakin's counting house?'

'Yeah, yeah, man.'

'What about the money that went missing? That million?'

'Was no money.'

Flynn punched Grant very hard in the liver, just under the right side of his rib cage. He squealed. Flynn allowed him to double over. 'Do not lie. I have no time for lies. If I think you're lying, I'll kill you. Tell me about the money.'

Cradling his stomach and emitting a noise like a broken foot pump, Grant angled his face upwards, saw Flynn meant every word and started to jabber. 'It were a massive collection that night. About three months' worth of collections from all over the place. By the time you guys hit the place, I knew most of it would've been counted and bagged upstairs – back bedroom. I worked out a deal with Jack. He had debts everywhere and needed cash to pay 'em off . . . and the cops'd still come up smelling of roses 'cos there was a load still being counted at midnight.' He looked warily at Flynn. 'It were all bagged up. Two holdalls. It were simple, 'cos simple is good, yeah? Jack just dropped it out to me. I were out back, waitin'. I got a cut, he got the rest.'

'How much?'

''Bout nine hundred Gs. I got a hundred. I only did it 'cos I knew the case against Deakin were good and he'd be going down for a long stretch.'

'How did you know about the money?'

'I heard. I got ears. I was a nothing guy, harmless piece o' shit to Deakin. He got careless talking when I were about.'

Flynn stood up to his full height, thinking about the hasty explanation and how it fitted in with what he knew.

'Where's Jack now?'

'Dead as far as I know. Fell out of a boat, I heard,' Grant said unconvincingly.

'You believe that?'

Grant shook his head. 'Don't know one way or the other.'

'Where's your cut of the money?'

'What?'

'Your cut. Where is it?'

Grant's red eyes rolled in their sockets. 'Where the hell d'you think?' He held out his arms, twisted upwards, showing Flynn the soft flesh of each inner elbow. Flynn recoiled at the sight of years of injecting, searching all the time for undamaged veins, often with old needles. 'I inject my tongue now,' Grant said. 'That's where my cut went, every last penny. To people like Deakin who took over his business. I got nothing left, so I'm back to shoplifting and fencing gear . . .'

'Nice of you to run it past me,' Kate said huffily. She drew the quilt all the way up to her chin, the message very clear:

nothing for you tonight, my laddo. She looked cynically at Henry.

'She's my sister.'

'And you're a soft touch, pal.' She turned away and within moments she was breathing heavily, but not as a result of anything romantic Henry had done to her.

He lay back, hands clasped behind his head, his mind too busy for sleep. His thoughts flashed back and forth, eventually settling on Steve Flynn, the surprise card in the pack, maybe the joker. Henry could not fathom why he'd turned up. The story about knowing as much as anyone about Deakin might well have been true, but as a reason for coming back? To Henry it seemed as thin as tissue paper. Something else was going on. Perhaps something connected with the PR woman who'd died on the plane? That was something Jerry Tope had discovered – that the police in Gran Canaria and the Met were running a joint investigation into her death, which was caused following an assault by two men who had tried to rob her and Flynn in a hotel in Puerto Rico. Two men . . . Cromer and Jackman? Henry thought. He wasn't going to spend time agonizing over it. If Flynn wasn't prepared to be upfront, then he couldn't expect anything from Henry either.

Then he thought about his conversation with FB. Had he given Henry carte blanche to do something illegal?

His thoughts tumbled as sleep encroached . . . He rather liked Flynn in a curious way; he was the sort of bobby who, when young, had gone on foot patrol around town centres, purposely kicking drunks on the shins to wind them up . . . just like Henry used to do . . . And Lisa, God what a pain! Involved with some very unsavoury people . . . Then Henry saw himself sitting on a beach, sunning himself . . . he needed a good, long holiday . . . He yawned and looked at the bedside clock.

Flynn had not bothered going to bed. He sat alone in Faye's living room drinking tap water, fighting the urge to pour a very large whisky. He needed a drink. His mind was a jumble.

He seethed angrily as he thought about Jack Hoyle, ex-partner, disloyal bastard, a man who'd stolen his wife (then dumped her) and a million quid. Bastard. Flynn's heart pounded against his ribs. It had been Jack who, twenty years earlier, had introduced him to sportfishing. In those heady, premarital days, they had holidayed together regularly in the Canaries and even once got across to Key West to have a go at some classic marlin fishing.

It had been a journey that filled them both with excitement and desire. Even at weekends, they'd go sea fishing together off one of the east coast ports or North Wales. Jack had taken his master's certificate and was an excellent seaman. No way, Flynn thought, had he capsized a fishing boat. He'd been too good for that . . . but a million smackers coupled with a coincidental disappearance? Flynn mulled it over bitterly. No body found.

And then Craig, his son.

Flynn's insides felt as if they'd been scraped out. He was out of his depth with a task he thought would have been well within his capabilities. He knew it was beyond him alone.

Henry's mind was now awash with disjointed images and voices. Sleep had almost overwhelmed him. Nothing was happening in his head that made any sense.

His mobile phone rang on the bedside cabinet. He jerked into an unpleasant wakefulness, his fingers searching for it.

Next to him he heard Kate mutter, 'Fuck!'

'Henry Christie,' he said thickly.

'Henry, it's me, Flynn . . . I need to see you urgently.'

EIGHTEEN

'I don't want any of you to feel obliged that you have to become involved in this – no pressure, honestly. But if you do want to walk away, all I ask is that you keep silent. I promise no one will ever know this meeting occurred and you will not be connected to anything that happens subsequently from here. What I'm proposing is illegal and if we get caught doing it, we're for the high jump – unless I can cover it up.'

Henry looked at the people gathered in his office, maybe not the most suitable place in which to organize a secret meeting, but probably as good as anywhere at five in the morning.

Four out of the five he trusted implicitly. The fifth he was still unsure about, but he was starting to warm to him.

Bill Robbins shifted uncomfortably in his seat. Bill and Henry went back a long way, but most recently had been involved in apprehending dangerous terrorists and bent cops. Jerry Tope had assisted Henry on some successful investigations and had already

shown his willingness to duck around corners, especially by
hacking into computers to get results. He'd brought Rik Dean
into this because even though he wasn't operationally fit yet, his
experience would be useful to Henry. He and Rik also went back
a long time and the fact Rik was now screwing his sister gave
an extra hold on him. Next was DC John Walker from the
Technical Support Unit; John had provided Henry with off-the-
record surveillance and recording equipment in the past and could
be relied on to keep his mouth tight.

Finally there was Steve Flynn . . . Henry glanced at him, still
in two minds.

The call from Flynn came at one forty a.m., almost two hours
after Henry had gone to bed. Many minutes of tossing and
turning, closing his ears to Kate's increasingly loud snoring. He
had almost told Flynn where to get off, but relented and told
him to make his way to Henry's house.

Henry dragged himself quietly out of bed, got dressed on the
landing and went to wait for Flynn.

When he arrived, tired and exhausted looking, Henry knew
something major was about to be revealed.

Flynn decided to tell everything, up to a point. Just the truth
he wanted Henry to know and nothing else that might complicate matters – such as the fact that two dead bodies and several
firearms could be found in a deep gorge in Gran Canaria.

He told him about Gill Hartland, the TV exposure following
the rescue of the boat people, and the subsequent visit of Jackman
and Cromer.

They had retired to Henry's conservatory, where Henry had
drawn the blinds and switched on the heater to ward off the chill.

As Flynn told Henry about Jackman and Cromer, he stood
up, pulling up his T-shirt to show Henry the triangular burn mark
on his nipple made by the travel iron. Henry gasped, appalled.

'Gill managed to raise the alarm and they fled,' Flynn said.
'They never came back, but unfortunately she had a brain haemorrhage from one of the blows and died on the plane home.' Flynn
had to gather himself. 'Never came back, never saw them again.'

Next he told Henry of the reappearance of his ex-wife, telling
him the story of Craig's kidnap and the demand for the return
of the missing money. Flynn said, 'I never really believed the
money existed, but it did. Maybe not a mill, but an awful lot.
And Jack Hoyle took it.'

'But you two led the raid. Surely you must have known.'

'I've thought it through and through. I mean, the raid was a mass of confusion, especially when the shooting started. I went in first, with Jack behind me, but I now recall looking around and he wasn't there. Other cops were, he wasn't. Then something happened and I turned back to the action. When I looked again he was at the foot of the stairs. He'd obviously shot up, found the bags of money and tossed them out of a window. His informant caught them, then legged it. He was back downstairs within seconds.'

'Why were no police outside, covering the rear?'

'We went in based on information from Jack – that the rear door was sealed and unusable. I took him at his word – why wouldn't I? – because I trusted him. But on reflection, how many drug dealers' houses exist without a quick exit? I was naïve,' Flynn concluded sadly. 'But the money existed. I tracked down Jack's informant earlier and he spilled the beans. But all that's past. All that matters now is Craig, but if Deakin gets wind the cops are involved, he'll be dead. I know it.'

'He's certainly capable – and desperate.'

'Oh yeah. When I was backgrounding him, a lot of stuff was unearthed about his violent streak. He's suspected of murdering rivals and people who short change him. One of them was a seventeen-year-old lad from Merseyside. Craig's fourteen.'

'But in cold blood?'

'I don't want to take the chance. So, Henry, are you going to help or not? If not, I'm off now and I'll take my chances.'

'Henry – stop beating about the bush,' Bill Robbins said. 'You know you can trust everyone in this room.' He glanced unsurely at Flynn, but went on, 'So spit it out. We'll either be with you or walk out and keep our gobs shut.'

All heads nodded agreement.

'It's not as though we haven't done anything illegal for you before, is it?' Jerry Tope said. Henry was horrified, because as he said these words, the office door opened silently behind them and a squat, bulky figure entered the room.

'I'll pretend I didn't hear that,' the figure said.

All heads shot around and they groaned collectively.

It was FB, the chief constable, his ever-increasing girth almost filling the doorway. He edged his way around the room and jerked his thumb at Henry, who rose from his seat and made way for the almighty to drop in his place.

'Morning, guys,' FB said. They muttered a muted response. 'Mr Flynn.' He nodded at Flynn who said, 'Morning,' then glared at Henry. 'I'm assuming Henry has told you why you're here,' FB said.

'No' . . . 'Nope' . . . 'No idea,' the assembled officers said in unison.

FB turned to Henry and raised his overgrown eyebrows. 'Hadn't quite got there, boss,' Henry said.

'Better get on, time being of the essence.'

'Thing is, the hunt for Felix Deakin has taken a dramatic turn. It's now gone beyond escape and murder. You might well be wondering what Mr Flynn is doing here. Even you, Jerry, because I know he hasn't told you everything. The fact is that Deakin believes that Mr Flynn, who you all know is a former colleague, and his one-time partner made off with a substantial amount of Deakin's drug money following a raid a few years back.'

'A million, wasn't it?' Bill Robbins piped up.

'That was the allegation,' Henry confirmed. 'However,' he wagged his finger, 'I don't intend to go into the whys and where-fores of the tale of the missing money, other than to say that Steve didn't steal a penny. The fact remains that Deakin thinks he did and he wants it back – probably to finance his life on the run.'

'Which means he's still in the UK?' Bill asked.

'Hopefully, but there's another twist.' Henry eyed Flynn. 'Deakin has kidnapped Steve's fourteen-year-old son, Craig, and wants the money as ransom.'

'Jesus,' Bill said.

'Fuckin' hell, Steve,' said Jerry Tope.

'Which is why we're here – even the chief, who I decided needed to be in on this. Steve's got maybe two days to get the money and then he'll hear from Deakin about the dropoff, etc. He's also stated that if the police are involved, he'll kill Craig, or if he doesn't get the money, he'll kill him. As he's a man on the run, we have to treat that threat seriously. He cannot find out about the police, or that Steve doesn't have access to that kind of money.'

'So what are we going to do, Henry?' Bill Robbins asked.

'I was coming to that.'

'What happens if the Home Secretary refuses permission?'

'He won't,' Henry said positively. 'The chief can be very persuasive.'

'But he won't be happy backdating the authorization, will he?'

'He should only have to back-*time* it,' Henry said. 'It should still be for today's date. It shouldn't be too difficult for someone who's claimed expenses for a house in Lancashire he only visited three times last year – expenses and a mortgage. And then he only visited the place with the rather attractive daughter of the Foreign Secretary, plus one of her extremely attractive horsy mates. And from what I hear it wasn't just tea and biscuits – it was spanking and wanking galore.' Henry sighed. 'One of the benefits of having a cabinet minister living on your patch. You see and hear things about them, not all above board. A few minutes on a clock shouldn't make much difference.'

'Well, when you look at it that way,' Flynn agreed.

Henry was driving a newly registered Transit van down the M65, east across the county. It bore the logo of a well-known satellite TV company, but the van didn't belong to them. It was the property of Lancashire Constabulary's Technical Support Unit, used with the secret permission of the company concerned. Henry had chosen it from half a dozen other vehicles, all bearing the insignia of national companies, kept in a small covered compound near Preston docks. They were used to provide transport and cover for Tech Support officers whose job it was to break into people's houses, flats, caravans or cars, and bug them without their knowledge. Overalls had also been provided, as well as ID tags hastily prepared by John Walker.

Walker was sitting next to Henry on the double passenger seat and next to him, by the door, was Steve Flynn. All three were in the same overalls.

Henry had been reluctant to have Flynn along, but he'd relented when Flynn signed a disclaimer concerning injuries and claims. It probably wasn't worth the paper it was written on, but it made Henry feel better.

They were en route to Barry Baron's house in the Rossendale Valley, which they planned to bug with listening and video devices. The first stage of Henry's masterplan.

Running parallel to this operation, back at HQ, was the task allocated to Jerry Tope. He had been given Flynn's unofficial file on Deakin and his job was to get everything from the official current Intel files on Deakin and start doing the work on them. Checking addresses, phone numbers, associates, enemies, trying to get something useful from it all. Henry wasn't sure what he was looking for. That was down to Jerry.

The next stage of the plan, should it come to it, was to wait for Deakin's contact call to Flynn about the money. Flynn would then claim he had traced the money, but would need a couple more days to get it together. Hopefully it would be the beginning of negotiations with Flynn for the swap – money for Craig. Henry had also arranged for the mobile phone companies to be on standby to triangulate Deakin's location.

While all this was going on, the chief would approach the Home Secretary to get the bugging authorization. He would also start making inquiries about getting a million pounds in cash together, should it all go as far as a transfer.

It was all very loose and unpredictable, but that was the way of kidnaps. Plus, Henry knew, if anything could go wrong, it would. He didn't share that thought with Flynn, but he expected the ex-cop had it at the back of his mind anyway.

'How come you didn't pick up on Baron's role in Deakin's life when you were doing the background?' Henry asked Flynn. 'The fact he was Deakin's right-hand man?'

'Don't know . . . we knew he was always around, but obviously didn't put two and two together.'

Behind the van were two cars that had been seized and confiscated from criminals. One was a sporty Ford Focus driven by Bill Robbins, the other an old-fashioned Granada Scorpio, once the treasured possession of a drug dealer who had wept as it was loaded on to a flatback and taken from him. Rik Dean drove this. Both were pool cars now used by the cops.

Barry Baron, it was discovered, was due to be at Rossendale Magistrates' Court that morning, defending another of his ne'er-do-well clients. It was Rik's job to go to court, make certain Baron was there and keep the others informed of his movements. The case he had up was due for a trial, but though it was scheduled to proceed, anything could happen.

The little convoy peeled off the M65 and headed towards Rossendale. They came off at the Rawtenstall link and Rik went straight on towards the latter town. Henry turned right on to a countrified road that had once been the main route from Haslingden to Manchester. It dropped into a steep, tight valley, at the bottom of which Henry turned towards a tiny settlement called Irwell Vale, right next to the river of the same name. Baron lived in a new development of big detached houses on a quiet lane here.

Bill pulled in about a mile from Baron's house so he could give Henry warning of anyone approaching.

Henry drove the van on, creeping down Hardsough Road – the river on one side, the one-track East Lancashire Railway on the other – in the way a service vehicle might do in order to find an address. They reached Baron's house and pulled up on the wide driveway in front of a lovely, expensive property. They knew Baron was divorced and lived alone, but weren't sure if he had a cleaner or a live-in lover or if there was someone else with legitimate access to the house. They'd have to suck it and see, and then wing it. At least Baron had a satellite dish on the side of the house, which was a relief.

'I'm at court,' Henry's PR crackled through his earpiece. It was Rik calling, confirming his arrival at Rossendale Magistrates'.

'Roger that,' Henry said.

Henry opened a flask and they had a cup of coffee each – something that would hopefully give them some credibility as workmen. Flynn perused a copy of the *Sun*. They weren't going to do anything until Rik confirmed Baron was definitely at court. The coffee tasted incredibly good, but made Henry realize how hungry he was. To complete the scenario, they should have been eating bacon sandwiches.

'You don't think Deakin's here, do you?' Flynn nodded at the house.

'Crossed my mind, but I don't think Baron would be that stupid – or would he?' In his experience, even top crims did stupid things, which is why they got caught, not because the cops were particularly intelligent.

'Nah, he isn't going to be that dumb.' Flynn sipped his coffee. 'What is it about flask coffee? Comes out better than it goes in.'

Henry's mobile rang. It was Rik Dean calling from court. 'He's landed, talking to his client in the holding cell.'

'OK, keep us posted.' He supped his coffee. 'OK, guys.'

The three of them finished their brews and, after shaking out the last dregs of each cup on to the ground, they went to the back of the van and opened the doors. Flynn dragged out a pair of stepladders. Walker picked up a toolbox and they went up to the house. Everywhere was quiet; only the hum of vehicles on the A56 somewhere away to the left could be heard, and the Irwell to the right. The house was divided from its neighbours by high privet hedges and well-trimmed conifers and was not overlooked.

A spit of adrenaline came into Henry's saliva as excitement started to get to him. This was like having sex with a mistress

at home while the wife was out shopping, he guessed. Always
the possibility of being disturbed and exposed.

Flynn extended the ladder up the side wall to the satellite dish.

'You climb up and pretend you know what you're doing,'
Walker said to him, handing over a small wrench and screw-
driver. 'Obviously don't do anything to it.'

'I won't.'

Walker beckoned Henry to follow around the back, and they
checked all possible points of access. He sighed when he saw
the alarm box high on the front wall above a window.

'We usually do this sort of stuff in the dead of night and don't
give anyone chance to see us. And we usually do research first,'
he moaned.

Henry shrugged. 'Tough. Is the alarm a problem?'

'Not if we get in cleanly and find the key pad in less than
thirty seconds. I have a magic instrument that will find the code,'
he said mysteriously.

'Cleanly?'

'Don't fall over and break our necks. Don't prat about like
the two stooges, that sort of thing.'

While they were having this conversation, they had returned
to the foot of Flynn's ladder and stood pointing meaningfully at
the house and dish as though they were discussing angles, just
in case anyone was looking.

'Kitchen door, I reckon,' Walker said. He gave Flynn the
thumbs up, then he and Henry went around the rear again. The
door was a modern, double-glazed UPVC unit that looked
extremely secure to Henry. 'Easy peasy,' Walker said, pulling on
a pair of latex gloves and delving into his toolbox to emerge
with a set of thin plastic keys on a ring that reminded Henry of
a baby's toy. Walker looked squarely at Henry. 'You sure this is
going to get authorized? If it doesn't and it comes out, we're up
the Irwell without a canoe, you know.'

Henry shrugged. 'What's the worst that could happen?'

'The chief'll cover his arse, so will you, and me, Bill and Rik
will lose our jobs.'

'So, hardly anything to worry about.' Henry gave him a cold
smile.

'Thanks for that note of reassurance.' Walker shuffled the
plastic keys, finding the one he wanted, inserting it into the lock,
easing it slowly in. 'Magic, these things.'

'*Henry – trouble!*' His PR crackled with the voice of Bill Robbins.

'What d'you mean?'

'I mean I hope you haven't gone in yet, because either way, get the hell out of there now! Just do it.'

'Doing it,' Henry said.

Walker had already repacked his toolkit. As they hurried around the side of the house, Flynn slid down the ladder as though he was coming off the flying bridge of a sportfishing boat.

'Move,' Bill said urgently. 'One minute at most.'

'What's happening?' Rik Dean interrupted over the radio.

Flynn let the ladders clatter back, hefted them on to his shoulder and hurried to the van.

They didn't need to wait for an explanation: Bill's imperative tone was enough.

Henry's mind raced. Had Baron managed to give Rik the slip from court? He could not begin to comprehend what had caused this scare, but he knew the three of them had to get back into the van, reverse out of the drive and get out of the way.

Thirty seconds, easily, had passed.

In that time they came close to becoming the *three* stooges. Flynn swung the ladder around. Henry saw it at the last moment and ducked. Walker opened the rear van doors, dropped his toolkit on his foot. Flynn brought the ladder back in the opposite direction and Henry sidestepped out of the way again. Hopping on one foot, Walker picked up the kit and flung it into the back of the van, where it burst open. Flynn slid the ladder in too enthusiastically and smashed it through the cab window. He turned and bumped belly-to-belly into Henry as Walker slammed the van doors and trapped a finger, emitting a yowl of pain. Flynn pushed Henry aside, causing him to twist on his right knee, which gave under him. He had to grab Flynn's arm to keep his balance, almost ripping the overall sleeve off. Meanwhile Walker had hobbled to the passenger door of the van and found it locked. Henry staggered to the driver's door, opened it with the remote and heaved himself in. Walker jumped in, quickly followed by Flynn, all three of them having to sit on shards of broken glass from the partition window that Flynn had smashed.

Henry fired up the diesel engine with a plume of blue smoke coughing out of the exhaust. He slammed it into reverse, mouthing, 'You freakin' pair of imbeciles.' He kangarooed the van back out of the drive, jammed on the brake, causing it to wallow, then found first and gunned it forward for about two metres before stalling it, managed to get it going again, then set off. Behind them, a Mazda sports car turned into the road and pulled on to Baron's driveway.

Henry, using the wing mirror, felt sick at the sight of the car. 'Did you guys make it?' Bill Robbins asked.

Henry was crawling along the gutter, pretending to look for an address. He swung the van around at the end of the road and drove back past Baron's house as the occupant of the Mazda climbed out and approached the front door, key in hand, not giving the satellite van a second glance, opened the door and stepped into the house.

Even so, just to be on the safe side, Henry dipped his head away. Flynn and Walker were unlikely to be recognized. But there was every chance that Naomi Dale, CPS prosecutor, would immediately make him.

NINETEEN

T hey regrouped in the car park of the Woolpack, a pub situated on a roundabout near the A56. Rik Dean was still at court, where Baron was still engaged. The other four clustered around the front of the van to discuss the latest development, staying out of sight of the road while keeping it in view. Henry explained who Baron's visitor was; he would have contributed more, but was completely dumbfounded by her appearance and its possible implications.

'Henry? Did you hear me?' Bill Robbins asked.

'Sorry, mind's suddenly a blank. What was the question?'

'What next?'

Henry scratched his ears and ran a hand across his scalp. 'Well there's no chance of getting any equipment into the house at the moment. We're probably going to have to go to Plan B.'

'What? Wait for Deakin to contact me?' Flynn said dismissively. 'We need to make the running here. If we start reacting to events and slowing down, we'll be stuffed.'

'And you are along for the ride, not the decision making, Steve – don't forget that.'

'It's my son they've got. I'm no passenger.'

'You'll do exactly as I say,' Henry bridled.

As the two men stared at each other, a kind of primeval psyche

overcame them and they started to square up. Both men
were of equal stature, Henry just an inch shorter, but whereas
Flynn's bulk was all muscle, Henry was turning to fat around
his chest and guts, and was nowhere near as fit – or as physically dangerous.

'Hey, guys,' Bill intervened, 'don't be pathetic.'

'*He's on the move*,' Henry's earpiece told him. It was Rik
Dean. 'His case has been adjourned and now he's leaving court.
What's your position, guys?'

'We've had to withdraw – someone appeared at the house,'
Henry told Rik, remembering he hadn't updated him on who it
was. 'Can you follow him?'

'Yeah, no probs. He's on his phone, incidentally.'

'OK.'

Henry and Flynn exchanged a fierce look and Henry shook
his head at him, about to say something else. Fortunately his
phone rang and he answered it. It was Jerry Tope.

'Henry, I'm in the control room linked to the mobile phone
people. Baron's on line, in contact with his office in Rochdale.'

'Thanks, Jerry – keep us informed.' He gave Tope a quick update
of the situation, then ended the call. 'Baron's phoning his office.'

'He's driven off the court car park, now heading up the six-
eight-one in your direction, guys,' Rik Dean piped up. 'He hasn't
spotted me and I can see he's still on the blower. He's in a big
black Mercedes.'

'Thanks, Rik,' Henry said. To Bill, Walker and Flynn, he said,
'Let's get back on board and wait to see if he passes us.'

'I can guarantee he'll be heading home for some totty,' Bill
Robbins said. 'I would.'

'Let's just get in the cars, see what happens,' Henry said
impatiently.

'I'll get in with Bill, if that's OK?' Flynn said. 'It'll even
things up.'

Henry nodded and climbed into the Transit with Walker.

'He's turning off at Lane Ends,' Rik Dean's next transmission
came. 'Coming your way. Could be going home.'

From where the two vehicles were in the pub car park, they
could look across the A56 and up to Lane Ends traffic lights
about half a mile distant. They saw a black car turn in their
direction.

The car, which as it approached could be identified as a
Mercedes, came to a roundabout that crossed the A56. It shot

straight over and passed the Woolpack, heading towards Irwell Vale. Rik's drug dealer's Scorpio was four cars distant behind it.

'You want me to stick with him?' Rik asked.

'Henry,' Flynn cut in, 'let me and Bill take over the follow.'

Henry hesitated, then said, 'OK. Rik, you pull into the Woolpack. Steve, you and Bill follow.'

'Roger that,' Rik said.

'And Steve,' Henry said, 'you do what you have to do, OK?'

Bill and Flynn followed Baron's car down the steep road into Irwell Vale. They watched him turn towards the small settlement and as they entered the road on which his house was situated, they saw him reversing the Mercedes up his drive. Bill drew in a hundred metres away and switched off the engine.

'Give them a minute,' Flynn said.

'Then what?'

Flynn regarded him squarely, his eyes hard and scary. 'I get out, go calling and you disappear.'

Bill nodded, understanding.

'Don't worry about me.'

'I won't.'

Flynn got out, gave a quick wave and strode towards Baron's house. He paused at the bottom of the drive, glanced briefly back at Bill and gave him a go-away wave, but then stopped as the satellite TV van turned into the road and stopped behind Bill's car.

Henry jumped out and trotted towards Flynn, who had dropped out of sight of the house by the gatepost, waiting for Henry.

'On second thoughts, I'll be coming too.'

Flynn eyed him and nodded. 'You know I'm going to hit the fucker, don't you?'

'Only in self defence, I hope.'

'No,' Flynn said. He spun on his heels and walked to the front door, which he rapped on. Henry followed, and flattened himself against the wall, out of view should anyone peer out before answering the door. Unsurprisingly, no one came. Flynn knocked harder and louder. An upstairs curtain twitched, footsteps could be heard. The door was unlocked and Barry Baron appeared in a shirt, trousers and shoes.

'What?' he asked, irritated.

Flynn had formed a pleasant smile on his face. 'I've come about your satellite dish,' he said.

Then Henry rotated into view. 'And so have I.'

Baron's face was one of those pictures to behold, the face that speaks a thousand words, as he instantly recognized Henry and reacted by slamming the door in Flynn's face. He managed to twist the key in the lock before turning and running through the house with a scream of warning.

Henry glanced up, catching a fleeting glimpse of Naomi Dale's face at a crack in the curtain – and a bare shoulder.

'He's going out back,' Flynn said, thrusting Henry out of the way and tearing around the corner of the house. Henry let him go and called the three other officers to come and join him. Then he knocked patiently on the door.

Baron fled through the house, out of the kitchen door, grabbing a knife from a wooden block. He ran across the lawn, diving through the hedge at the back of the garden and tumbling down the banks of the River Irwell.

Flynn saw him disappear into the trees and followed, unaware of the knife.

The door opened. Naomi Dale faced Henry Christie. She was buttoning up her blouse, a guilty but resigned expression on her face. They regarded each other for a long, awful moment.

'I love it when people panic when the cops come a-calling,' he said.

Somewhere in the distance Henry heard the sound of two cars approaching at high speed.

'You've got nothing on me,' she said coolly.

'I'll say this before anything formal gets spoken,' Henry said. 'I don't know what's going on here, but I'll lay odds that I find evidence in this house of the whereabouts of Felix Deakin and the young lad he's kidnapped. Mobile phones will be a good start,' he gambled. 'Whatever, you're going to have to get your thinking cap on PDQ, lady, because when Mr Baron gets gripped, I guarantee he'll squeal like a piggy.'

She eyed him, then suddenly turned and rushed into the house, cutting right into the living room. Henry was behind her as she dove for her handbag and tipped it upside down, scattering its contents on the carpet, falling to her knees and trying to get hold of her mobile phone. She grabbed it, but Henry wrested it from her grip.

'Mine, I think.'

Then he saw a folded piece of yellow paper in among her

clutter. A memory came to him – Deakin passing something to Baron in the prison interview room. A yellow Post-it note. Henry picked it up and folded it open, reading the words, 'Get her to fuck him', scribbled thereon. An instruction from client to brief.

Flynn burst through the hedge like a rhino charging through a thornbush and was immediately faced by the almost perpendicular bank of the river. He was travelling so quickly and came across the slope so unexpectedly that it was all he could do to stop himself plunging headlong into the gurgling, but shallow water ten feet below. He skittered sideways down the bank, just about staying upright, and finished up with his feet in the water.

Baron was running along the bank, one foot in, one foot out of the water, some fifty metres ahead of Flynn. Then he turned ninety degrees and scrambled up the bank on all fours.

Flynn went after him, trying to keep on the bank, but because it was so steep, he found it hard to stay out of the river. At one point his foot slipped on a slimy rock in the water, but he stumbled on, his momentum keeping his balance. Then he turned up the banking in Baron's tracks.

Flynn fully expected to find himself on a road or farm track, but as he emerged he was surprised to discover he was on a single-track railway line. He didn't know this, but it was part of the East Lancs Railway running from Rawtenstall to Bury, via Irwell Vale.

Baron was now well ahead of him, running along the tracks.

Flynn's mouth curved into a sneer as he set off at a loping run. His long legs stretched easily across two sleepers at once, eating up the distance between him and his quarry in no time – assisted by the fact that Baron was clearly flagging now. Flynn could see it in the way he was running, his legs looking like lead.

Flynn was hardly out of breath and there was perhaps twenty feet between the men when they reached a bridge spanning the width of the Irwell over a tight, steep gully, with maybe a thirty-foot drop to the water below.

It was here that the exhausted Baron turned and dropped into a combat stance. He flashed the knife and confronted his pursuer.

'Come any closer and you're dead. I'm an ex-Marine and I know how to kill.'

Flynn stopped running, his eyes taking in Baron. Ex-Marine he may have been, and he may have looked pretty tough, but Flynn could see the guy was totally unfit. He approached Baron slowly.

'Who the fuck are you anyway?'

'I'm Steve Flynn – also an ex-Marine,' Flynn said, unfazed by Baron's revelation about his background.

Baron's eyes widened with horror.

'Yeah, that Steve Flynn. Felix Deakin kidnapped my son,' he growled, 'and I have nothing to lose here.'

'I have everything to lose.'

'You chose your track, pal, not me.' Flynn took another step. Baron jerked the knife threateningly. Flynn snorted derisively. 'You are joking, aren't you?'

'No, I'm not.'

'Where are they?'

'Who?'

'Deakin and my son.'

'Don't know what you mean.'

'You idiot. It's too late for that, don't you get it? You're finished. You can go down with a fight if you want to, but you will be going down. I'll have that knife out of your hand within a second and an elbow in your throat.'

Baron hesitated.

Flynn moved closer. Three more steps would put him within striking distance. 'Drop the knife, because if you don't I've decided I'll break your wrist and then hang you over the side of this bridge by your ankles. I might do that anyway.'

Baron considered the options, then opened the palm of his hand. The knife fell to the ground. Flynn moved in like a flash. Before Baron knew what had happened, he found himself looking down into the River Irwell.

Henry's mind worked quickly as he skimmed through the numbers on Naomi's phone. He looked at the calls made and received – many to and from 'Barry My Luv' – and the texts, which were obscene in content.

She was cuffed now, sitting in the back of the Scorpio. Henry was standing by the car door, tabbing through the phone.

'How long?'

'How long what?' She had been particularly obnoxious and resistant to anything asked of her.

'You and Barry-My-Love?'

'Fuck off,' she said and turned away disgustedly.

'What was it – lonely woman syndrome, looking for excitement? You've been feeding him information about everything we've been doing, haven't you? And it was down to you that

Deakin got the chance to get to court, wasn't it? Something that resulted in the death of a good cop.'

She shrugged.

'And something that was bugging me, too – how Baron knew so much about the weakness in the case against Cain. He could only have got that from you.' She shrugged again. 'If you've any compassion about you, you'll tell us where we can find Deakin now. There's a kid's life at stake.'

Henry turned and saw two bedraggled figures in torn, wet clothing coming down the driveway towards him. Baron was being herded along by Flynn, who kicked and pushed and dragged him by the scruff of the neck. He roughly deposited him on the ground next to Henry's feet.

'Meet the man who snatched my son off the street,' Flynn breathed, 'the man who's going to tell us exactly where he is. Aren't you, mate?'

Flynn kicked him hard in the ribs.

It was a textbook rescue. Acting on the information provided by Baron – and eventually Naomi Dale – the police surreptitiously surrounded an old farmhouse on the moorland between Rawtenstall and Burnley and Henry handed everything over to trained hostage negotiators. The farmhouse, it transpired, was one still owned by Deakin and had been overlooked in the seizure of his assets, although it was listed in Flynn's unofficial file.

If anything, Deakin was a realist. The sight of armed police, dog men and uniformed officers surrounding the farmhouse made him walk out within about fifteen minutes of being contacted by the negotiators.

Craig was allowed to run out first into the arms of two uniformed constables. He was bustled quickly away to safety. A few minutes later, Deakin stepped out, hands held high, defeated.

He was probably one of the best assassins in the world. A former SAS sniper who had seen action in many fields of war, his skills with a rifle were much sought after when he discharged himself from the army and set himself up as a gun for hire.

His usual targets were politicians or businessmen, but his target that day, for which he had been paid a serious amount of money, was Felix Deakin.

From his position over a mile away from the farmhouse, secreted in a dip, but in an elevated position looking down and across to the building, he watched the hostage negotiations taking place. He had arrived many hours before the police, and their arrival, while unexpected, did not faze him. He had a job to do, had a good escape route and had been paid. He knew he would escape. And in fact, the police turning up was a bonus that made his job so much easier. He had expected to be waiting for hours, maybe days, for his target to present itself, so the cops doing their job saved him a lot of time.

He saw the release of the young boy.

Minutes later, Deakin himself emerged and was instantly surrounded by police officers. They spent some time cuffing him, then led him to a police van that had drawn up outside the farmhouse.

The sniper relaxed. The shot would come. He wouldn't have long to make it, but he was confident it would happen.

And it did.

For a few moments, Deakin stood handcuffed at the side of the white van while the rear doors were opened. The van provided a superb backdrop, highlighting his target brilliantly.

The sniper looked down his sights at the cross-hairs and fired.

The bullet ripped through Deakin's head, almost slicing it in half, killing him instantly.

The sniper did not wait around to watch the chaos a mile away. He collected the spent shell, withdrew unhurriedly, and moments later was in his Land Rover, freewheeling away down the hill until he reached the road, when he let out the clutch and engaged the gear. By the time the cops found out where the shot had been fired from, he had changed cars twice and was at Manchester Airport climbing aboard an EasyJet plane to Barcelona.

He did not know why he'd been hired to kill Deakin. He was not bothered either, though he thought it might have had something to do with him having given evidence against another man. Whatever. He smiled at the stewardess and asked for a coffee when she was ready.

TWENTY

Three weeks later, the review panel was much more lenient on Henry Christie, and listened with interest as he gave them a blow-by-blow account of the investigation into Felix Deakin and everything else that surrounded him.

It had taken Henry that long to pull it all together, for him to keep a strategic eye on its progress (as he was keen to point out) and to say where it was all going.

He started at the beginning with the murder of the security guard at the supermarket. Some dogged police work by a couple of detectives on the murder team had resulted in the arrest of a gang member, who instantly pointed the finger at Richard Last as the man who had pulled the trigger and killed the guard. Further arrests were imminent, he assured the board.

In relation to the double murder of Richard Last himself and his partner Jack Sumner, Henry told the board the murderers were Teddy Bear Jackman and Tony Cromer; they had been contracted by Barry Baron, Deakin's solicitor, to get information about the whereabouts of the money from the supermarket robbery, because it had not been paid over. Baron claimed he did not want the men killed, but Jackman and Cromer had been overzealous and had failed to elicit the required information anyway. Jackman and Cromer were posted as wanted, but their whereabouts remained a mystery. He added they were also wanted for the unrelated murder of a British woman in Gran Canaria during an unsuccessful robbery.

Felix Deakin, he went on, had been getting money together to finance a life on the run. Working with Baron and a CPS solicitor called Naomi Dale, they conspired to get Deakin to court to give evidence. Deakin, again through Baron, hired a professional gang to spring him from court, which they did. But because he did not have the money he needed for his life on the run, in desperation he kidnapped the son of an ex-police officer who he mistakenly thought had stolen money from him in the past. The kidnap was successfully resolved, but an unknown gunman killed Deakin as he was being arrested.

Henry said he thought this was in retaliation for Deakin's offer to give evidence against Johnny Cain in the murder trial that subsequently collapsed, even though that offer was simply a means to give him chance to escape. Cain, ironically of course, did not know this. That was a line of inquiry that was being pursued, but as Cain's whereabouts were now unknown, it was problematic.

He made mention that Barry Baron, Deakin's solicitor, was being extensively investigated for his role in these matters, as was Naomi Dale, who was Baron's lover and had obviously been under his spell for some time, passing on sensitive information.

He wound up the review by saying that the gunman who had taken a shot at him and DI Dean at Blackpool Victoria Hospital was still being sought, and the incident may or may not have any connection with the cases Henry had been dealing with.

He got a round of appreciative murmurs and a wink of approval from FB. He left on a high, returning to his office with a smug look on his face. All the right notes, he thought . . .

Sitting down at his desk he saw the little red light flashing on his desk phone, indicating a voice message had been left. He picked up the phone and dialled the service.

'Henry, hi, it's me,' the recorded female voice said. 'Detective Superintendent Andrea Makin from the Met – remember me?' How could I forget her, he thought. 'Give me a call back on this number. I'm working Organized Crime now, by the way. Look forward to hearing from you. Bye.'

He called immediately. 'Andrea – Henry Christie. How are you?' he cooed. He had no trouble visualizing her, although he did redden a little at the memory of him being on top of her and, for some unaccountable reason, not being able to get an erection. But that was another story, so he blanked it out of his mind, had a bit of chit-chat with her about a case they'd fairly recently worked on together, then asked her what he could do for her.

'It's actually what I can do for you,' she corrected him nicely.

'All ears,' he said.

'We have an ongoing investigation into a crime family down here . . . and, to put it simply, we've used a bit of a honey trap which uncovered a plot to have someone murdered . . .'

'Sounds interesting.'

'Scenario: single woman comes along, starts a relationship with a married man. Married man, unfortunately, is married to the mob. His wife is the daughter of a very big player down here in north London.' As Henry listened, everything inside him froze up, as did his skin, which contracted and became tight on him. Andrea Makin continued, 'The marriage went pear shaped because of the arrival of this single woman, and as you know, there's nothing worse than a woman scorned. Unfortunately this woman, being the daughter of the crime boss, wanted this loose woman killed, so they contracted someone to do it. With me so far?'

'Hell,' was all Henry could say.

'And that contract killer, a rather pathetic figure if truth be known, is sitting in a cell in Lower Holloway, singing like Tweety Pie. Saying it all went wrong, he panicked, missed his target and shot a guy by mistake, instead of the woman he'd been contracted to waste.'

'The guy being my DI.'

'That just about sums it up.'

There was a pause. 'And the name of the single woman?' Henry asked, half-hoping it couldn't be who he knew it was.

'She's known as Lisa Christie,' Makin said. 'Ring any bells?' she laughed.

Henry closed his eyes. Then said, 'I'll dispatch that DI down to see you immediately, work out what needs to be done.'

Flynn had already done one of the two things he needed to do. That was to visit a west London cemetery to lay flowers on the grave of Gill Hartland. He spent about an hour with her, chatting about what might have been, but not getting too upset, because what they'd had, had been brilliant, even though cut short. When he walked away from the plot, he did not look back.

He was in the process of doing the second thing, sitting in the open air eating breakfast at the Two Friends Patio Restaurant in Key West, Florida. The food consisted of a ham-and-egg omelette with potato bits and wheat toast and a large, strong filter coffee, accompanied by a Grey Goose Bloody Mary, which really hit the spot. He was enjoying the food as he looked along Front Street. It was still early but already the heat was rising and approaching eighty degrees.

When he'd finished the food and was suitably refreshed, he paid the check and sauntered along Front Street, in the general direction of the Key West Bight and Charterboat Row. The plethora of boats made Puerto Rico look sick, many of them far more expensive than *Lady Faye* or *Faye2*. A sportsfisher's paradise, but a little over the top for him. He liked how basic Puerto Rico was, much more down to earth and seedy, even.

Of course, Key West was every big game fisherman's dream location, made famous by the exploits of people like Ernest Hemingway, and many years ago Flynn had thought he would love to live in a place like this. No longer, though. He'd found what he was after in the Canaries, understood the place, loved the people and had no desire to relocate and start again. If he'd had the chance twenty years ago, maybe the whole story would have been different.

He paused and looked with pleasure, not envy, at the boats and their crews – and the many lovely ladies adorning them. Maybe Puerto Rico could pinch one or two ideas, he thought.

He strolled to a pavement café with a pleasant view of Charterboat Row, and waited patiently with another coffee for company.

Moored in the water opposite him was a fine Albemarle sport-fisher called *The Riff*. It was a forty-one footer with everything a client could want. The skipper was busy preparing the boat for a charter and did not see Flynn cross the road and approach the stern.

Flynn watched him for a few moments before the guy glanced up, squinting against the sun that was behind Flynn. It took a while for him to focus, and then he stood up slowly to his full height.

'I knew you'd come,' Jack Hoyle said.

'You're so predictable, Jack,' Flynn replied. 'Not very hard to find at all.'

'Yet you're the only one who has.'

'Trust me, pal, I'm probably the first in a long line.'